TOWARDS THE ONE & ONLY METAPHOR

MIKLÓS SZENTKUTHY

Selected Other Works by Miklós Szentkuthy

Prae

Chapter on Love

St. Orpheus Breviary

Divertimento

Face and Mask

Cicero's Journeyman Years

Narcissus' Mirror

Europe is Closed

Testament of the Muses

Frivolities & Confessions

While Reading Augustine

TOWARDS THE ONE
& ONLY METAPHOR

MIKLÓS SZENTKUTHY

TRANSLATED BY

TIM WILKINSON

Contra Mundum Press   New York · Berlin

Library of Congress Cataloguing-in-Publication Data

Szentkuthy, Miklós, 1908–1988

[Az egyetlen metafora felé. English.]

Towards the One and Only Metaphor/ Miklós Szentkuthy; translated from the original Hungarian by Tim Wilkinson; introduction by Rainer J. Hanshe.

—1st Contra Mundum Press Edition
408 pp., 5x8 in.

ISBN 9781940625003

I. Szentkuthy, Miklós.
II. Title.
III. Wilkinson, Tim.
IV. Translator.
V. Hanshe, Rainer J.
VI. Introduction.

2013948333

TABLE OF CONTENTS

Entering the World Stage: Miklós Szentkuthy's
Ars Poetica: Introduction by Rainer J. Hanshe   0

1 ⟹ My aim is wild, absolute imitation, prodigal
precision. A *Catalogus Rerum*   2

2 ⟹ The eternal game: to get to know the world? —
to preserve the world?   2

3 ⟹ 'Vision' of the black throats of stridently
chirping, invisible birds   3

4 ⟹ Two kinds of heat: the summer heat of Nature
and a sick person's fever — Fight it out!   3

5 ⟹ A hymnal life — an analytical life. Fever.
Summer. Pindar. Proust   4

6 ⟹ The perverse marriage of banality & rhyme   5

7 ⟹ The feverish fiction of possibilities and
imitation: the most brotherly brothers   5

8 ⟹ Drawings cool one   5

9 ⟹ Two female gestures   5

10 ⟹ Eros. Its animal and floral parts   6

TABLE OF CONTENTS

11 ⟹ A little moral-philosophical typology from plant portraits 7

12 ⟹ Form: a concept conferred by plants 8

13 ⟹ An auburn-haired woman is stretched out on the hillside. Alien? acquaintance? mother? lover? 9

14 ⟹ Women known by sight: the most important liaisons of my life 10

15 ⟹ The above-described forms of seduction 11

16 ⟹ More on the auburn-haired woman: the platonic flirt of eyes 12

17 ⟹ *West-östlicher Divan*: sobriety and colorful story setting 12

18 ⟹ Bedroom in summertime at daybreak: laboratory and fate 13

19 ⟹ Huberman 15

20 ⟹ Three things distance me from life! The state of *love*: my desire for a synthesis; to unify the lyric and objective worlds. Mathematizing *scientific* realism: my astronomer friend is a non-lyrical, objective person. After women and science is an exit out of life supplied: by *dreams?* 22

21 ⟹ The three-fold metaphor or biological phases of love: flower, worldliness, illness 27

22 ⟹ My essence: an absolute and unbroken need for intensity. But let there also be orgasm: form! 29

23 ⟹ Comedy. Amatory phobia 35

24 ⟹ The most fictive, most null part of our life: self. A woman who adores one alone calls one's attention to this. Ecstasy and idyll: are there two more such lies in the world? 36

25 ⟹ Psyche, hetæra, beauty: can we ever be freed from these three eternal forms of woman? 38

26 ⟹ A journal-like work: a mixture of the ultimate formula and a set of impressions in which time is the main protagonist 48

27 ⟹ Absolute suffering: a dream about a sick old woman's young-girl anguished nude act. I read all the poems of Goethe: the opalescent contradictions of Goethe myth and Goethe reality. I saw the beast most horrible: the monster's feast. A deserted park as evening closes in: immersion in quiet 48

28 ⟹ Jewish burial 60

29 ⟹ Morn awakening: to be born chaste in the
tormenting totality of freedom. Should I be life
or work? 73

30 ⟹ A metaphor: an embryo; a clarified thought:
a fully-grown human body 80

31 ⟹ Action and thought. Elemental eroticism,
abstract metaphor 80

32 ⟹ Two Jewesses with fairly wide-ranging
anthropological and psychological
consequences 82

33 ⟹ Out of a love triangle an ethical Holy Trinity 87

34 ⟹ Leaving an incipient love as a beginning 91

35 ⟹ An apartment: the height of metaphysics and
practicality 94

36 ⟹ Novel of Charles II Stuart. The official emblem
of royal *immorality*: "Fantastic as a heraldic
device, tedious as a document" 98

37 ⟹ The furor of self-criticism 118

38 ⟹ A flagellant stylistic analysis: leaden
weight of eternity bound up in the hairs of
ephemerality 118

39 ⟹ The splendor of a lonely room in a summer
storm 120

40 ⟹ The young Goethe: insipid myth etiquette, naively crude sensuality 120

41 ⟹ *Questionnarium doricum* 121

42 ⟹ Holbein: Portrait of a Young Girl 122

43 ⟹ Haydn-sonata and a cactus. My experiments at a novel: they are that in a concrete *biological* sense 131

44 ⟹ Apropos, Haydn: form-breaking classics, form-palsied Romantics 132

45 ⟹ The fugue as mathematized music and as deliberate sensuality 133

46 ⟹ Two motifs 136

47 ⟹ The compilational character of beauty 136

48 ⟹ Now leave me alone 137

49 ⟹ Is there a separate life and art? 139

50 ⟹ Our Father 140

51 ⟹ Love is a suffocating greenhouse flower disease 147

52 ⟹ "My political adversary" 149

53 ⟹ Two kinds of knowledge of human character 150

54 ⟹ The absolute diversity in substance of historical protagonists 151

55 ⟹ The humbug of the press, the abject poverty of newsvendors, the ignominy of snobbery 152

56 ⟹ Of what does a crisis of something consist? 155

57 ⟹ To become immersed in the fateful human reality: in the service of *today* 157

58 ⟹ Demos, lust, solitude: Don Giovanni's three punishments 158

59 ⟹ My two Alphas and Omegas of inspiration: nature and worldliness 159

60 ⟹ Hymn to Destiny 163

61 ⟹ The two big extremes of my life: the 'hymn' and a 'scheme of sensations' 167

62 ⟹ The difference of death originating from disease and from accident 171

63 ⟹ Ethos and truth 171

64 ⟹ Artist and petty bourgeois 172

65 ⟹ Architecture, disease, eros: all three seek plasticity 173

66 ⟹ Plan for a novel (Charles II Stuart) 174

67 ⟹ Conversion. Augustine's. My own. Its worth & worthlessness 179

68 ⟹ Why don't I write plays? 182

69 ⟹ It is of secondary importance whether I am a painter. Sketch! Sketch! 186

70 ⟹ My style is a rag like St. Francis' clothes; my style is tuberculosis like St. Theresa's; my style is blood like that of the martyrs 187

71 ⟹ The Saint (plan for a novel) 188

72 ⟹ The Christian Socialist (report) 190

73 ⟹ The love of James I and Jane Hobson, or the parable of disproportionate anger 191

74 ⟹ Vitriolic plan for a novel (Dedicated to the Compagnie de Quinze theatrical company of Paris) 193

75 ⟹ Raving charity. Gratitude or murder? 197

76 ⟹ Harmonious dream visions 198

77 ⟹ The (ancient) ethics of the humbuggery of wealthy businessmen 200

78 ⟹ The parents' secret. The secret of faraway lands 203

79 ⟹ A false equation between canned food and humanity 203

80 ⟹ The opposition between worldly and unworldly 205

81 ⟹ The two extremes of sexual biology and sexual aesthetics. J. C. Powys: *Jobber Skald* 205

82 ⟹ Caracalla's dream. Plan for a novel, fantasy, analysis 206

83 ⟹ I always have one subject 210

84 ⟹ Which is the 'right'-er flower? 211

85 ⟹ The four models for Raphael's Madonna 211

86 ⟹ A departed person. Lack, absence: absurd mathematical points of departure and everyday realities 212

87 ⟹ Analysis and style 222

88 ⟹ One cannot serve two gods at the same time: art and morality 222

89 ⟹ An unbridgeable and disheartening difference between: my writings and my thoughts 223

90 ⟹ After & in the footsteps of the departed one 226

91 ⟹ Summer: the greatest chaos and greatest order 227

92 ⟹ What alters the portrait of a novel's hero as written down 228

93 ⟹ When the physical center of gravity falls *beyond* objects (words) 229

94 ⟹ From the hours of young Bonington. Fantasies while looking at his watercolors 229

95 ⟹ The relationship of dream and prose. Is our instinct for reality or for unreality 'truer'? 230

96 ⟹ A genealogy of the sufferings of 'Charles VII' 237

97 ⟹ Someone in the neighborhood is practicing the piano; I am reading a mystical novel; I am meditating on my fate: three dazzling and excruciating worlds 238

98 ⟹ What if a person is not truly born for anything? 239

99 ⟹ The individual's ailment and society's ailment. Plan for a novel 242

100 ⟹ Should I write a hymn or a novelistic catalogue of data about the impossibilities of all love? 244

101 ⟹ It is eerie *to see* art's poison in the center of art 248

102 ⟹ Three different figures, three pointlessnesses, three sufferings 250

103 ⟹ A summer afternoon in my study. Conversation with my mathematician friend. Topics: war and number theory. That is to say? The paths of death & reason to incomprehensibility — ghostly stone guests 258

104 ⟹ Two possible programs of mine: ascetic-Catholic morality or sacrificing my whole life to mathematics 262

105 ⟹ The June 20, 1935 issue of the *Boston Weekly*. Commentaries, synopses of planned novels 268

106 ⟹ Three determining pillars of my life and oeuvre: dreams, worldliness, plants 273

107 ⟹ Parable about unrealizable dreams and impossible realities. Plan for a novel 280

108 ⟹ Henry 'the Merchant,' King of England, Philip 'the Pallid,' King of Spain, Queen Ydoleza of Spain, Princess Ucia d'Avar of Spain — the four main characters of a planned novel 285

109 ⟹ Two worlds. One of them: God, man, suffering. The other: nature, beauty, happiness. Do they exclude each other? 289

110 ⟹ A symbol of unproblematicalness: a bunch of daisies that have begun to wilt slightly 295

111 ⟹ The magic-making-medicine-man effect of languages. Readings of Sir Thomas Browne and François Mauriac   298

112 ⟹ Towards the one and only metaphor: or out of a million metaphors towards the one & only *person?*   307

Endnotes   310

ENTERING THE WORLD STAGE: MIKLÓS SZENTKUTHY'S *ARS POETICA*

He who is born in imagination discovers the latent forces of Nature... Besides the stars that are established, there is yet another — Imagination — that begets a new star & a new heaven.

— Paracelsus

I N 1827, LONG BEFORE GLOBALIZATION and the institutionalization of multiculturalism, Goethe forecast the disintegration of national literature and the burgeoning of *Weltliteratur*, whose epoch he saw near at hand and sought to hasten. To achieve that, he accentuated the necessity not only of reading works in their original languages but of studying their times and customs in order to best understand them; this was not to offer world literature as a mere cultural product but had the more elevated aim of fostering the "true progress of mankind," which Goethe thought could be achieved through the concerted efforts of all cultures. The bane of progress aside, that was the grand project. And despite its shortcomings and limits, Goethe also recognized the fundamental role translation would play in acquainting people with world literature, and the eventuality of it supplanting national literature, which he adduced would be swiftly realized due to the "ever-increasing rapidity of human interaction," "vastly facilitated communications," and the "constantly spreading activities of trade and commerce."[1] What Goethe envisioned, at least superficially, we have in part witnessed, and many would affirm that we live in a compact global community where literature and the arts are less and less dominated by a central canon, though such utopic pronouncements and empty optimism necessitate scrutiny. In the late 20th century, Gadamer and other critics questioned the validity of Goethe's concept of *Weltliteratur* as Eurocentric, potentially homogenizing, & possibly normative, while Erich Auerbach made the incisive observation that, "in a uniformly organized world, only one single literary culture — indeed, in a relatively short time, only a few literary languages, soon perhaps only one — will remain alive. And with this, the idea of world literature would be at once realized and destroyed."[2] If the once largely Eurocentric canon shunted other cultures to the margins, at least there were margins in which to exist — Auerbach's analysis of *Weltliteratur* is that of a tenebrous, near-apocalyptic dialectic where nothing remains.

Whether these critiques of Goethe's more nuanced concept are entirely accurate is open to question, as is

1. *WA I*, 42.2, 502f; *WA I*, 41.2, 299; *WA I*, 42.2, 505. Goethes Werke. Weimarer Ausgabe (Sophien-Ausgabe). 143 Bde. Weimarer 1887–1919.

2. Erich Auerbach, "Philology and *Weltliteratur*," tr. by Maire & Edward Said, *The Centennial Review*, Vol. XIII, № 1 (winter 1969) 3. Translation modified.

exactly what world literature is or can be, if something of the kind is even possible. However, such appraisals warrant reflection and, in our epoch, where the speed of human interaction is Zeus-like, world cultures make contact with a rapidity that outstrips our ability to digest them, even moderately. In an interview made just prior to his death, W.G. Sebald spoke of the utter impossibility of keeping abreast of contemporary literature and cited the near-manufactured yields of Germany and Switzerland as particularly imposing examples. Due to the state subsidization of literature, Sebald laments, writers proliferate, multiplying by the hundreds, as if some kind of pestilential phenomenon: "Just look at Switzerland, there must be about 5,000 published authors there today. Twenty years ago, there were only two known ones, Frisch and Dürrenmatt, and today there are two dozen just in the city of Basel."[3] If to most the prospect of two-dozen writers in a single city isn't unsettling, Sebald noted with alarm that, if one thinks of the sheer "thousands of novelists" in Germany, the possibility of wading through their work is too daunting to countenance. As his anxiety reveals, while we may have a more global consciousness and culture, its sheer abundance often leads to its near figurative obliteration, certainly to

---

3. Jens Mühling, "The Permanent Exile of W.G. Sebald," *Pretext* 7 (spring/summer 2003).

obscuring what is there, waiting to be discovered, with even the moſt noteworthy achievements often being left unrecognized. If Germany and Switzerland can hardly be said to suffer neglecŧ, Hungary is one culture long marginalized by the world ſtage. Although Hungarian composers such as Kodály, Bartók, and Ligeti are known throughout the world, and were during their own lifetimes, that has not been the case with many if not moſt Hungarian writers. While literature is not as immediately accessible as music,[4] writers such as Sándor Petőfi, Imre Madách, & Miklós Radnóti ought, certainly at this date in hiſtory, not juſt to be better known but better read, eſpecially if one wishes to ſpeak of *Weltliteratur* with even a modicum of probity. In the laſt two

---

4. Consider Schopenhauer's metaphysics of music: famously, he argues that music, which he equates with the *Ding-an-sich*, "provides the innermoſt kernel, prior to all form — the heart of things. This relationship [between the universality of concepts and the universality of melodies] can be expressed extremely well in the language of the Scholaſtics, where it is said that concepts are the *universalis poſt rem*, while music gives the *universalia ante rem*, and reality gives *universalia in re*." Cf. Arthur Schopenhauer, *The World as Will and Representation*, trs & eds Judith Norman, Aliſtair Welchman, Chriſtopher Janaway (Cambridge: Cambridge University Press, 2010) 291. However contentious Schopenhauer's position is, and it is not without critical weaknesses, music does not need to be translated to be heard, making it more inſtantly digeſtible than a work of literature in a language foreign to a reader.

decades, a considerable shift toward expanding the impact of Hungarian culture has occurred; as its literature gains more and more prominence worldwide, contemporary writers such as Péter Nádas, Péter Esterházy, and László Krasznahorkai are becoming nearly as familiar to readers of world literature as Saramago, Banville, and Bolaño. Yet, whereas Nobel laureate Imre Kertész is widely known, another Hungarian writer, Miklós Szentkuthy — who has at times been compared to the holy trinity of Proust, Joyce, and Musil — still remains something of an obscurity even though his work predates that of Kertész & the others just listed, who represent the new, late-Cold War generation, and didn't begin publishing until the end of the 70s and early 80s, long after Szentkuthy had produced all of his major works and established himself as Hungary's foremost modernist. In fact, many if not all of Hungary's leading writers have sent signed copies of their works to Szentkuthy but, in the West, they have largely eclipsed their prodigious herald — Krasznahorkai advancing more swiftly to the world stage in part due to his association with Béla Tarr and Ágnes Hranitzky, Kertész by writing novels on the Holocaust, which accord instant caché and significance. *Fatelessness* will receive more critical acknowledgement than Szentkuthy's *Marginalia on Casanova* strictly because the former will be perfunctorily deemed 'more important' given its subject (which is not to cast aspersion on its merits). Topicality blinds and trumps.

If Szentkuthy is Hungary's foremost modernist, in some ways, he is not really a "Hungarian" writer — not in any folkloric or nationalistic sense — his work doesn't deal with Hungarian reality or culture, except perhaps in extremely covert or complex allegorical ways.[5] "Homelessness," said László Németh, "is one of [Szentkuthy's] main distinguishing marks, as compared with kindred Western writers." Elaborating further, Németh suggested "homelessness to be a higher form of protection of the mind."[6] Since the first volume of Szenkuthy's *St. Orpheus Breviary* was banned and he was forced to vet each of his further publications with the Hungarian state, and eventually interrupt the writing & publication of the *Breviary* — only to return to it 30 years later — to write biographical 'fantasies,' essentially for hire, on the likes of Dürer, Goethe, Mozart and others, the fortification of that homelessness was clearly vital.[7]

---

5. For one analysis of this in English, cf. Nicholas Birns, "Startling Dryness: Szentkuthy's *Black Renaissance*," *Hyperion: On the Future of Aesthetics* (summer 2013) 227–242.

6. László Németh, "Miklós Szentkuthy, *Az egyetlen metafora felé*," *Tanú*, № 1–2 (1936). Tr. by Tim Wilkinson.

7. For Szentkuthy's own account of his being charged with "offending against public decency and affronting religious sentiment," *Casanova* being banned, and his subsequent books requiring state approval before publication, cf. Miklós Szentkuthy, *Prae: Recollections of My Career*, tr. by Tim Wilkinson, *Hungarian Literature Online* (April 23, 2012) §34.

Although Szentkuthy was not *persona non grata* under Rákosi's Communiſt regime, and his Jewish origins were unknown at the time, he was certainly forced to become a kind of internal émigré. Yet, that he did is noteworthy, takes us to an atomic crux of sorts. After receiving the Baumgarten Prize along with seven other recipients, Szentkuthy was sent to London from February to autumn of 1948 after being chosen by the Miniſtry of Education — along with Gábor Devecseri — to eſtablish at the University of London, Oxford, or Cambridge a one-to-one language department.[8] That never came to be but, at that time, inſtead of returning to Hungary, Szentkuthy could have defeċted, and since his English was expert enough, could have written in that tongue — like Conrad or Nabokov — without fear of censorship. But, although he was not a folkloric writer or a social realiſt, let alone a nationaliſt, emigrating remained a form of betrayal for Szentkuthy. Not of some political faċtion, hardly so, but rather of something intimately

---

8. There were a total of eight recipients of the Baumgarten Prize. The others included György Bölöni, Károly Kerényi, Iſtván Vas, Zoltán Zelk, Sarolta Lányi, Iván Mándy, Ágnes Nemes Nagy, and Endre Vajda. During his visit to London, since the language department came to nothing, Szentkuthy "roamed round half of England, with cathedrals remaining [his] 'burning' obsession." Cf. Miklós Szentkuthy, *Az élet faggatottja: ʾBeszélgetések, riportok, interjúk Sz.M.-sal* (Budapeſt: Hamvas Intézet, 2006) § 36.

connected to his being, something he himself might almost see *biologically* — a betrayal of his linguistic identity. As Mária Tompa, the executor of the Szentkuthy Estate, points out, "being a Hungarian writer, he wanted to live out his personal identity, along with all of its difficulties, in his native country."[9] A keen decision, and one which clearly preserved Szentkuthy since, as expert a writer as he was, even Nabokov lost something fundamental by adopting English as the base language of his art, which he explained in a rare admission:

> Of the two instruments in my possession, one —
> my native tongue — I can no longer use, and this
> not only because I lack a Russian audience, but
> also because the excitement of verbal adventure
> in the Russian medium has faded away gradu-
> ally after I turned to English in 1940. My English,
> this second instrument I have always had, is
> however a stiffish, artificial thing, which may be
> all right for describing a sunset or an insect, but
> which cannot conceal poverty of syntax and pau-
> city of domestic diction when I need the shortest
> road between warehouse and shop. An old Rolls-
> Royce is not always preferable to a plain jeep.[10]

9. Mária Tompa, "A végső kérdések kulisszái," *Orpheus*, Vol. V, № 1 (1994) 45–52. For an expanded, English version of this essay, cf. "Backdrops to the Ultimate Questions: Szentkuthy's Diary Life," *Hyperion: On the Future of Aesthetics* (summer 2013) 282–318.

10. Vladimir Nabokov, "The Art of Fiction № 40," Interviewed by Herbert Gold, *the Paris Review*, № 41 (summer/fall 1967).

Szentkuthy was sensitive to this potential risk and, in choosing to return to Hungary, skirted it, yet knowing full well the conditions under which he would have to live. But it was only in Hungary that he knew he could sustain and cultivate his vision, and his attitude toward tragedy was spartan and stoic:

> It is not meant as idle chatter when I emphasize that I live with ... distant stellar constellations... From *that* huge perspective, from among such backdrops, please don't take it as boastfulness on my part that on such a small territory I can't take a historical period like that too tragically... I was one of the regime's victims ... but that way of looking at things has consequences for one's general state of health & character: those few years of dictatorship ... were an insignificant miniature, a weekend compared with the milliards of years of the universe. It would be ridiculous for me to speak about *sub specie aeterni* and meanwhile whine on about tragedy..." [11]

To recount this is not to cast Szentkuthy as a martyr for writing, but only to suggest a steely, unblinking reserve, and the character of one who embodies and lives by the principles elucidated in his writing. It is not mere words; it is a living praxis. Out of a cosmic vision,

---

11. Miklós Szentkuthy, *Frivolitások és hitvallások* (Budapest: Magvető, 1988) ch. XII, p. 340.

an ethics. Tompa explains how Szentkuthy "thought it was grotesque and, above all, senseless to light his imagination in voluntary exile, a thousand miles from his native land, and set down on paper the offspring of an imagination which luxuriated in the Hungarian language and artificially create a substratum for that mother language."[12] If in his subject matter Szentkuthy is not Hungarian, it is then in *language* that he is, through and through — and it is then in language that he is *not* homeless, but profoundly *bennszülött*. A cosmopolitan, indubitably, but autochthonous.

When *Prae*, Szentkuthy's first novel, appeared in 1934, the book was so startling that András Hevesi deemed him a "monster," while Szentkuthy, despite his own misgivings about the term, essentially inaugurated the Hungarian avant-garde. He would see such experiments within a vaster historical continuum, "amply demonstrating" that what were "imagined" as "revolutionary innovations" by Surrealists and others, "also played a part, to a greater or lesser extent (better too), in the history of the arts."[13] To Szentkuthy, the style of the ultra-modernists was outdated. In *Towards the One and Only Metaphor*, he outlines what he sees as the two principal forms of experimentation: "one is strictly rational, self-analytical,

12. Tompa, ibid.

13. Miklós Szentkuthy, *Prae: Recollections of My Career*, ibid., § 21.

& overscrupulous, simply a pathology of consciousness,"
and the other is "the perennial experimentation of nature,"
such as biological forms of development, where there are
no distinctions between 'final results' and 'undecided, exploratory trials.' "If *Prae* & other works I have planned
are 'experimental,'" he counters, "then they are so in a specific biological sense: not an apprehensive, exaggerated
self-consciousness, but experiments of primal vitality,
which are in a special biological relationship with form
(cf. the 'forms' of protozoa: experiment and totality of
life are absolutely identical, they coincide)."[14] Similarly,
Szentkuthy speaks elsewhere of "the experimentalist
playfulness of Nature, the thousand variants of sex,"
and of how "the art of the Mayans & Africans" was
never "detached from the iron positives of reality."[15] Despite that anchor to reality, the mercurial *Prae* was considered "an eerie attack on the Hungarian realist novel"
and denounced as non-Magyar — a curse, then, against
nationalism and folk-culture, with Szentkuthy suffering from the reprehensible malady of cosmopolitanism.
This raises a thorny political question to which there
is perhaps no definitive answer, for what does it mean

---

14. See § 43 of this book, which begins with the phrase: "A Haydn
sonata and a cactus." Haydn is representative of the first form of
experimentation and cacti of the second.

15. *Prae: Recollections of My Career*, ibid., § 16.

to be Magyar, Asian, or, for that matter, Sicilian? If modern physics has sundered the very solidity of matter, how can any form of identity be sustained as solid and absolute, let alone infinitely sustainable? If Szentkuthy is to be critiqued for being cosmopolitan, what happened to the sea change from national to world literature that Goethe envisioned? The Magyar of 1848 is no more, nor the American of 1950. To Nietzsche, "what is normal is crossed races," and they "always mean at the same time crossed cultures, crossed moralities… Purity," he continues — upending any nationalistic conception of the term — "is the final result of countless adaptations."[16] Our artists and philosophers, the visionary ones, are generally far in advance of our politicians. Over 50 years after Szentkuthy was denounced for being non-Magyar, Kertész would suffer similar attacks after winning the Nobel for a body of writings that do not glorify Hungary, prompting many people to question whether or not he was "a real Hungarian writer."[17] An intractable question, and as Szentkuthy himself knew all too well, cultural diversity has its perils; but then, if, as Nietzsche argues, hybridization and adaptation

---

16. Friedrich Nietzsche, *Daybreak: Thoughts on the Prejudices of Morality* (Cambridge: Cambridge University Press, 1997) §272.

17. Florence Noiville, "Imre Kertész's Hungary: A Country on the Wrong Side of History," *The Guardian* (February 12, 2012).

is what ultimately creates 'purity,' the whole swindle of essentializing races and cultures is rendered impotent. Modern physics further obliterates it. And since no language is entirely and absolutely indigenous, then Szentkuthy (as Kertesz, and others who have been similarly questioned) remains thoroughly Hungarian in being both autochthonous and allochthonous.

Although the *monstrum* had its champions, aside from an excerpt translated into Serbo-Croatian in 1970 and into French in 1974, *Prae* has never been published outside of Hungary, severely circumscribing its legitimate place in *Weltliteratur*'s genealogy.[18] Despite the fact that it foregrounds and presages many of the innovations or techniques of later literary movements, *Prae* currently remains lost to the world, despite the initial intrepid efforts of the Serbo-Croatians, and the French, generally in advance (as they are) in literary and artistic matters. If, as József J. Fekete observed, "linearity of time, coherent characterization, & plotline disappeared from his work and were replaced by something alien, a mysterious secret: authorial method,"[19] Szentkuthy is

---

18. Miklós Szentkuthy, *Prae*, tr. by Imre Bori, *Polja*, 138 (Novi Sad: 1970). Miklós Szentkuthy, *Prae*, tr. by Philippe Dôme, Pál Nagy, and Tibor Papp, *D'Atelier*, № 6–7 (1974) 7–58.

19. József J. Fekete, "Outprousting Proust: Szentkuthy, the Proteus of Hungarian Literature," *Hungarian Literature Online* (July 3, 2008).

then a true pioneer whose work will force us to re-consider not only the genealogy of the *nouveau roman,* but perhaps other genealogies, too. Countering the parallels often made between Szentkuthy and Proust or Joyce, parallels that even Szentkuthy rejected as misconceptions "on the part of people who have never read either Joyce or myself," [20] Németh perceives a more accurate corollary in Kant:

> What is important here is not the sensual mate-rial but the introspection of the artistic spirit that goes with it. If we wish to compare him with one of the big monsters, then Kant is much nearer the mark than either Proust or Joyce. *The Critique of Pure Reason* in point of fact is an introspection of the emptied mind. The mind jettisons the world from itself and strives to grasp what is left. As an experiment, it then again repeatedly gobbles one thing or other from the world and watches how space, time, and the categories chew it. It is not the item of food that is important, but the chew-ing itself; the food is only placed in the mouth so that there should be some chewing to investi-gate. It is like that with Szentkuthy as well, with the difference being that it is not the scholar's brain that is observing its own mechanism of chewing, but the on-looking and shaping artist.

20. Szentkuthy, *Prae: Recollections of My Career,* ibid.

> He is the sort of poet who, before throwing himself into his poetic work, carries out extraordinarily extensive prosodic studies, though not in the way that scholars of prosody usually do, but as only a scholar-poet would do it, who, struggling to reach for a novel system of poetry completely suited to his temperament, practices the ideas he has for substitute meters and contents on a hundred different examples. Any of those examples might be a masterpiece in regard to its meaning and content, but the true goal is a prosodic foundation carried to an unheard-of scale.[21]

In effect, a Kantian, but an artistic-poetic one scaling every domain of politics, literature, science, painting, history and the self, down to its biological and quotidian registers. Although this risks hyperbole, to convey the genuine significance of *Prae* as a Rosetta Stone of Hungary's role in the development of world literature, imagine Joyce's *Ulysses*, or Einstein's theory of relativity still being unknown, and the shock — & knowledge — our encounter with them would now bring. But that is the mantle of the posthumous; the works of those who are *Unzeitgemässe* are always in advance of their time. Thus began Szentkuthy's strange fate, with him struggling in the shadows during Rákosi's rule, yet all while

---

21. Németh, ibid.

writing original tome after tome, producing a prodigious and startling body of essays, novels, biographical 'fantasies,' to translations of *Gulliver's Travels*, *Oliver Twist*, & *Ulysses*, as well as a host of other works, including a diary of almost 200,000 pages spanning nearly 60 years, which late in his life the author declared contains his 'real' writing.[22] The first part, which dates from 1930–1947, an undeniably fertile and significant historical period, was opened on the anniversary of his death in July of 2013. Revelations surely await, especially since Szentkuthy probably appears in the diary as unmasked, for it may have been the one place where he could stand naked — as naked, that is, as anyone can be. But then, as he himself warns, "the diary is not always a sanctum of frankness; indeed, it is very frequently one of role playing. Particularly with me, being a born comedian... I am always jesting, so in the diary there is a lot of role playing; sometimes outright lying. A person stylizes himself."[23] If the mask remains, or a host of yet others

---

22. Szentkuthy first made this statement in 1979 for the *Who's Who Encyclopædia*, then in *Film-portrait of the 75-year-old Miklós Szentkuthy* (1983), and in *Frivolities & Confessions* (1988). *Film-portrait* was directed by Ilona Török and screened on Magyar Televízió in 1983. Pál Belohorszky was the interviewer. Cf. Miklós Szentkuthy, *Az élet faggatottja*, ibid., 102–114.

23. Szentkuthy, *Prae: Recollections of My Career*, ibid., 116.

are adopted in order to achieve that ſtylization, then plainly, in the diary, Szentkuthy is at very leaſt free of fortifications, at total ease in the safety of — *a home.* Here the internal émigré is no longer *hajléktalan.* With the Duc du Saint-Simon, Amiel, and Pepys as but several of his models as a diariſt, a certain circumſpect *Redlichkeit* surely guided his diary entries and, even in fancy, there is truth — the fantasy reveals the conſtruction of that particular mind, self, body. Through the mask of St. Orpheus, Szentkuthy did avow that, through the perſpective of his own life, he could "provide (the malicious of course will say 'to mask') a rationale for the diary ſtyle of my entire oeuvre, my utter *homesickness* for an endlessly complete diary," for it is the diary which is his "ultimate ideal in place of the honeſt superſtition of the old-fashioned 'objective opus.'"[24] Like all the great confessional artiſts, Szentkuthy is laying his heart bare, with even his biographical fantasies being masks, in part, of himself. Yet, in taking on a multitude of hiſtorical personages, there is no mere personal subjectivism in his revelations, nor the torpid self-obsession that rules our age but rather the x-ray of a *typus.* And if in his pursuit of fulfilling the Delphic injunction Szentkuthy betrays what he himself called a "myſtic penchant

---

24. *Marginalia on Casanova,* tr. by Tim Wilkinson (New York: Contra Mundum Press, 2012) §73, p. 134. Emphasis added.

for self-torment," that is oft (if not consistently) temper-
ed by humor, a genuinely comic — not bilious — irony.

While Szentkuthy's work would experience a renaissance within Hungary during his lifetime, following his
death in 1988, his reputation broadened even more: his
works were also translated into French, Spanish, Portu-
guese, Romanian, and Slovakian, earning him some recognition outside of his native country.[25] His lack of such
a reception in the Anglophone world is in part ironic
considering that he began as an Anglicist, penned a dissertation on Ben Jonson, and would later translate into
Hungarian not only Poe, Twain, and Eliot, but Donne,

---

25. I refer here to entire books since, actually, translation of Szentkuthy's work did begin in the mid 30s, when excerpts of *Prae* and
other texts (mostly essays), were translated into German but then
never published. The very first published translation of Szentkuthy's work was of an essay he wrote on Thomas Mann's *Joseph
and His Brothers.* See "Joseph-Geschichten," tr. by Pia Razgha, *Sinn
und Form* (1965) 205–217. Mann read the essay and expressed
his admiration for it, writing to Razgha that he found it an "exceedingly artistic, spirited, and chromatic review" and that Szentkuthy is "an amusable, very astute, sensitive, and susceptible spirit,
blessed with a supreme degree of humor..." Mann concluded his
letter by noting that Szentkuthy's critical tone reminded him
"very much of something Russian; in the manner Mereschkowsky
writes about Gogol, for instance. Anyway: I read his whole study
feeling true pleasure from the first to the last word..." The original German letter precedes Razgha's translation of Szentkuthy's
essay: "Thomas Mann an Pia Razgha," *Sinn und Form* (1965) 204.

Milton, and even Sir Thomas Browne (who figures — along with Mauriac — at the end of *Towards the One and Only Metaphor* as a key *typus* for Szentkuthy's conception of writing).[26] And that Szentkuthy still remains almost entirely unknown to most readers of world literature, despite circulating in translation since 1990 (in book form),[27] lends heft to Auerbach's foreboding dialectic, and confirms that it is only with his translation into English that he will enter the world stage. Yet this is itself peculiar since, as is well known, the number

---

26. Szentkuthy also met both T. S. Eliot and Dylan Thomas at a reading in England, corresponded in brief with Thomas after asking the poet to revise his wife's translation of an essay he'd written on Joyce, and met with Robert Graves in Hungary in May of 1968. Despite these encounters with three of the foremost writers of the 20th century, it did not lead to any greater notice of Szentkuthy's work, nor efforts to translate it into English. For Szentkuthy's own account of his encounters with Eliot and Thomas, see *Prae: Recollections of My Career*, ibid., §36. For his translation of Eliot's "Tradition and the Individual Talent," see "Hagyomány és egyéniség," Uő: *Káosz a rendben* (Budapest: Gondolat, 1981) 61–72.

27. As noted above, Szentkuthy was first translated into German in 1965, then into Serbo-Croatian in 1970, into French in 1974, into Serbo-Croatian again in 1985 (the essay "Makrokosmos"), and into Polish in 1986 (an excerpt from the *St. Orpheus Breviary*). The first complete work of Szentkuthy's to be translated into another language was *Divertimento*, his novel on Mozart, which published by Tatran in Slovakia in 1990.

of translations published in English every year is scant. Such is the magic of hegemony. With the publication of *Marginalia on Casanova* in 2012 — volume I of Szentkuthy's *St. Orpheus Breviary* & the first book of his to be translated into English — Contra Mundum Press sought to make his work more well known. In selecting him as our featured author, we will publish further translations of his work — all to be rendered by Tim Wilkinson — over the coming decade, including *Prae*, at last exporting that infamous text in its entirety. And now, with *Towards the One and Only Metaphor*, we offer the second English translation of Szentkuthy's work to date.

Originally published in 1935 and republished in 1985, *Towards the One and Only Metaphor* — Szentkuthy's second book — is comprised of 112 numbered sections ranging in length from one sentence to several pages. While a unique work of its own, something of a centaur in fact, it is also the seeding ground out of which much of Szentkuthy's future work would come. It is a text that defies classification into any particular genre, yet is perhaps most accurately thought of as *literature* in Blanchot's expansive sense of the term; as he defines it, literature is that which 'ruins' distinctions and the limitations of whatever genre in its creation of a unique, hybrid form. When reviewing the book in 1935, Dezső Baróti observed that *Towards the One and Only Metaphor* is comprised of "unconventional journal-like passages expanded into short essays, plans for novels, poetic meditations that have the effect of free verse, & paradoxical aphorisms," all of which reveal a moral philosophy, a politics, an erotics. "Its predominant motifs (insofar as one can succinctly describe it in a few words) are most especially nature, love, eroticism, sex. All that, however, is constantly painted over by the *vibration* of the unconcealed presence of a writer constantly in search of himself, & rife with beguiling, stimulating, and ever-renewed surprises."[28] This accords with Szentkuthy's grandiose if not quixotic goal of creating what he repeatedly called "a *Catalogus Rerum*, a listing of entities & phenomena, a Catalogue of everything in the Entire World."[29] Did Flaubert see Szentkuthy in a flash of prophetic light before conceiving of *Bouvard and Pechuchet*? Recognizing the absurdity of the *Catalogus Rerum*, similar in kind (as it is) to the totalizing projects of the Encyclopædists, if not the arch aim of the Enlightenment epoch — *das absolute Wissen* — it gives rise to laughter, even in Szentkuthy himself. Nevertheless, and at the same time, it was to him "a truly noble, Faustian goal" in which he sought to summarize "the untold thousands of phenomena in the world."[30] This included cataloguing "all of nature's

---

28. Dezső Baróti, "On *Az egyetlen metafora felé*," *Új tükör* 21, № 1 (1985). Tr. by Tim Wilkinson.

29. *Frivolitások és hitvallások*, ibid., ch. XIII.

30. Ibid.

accessible phenomena, all the heavens & hells of love, the whole world of history, and finally a universal review of mythologies (the universal show), all the way to Christian mythology."[31] What differentiates Szentkuthy from the Encyclopædists *et alia* is that this is only a cataloguing, not a Promethean attempt to harness and dominate nature; and what further differentiates him is his very jocularity, as well as his recognition that the Faustian target will never be reached.[32] The fool is the saving figure, the moral fulcrum, he who sabotages the Socratic project when it stretches toward extremities (the Revolution, the Terror, the Napoleonic Wars) since he knows its perils. Echoing the *ne quid nimis* of Pittacus of Mytilene, both Horace and Ovid respectively warn: *aurea mediocritas* and *medio tutissimus ibis*.[33] Still, Szentkuthy aims for the target, albeit with the rarely recalled second Delphic imperative always in sight: "Not too much!"

---

31. Ibid.

32. To András Nagy, Szentkuthy's *Catalogus Rerum* is "modeled more on medieval monks and on patristic & scholastic thinkers … than on the encyclopedia-champions of the Enlightenment…" Cf. András Nagy, "Masks Behind Masks: A Portrait of Miklós Szentkuthy," *Berlin Review of Books* (March 25, 2013).

33. Terence, the Roman comedian, issues a variation on this warning: "Do not pursue an object too far, too eagerly." Pittacus of Mytilene is considered one of the seven wise men of ancient Greece.

What, one might wonder, informs this strange *boke?*
Szentkuthy is guided or prompted into his Faustian
venture by sources as varied and diverse as Paracelsus,
Spengler, and Viennese psychology. There is an agonis-
tic element here as well, for *Towards the One and Only
Metaphor* is a response to criticisms directed against
Prae, a novel that so startled the Hungarian literary establishment that its author was viewed as "some sort of
book-bug homunculus, a horrific monster, who only ever
encountered sciences, philosophies, and mathematics."[34]
"Where," we can imagine some critics lamenting, "is your
humanity?" To combat that image of a *lusus naturae*,
Szentkuthy wrote *Metaphor* to establish his humanity,
and with a title that signifies the arc, movement, and
revolutions through which the book moves, from the
maniacal cataloguing of everything in the world to the
one and only crystallizing metaphor that will contain
it all. First, Paracelsus:

> Just as Paracelsus brought the human body, the
> stars, and minerals to a common denominator, or
> the way modern physics has a tendency to crop
> up every now and again, bringing to a common
> denominator all the material phenomena of the
> world (material is actually a property of energy,
> energy is actually a property of space…), so I

---

34. *Frivolitások és hitvallások*, ibid., ch. XIII.

wished to offer some kind of *summing-up* of art,
theology, love, life, death, the everyday, mythology,
games, tragedy, the cradle, the grave, jokes, a revelation. A listing is not moonshine: with me those
are true 'contrasts.'[35]

And so it is, with Szentkuthy taking up (on his own
terms) the Paracelsan ethos and tracing out through his
'lists' not only contrasts, but affinities and analogies: the
vibrating correspondences that reveal the very fabric or
threads underlining the universe. This is — as Szentkuthy
explicitly avows with a distinctly spiritual word — a *revelation*. What is it, the indefatigable searcher asks, that
underlies all things? What is the common denominator
that can link one's organs, a chemical substance, and the
most distant nebulae?[36] How can these disparate things
be united? Szentkuthy's lists then are not mere lists, not
"moonshine" (as he objects), but are gathered from that
sub specie aeterni perspective; if he catalogues, he does
not descend into a mere grocery list of items. Instead, his
cataloguing is more mercurial, more chemical, a trans-
planting of mathematical formulæ into literary style. In
this, in the Paracelsan ethos, we have the methodology of
his book, though that word sounds too theoretical for a
clowning, prankish, iconoclastic author like Szentkuthy

35. Ibid.

36. *Frivolitások és hitvallások*, ibid., 325.

who, much like Paracelsus, believed that "knowledge is experience" and since the "high colleges manage to produce so many high asses ... a doctor must seek out old wives, gypsies, sorcerers, wandering tribes, old robbers, and such outlaws and take lessons from them."[37] Experiments are for Szentkuthy biological, *essais* of primal vitality.

While a *Catalogus Rerum, Towards the One and Only Metaphor* is also a *confessio*, and this transports us — briefly — into Spengler and Viennese psychology, into the practice of analysis. For Szentkuthy came of age amidst the birth, struggle, & apotheosis of modern psychology, and by the time he wrote *Metaphor*, Freud, Jung, & Adler had published almost all of their major works while the International Psychoanalytical Association had not only been in existence for a quarter-century but had suffered its major fractures and faced its strongest opposing theories, most prominently with Jung's *Psychology of the Unconscious* (1912), *Psychological Types* (1921), & *Dreams and Psychic Energy* (1928), Rank's *Trauma of Birth* (1924), and Reich's *Function of the Orgasm* (1927). In 1933 — one year before the publication of Szentkuthy's

---

37. George Constable, *Secrets of the Alchemists: Mysteries of the Unknown* (Alexandria, VA: Time Life Education, 1991) 63. For similar pronouncements by Szentkuthy, cf. *Prae: Recollections of My Career*, ibid., § 22.

Prae — Hitler rose to power, Freud's and Reich's books were destroyed on the infamous night of book burning, and Jung published his seminal text, *Modern Man in Search of a Soul*. In fact, the quite exacting and singular definition that Jung outlines of the "modern man" could very well apply to Szentkuthy:

> ... the man we call modern, the man who is aware of the immediate present, is by no means the average man. He is rather the man who stands upon a peak, or at the very edge of the world, the abyss of the future before him, above him the heavens, and below him the whole of mankind with a history that disappears in primeval mists. Since to be wholly of the present means to be fully conscious of one's existence as a man, it requires the most intensive and extensive consciousness, with a minimum of unconsciousness. It must be clearly understood that the mere fact of living in the present does not make a man modern, for in that case everyone at present alive would be so. He alone is modern who is fully conscious of the present.
>
> The man whom we can with justice call "modern" is solitary. He is so of necessity and at all times, for every step towards a fuller consciousness of the present moves him further from his original "*participation mystique*" with the mass of man — from submersion in a common unconsciousness. Every step forward means an act of tearing himself loose from that all-embracing, pristine unconsciousness which claims the bulk of mankind almost entirely.[38]

With his *sub specie æterni* perspective of human history, his penetrating investigations of con- and un-consciousness, & his hyper-ever-presentness, Szentkuthy is — if not a modern man — damn near to the mark. Jung's characterization aside, it is in the ferment of a continent-wide political upheaval and intense psychic exploration that Szentkuthy begins his life as a writer. While as a Catholic, albeit a highly unorthodox one, the rite of confession was central to his life, the act of analysis or ruthless self-examination was intensely heightened by his impassioned study of the works of Freud, Jung, and Adler. If there is no explicit trace of their terminology in his work, or overtly psychological representations of characters in them, an *impact* is there, transfigured and digested in Szentkuthy's own way, most prominently in his obsessive, persistent, and dogged pursuit of *the question*. For one of the most conspicuous features of *Towards the One and Only Metaphor* is analysis. "My endeavor," he revealed, points

> to a world concept [*világkép*] in which I am able to offer a summation of the ultimate questions of life. (Like the figures seen in old coats of arms — the stylized images of a lion, the moon, stars, a chess table, an arm with a mace, hillocks & stretches of

---

38. Carl Jung, *Modern Man in Search of a Soul* (New York & London: Harcourt Brace Jovanovich, 1933) 196–197.

water, *et cetera* — a lot of fine things fit into a small space...) Ultimate question is a very good term because in this world of ours everything *remains a question*, at least for the examining brain. As a result..., it is of much more value to catalogue issues that reach to the very foundations of the world than to give premature answers and solutions.[39]

No answers, no solutions, but a catalogue of questions, though even that is not meant literally: one will not find in this book a single 'list' in the common sense of the word. *Metaphor* is not in any way pedantic; it is a work of aphorisms and *essais* and Szentkuthy is as candid (and as entertaining) as Rousseau. Whatever came to hand, ear, eye, or skin was analyzed by Szentkuthy with exactitude and assiduousness for, to the extent that it lay in his powers, he "endeavored to get to the bottom of things with the same passion as that exerted by the Viennese physician."[40] This is the manner in which the question prevails: in *a thinking in action*, in an elegance of cogitation. Szentkuthy *dances*. And this persistent mania for analysis and summation was also "vindicated," he said, by Spengler's *The Decline of the West* (1918). In particular, as Szentkuthy describes it, Spengler's biological view

39. *Frivolitások és hitvallások*, ibid., ch. XIII.

40. Ibid.

of the life cycle of cultures solidified his search for the unifying Paracelsan metaphor:

> According to Spengler, the history of the Chinese, Jews, Greeks, Egyptians, Arabs, etc. all displayed one and the same biological progression and formula, the primitive epoch of birth may be seen everywhere, the most splendid era of flowering, and then the over-ripeness in every area at harvesting time, which in turn leads on to total withering and an almost sickly unproductive decadence. Thus, for Spengler at least, world history shows a single picture or recipe — a one and only metaphor! — as, indeed, in several other respects, the histories of plants and animals also do from the earliest times until the present age. [41]

Early critics such as Gábor Halász saw in *Towards the One and Only Metaphor* only a chaos of orality devoid of any organizing principle, let alone a calculating geometry. Instead, it was pure excitability, tension, flair, nerve, intellectual paroxysm; not a unified work, only the precursor to a work; all that "is left is this *prae*," Halász concluded his review, pointing back, acidly, to Szentkuthy's audacious first novel, and then remarking, dismissively, that Szentkuthy had still not learned how to write but was

---

41. Ibid.

simply casting "raw material"[42] at his readers. Clearly, Halász could not recognize the Paracelsan aim of the book, nor that its organizing principle was entirely unique. As with any fragmentary work, its lack of a systematic structure does not betray a lack of *design*, nor the absence of a guiding *vision*. True, *Metaphor* is an essayistic and confessional work *à la* Montaigne's *Essais*, or Lichtenberg's ruminative waste books, or Joubert's keen-eyed observations. Yet, if it is as fragmentary as those texts, *Towards the One & Only Metaphor* is at the same time ordered like a group of disparate stars: when viewed from afar, they reveal or can be perceived to form a constellation — they *are* sculpted by a geometry of thought, for, as András Keszthelyi observed, the text is essentially something of a manifesto, "an explicit formulation of the author's intentions, his scale of values, or, if you wish: his *ars poetica*."[43] And when reviewing the book upon its original publication, Németh elucidated its geometrical and biological dimensions, noting how, through dehumanization, Szentkuthy returns us to the embryo and the ornament. This is done, however, in order to bring us into closer alignment with Szent-

42. "On *Az egyetlen metafora felé,*" *Napkelet,* № 12 (1935). Tr. by Tim Wilkinson.

43. András Keszthelyi, "Mit üzen a 'monstrum'?" *Élet és Irodalom* (November 7, 1985). Tr. by Tim Wilkinson.

kuthy's gestures and words, to take us into the very *particles* of existence, and the word is germane. To Németh,

> There is no form and content in humanity; our protoplasm is more geometrical and our form more formless than the geometry and biology bubbling up in Szentkuthy's U-tube. His method is dehumanizing; he dehumanizes man by mutilating him in the direction of the embryo and the ornament. The dehumanization, at root, is irony, and the type of writer who simply wishes to keep on smiling during the puppet show and gut-wrenching may well feel just fine. But Szentkuthy is not that type; indeed, he is greatly preoccupied with humanity, and in his ecstasy as lyrical agitator-cum-preacher would far sooner push our eyes, ears, and heads under his gestures and words.[44]

And in *Marginalia on Casanova*, through the figure of its narrator, St. Orpheus, Szentkuthy offers a key to his very art when he describes 'the most savage battle of his life': "the battle of the 'descriptive' versus the 'anecdoticizing,' the Romantically luxuriant in statics versus the French moralizing style of a La Bruyère or La Rochefoucauld." While both styles figure prominently throughout his oeuvre, description is undoubtedly victorious, since Szentkuthy finds in it "many more novelties, variations,

---

44. Németh, ibid.

elements, and shades than in any kind of so-called rational thinking. The most complex thoughts, poetic sensibilities, or philosophical sophistications are all stupefying platitudes, oafish homogenizing beside the infinity of nuancing an *object*. Thinking, however, imposes a demand for nuance, a microscopic madness; it goes where it can best satisfy that *insatiability for atoms*." [45] And so he brings us into the very particles of existence through his Paracelsan principle of analysis, his search for affinities & analogies, and his tracking of correspondences, all of which are forms of nuancing. Nevertheless, it is not only objects but concepts, historical phenomena, consciousness, and a host of other things, including language itself, that Szentkuthy nuances, turning them into living creatures, animating them with endless undulations, making them vibrate, viewing them as number, endowing them with color and sound. For to him, words are "chance reflex crystals" which he plays with like a chemist and an alchemist. And through this play — in every book, whether masked or unmasked — Szentkuthy's *ars poetica* yields up a philosophy of love. It is always Eros which is put through a thousand and one permutations, and which is repeatedly — tableaux-like — animated out of Szentkuthy's efflux of materials, like the thousand &

---

45. *Marginalia on Casanova*, ibid., §73, p. 130. Emphasis added.

one figures of Asian temples, such as the Kharjuravāhaka monuments, which are equally spiritual, geometric, and erotic.

It is hoped that the 21st century will see Szentkuthy's transcontinental reception and renascence, and that — as Nicholas Birns predicted in a review of *Marginalia on Casanova* — "Szentkuthy will enter and alter the canon of twentieth-century literature as we know it."[46] For the canon will not be closed as long as *Weltliteratur* is moving — like Szentkuthy, & now *with* Szentkuthy — towards the one and only metaphor.

Rainer J. Hanshe

April / July 2013

Berlin & Budapest

---

46. Nicholas Birns, *Tropes of Tenth Street* (October 6, 2012).

TOWARDS THE ONE
& ONLY METAPHOR

I

IN STARTING this book, what else can I take as my introductory precept (or desire) than this: I have no other aim than wild, absolute *imitation*; around me suffocating, swooningly torrid air, in this steamy yet nevertheless certain gilded death the warbling darkness of a pair of sparrow throats &, above all, these million lines, the analytical richness, of foliage, grasses, and nameless meadow flowers. These *lines*, the fantastic richness of this prodigal precision — *they* are what intensifies my desire for imitation into a mania. A *Catalogus Rerum*, an 'Index of Entities' — I am unlikely to free myself of this, the most primeval of my desires.

2

THE ETERNAL GAME: *to get to know* the world — *to preserve* the world. When I am excited by imitation: is that a sentimental fear of death guiding me, I wonder, a grandpawish fondness for *bibeloterie*, or some desire for universal knowledge, a Faustian gesture? You, you little blade of grass, here beside my pen: are you the graceful seal of ephemerality of a selfish moment of mine, a small witness of my frivolity — or are you a secret of Nature that is to be discovered?

3

HOW INTERESTING the chirping of birds: when I am listening I 'hear' virtually nothing, I only *see*: the black throats of tiny birds, the swelling miniature yet nevertheless *quantitatively* tragic night of cuckoo lungs — those little midnight horns arising in the trail of the chirping are the sole blackness in the morning light.

4

TWO KINDS OF HEAT: the summer heat of the out-side world & a sick person's fever. Fight in the blue-grey daybreak of the bedroom! That, too, to the 'imitation': the lathes of the roller blinds, the moonlit, milky-blue leaves of the plant creeping onto the ledge (at 2:30 in the morning), the lightness of the street, the gloom of the bedroom, the crumpled-apart eiderdowns, the visible nude-figure syllables — those impressions of mine are the most important, they are *everything* to me.

My body's inner fever, *'paysage intime de la maladie'* [1] —
& the summer heat fermenting at daybreak — fight it
out. Which wins? Which is due to the girl and which
is for the girl? Woman = I wonder, do you, too, come
from the daybreak? Stars, flarings-up of marine horizons, birds and avian throats falling maturely to the
ground among the loosening foliage hawsers of the
trees; in short, the outside world, the Greek or Gundol-
fian 'cosmos,' [2] are these your anatomical continuations
— or is my fever, my body's inner turbulence, your
true brother; indeed, your identity? How gratifying
both notions are — whether you are an inner hallucination of my heart, my gall bladder, my vagrant hormones
('myth secretions'), or a strange palm on some strange
Riviera, an Artemisian, cruel 'objectivity.'

5

CAN A HYMNAL LIFE be separated from the analytic
life; are a separate Pindar and Proust credible? That
question of the two kinds of heat preoccupied me the
entire night: with the frantic persistence, the stubbornness of my half-asleepness, I sought an absolute dis-
criminating definition, & at the same time the dream,
the semi-reality carried me at a quite dizzying and
irresistible pace towards the rich, swirling nullity of
the dithyramb.

⟰ 6 ⟱

I READ SOME POEMS BY GOETHE before going to bed: perhaps the perverse marriage of banality and *rhyme* caused this thirst for dithyrambs. *Voyage curieux*: the *Spieß*-ness of the *rhyming* makes one more anarchic than the anarchy of the rhyming.

⟰ 7 ⟱

THE MOST BROTHERLY BROTHERS, the sole relatives: they are here beside me — sleep and precision, the feverish fiction of possibilities and imitation.

⟰ 8 ⟱

DRAWINGS COOL ONE: if I look up at the optical mosaic of trees, the sharpness of a million contours is cooling.

⟰ 9 ⟱

Two female gestures. One of them, really petite but, in terms of her curves, a plumply, well-proportionately skinny woman (fairly elderly), adjusts her dress in the

Street — but how? She *picks at* the silk on her shoulder blades with the thumb and index finger of her right hand — on precisely the part of the body which is par excellence the place for being caressed by a man's hand, a broad and wavy *planar* sensory area (in itself a constant curved Minkowski erotic *space* or *plane*):[3] the woman picks at *points* there just like a bird with a sharp beak picks at a cherry. Of course, it is all much more unashamedly provocative than if she would smooth her dress by stroking it. Elderly woman — girlish figure — silk dress: good.[4]

The other: a woman on Gellért Hill in Budapest is cutting her toenails in the sun. That, too, is 'coquetry', there is no doubt about it. The vulgar intimacy is erotic. Go your double route, Eros, on the high-minded ways of geometric metaphors and facts — go on the kitchen-smelling pathways of vulgarity & demotic sloppiness.

⇇ IO ⇉

EROS: something geometric, something ethical, something demotic, something natural. — The two kinds of primitiveness: demos and nature.

Demotic = the *animal* part of love.

Natural = the *floral* part of love;
it is also evident here that animal and flower do *not* denote the same nature — they are two different worlds.

⇐ II ⇒

A LITTLE *moral philosophical* (yes: moral philosophical) typology: from the portrait gallery of plants =

a pine: each cone a brown central point around which the needles branch out like a porcupine or ſtar, with each such ſtar ball sweetly taking up position next to another — they barely bump into or interſect with each other;

a young acacia: pure half-light & half-shades, in point of faċt, optical hypotheses incarnated as lamellæ. What a significantly different *moral* physiognomy from the pine tree. How different the deer-paw graphology of the branches, the Io-embracing with the winds, the swaying, skirt-like rubbing againſt themselves.

When they turn out in the wind and suddenly diſþlay their silver reverse sides; pine needles are unable to turn out like that (different psychological temperament).

The 'monotony,' the faċt of the repetition of forms with the pine-tree and the acacia — there are *many* pine needles, *many* tranſþarent acacia leaves, but how fantaſtically *differently* many those two manys are;

unknown bush: Corot-like, it reaches into the picture from the side of the picture — its branches display some kind of aquarium-like eternal and nostalgic horizontality, the leaves are also sparse, resembling samples of bridge cards, and amazingly flat. Full of waving horizontal silhouettes as if one were looking from the bottom of a lake at lotus leaves swimming on like embodied shadows over one's own head.

Are these not world historical profiles, the teachings of saints, the victories & fall of politicians, the 'grand' style and petty mannerism of poets =

pine needles
acacia ovals
lotus shadows?

Or if you prefer it, the reverse — hence a little *botanical* (yes: botanical) typology — from the human portrait gallery: St. Francis, Hitler, Rabelais, Lincoln, Jacob. (To elaborate, *ad libitum*.)

 I 2

'FORM' and 'order': different entities.
The nature of 'form' will perpetually have light cast on it by *plants* (conformation of leaves & flowers; clustering

of leaves & flowers; relationship of leaves and branch-es; wind and resistance of foliage; directions of roots).

On the nature of 'order': consistent Freudianism = *botanical* harmony (conformational harmony).

⇐ 13 ⇒

Foreignness — sibship
Motherhood — lover

— An auburn-haired woman is stretched out before me on the hillside. She is lower down, I am higher up (who is below and who above is just as decisive an issue here as it is for an army at war): when we look at each other and our eyes meet (how plastic & precise an 'en-counter' like that, excluding any misjudgments — when one can sense fancying a person more objectively than the most sensitive physical sensor). I wonder what causes the pathos: one another's human *community*, our bio-logical sibship — or the *foreignness*, the space between our 'individualities'? Can it be determined which sensa-tion is the 'more justified': animal attraction to a fellow animal or a burning isolation from the eerily other and *different* ego? How do both simultaneously have an in-fluence on Eros: it is the biological common denomina-tor at the bottom of the entire human race yet equally the most fiercely *personal* thing, the individual's chief individualizing and isolating factor. This woman: how absolutely familiar, familiar to a *cosmic* degree, we have between us an acquaintance going back millennia, dating to Paradise, our 'geological' memories are shared — the natural history epic of the Homo animal makes its mark in every urban nuance and 'flirting' dodge, "... when we were as yet still *fish*, on the third anniversary of the Creation — Do you remember?" — And at the same time how *alien*: how rigidly, fatefully, and furiously, how impossibly alien.

She is feeding the child cherries, piece by piece: the child cannot even be seen, it's lying in the grass, hidden by green — it's as if the woman were throwing the fruit on to the ground. Whether she is a mother or *Fräulein*, I do not know. But there is something uneliminable in that feeding cherry by cherry, something elementarily *amorous*. The most coquettish, shallowest dodge, it seems, is: maternity.

⟸ 14 ⟹

THE BIGGEST and most important liaisons of my life were these: at certain intervals to see the same female face in the same surroundings without our ever having met before. For instance, at the opera: the girl has a ticket for the same performances as I do. At times like that there is something dream-like, a silent confidentiality between us: the infinite richness of time, the past, of memories, which is to say the principal nutrients of love, and all the same I don't even know the girl's name; we are strangers. Is this not the chief charm of holiday places: the *familiar* unknown? That is why they are the greatest *loves* (the word can never be written down with such total justification as in precisely these situations), because in that kind of liaison truly the *only* thing which plays a part is the essence of Eros: a lovely portrait and passing time: the *nude* figure of Venus being born from the billows of *time*, which reimmerses into time — "for out of it wast thou taken."⁵ What fantastically unsettling moments those are when, years later, one again meets such a pseudo-acquaintance: greet, no, not just greet, but hug and kiss her, and only at the last minute is one able to hold back one's pathos, reminding oneself that one is not meeting an old acquaintance but, quite the reverse: an old unknown.

15

HOW MANY forms 'seduction' takes:
    cutting corns from unwashed feet,
    feeding flipped cherries to children,
    stretching out lazily, eyes closed on the grass:
    animal nonchalance, playing mother, playing death.

⇐ 16 ⇒

THE STRANGE SITUATION of the woman's body: both the woman & the man 'ogle' — meanwhile a three-year-old girl is combing, or, to be more accurate, she is tearing the woman's hair with a comb, and the woman is lazily letting her. Through what meandering paths nature introduces the body (*"tiré pas les cheveux"*[6] — once in earnest!), an indispensable character, into the eyes' flirtatious-Platonism. Laziness, vanity, game, a touch of idyllic sadism, Narcissizing, pose, desire, blasé indifference — for how long is it possible to string more nouns onto this auburn hair?

⇐ 17 ⇒

IS ANY GAME in the world more refined or verity more poetic and live than the underlying tone of Goethe: the *West-östlicher Divan* = sobriety & banality, triviality and an eastern story-setting which is as colorful as *A Thousand and One Arabian Nights*. Is it not *immoral* to awaken one's desire at one and the same time for a peasant-axiomatic, level-minded 'common sense' talking in adages — and also for the night, for the Orphic mystery, and the anarchically kitsch (i.e., true) East?

⟞ 18 ⟝

THE PROLOGUE to a summer morning: the agony of the bedroom at daybreak — the secret of dreams, the secret of *raison*, the secret of infiltrating flowers, the secret of secrets. And the epilogue in the boiling midday heat? Conversation with a tram driver: he had drunk no beer for two years as that made him fat; he preferred a pint of wine ("if it is good," he emphasizes) with soda water, beer is dreadfully expensive here, the big heat wave had arrived quite unexpectedly. It is fair enough that I am reading the *W.-Ö. Divan*: is that not what I am experiencing? The eternal duality of banality and demonics (never its *battles*!).

I like a bedroom at daybreak; there is something universally human about it, a laboratory and fate simultaneously. The laths of the roller blinds: with their blackness, their complicated systems of filtering light, and their even more complex reflections on the open panes of glass — those laths are symbols, realities, of line, geometry, form, dramatic monotony, baroque simplicity, satisfiers of a primeval instinct of mine. It's the same as the keyboard of a piano: at home I keep the lid of the keyboard constantly open in order to see the sensuous abstraction, the amorous cubism, of the white and black lines. Just as non-linear black roses of music grow into the air out of the primitive linearity and numericalness of the keys

— so here the billowing, highly non-*orderly* paradoxes of the lighting propagate out of the fairly cheap physical orderliness of the roller blind. Every parallel, refrain, and repetition excites me: the rings of ripples on lakes, the escaped powers of ovals on branches, of acacias, fence laths, etc. *Un poète des parallèles*: that poet is *not* classical and does not write rhyming couplets, that is for sure. From the bedroom can be seen the Moon, stars, flowers, every muscle, mask, and *décolletage* of the atmosphere step by step. 'Garden': that is some magnificent middle way between biological wildness and scientific laboratory, resembling the old pieces of the goldsmiths' art on which crystal, a diabolical 'libertinage' of precious stones, and the pedantic ordering business of a working craftsman and artist are brought together. The tree that happens to be overlooking the window and is in keeping with it is quite different from trees in general.

In the bedroom is the clock and a sleeping woman's body, there are morality, death, and Eros. Human beings in a bedroom are *ethically* rather than physically naked. A bedroom is simple; smooth walls, hygiene. And between hygiene's nurse-like walls the poppy of dreams grows: dusted with poppy seed, sooty, rancid, opiate-dosed, cyanic blue, and with a black calyx. A wife: the morality of marriage. A dream: the freedom of *nihil*, its all-toppling anarchy, its orgy of problems. That is all *together* in a bedroom — hence it is a great big place.

I grasp this arch, shall kiss it to the day I shall die: woman, garden, time, dream, morality; from the daybreak pillar of geometry to the tram driver's noonday pillar. ("A pint with soda"? *Benedicte!*)[7]

19

Huberman[8]

FROM THE MOMENT the first notes of the F minor Adagio sounded the violinist could not be seen, all the more the violin: it suddenly appeared, as in a vision, in a pale Moon sheaved in chandelier-light, with infinite tenderness and energy as it were cast into the air, just like a long-lost jewel that is now thrown up at the head of a suddenly breaking high wave (not like an openmouthed sack but one forcibly slit at the side) or a communion wafer waved towards a packed church congregation — the violin's greyish-brown wood: whereas most musicians had a bright yellow, vividly blackish-red colored violin, this one hovered in provocative neutrality between sky and earth in front of the half-built organ.

The vibration of the initial notes and the drawn-apart slow rain of the light were in the closest relationship (the individual rays twisted and the solitary sparks drew apart as when someone stepping through a vertically hanging curtain composed of strings of pearls is forced to deflect the vertical strings slightly to the left & right).

The voice was so precise and soft, so airily dreamy and Annunciation-style dogmatic, that the choir and the rest of the audience thought that it did not derive from the flying violin suddenly thrust into the air but from somewhere else, and the arrow-shooting of the body of the violin into this agonic high was just a mysterious semaphore signaling that one's strings and bows should be sent away, all earthly violin playing should come to an end and one should listen to the celestial philharmony.

The notes were so gorgeous that there was something perverse, an immoral 'negativity,' streaming out of them: as if they were surprising from behind the bars of the cadence, plastic in their uncertainty, like the elders spying on Susanna [9] — in itself it was a bathing of notes which had been stripped nude, chastity in a crystal-clear ethereality, with her provocative, unmistakably whorish gestures. The dead-beat choral singers closed their eyes; with a helpless smile of awe the conductor chewed the tip of his baton as if he wanted to play flute on it. With a curious, ornate Moon-round hand, the tones inscribed into intoxicated souls; there with a harpoon of melody at its edge while others, coming directly afterwards, paraded with their golden surfaces among the foliage of their dreams to build a triumphant, reverential-coquettish nest.

In the subsequent minutes the violinist, too, became visible under his crookedly hovering violin: the instrument continued to rock like a gold-leaved branch in the wind, with the violinist virtually hanging from it like a sleeping bird dangling on a branch, a hanged man, or a black rag. He threw the violin so high from his shoulder that his head slipped right underneath it, and for a goodly time it pitched & rolled there in the shade. The contrast between the sloth, so to say, clasping to the violin from below and the inhuman sweetness of the music was marvelous: it was evident that, out of asceticism, virtuosity, and lust, he was tossing his soul, his pathos, and his instrument too far and too high from himself, and now only, with distorting grimaces of fingers, arms, & face, was he able to catch up with himself and again completely cover with his body whatever remained of the melody in his soul.

When the orchestra began to accompany him with a quite soft pizzicato, the violinist's pose suddenly changed: within a trice the violin swooped into the depths, as if the unexpected weight of the bubbling passages had carried him down from on high and he was now struggling under a hailstorm. At that point the violinist's face could be seen well. An enormous skull was placed above a short, flat-footed, rickety-kneed hunched body. The size of the skull is to be understood as residing in its width: there was a horizontal, virtually flattened monumentality about it; even his 'lofty' forehead was somehow 'spiritually' lofty, though in reality it was rather broad. On certain Aztec idols, on the slightly puffed-up belly, drooping to left & right, of statues of

Buddha, and on the lazy and tragically melting diadem of archways of Babylonian gates, one can sometimes see this paradoxical melting into each other of domed height and the flat sprawling & slipping to the ground of swelling, half-leavened dough. Spirit and animal bone, artistic Gothic and mineral Romanesqueness are good expressions of the fundamental problem of art: sentimental transcendentalism and material dormant-swirling mass, which predicate, murder, and demand each other. The brow was pale, combining the tints of the Moon's Astarte silver & a nervous *Schwächlinging*[10] standing outside life (mystery and bad neurasthenia — is there not something *par excellence* 'artistic' about this fist-mimicking head?); shades of ash grey 'secondary planets' spread across these pallidly gleaming fields, especially two large bumps, with those pale-strong contours that snails usually leave as a trace on green leaves when they slide further.

Why that, after all, flat hunk of a head, inclining to left & right into the depths, nevertheless created an impression of 'loftiness' was easily explicable by the fact that bodies rising on high from the depths usually display those kinds of arched forms, and willy-nilly one saw in the material the strength which was pushing it towards the spheres; an arc of distant hills which just managed to rise up at the edge of a desert: a ribbon which was still half-submerged, but one could sense that a big internal spasm of the earth had squeezed it out of the darkness into the sky; the backs of seals and whales popping up for air from underwater; the rising sun's horizontal yet nevertheless tower-spined arc: the whole enormous skull was, in point of fact, a parallel band above barely curved eyebrows, which stretched from the nose practically to the ears.

The gesture was the most congenial gesture of art: the amorphous, barely analyzable big mass, rigid rather than waxily melting, sheer weight, dream, slow-breathing, nervelessness & pulselessness, but the whole was nevertheless raised and driven by something, a hidden divine leaven, ferment and flood-tide. How much more intellectual is a head like this, resembling a sea-rounded egg-stone, than a so-called Gothic truly tall & therefore 'intellectual' head, towering like a cone set on its apex.

The geological strata of horizontality were repeated right through the head: the gigantic (but only occasionally presenting) furrows of the forehead, the eyebrows, the eye movements, the frames of the nostrils, the black continuo of the lower jaw, and the closing curve of the chin all ran from right to left. The eyes were narrow and, as has already been pointed out, reached back all the way to the ears. At times two dark cavities were apparent like the ineffective channel of a reed cut lengthwise in two — an expressive, unrepentantly melancholy blindness emanated from them: while the diluvial globes of the brow shone their sporulating whale's belly in the moonlight, ghostly spaces under the eyes gaped a demonic night with the slogan of "not worth looking at, no need to look, color & form are sick heresies vis-à-vis the sound" — a night which, besides all its mystic nihilism, seemed to be a concrete, slightly dirty, gummy eye disease: chaos and trachoma simultaneously.

One of the eyes had an outward squint: this alternatively dancing pupil at once intensified the protozoan-style amorphousness of the whole face and look running across it, continually recapitulating the horizontality of the earth's surface. The pupil sometimes raced lightning-quickly from the nose to the ear with its sick muscular freedom, the whites not even evident at such times, and with a dark spot filling the eye. On other occasions, in sharp contrast, the eyes grew totally confused, darting frantically here and there in the huge eye area, hummingbirds in their cage, so to say. The eyes slipped almost into the forehead so that they had to be jerked back into position with the butterfly net of the upturned eyebrows; on other occasions they sank behind his cheekbones so that they had to be spooned to the surface by the elevators of the neck muscles, then again lose their way in the whites of the eyes, and the eyelids tormented them with all manner of painful, eelish waves; in the end, it often happened that the eyes more or less catapulted the pupils from the corners of the eyes, over and beyond the ecstatic boundary — the *limes* — of cross-eyedness, among the choral singers or the audience.

His nose, in relation to the archaic plasma tempi of other parts of his skull, accommodated to vulgar ghetto clichés: it was hooked and at the lower end a swollen printing error in the text of the alluvium. The lower lip detached from the face like one side of boiled fish from vertically placed fish bones: drooping, curled, twisted under itself, like a black scroll of papyrus, or stretched nostalgically forward, like Oriental vases or the rim of a well. The sometimes gigantically dilated eyelids and this black fin or salad leaf followed a uniform rhythm as they were also uniform in their lobular outsizedness. It was also obvious that there was a close agreement of muscle between the shadow flesh of the mouth and the nose, constrained as it had been into a hook by all the horizontality: it was gratifying to pull apart the nostrils in the 'maelstrom' of horizontality, to annihilate the entire nose by endlessly straining forward & rolling the lower lip up under itself — or *vice versa* to tuck an enormous plinth from the mouth, after a brief drooping, beneath the flattening nose.

How much more expressive, more defined, & more analytical a mimic is that pair of hawser-thick wrinkles on the brow, the sick & 'senseless' cross-eyedness of the eyes, each sudden sea-swelling on the chin of a lower lip provocatively fattened into a caterpillar, the movements of the head clumsy in an octopus fashion — than the confused and indiscriminately psychologized and humanized play of features of a professional actor able to control every muscle and nerve. That head and rhythm were the true, the sole possible parallels to the string of tones, uniting as they did all the bestiality and mathematical character of the sound, which beaded out, crystal-clear, from the violin. The enchanting *'dulcor'* [11] of the Adagio did not call for a portrait of a transfigured seraph but this sort of sloth-bodied & moldy-skinned Caliban above the bone cushion of the violin.

⇐ 20 ⇒

IT IS POSSIBLE to 'distance oneself' from life — possible to 'draw nearer' to life, to reality. Distancing or nearing — all the lyrical perfumes of imprecision issue from those words, but still they are justified & possible from some viewpoint (I am too lazy to define it).

I frequently experience three such distancings: through the techniques of love, science, and sleeping.

Is it not the chief distinguishing mark of the state of being in love that one has no connection with the world: the image of the girl hardly crosses one's mind, the time of the next rendezvous barely presents itself to one's consciousness, one's sensual desires (in a positive direction) are negligibly slight; by & large: the woman is zero from a practical point of view — admittedly, a 'dynamic nil.' What one actually experiences, by contrast, is a certain inner relaxedness, looseness, spleen, a sleepy objectivity

vis-à-vis matters of this world, a 'precise indifference' —
the whole thing is a 'grey magic,' 'listless ecstasy' insofar
as one becomes alienated, on the one hand, from the
world, from other people's functions, the whole history
of the rest of humanity, from the nature of nature (this
is somehow an 'ex-static' feature) and, on the other hand,
a passionate viewing, a hallucination, a satisfactory possession of a new phenomenon (of the girl, for instance)
is missing — one's last remaining individuality is not a
blazing fire rose in the world's gloom of boredom, but
a flickering rose of boredom, just as pale as the world
(that is what is listless about it). There was a time when
it irritated me dreadfully if, in my amorous condition, I
was obliged to meet men carrying out intellectual labors:
poets (1°), essayists (2°), theoretical physicists (1,000°).
I felt an excruciating antithesis between my self, who
was finding nothing positive and pleasurable, and my
friends, who were finding many positives and much pleasure in the electrons and expanding fogs of the world. If
it had at least been in my power to confront the woman
and her raw film negative or her fruitful-fermenting
mythology with their poems, judgments, and realities,
but no: love's biggest torment was that it withered from
the world, it made me foolishly negative, the woman
was shrouded in obscurity. Is there a bigger antithesis
(I wondered) than that between my little sexual hypochondria and, let's say, Eddington's *Mathematical
Theory of Relativity?*[12] Never did I feel the lyrical person-

ality to be more of a nullity, more parodical, and sicker than at times like that — mathematics more dehumanizedly true or more lethally objective. Of course, as in every *minderwertes*[13] and neurotic person (cf. the pursuit of paradox, synthesis, and morphology by German humanities) there suddenly awakened desires for synthesis: maybe I could be the person who was able to unify in my life the absolutely 'limited' hypochondria of the lyric poem, the shivering filth and qualm oozes of the *ego*, and the most sadistic objectivity (sadistic in relation to the lyricizing), *fact* character, and mathematical perception of the objective world.

Yesterday a friend of mine, who for me will be a permanent symbol of a *non*-lyrical, 'objective' person (an absolute musician and absolute mathematician temperament, with heaps of ethical *'douceur'*) took me into the observatory and, among other things, pointed out a ball-shaped star cluster (Messier 13)[14] on the telescope; on his table I found masses of mathematical books (afterwards I bought Eddington's *New Pathways in Science*). Nowadays I do not perceive nil in love and a mathematizing scientific realism as being an antithesis: these scientific truths can lead 'out of' life just as much as poetic lyricism. Life is: *comble d'imprécision*. What do I mean by life, I ask myself? In what way do I arbitrarily narrow down and broaden out the word, the elastic boundaries of which everyone has already exceeded with the most comical irresponsibility, whether they be a buffoon politician or a dogmatic religious nut. By life I mean the life of an average man on the street, an ordinary Joe, but at the same time also of a few sober 'heroes.' For him poetry is not infralife, science not ultralife.

The face of the star cluster: on a dark grey or blue-black or numb-brown background a silvery, glaucous comet's tail the color of a genuine pearl — a whitish gloom in a darkish loom — how marvelously the picture united the laboratory, geometrical staginess of a magnifying glass, the natural, elemental solitude, and the biological material of distance.

The antithesis between the huge apparatus of the telescope and the extraordinary narrowness of the aperture through which one looks at the stars — how much smaller it is than those of a pair of binoculars. That is why one has the impression one is observing the star cluster by chance as the eye can barely gain access: there are sharp screws grazing and digging into the nose, needles, scales, screws and tubes into the ears, temples, and upper jaw at the least movement — to a lay mind *those* are the essence of 'scientificity': there is an instrument, the object of which is to see afar, and on that the fitness for seeing is hardly apparent — such an absolute visual device that one's eyes can at best only just get near to, and if one has somehow managed to get close to it, the visual field is as restricted as in those unpleasant dreams when the eyes stick together and one is unable to read anything at all even if one were to sweat blood.

I am unable to shake off the contrast: the teeny-weeny regular round opening, the screws, arms, the pulsing of the timing machine, the forced contortions of the neck resembling tortures by the Inquisition, and at the same time the Pascalian horror of the celestial night sky, the velvety, embryonic intimacy. The perpetual prank of magnifying lenses: one is both 'there' and far away at one and the same time.

It seems it is impossible to live: women & telescopes show the way *out*. Dreams also show the way out — especially those in the daytime (morning and early-afternoon dreams). While tree boughs, birds, lights and vehicles chirp in the streets, I freely indulge the laxity of my guts, my blood, and my fever: I stew, stammer, and swoon on a sofa. Oh, poor body of mine, sailing as it is to death, you '*materia*': you most show the way out. My uncertainly vibrating cross eyes, my horse's head crowned with its giddy-rainbow-hued turban, my truly chronic inner ear, my nervously sporulating bowel juices, my puny, rotting legs, my fiery, eczematous mitts, in short, my 'positive' idol and statue part: you are the greatest bar in my way towards a 'normal' life. Should I curse you: girls desisting due to love, heavenly secrets dressed in mathematical constellations, & neurotic body? Or should I bless you? The motto of my agony will be of the following sort: "Had I not been enamored, had my body not had the body it has, had I not been 'true': might I perhaps have been able to live?"

⇐ 21 ⇒

To LOAF ETERNALLY between these three *styles* (metaphors or biological phases) of love: flower, worldliness, and illness?

The blind leafy boughs of gardens stand in spring-like plenitude in the broad, unexpectedly frosty night as if they were bursting breasts and udders of death; the air is full of the smells of roses, olive trees, and elders: these summery (not to say 'washable imprinted') fragrances are odd in the icy cold, much the same as prepared smells under glass — summer & winter simultaneously. How stiffly, and yet with a humility undulating from inside, flowers stand there: gamo- and polypetalous, sheer crystal, symbol, each one bloody form. Is that Eros? When will the ultimate connection of *sex & flora* become clear?

A slender Horch automobile by one of the garden fences, a woman alone in the dark upholstery of the back seat. A small white hat, a feather stuck slantwise into it (like the arrow in hearts carved on tree trunks), legs crossed in a skirt that has ridden up and is anyway broadly slit, & fishnet stockings full of huge holes. She is powdering her cheeks: in the wake of her puff, tiny gleaming galaxies wander in the depths of the automobile, a mirror is also fished halfway out of the handbag as if she were going to examine herself not so much from out of the mirror but the whole handbag, and the mirror (together with the handbag!) was higher than her head, looking at herself in it, the eyes virtually out-turned, from below, the snake of her tongue sometimes glinting all the way along the rim of lipstick like the automatic wipers on an automobile's windshield, giving little pats to her cheeks, tweaking a maenad curl medallion from her hair forward from under her hat, and tapping with fingers, magnetized around a solitary flat ring, to set the hat straight, then the handbag is closed, or rather rolled up with a quiet rustle and she drops it down into her lap as if a jolting roller blind were being let down her chest by a motor which had started up and was spraying it with some kind of motile dew. *Vogue!* Dresses, the geometry of poses, the chemistry of masks, the abstract, sexless world of the mirror & vanity, the dehumanizing tricks of the desire to please: what is *your* relationship to Eros? A riddle just as is that of a flower.

Finally, a badly curtained bed-sitting-room in a railway workers' flophouse: bed, unclothed, vulgar bodies, mashed and spongoid skin of sickness or health (the *health* of the average man is in itself *de profundis* pathological). Here love means either ten children or an abortion in a suburban quack's shack, either suicide by drinking sulphuric acid or a good meal, or syphilitic material for bespectacled physician automata (*Review of Syphilology* — what a farce!) — there love is always equivalent to some disease (even if it is healthy, because it has no mask: for example, a flower or fashionable dress) or with some moral crisis; those hugs and kisses are always dancing among microscopes, clinics, and churches. The biology of flowers and humans may look similar from some angles, but for the time being, for me, there is a crevasse between the two. What pallid skins, what evil-smelling condoms, what dislocated washbasins, what deathly, funereal purple potassium permanganate. Sir, bridge the gap between drawings of syphilis and the sketches in *Vogue*.

 22 ===

THE MOST mysterious, most powerful companion of my life (apart from a constant physical malaise and episodes of vertigo) is boredom. It is hardly possible, I think, for someone to become so utterly bored as I do. At such times I ask with crazed obstinacy, "What is the other person doing now?" Such a ridiculously tiny percentage of books excite me and inspire me that I can quite safely exclude reading as a *pleasant* experience from my life: I perennially prowl in front of the book stacks, but they only induce atrocious tedium. That is a fairly important matter and symptom: a writer for whom books cause the least pleasure. Why? I have already read the really good books; and I so much expect from new literature precisely what I would like to accomplish myself that, naturally, I am unable to find it in anyone else.

And here before me stretch these long, oh so long afternoons. I cannot write just any time — what am I to do? Only *people* truly excite me: portraits of women. And architectural tricks, outrageous plans, though there again preferably things that I myself imagine. As to acquaintances, however, I have hardly any; I am not an engineer. How should I spend my time? In order to be able to see pretty portraits I ought to play sport, go to parties and dance, have money, but I have none of those. I am unutterably happy if I can find one teeny-weeny reason to go out at times like that: if I need to go to the barber's to get my hair trimmed, or go to my school in order to check some footling notice, drop in to see my mother, go to some far-flung shop (one that has no telephone) in order to cancel an order — those are my salvational diversions.

From where, from where on earth, do I get this utterly suffocating potential for ennui? Have my nerves, my sensory organs, & my logics unduly identified life with ecstasy and mystic wonders, so that if there is no Bacchic upheaval I am already bored? It could be. Or did I as a young boy become fatefully accustomed to endless impatient companionship with little girls, accustomed to the poisonous equation of 'pleasure = receiving gifts,' and that is why I am now dozy and sour even among so-called 'good' books? Gift, relentless erotic need, relentless need for charity, ascetic-snobbish high-grade demands from art's every moment, maybe even a mistaken career choice: literature instead of architecture — those kinds of things certainly may be the causes of my endless boredom. Not in any event, then, a book, but women: women as 'inhumaine' formulas, biological architectural schemata — and women as 'guests who like to be with me.'

The 'guest' is one of the central problems of my life, closely connected with boredom. If someone (who is moreover a burden to me; indeed, whom I cordially detest) telephones to call off a visit or to announce that they can only come at a later time than we have agreed, my heart sinks and I become quite ill. If someone departs, I am barely able to disguise my abrupt desperation, for I know that afterwards comes the vacuum, the lethal gloom of tedium. These 'afters' are the most intolerable. What am I to do, for instance, 'after' an early-afternoon film showing? Going to the cinema is for me always a great pleasure, making me laugh and cry uninhibitedly at the most idiotic films. But then 'after'!

I suppose a huge mass of petty-bourgeois primitiveness or vulgarity must have accumulated inside me, choked off and distorted by a smarminess with roots in worryingly tragic, religious, and self-tormenting toadying — for trash is what corresponds to my inclinations, mechanical debasement to my form of life, but I forcibly threw myself at 'great' works, which may have deflected me from potboilers but they leave me distressingly unmoved. Here I stand now between a parlor-maid's romance and Heidegger's philosophy, between the cinema and truth, with my one and only vocation: a tedium of mythical completeness.

Or do I, perhaps, have undue regard for the scale and complexity of the big 'problems' (*pauvre mot*) and simply dare not set about them when I am alone (= 'when the *guest* has gone'), just mooch about? If boredom occupies my every minute & every hour (when does it not?) — the haphazard character of every biological performance stands totally naked before me — am I not one of the greatest vagaries and 'nonsensicalities' (if indeed those words have any meaning in biology)? Nothing but a wild penchant for the fashionable, yet at the same time a loathing of any fashionable person. Nothing but wild intellectual penchant, yet at the same time an eternal flight from books and intellectual society towards peasants, amiable oafs. The only good thing about it all is that if this is a neurosis, then it is in no way a neurosis like Kierkegaard's, or the kind that a state-licensed psycho-analytical organ-grinder would crank out if I were to fall into his hands.

Although I am suffering and sense myself as being tragic, I do that more out of convention than true instinct. I am a 'figuration,' a biological sample, a flower, & as to whether that is a tragedy or success, a value or a lie, a pose or revelation, an illness or some absolute verity, I know not. 'All sorts of things happen in life, and this too has happened': I simply stick labels on such maxims for myself. It is never an aim in life that an individual should be happy. Neither blind '*élan*' nor the God of the Catholics wishes that each and every person here on Earth should be happy. That is quite evident. I was not born an architect or a writer, a rampaging Don Juan or a philosopher, but what I am — an anonymous, indefinable variant. These are matters of atavistic propensity & life necessity, intrinsic talent and routine, which have developed by chance in life; the interconnection of these facts is very complex. Someone is born an architect and becomes a writer under the active pressure of circumstances, & hence on the basis of a bunch of 'inhibitions'; but if circumstances could carry him that far, then in truth he was born a writer and not an architect. On the other hand, throughout life he carries architecture as an imagined salvation. Who, one may ask, decides whether this 'architecture' will be an eternal *idée fixe* or some quite different propensity in a randomly *ad hoc* mask of 'architecture,' or else the eternal wish of an atavistic 'predestined' talent to break free of enforced literature? It is true that it is very easy to imagine of life, insofar as we know it, that it brings architects into the world who become writers: it was never the goal of life that individual flair should realize its full potential. The hybrid: that is life's prime *métier*.

Might a religious instinct be at the bottom of my boredom? Invariably my one & only question, whether consciously or with Freudian discretion: 'how to be *saved'*? It could be that books bore me because they do not transport me into the kingdom of heaven.

What do people do to occupy — not so much their afternoons as those five- and ten-minute gaps? For instance, I return to the house, my wife is not at home, & I have to wait a quarter of an hour. What should I do in the meantime? "It's not worth making a start on anything," I tell myself hypocritically. Although if, just once a month, it should so happen by chance that I find something of *interest* (oh, adored mysterious, fugitive word!), then it does not bother me that I shall only be able to buckle to it for five minutes, I just buckle to it. I pace up and down, sit down, leap up again — is that what parlor-maids and private tutors call 'nervousness'? These tormentingly unoccupied moments are the subtexture of my life, that is my body. How happy I am if some totally unproductive and irrational bit of business crops up: conversations or discussions with narrow-minded figures. These are occasions when heaps of my acquaintances whine, agonize, and complain that 'their precious time is being stolen away from them,' oh, how I would love to ask them — enviously! — *what*, exactly *what*, is it that they do with 'their precious time'? The only option is to sleep through the spare time, but that gives one the most horrible giddiness, headaches, and nausea. One ought to chatter, chatter, chatter endlessly: women would come and women would go; their looks would be far more than a matter of indifference but much less than love.

Women: mobile architecture. Architecture: mathematized sexuality. What is my essence (which might also be a satisfactory explanation for my boredom)? My essence is a need for absolute and unbroken *intensity* (God, politics, a woman, perpetual chatter — it doesn't matter what) and a perpetual need for *form*, pure or concealed plasticity, biological or geometric design. That, too, just goes to show that behind great vitality is a big neurosis, and behind a big neurosis, a great primordial *élan*.

COMEDY: a husband is on 'good' enough terms with his wife to be able to tell her that he has a date with a woman at nine o'clock on Thursday evening. Until quarter to nine the husband and wife had guests, and after they had left the husband and wife set off together for the place of the assignation, and once they get close they will part as in point of fact the wife is also curious about the lover-designate and wants to see her. While rushing towards the meeting place they run into their slowly strolling guests. The husband leaves his wife with the dawdling guests — after all, it is impossible to confess to them that they are going together to a rendezvous of the husband's. After which the husband waits in vain, the woman *doesn't* show up. The husband *happily* goes back home: the constant game of the intellectual lover

— minute by minute he becomes happier when he sees that the woman is not going to turn up. She lies at the intersection of *two* disturbing perspectives; for one thing an empty puppet topic of the most highly cynical escapade — (the wife knows about it, etc.), while second, internally, to get to the woman the husband is subject to the torments of a thousand phobias all the same — before the rendezvous he vomits, shivers, & has attacks of hiccupping. When the woman fails to turn up: peace, a gentle doze, siesta — far from the frivolity of the 'caper,' far from the suffocating darkness of 'phobia.'

⟨ 24 ⟩

WHY that dreadful & tedious sense of dissatisfaction when the woman says to the man that she loves him, him alone, she adores him, there is no other sense in living than the man? Yet when instead of such charismatic psychology a woman gives her body — that, too, is boring. It is not a matter of *faux* blaséness, not simple premature senility or affectation, but of fleeting bad humor. I consider it as being frightful stupidity to love me: my logical sensitivity is offended by a woman who is so 'uncultured' as to be capable of loving me. Me of all people: what am I? A pick-up, a record for the world — I barely exist, only the world inside me; I do not like myself, I love only the world, for 'I' am only a fictive frame. That frame is what the woman loves, failing to notice the world it encompasses. That is why women who are devoted to one do one the worst possible service in the world: they draw one's attention to the most fictive, most null and void aspect of one's life. Me? If I say 'fictive' frame that is still saying too much — less than that, given that the 'me' is an inexplicable, never finished, fluctuating, soluble, tattered, unexpectedly and clumsily crystallizing something: how is it possible to adore that stupid amorphousness as precisely as that woman does? A dreadful malaise within the devotion: being adored restricts, suffocates, a worshiping woman distorts to a cut. That is why if I am not feeling well, for example, & the 'devoted' woman makes an appearance in my room, right then, with the accuracy of a stopwatch, I feel a hundred times worse simply because as long as I was on my own my indisposition was just as diffuse and misty an entity as my entire 'self,' a wandering spiral — as soon as the woman entered, with a single witch's glance my illness, which had been resting on objects, was also strangled & restricted into 'me,' rarefied, suddenly focused onto a small place, into myself. It's no use the adorer spouting any hymn about one, she can only evoke the impression of a barrel organ because she is in error, in error, in error: the world is what is fine, God is fine, not I. A failure of hetæras, a failure of Madonnas.

The adoring woman's adoration is either an ecstasy or idyll: is there any other lie in the world besides precisely these two? Idyll: that is to say reaching the goal in a small circle, in one-member, unarticulated roots of the 'nous, we, wir' type — in a little sub- and slobber ethics, cocooning oneself away from the 'élan agonisant' of all phenomena? Ecstasy: i.e., reaching the goal in a wide circle, the myth, kneading god into and from love as if there were something truly final and infinite. Idyll and ecstasy are the two *main* imprecisions vis-à-vis the world's phenomena, are the heresies which are most to be rooted out: a flower, a kiss, a slice of history is not a 'god,' not a 'humane nook,' not metaphysical maturity and petty bourgeois choice morsel, but something else, and I could not even say something intermediate between the two. And women are only familiar with and propagate these two grubby heresies. *Obsta*!

$$\Longleftarrow 25 \Longrightarrow$$

CAN A PERSON ever free oneself of these three forms of Women: the eternal Psyche, the eternal hetæra, and the eternal beauty? (Not that a Psyche could not be pretty or there could not be a psyche in a hetæra.)

Let us take the 'Psyche'; in the clothing of the psyche (i.e., a woman for whom the psychology of love dominates) there is always something that has gone out of fashion, at least a touch of antiquity: to every explicitly psychic phenomenon there always belongs some anachronism. My psyche illustration is something of this kind: a very big floral, airy, streaming dress, nothing but split petals, a convergent pattern, the whole thing a haze. But that airiness is not a featherweight like that of modern sporting-Ariels, [15] more the feverish decadence of a 'lady of the camellias,' [16] when — as a result of a paralysis of logic — neurosis, tuberculosis, love & art were able to seem to be equivalent. Brilliant buckles on the shoes — who wears things like that nowadays? On her head a fashionable hat with a huge, wavy brim: the various stages of waviness differ as sharply from each other as the states of an umbrella when it is closed and when it is turned inside out by the wind. Jellyfish are able to shrink that much into themselves while ascending and spread themselves flat as a lotus while descending. The dying-foam flowers of the dress, the gill-like breathing of the hat — is there not something typically psychological about it all? A strong noonday sun, sleepiness, menstruation, & sorrow, sorrow, desolation: how much longer will people go on doing this? Man and woman — one of them is weary of the other. Is that not the whole psychology of love — the small asymmetries of *charis*, instinct, boredom? All the withering, suicide, hysteria, and illness — *mon Dieu*, how much longer will it last? What is that soul, that psychology, all that artistic and crazy sensibility to us? *Voilà*: there goes that woman on the hillside — every item of clothing, glance, & pulse is death. Death and a bit of unfashionableness: is that how the amorous psyche is prepared? Why, God, do you allow women to adore a man so greatly and men to adore a woman so greatly? This woman with her clouding imprinted agony is 'madly' in love with a man and is unable to live with him. How divine and how doltish that is, how Olympically cretinous. That may be the most tragic in overpsychologized loves: that all the scads of bleeding mental experiences, & the thousandfold incarnating deaths, which accumulate with each amorous opus: they have *no* credibility, no smack of veracity & justification — the character of comedy is ineradicable. That woman may be swaying towards death with her rhythmic, Parnassian steps — the man for whom the woman is pining is, perhaps, already dead. The poison of the psyche is sure because it is insane. Is not the *Burlesque* the most triumphant muse over the white corpses, over the graves of Romeo & Juliet?[17] How much loving couples speak and lie, how many self-sacrifices they make, how much they write beside candles, labor in hysterics over, how much they bicker, promise, doubt, gossip, masturbate, and die; why is that so? Is it not due to some awful mistake, a misprint or shift of accent? Is heroism going on here or slitting of stage sets? Or am I just naïve for imagining there is a difference between the two?

Is it the automatically arising basic asymmetry in love that is called the 'psychological part'? Is there any sense in drawing a distinction between the primordially unequivocal tendency of love and the mental 'complications,' which result (and are apparently superfluous) from social life? Are not the 'complications' just as much primordial endowments as 'primitive' instincts? What a hodgepodge, heterogeneous thing an amorous relationship is: from passion to *convenance* purely an unclean patchwork of the elements of biology, law, and cultural history: a flea market.

When I see that suffering, tragic female form: I sense, at one and the same time, the most lifelike aspect of life (that aspect comprises a union of absolute emotional infuriation and absolute 'futility') — and also the ignorance, the mistake, which awakens alienation and not sympathy. One is confronted by such a dilemma with every 'grand' sentiment: on the one hand, one sees in it a plenitude of vitality, the wallowing '*élan*,' exaggeration, mania for reality of blood, monsoon, sea, steppe, snow, and goldfish-spawn, yet equally some logical *error*, a screwiness of brain and rationality, puppetry, flailing in the air, a disproportion, a miscounting: "After all, it's not worth kicking up such a big caterwauling for any man or woman."

Things of minor significance are what is important: lovers usually quarrel about 'trifling' matters. In the arena of irrationality (love), however, is there any sense in the difference between 'minor' & 'important'? Is an abandoned lover tragic or not? One has the feeling that custom turns loves into love, or in other words, in a fateful desire 'destiny' is nothing other than run-of-the-mill routine; they saw each other daily; passively, they stuck together through inertia — destiny is nothing but a technical chance, 'faute-de-mieux.' Is it worth giving up life for a lazy automatism like that?

'Feeling': that is life's central problem: the battlefield of the human duality of irrationality and logic. The essence of life, it seems, is precisely that, by the strength of inner *ananke*,[18] one *must* die for what is *not* worth dying for. Emotional life = constant *de*-climatization, constant rupture, standing in disproportion to the phenomena of the world. Sometimes the most delirious ecstasy nevertheless raises the impression that the feeling is 'proportionate' to a thing — sometimes with the most 'normal' emotional reactions one has the feeling that it is incongruent, disproportionate *ab ovo*, because it is a feeling. Does psychology really, organically, truly belong to us or is it an *error* — are amatory tragedies tragic or ridiculous — that tormenting ethical issue hovers around you, georgette-costumed, petal-hatted Psyche.

If I were to paint you, I would search out somewhere around Manet and Courbet, from the age in which impressionism & naturalism were manifested at the same time, from the age which is already of historical interest but with the demonics from those past years still striking at us from behind the mercantile price grilles of auction catalogues. The impressionists would provide the optics, the glistening uncertainty of lighting, the dancing, iridescent backdrops of relativity, without which there is no 'psychology': noontime vapors in the treetops, transparent colored shadows, summer birds dropping onto the pastures like sealing wax from the heat, the frolicking wrinkles of clothes, a frivolous confluence of camiknickers and dress — that would be the business of Manet & Co. Then the naturalists: the tragic, the gloomy destiny, the fanatics of deadly life; they would give the figure of your body, the womanly duality of sensuality and ethos, they would give all the slovenliness, imprecision, and sickness of death to your half-daubed lips, your powder-lumpy cheeks, to your hair as the chignon falls apart. All the same it was post-1850 that fading and disillusion could be rendered with the greatest gusto and 'fidelity.' You will be the eternal riddle in my life, Psyche; I shall always doubt in your existence and always recreate it. If you are so inevitable, whence my savage belief in your avoidability?

The other eternal something: the hetæra in every variety; for these kinds of almanac purposes the most vulgar are best of all, of course. What a pity it is that one's delicate salon morals do not permit one to make a 'definitive' (splendid word) portrait, after the decadently moral and aesthetic Psyche: of the eternal whore. With the logic of medieval allegories, the greed for the concrete of verists, the analytical mosaic monumentality of Proustians: each style should discharge its debt to this Second Uneliminable. That is not a simple being either:

in her trampish gestures, her grunting, her tongue-wagging, her squawking for money, her hair dyeing and her idiotic parasitizing there is every biological move of primitive submarine beings, but also the style of indigence, of poverty, which happens to be prevalent in society. Whether the naturalism is French or Russian, with a flavor of puberty or Santa-Claus-bearded prophesizing: it made a 'Casta Diva' out of the whore, needlessly compromised her, made her laughable: apologized for her. Miraculously, the harlot survived that, even though matters that have been defended do not normally stay in life. A harlot is the artisan and smith of love, each of them a brawny-grubby Hephæstus who throw deadly-pale grammar-school boys onto their filthy couches like iron onto an anvil or a side of beef onto a butcher's stall: "Let's go, then." And the work proceeds: serviette, bottles of permanganate, bowls, condoms, tips rattle on: *malgré* Zola. What, in point of fact, is the reason for speaking of a 'biological move'? It crosses the minds of, at most, consumptive philosophy students while the straw-haired carnal butchers work on them. This type of home-craft lust is neither known nor made to be known by hulking-hatted Psyche — that deadly spleen of the psyche is never known by a hetæra: if a sort of polytheism is justified somewhere, then it is in love — if something is two, the psyche and whore are two.

But a 'pretty woman' is exactly that kind of self-sufficient entity. A pretty woman whom one sees on a bus, in a dentist's waiting room, on the balcony of a coffee-house by the Danube, or on the beaches of Florida: a constant feast for the *eyes*, whom one never knows, who will never become a psychology or lust, but will remain forever an attractive color and shape, a *Vogue* formula, a bodiless, mindless surface or retinal mask. Today I traveled with one on the bus. Whereas the necessary background to Psyche is open country (foliage, flowers) and for a hetæra a bed-sitting-room, for this alpha-beauty (somehow it is fitting to name abstract things that way) it is an inner-city shop window caged in by a great deal of glass — a bus window is a clear profit alongside a face like that. There was a marvelous economy in the frame of her body, her dress, her looks, and her movements: *moindre effort*. A dark blue dress with white polka dots — in itself that is fairly puritanical, a provocative 'minimalism.' She has no need to be showy — she herself is beauty enough? Or she genuinely wants to be simple: she has no wish to highlight her loveliness but to hide in the morning ornamentality of dots? Those are not mannered, specious questions. On her golden-yellow, cropped hair is a small, brown cap, on one arm a small, spare, antique chain. The hair is clipped quite short, as if practicality had been the main goal, but that short hair has been elaborately frizzed in a small area, all Praxitelean punctured thimble[19] and frothing shavings, though those are not in such whimsical countlessness as the furrows in grains of sand or the crooked initials of wild grapes, most definitely not: they are numerable, exactly; it is clear that the woman ordered them piecemeal and paid for each one individually. Although every single curl is a stiff, mechanically prepared molding, the positive of a schematic barber-negative, the whole is fanciful, vibrating, life-like. But how economical, on a teeny-weeny autarchic area, on the most Harpagonesque island of the Harpagon globe.[20] The cap is also small: in itself an amulet of coquettish thrift — a snub precisely on the 'i' of the woman's body. But how consistent with an 'I' is the nude figure: legs, breasts, shoulders, are just symbolic curves, circumflexes, which have been blown elegantly and modestly into place. I can almost hear her saying to a woman friend: "Oh, I just threw on those circumflexes so as to have some covering over those places: that's only proper, isn't it?" The broad belt is like the matching twine on parcels bought from the shop — back at home a box can never be tied so snugly, the twine slips. The eyes lie far apart, like two outdoor tables on a balcony: one can immediately spot that the same family drops by both tables yet the two branches are not on good terms with each other and only sit on one and the same balcony as a formality. She adopts a half-asleep, half-philosophical gaze ('philosopher' in the sense that Don Alfonso of *Così fan tutte* is a philosopher): grey, like a cross-section of water. The lipstick is applied in a conspicuously broad stripe on the lips, her whole body is so Miltonianly simple that if twice as much were applied it would not seem exotic or wild, far from it — how paradoxical the world is: the very thickness of the lipstick gives an impression of puritanism. At one spot the paint is a little bit (ever such a little bit) askew — that makes her look even more scornful, more sour. These *just*-pretty faces are the prettiest at a point of the semi-profile where all the play of color and line (the eyelashes, tip of the nose, lips) has just vanished in the amorphousness of the facial muscles yet by implication is still perceptible to vision. For example the eyes: all they are in semi-profile are small indentations under the forehead — in the center a greyish-black glass sludge or point, and above them (the eyebrows as well are by then quite amorphous), by contrast, the lashes are visible in isolated sharpness like a radiating fish-bone stuck on Mount Ararat. Nothing is prettier than the spokes of lashes under the forehead fanning out around an eye which is submerged like that, like the stalks of flowers aspiring for height from out of the heart of a dead body above balladic graves.

So, that is 'beauty,' the third of the three gods, who has nothing to do with the other two. (It would be interesting to compare the fashionability of Psyche with the fashionability of Beauty: the former is all dispersion, aesthetics, floating, watercolor, the latter — plastic, hygienic, electrically, dryly coquettish, resembling a precision instrument.

⇐ 26 ⇒

THE perennial problems of any journal-like work: on what should the emphasis be placed: on the individual as a picture of a unique unit or biological system, the sketching of certain structural ground plans; in other words, a final *reductio ad unicam* formulam (a 'formula' which, of course, is simultaneously flora and metaphor — and that's not a play on words)? Or else the polar opposite of that goal (at least opposite in its practical execution), being a record of the most fleeting ideas, perceptions, barely thought-out thoughts, hesitantly wraith-like possibilities — a set of impressions picked up *about the world*. Or else neither explicitly the basic formula of the Self nor explicitly the million shards of the phenomena of the *world*, but a compromise between the two, i.e., a true *journal* in which the protagonist is *time*: thus, both I & the world considered from the viewpoint of temporality — everything fitting into the single absolute unity of 'from dawn to dusk.'

⇐ 27 ⇒

1) *Absolute suffering,*
2) *Goethe,*
3) *"I saw the beast most horrible,"* [21]
4) *A deserted park as evening closes in.*

1. I dreamed about a naked old woman, who was deadly sick and her child (or some younger relative) was also on the point of death: the child was lying in bed, the old woman was up and about. In my dream there was *no* naturalistic episode of horror (at least I barely recall any): illness, death, and merciless fortuity in all their own abstractness were absolute as *thoughts*, not as sensory perceptions. Of course, that was the most dreadful imaginable. The sole bit conveying a sense of horror was perhaps that the old woman's nudity was like that of a young girl, and dotted all over she had fairly sparse tiny grey spots, little punctures. The nude figure of a girl: the classic *lines* of the figure were expressions of a *precise* absolute of suffering — an old, wrinkled, dirty body becoming mangled into shapelessness would not have expressed the *mathematical* totality of the pains of death & illness, yet that experience was the aim of the dream — over and beyond the daily dilettantism of sentiment and sensation to undergo the divine rationale of pain, to live through its transcendental *logic*. It was spine-chillingly stylish to have the death-freighted illness (not ill)-old woman appear as the nude figure of adolescent Diana. The grey points sketched the corporeal dissolution — also with geometrical schematism, not realistically (one is sensual by day, logical by night, at night one *thinks*). (Incidentally, I heard today that an acquaintance's daughter really is on the point of dying.) As if every imaginable intellectual connection with mortality

had been gathered together in this dream: I continually sensed how kitschy that double death could seem, and how much, how very much, it was not so — the thought that "death is lying at wait for us at every moment" stood before me in such fullness of truth, in the brightness of an operating-room lamp, that I found the two 'performers' inadequate, too discreet, by comparison. "*Le rêve est le pays des* accents": [22] that maxim was more emphatically *true* than at other times. Meanwhile there was no blood, no rattling, no mourning, no ugliness and distorted mask of agony: all existence was a clean & transparent axiom of death and an absolute agony that could not be shaken off. (Logic and superstition.)

2. I am reading the complete poetry of Goethe in chronological order; right now the poems from between 1814 and 1822. It is a perpetual problem, a matter of perennial unease, the nub of which is obvious, and that is whether he was a poet or not. There is a curious blend of painful dissatisfaction and rapture in one seeing here the facts of nature and art constantly being raked up, adverted to but not elaborated, not lived through, simply 'exploited.' Here it is not a question just of the rococo Goethe and his rococo technique in general. His motifs are always the same: *Mitternacht, Nebeldunst, Sonnenschein, am Meere Schiffer, Tag & Nacht, das Grenzenlose, Farbenglanz und Übergänge* —"*Das ist denn doch das wahre Leben, Wo in der Nacht auch Blüten schweben.*" [23]

This mood of horticultural ecstasy, parkland '*Entzück-ung*'; when the poet does not move one by thoroughly soaking a chosen subject (Grecian urn! skylark!) by a faith in analysis, by metaphor, but he keeps all the 'items' of existence in play, from chaos to memorial volume, balanced between triviality and mildly meditative nihilism. For me, for whom art was always identical with absurdly thorough intellectual analysis, exhaustion of nuances (outprousting Proust) and hyperbole of metaphor — naturally that Goethe style is the most remote, the most mysterious, and only possible for moments. How is it possible to *half-* or quarter-touch on something? For me that is the excitement in Goethe. On many occasions I enjoy him hugely, but is that sincere, I wonder, or a feigned pleasure? Or could it be that I delight in the extraordinarily handsome and sensuous edition (Insel Edition, Vols 1 & 2), the opalescent contradictions and congruences between the Goethe myth and the Goethe reality, the temporal thrill inherent in chronological ordering, the completeness? I suppose that in prose one needs to be analytical and metaphorical in the extreme, because there is no *rhyming* scheme in it — whereas since in poetry there is both rhyme and rhythm that can make up for the lack of analysis and metaphor: simple balance. *Banalité et musique: quelle royaume étrange!* [24]

3. There is a tree by the roadside at the tip of an infinitely slender trunk of which is a single fraying ball of

foliage: maybe that is how pines grow weary yet soar in Rome, or the soul of dead Mary Magdalene flittered into the heavens when she quit her wire-slim body. There is nothing lovelier than a ready-to-travel rocket of a bough like that at the end of a stem, resilient as a dagger: a butterfly at the moment it seeks to release a flower which is nevertheless nodding under its feather-light weight; a fishing boat passing in a Claude Lorrain harbor at precisely the moment when it pulls out its anchor dart from the sea's Nereid flesh: a camel's tur-baned back when the *seated* animal is just setting about rising to its feet, and all that announced by a rather mild tremor: that's the way, that is how it stands up & sets off, that is how the bough goes to sleep and arches into the sky. If anything is an evening metaphor for the Christian soul then this crown of foliage is it. *"Die Seel"* — as it is put in the texts of Bach chorales, express-ing the essence of the baroque soul with an apostrophe.

But I could not watch the bough's silent travel in si-lence; this evening a bronze laurel wreath and black halo were not granted to me. At the end of the road, from a little marsh, on which all manner of poison and ill-willed fever casts a rotten dome, a white monster climbed and threw herself on me. She was a beast, she was a woman most horrible.[25] Above my head the stars danced in white like snow in July, which never reaches the ground, being all bell-ringing blind butterflies, the sparkling pollen of flowers, gently yet nevertheless darting about in zigzags.

Christian yet nevertheless in masquerade. How I longed to be among them, just like the sword of the trunk at the end of that solitary bough: the sky pulled, sucked at, inhaled, but the monster below did not go on the loose. How often I myself have sought loveliness, how often I have cheated, lied, and played the hero in order that a little lust trickle into the dumb cup of my hollow body — now here, uninvited, was 'joy' with its entire weight, its entire logic and its blind selfishness.

Her skin was white, the kind of white that only aging women have: not snow, not linen, not death, not clouds, not candles, not sugar but fattened and yet anaemic, nacreously reflecting and farinaceously lustreless, a disgusting whiteness. Before storm darkness a grinning horizon, gloating over misfortune under black clouds, often flashes white; sometimes before a crepuscular clouding-over a spooky lightness is unexpectedly spilled on the world, a senseless white between twilight and night: the body was like that, on the threshold of oldness it was enveloped in a hysterical ephemeral blooming, a *chemise d'agonie* (Worth).[26] Her hair was black, rough, dry, coarse Negroid tow, full of tawdry curls, stiffened flourishes: when she pitched herself at me, she daubed me all over with that black purulence, the black "locks" wriggled on my arms and between my legs like woolly grubs on a dead body.

"*Voilà le plaisir!*" I might have said, crying from fury and laughter while the late bird chirpings traced a few diagonals in the sky like physicians make on a person's back to test the skin's sensitivity. I could not even see the birds, they had been soaked into the night-flavored late blue or the watered-down gold of the setting sun: all that remained of their form and wings was some delirious ash in the big melting pot of spaces, lights, and distances. While every feather, bone, and throat of the birds slowly melted away from its anatomical form like a postage stamp soaked from the envelope, I took the opposite, agonizing way — what the white monster needed was precisely my form, my arm more armed, my mouth more mouthed, my tongue more tongued, the keys of my sex & my sex bookmarks more sharply. She was a maniacal bloodsucker of idiocy: from behind her quacking lips glinted her sparse, short, yellowing fangs; her tongue jumped hesitantly in its own cavity or around my strangled body — were twelve devils to take possession of twelve apostles the baleful flame would assume that sort of shape.

The three parts of her muscles, bones, and skin were already a bit displaced to the side: she pawed me only with her bones, her flesh only swung sluggishly after those, like a towed ship at the harbor's edge, the skin having slipped away from the flesh like an outgrown dress. Sometimes thin wrinkles and slight fissures run across an intact snowy meadow, minute swellings & dimples due to the unexpected warmth: ever since the monster bit into me, lust will always be for me synonymous with the gaps of shading which precede melting. Rag of rags, theatrical villain: your mask was not primitive life or absurd masquerade, not the schooled formula of sadism but a metaphoric pose of death, no — the whole thing was a disenchanting pack of nonsense. As you simultaneously wanted Elysian lyricism and suburban cussing, as you sought simultaneously some kind of Polynesian superstition and street-wise cynicism — I could not say you were even disgusting or grotesque; you were the neutral boredom of nonsense.

So why is it you elicit from the Adam's body of my ropy prose the vacillating Eve's bones of potential poetry? Were you a myth, after all, some negative absolute? Or were you a caustic lye: a lust of lusts, which did not produce any pluses from the soil of my body but ate away, washed off from it, any surplus — your embrace peeled, tore off the desire to be embraced. I no longer have any skin, no sense of touch for women, you burned off the lechery attire (with the Rachel-lace fripperies of its nerves), licking it off with your prickly serrated tongue; our unification was such a pincer neurosis that you retained all its devices for yourself forever; I have no more slender soft wax, from the stubs of which the flame of night-time candles might let drop proud vignette seals on rolling scrolls of letters; kisses were not the encounter of two sets of lips on a shared plateau of pleasure: you devoured, wolfed down the other's lips, leaving me bereft of kisses from today forever. But that may be the logic of lust: one grows fat on the other's chewed-up body, the other stays slim in classic or cubist nakedness, without leaf, flower, or fruit, like an ascetic, like a fish worn to the bone, like the stalk of a grape. It was all just 'nourishment': you only ever just swallowed, gobbled up, and bit off, then, once bloated, trundled back into the roadside bed of reeds.

I regained my freedom: you nibbled from me every teasing bud and thorn of sex — I am just a little bloodied, I have to bathe my wounds. As to whether this will be a baptism or the laziness of Roman thermal baths, for the time being I shall not ask: perhaps morality is being born inside me, perhaps sleepiness, perhaps an unquenchable desire for the white beast of the reeds from the marsh. But right now *water is a must*: it does not matter which. The *sea's*: all foliage, cold, the whole of Neptune's farmstead is liquid forest, the fishes are leaves, the waters leaves, the bottom of the sculler is a leaf, the surf is a leaf, the light ray diffracted by the denser water is a leaf, I myself will be a leaf among the rest in delirious baptism — swim, Oceanides! How different is your embrace, Oh, water, than yours, Oh, woman! — though schoolmasterly specs teach that the two are the same. That is the sole sensory sensuality, when the entire body is caressed everywhere by a free and amorphous element: a rushing wind, racing water, a scurrying ray. Wind & water do not 'feed' on me, do not amputate me, do not fish in my hormones, they do not place me between hard rails, like a broken leg. Water is nothing more than the minimal plastic threshold of space and freedom: barely a graphic of one perspective. That is what I need, that, only that, but all the time.

But a *waterfall* is also a good combative baptism: water striking big, mushroom-shaped, moss-pubed stones, all sharp thorns, noise, whiteness, a million pearls, a billion pins, which burn the skin like fire if they pierce down on it. What disorder: in places where the water drops on the precipice is a mixture of smooth, total, voraciously eager, whisperingly whooshing, deep-forest S's & R's of agony, swirling in the throats of moribund titans: a standing-dizzying paradox of a curtain. In places where it strikes on stone: nothing but glaring zinc-white lesions, white cries, white blood, white lances, and white skeletons — this is an ecstasy of whiteness, its fateful inevitability, its roaring & clattering nakedness will be a good christening for me after the monster's banquet. After a smooth curtain-green & thousand-dislocation whiteness, the precious waterfall has a third grimace: calming down between two rocky walls, the water bubbles like a smeared-out frog does with its popping eyes, its croaking, and its transitional protective coloring as if it were being cooked, half-boiling, not knowing whether to be a peace or a revolt.

Sea? Waterfall? Why not the dawn-time *rain* of spring? Trickling down along grey-blue branches, the water does not burst on me directly from sky or ground but via the delaying time beats of leaves, filtered, in a staggered fashion: every single drop roaming on its own separate way towards me. How complex a cross-section of a drenching wood like that, what a steeplechase for gravitation's small glass arrows; I am baptized in that refined sieve christening. — (*Bestia te benedico*.)

4. One can never get enough of the antithesis between women & flowers, the *furor* of embraces, and the evening tranquility of a park. Both the one and the other are 'nature.' Both the one and the other are vital: — but one wonders: are they justifiably so? What sort of '*Philosophie des Organischen*' can that be which has the ability to lump together the above-mentioned 'white beast' and that swimming, mystical, angelic blue umbrella, that flat, mist-wafer, night-wafer of a tree leaf, which swims mid-air among gossamers, cobwebs, and half-woven shadows in the greenish tangle of the stars like a deathly *billet doux* of the empire of the Moon towards a well statue? The form, life, organs, sense & nonsense of a flower are totally the same as a human being's *mental* life: the primitive *élan* and examination of the relationship, the minimal forms necessary for that, are the one & only justified psychology. That recent lyrically flagged episode of lovemaking, on the other hand, was a *physical* affair, so it was truly the antithesis of a flower, a vespertine leafy bough. A park run half-wild, with a solitary statue in antiquated style — that is nature's finest form.

How lovely its color is in the evening: grey dust coated on green, the watery yellow of the barely awakened stars, the spinning tulle of the gloom, the dusky sky's unexpected pre-night night-blue, the brightness of the Moon more unsure than the gloom — all that together, spliced by silence, is the *no*-woman *par excellence*. How infinitely splendid it is thus, with no woman. The two paths against women: wild, dramatic asceticism as sketched by El Greco, & this parkland loneliness, dazed eremitism swooning underwater. Silence — it is life's greatest gift; that is god, the opium-laced initial letter of dogmas. The clumsiest relationship between man and the outside world is an embrace with a woman; there it is veritably a matter of a 'link' or 'fastener,' a Palæolithic rattling, bleeding, and rusty tool of arms and lips. The submersion in water is already a much more highly 'advanced' form — in this case a velvety 'not-I' envelops the whole body: that bears much the same relation to embracing as a streamlined automobile does to a top-hat-high stagecoach. Finally, the most modern version: quiet absorption in an evening park — heart, blood, stomach, sensory organs, lungs are each transformed in a trice from this universal medicament, which transforms the entire physique as a whole all at once, the sole agent which deserves the name medicine. Naïve therapy, hymnic poetry, a theology full-blooded through truth: all three are together in the quiet of a park. (The problem of 'mood' is the only important medical & religious problem: a 'mood' is explicitly a temperamental matter, an attribute of the whole 'Geſtalt.'

⟵ 28 ⟶

AT A JEWISH burial. Cemetery, railway ſtation, factory: these are always outwardly direcſted; penury, death, diſtance, capitalism's metaphysical zone. Even flowers and animals grew only in certain places, under certain climates — the dead and workers as well. The pooreſt burial: the minimum. Man revolts — do firſt, second, and third class apply here, too?

Near me is a so-called 'vulgar' person going to the same funeral; I can hear him joking acidly about exacſtly the same thing. The moſt refined intellecſtuals and the moſt poverty-ſtricken dolts are on the same level when it comes to great events — which shows that life's basic realities, like death, do not impinge on the circle of irrationality, *raison*, myſticism, and prose — those juſt *are* & are forever unworkable, forever unſtylizable. The great events evoke a single reacſtion in everyone at all times and for ever more, whether one calls that ontology, the banality of banalities, a reflex, a convention, or helplessness.

Yes; so there is firſt class here, too? *Mort de luxe?* [27] What a lot people have jabbered together about the antithesis between a 'ſplendid' and a 'dead simple' funeral

— and how often I have been disgusted by those pretentious last wills and testaments in which the testator
wishes to be buried in secret without music or wreaths
("at most one stem of…"; at this point the name of what
the testator considers to be some horrendously 'simple'
flower usually follows), at night, in an unplaned coffin,
under an old walnut tree in a deserted garden. In that
requested simplicity I sensed there was a great deal more
theoretical, more affected, naively more intellectual, &
more theatrical posturing than there was in a resounding,
thousand-candle, choral requiem stifled in flowers. Man,
primitive man (*pauvre animal*), always responded to the
facts of love and death with rites, big boloney, posturing, and gaudy backdrops — 'ceremony' is simpler than
'simplicity,' the latter being a simulated style, mannered.

I once saw in a film the 'initiation' rite or some such
ceremony that is conducted by Japanese geishas, the pro-
cession of these courtesans — on their faces a stiff mask,
cracking burial paint, on their limbs robes heavy as lead
and having the most inhuman conceivable bulges, curtains and troughs: the dress did not coincide at a single
point with the human anatomy — was invested by an
onerous, complex liturgy. Mummy masks, hair harassed
into a tower by instruments of the Inquisition, pennants,
a 'dress' overcomplicated by parasols and gas balloons —
those were a woman of pleasure's obligatory ornaments
— they did not gad about naked or in simplicity closest
to amatory functions; hugs, kisses, smiles, and sensual

gestures were infinitely remote: *respect* for carnal pleasure demands significantly different forms than does the
pleasure itself. This insane degree of etiquette in which
a person has become a puppet, a metaphor machine:
that is simplicity. To prescribe a programmatically simple
burial (if one had the money for a sea of chrysanthe-
mums & Mozart's *Requiem* as conducted by Toscanini)
is always repugnant.

But a simple burial for want of better, the burial of
a wretchedly poor person, is a very fine affair. Perhaps
lurking at the bottom of all my literary works or plans
is the morphology of an infinitely superb funeral: funeral of a pope in which history, God, mankind, art,
Golgotha, and so on are combined. That is why it did
me good right now also to see simplicity.

The door to the display room of the funeral home is
open; perhaps it doesn't even have a door: as if the coffin might seek to go outdoors but did not dare, or the
trees and sun go inside to the dead individual but did not
dare — on the threshold a timorous debate between two
modestly disposed worlds drones on. A stone-flagged
floor as in a kitchen, crack and large, fresh water stains,
puddles like in kitchens. The draped coffin is lying on a
stretcher, a candle behind it. Death sucks people out of
the world and restores to objects their own abominably
selfish objectification: the shoulder straps of the stretcher will become all at once just shoulder straps, the slim
triangle of the coffin a slim triangle, the single candle at

the head of the dead person — Oh, will wonders never cease: a candle! I have a gloss, a marginal note, for each of you, in the clumsy, pottering style of the living, which may rouse an indescribably soft-headed impression in the eyes of a dead person: I would like to add something about stretcher, coffin, and candle.

By holding onto the strap which the cadaver, pressed back into the bud of the coffin, will be raised one day in order to flourish for God — that strap betokens the unsettling oddity that the dead person is among us, the living, in just the same way as a living person — one must reckon with him, with his weight and length, and will have to do something with him. The dead do not quit us, no mysterious assumption occurs: they stay with us. Your weight has not changed — yesterday you were balancing on the white weighing-scales of a clinic, white men and women read off your evanescent or persistent decagrams from a white scale — your weight today is the same, it's just that a yellow, lallating corpse-coolie will feel it on the shoulders. Are the dead not bothered by the contrast of color that man devised for them: white as a sheet in the clinic, pitch-black in the cemetery? The shoulder straps: it is in contrivances like that that broken-down old nags are harnessed to a cart or a millstone; that is the kind of thing to which galley slaves were manacled. You are an instrument of 'work,' of coercion (the word 'symbol' is highly vacuous in the concrete-dense atmosphere of death): the dreadful paradox of 'work,' its secret, its human nonsense and power accompany you on your last journey.

But then by your head is the other object, perhaps the finest and most important of all objects in life: the tall, solitary candlestick. If a strap signifies 'work,' the dumb monotony of lugging things, then a candle is an eternal metaphor, beauty, the demonically enticing eternal aesthetic over your poor worker head. The dish of the candlestick holder collecting the wax drops seems a little bit like my two hands cupped together: half-prayer to the horrendous decrees of an unknown God, half-pious apprehension of all the world's phenomena, flowers, omen, and diseases.

What a fine and what an infamous thing it is that in a minimal funeral just one candle burns, and not three or five. How existential philosophy, existential poetry, and Harpagonesque miserliness, nauseating pettiness, coincide. How much saints & heretics, petty bourgeois and canonists anguished over the relationship of Church & money, ceremony and payment; can it be any other way? Why, why, the eternal why: Why should a person who pays more be buried 'more nicely,' and why is a worker buried the other way, from a puddly stone-flagged floor with just a single candle? Why is there not just one & the same kind of funeral for the rich & the poor: one sort in regard to the church? Secular relatives, counts, currency speculators, states & cities may then throw in whatever they wish, but the Church should only grant one kind.

Dearest slim candle, the sole human being in the congregation, have you any idea what a microscope is? Yesterday the poor worker's blood sample, a slide of a section of his tumor was on display under a microscope: yellowish-green blotches, tiny black hooks, and smudged bubbles could be seen, all of which had a name but in a language impenetrable to the dead individual as Hebrew today — poor guy, in his final days he was beset by such grotesque and fudged languages. One of these days chatter yourselves well and truly out, candle and microscope, you, necrology, and you, metaphor of death. Are microscope and chemistry, those smart numbers (0.000031, 0.002, 0.00009, etc.) worth anything if anyway the candle will always have the last word? The grandest and most mysterious thing in life is that it is capable of producing such opposed perspectives, viewpoints, and realities as the standpoints of positivist learning and nihilist metaphor: that worker is all at once a chemical experiment in a laboratory shivering from electricity or a capricious metaphor, a biological game of chance in the nothingness. Beside a candle, how grotesque are a medical library, a surgical appliance, a photograph of a world-famous professor on the cover of some magazine of the gutter press, there is *no* transitional position between clinic and cemetery — the undissolved crumbs of the medication that was administered last still swim in the blood as a green island, and on the crumpling skin of the cadaver of the corpse is already falling the first candle-drop of liturgy, God, and theatricality — the cadaver plunges from positivism straight into poetry, from mathematics at once into lyricism. One finds it hard to desist from the enthralling comparison: the form of the injection needle, with the form of a sodden handkerchief that has been soaked with tears — is there not in each one of these the precision and imprecision of science and death? I cannot resign myself to dying in such a way that I was neither an absolute physician nor an absolute priest: I seek to unite in my frame the whole of clinical and the whole of liturgized death.

The third object, then: the coffin. How slim, well-proportioned, elegant, and discreet as its edge is raised, ever higher, towards the head, & the sides become ever broader; was it not on designs like this that we studied drawing at grammar school? The form is the *nude* of the dead worker, & I know I shall not be committing blasphemy if I compare it with the taut, clear-cut bodies of swimsuited girls. The coffin is precise, and shapely as a Venus drawn with a pair of compasses, and the coffin 'fits' like a yacht or arrow, or a dart aimed at a target. It is as if it were showing Virginitas *mortis*. How agreeable those very simple tassels at the edges of the black shawl; there may well have been something like them on his table-cloths. The *edge* of the coffin lid: that is the most formal form, the most baroquely distinguished — a single, one & only line is all that is retained of the suffering human being, *Homo sapiens*, the million wrinkles and nooks of an aging body: a *summa hominitatis*.

Everywhere in the room hang the same tablets, inscribed in Hebrew, illuminated here and there by bare electric lamps: just wires and bulbs — how much more impoverished, more proletarian, modern technology is than candles. A woman in black overalls & headscarf is getting the relatives to pray, who place their right hands on the coffin. It would be in my power now 'to observe' certain figures, as after all that is what writers do: 'they observe,' but I don't want to do that. I observe willy-nilly, but on the spot I keep them secret from myself. The mourners? There are two extremes: the wailers and the chatterers, the very mournful and the deeply indifferent. I am also torn between two feelings within myself: to jump into the grave alive — what's the point of a lifetime spent in mincing matters so much — but meanwhile thinking about some other things, literature, Hitlerism, & life itself. Weeping is also justified, as is boredom — weeping is a mistake, just as indifference is also a mistake. Is there present somewhere here: in the mourners, in an object, the rite, the priest, a 'truth' relating to death — a reassurance or at least an attitude similar to definitive? No. Everyone goes home just as stupid and ignorant as they came.

Meanwhile I formulate my dissertation about the Catholic and Jewish conceptions of death. Priests or quasi-priests start praying & stuttering, appraising the public, one of them with both hands stuck in his pockets. Two civilian chaps in light suits and black bowler hats take a collection — Right now? Here? Is this an appropriate occasion? I myself would be hard pushed to define precisely if it is excruciatingly distasteful, or in a paradoxical way can respect be aroused that this ceremony is carried out with well-nigh characteristic casualness? Because this is not humdrum offhandedness: this degree of scratching nonchalance is already in itself a mystery, so to say, a spiritual exoticism tantamount to a religious trance. In the background an old man is picking his nose, first tidily casting the solid matter of one of its apertures beside the coffin, then the other, meanwhile yawning without covering his mouth and scratching himself, sometimes tipping his top hat to the back of his head, sometimes pulling it forward: I immediately felt that such a bored figure within religious intercourse with the dead could not evoke from me any kind of Lutheran or whip-wielding Jesus attitude — that species of indifference is something beyond human, dehumanized, and as such interested me more than it needled me into rebellion. The fellow leading the service, without even minimal inner contemplation, looked around the audience while he sang; indeed, he gawped at it so hard that his swiveling eyes were reminiscent of the eyes in shop-window automatons.

Is the 'soul' really a feat of Christian anthropotechnology? This rite signified an absolute absence of psychology: I do not know whether at the end of my days I shall be critical of it or affirmative. Perhaps I am too young to be able to establish a definitive hierarchy among the considerations of 'truth' & 'biology': there are times when a wild 'trance' of Catholicism runs away with me, and times when I sink into the biological determinism of primitive fish, primitive flowers, and primitive peoples — at this Jewish funeral those two considerations also wrestled within me: religious critique and an acceptance of natural science.

Here as well it is the principle game in life, the possibility of various points of view. This Jewish group from the viewpoint of natural science, popular psychology, chance literature, or that of Hitlerism. Alternately and intercrossed with each other the various points of view poked me in my chest like a sick heart pokes the ribs of a dying man: I was a writer, saint, Jew, primitive fish, Hitlerist, common man, sadist, moralist, bourgeois, and so on & so forth. When an assistant strolled before me with both hands in his pockets some kind of Christian moralist happened to be at work inside me, and I upbraided him angrily.

I sketched out schematically, irresponsibly, & from a layman's angle yet, all the same, with the seductive chances of truth: there is a Greek funeral, there is a Jewish funeral, and there is a Catholic funeral.

A Greek funeral is the burial of a *natural* religion: death is just as much a frugal part of existence as a fruit, or rather a fruit is also death, death is also a fruit. (As to whether or not this is a German *trouvaille* rather than a Greek reality is a very justified question.)

A Catholic funeral is the polar opposite: a burial of super-naturalness & *extra*-naturalness: it talks about everything except precisely nature: about the soul, which is a *non*-fruit *par excellence*.

And where is there place for a Jewish funeral in this primitive scheme, next to Greek *intra*-absolute and Catholic *extra*-absolute? The essence of that ceremonial nonchalance is that one cannot perceive in it the biological totality of nature; death is not a fraternal part of life along with trees, stars, and bodies of water, as it *may* be with the Greeks — and death is just as much not a supernatural, metaphysical phenomenon, divine and heavenly, as with the Catholics. This distancing equally from primitive physics and reckless metaphysics was magnificently signaled by the two light-suited *civilians*: the civilian suit of the town is very much unnatural & very non-divine but very much a forgetting completely about both. As these people conceived of being chosen by God as God being within each of them, and if 'chosenness' becomes such a nebulous and less-than-conscious 'identification' with God, then it is quite natural to yawn and pick one's nose during a funeral as God is not a remote & foreign metaphysicality, God is not the trees, stars, and seas, but they themselves: God's gestures are their gestures.

What contrasts are on view in this small group: first and foremost, two major variants of Creole melancholy and gaudy-redhaired chutzpah.

The Creole: chocolate-brown skin, the maturity of time shows on him as on a wine or a fruit or an unusually early-autumn leaf; time refines it, makes it more porous, more noble. There are two very important groups of phenomena in the world, one of which time beautifies, crystallizes — the other it distorts and spoils. Time undoubtedly makes this Creole skin aristocratic; indeed, it is explicitly time-skin. The eyes are huge, a bit extruding, the face and the muscles of the whole body are a mixture of sporty tautness and slothful laziness; gestures, reflex actions, the wrinkles on the surface of the skin are capable of all sorts of analytical work on the detail, the manner being characterized by eastern softness, mild spleen, an affectation swinging between sober measures, a bit of arrogance. The lips are usually finely outlined: they are never red hardly-visible 'openings' on the mask but arched and sharply outlined — they may be thin or thick, the essence lies specifically in the way their precise ornamentality is achieved. (Cf. for instance Bruno Walter's head, or the heads of Lysimachus and Ptolemy on page 13 of the picture album *Zeitlose Kunst*.) [28]

The other extreme is the red- or white-skinned type: while the foregoing one was characterized by its sheer linearity and analytical capability — on this second type tumors, puffiness, and a general insusceptibility to analysis predominate. It is as if the complex forces of biology had divided: in the firſt type, the energy that in trees seeks an analytical separation of veins, outlines, and individual organs prevails, and in the second — crude lolling, hormonal welling, and a suffocating, continued pumping of forms is in operation.

What naivety it is to play down these kinds of ways of looking at a constitution juſt because there are a great number of transitions and intersections: it is juſt as naïve as someone denying the faċt of musical sounds because there are a million ways of harmonizing them. After all, the ultimate goal is not to attain clean anthropological formulae but to trace the ſtyle of a certain morphological pattern of life, and follow the ſtyle of that pattern along a couple of rambling lines.

The end? The priest gets into an auto and rudely dismisses beggars from his path: just as in a Communiſt book of fairytales. Another demands that they "line up." *Quelle idée:*²⁹ to make these wretches exercise. Wretches? I am not mentioning this as a punch line but these were the beſt-looking people: time and fate permeated them like old Italian palaces; they had acquired moss & patinas as if they had become mineralized.

⇜ 29 ⇝

"UNE *toute petite série des négativités*":[30] to wake up in bed in the morning behind roller blinds — as it was chilly, a winter duvet was on my legs, and as it was dark, the lights had to be switched on. When the family gets ready for the official summertime, then it's always this cold, autumnal weather, and the lights are on just as in December. Bad headache. Morning: nothing has remained of yesterday; nothing ever remains of anything that would be *worth* continuing or that at least *ought* to be continued — there are just the bodily malaises, indispositions. Oh, illnesses: school assurances of composition in life, morning — does it have any sense when lights are on inside but outside is greyness, fog, rain? Is anyone born virginal every morning as I am, with freedom in such tormenting totality? No work, no woman, no language, no music, no stroll: I can choose them all myself. The wrinkles of the duvet are in particular contrast to this absolute inner freedom: it is full of misery, superstitious memories, the steaming past — but only a formal past, a mask-past: my yesterdays are never left to me. A person who continues his work of yesterday cannot imagine what effort is needed for the time-Robinsonade: I myself carve parts of the day and minutes, carve invented jobs of work for myself. My flower impressions from yesterday are unusable for today's flowers, my window is a new window, my eyes — new eyes; everything has to be begun again from the beginning. The *day* is the sole existential unit — every other concept of time is a fiction: can one manage to fabricate gods for even a single day, and can they be satisfied? — that is the positive question. A program for *life*? Nonsense. A program till the *evening* is more like it!

Day by day, every morning, in front of the clock face's Gorgon visage, I deliberate under the coverlet's dreadful wrinkle phantasmagoria: maybe sport would make me happy, tennis or the high jump, some '*action gratuite*,'[31] a senseless action as I never trusted in reason; I may well be fashionable hotel fodder as in recent times practically only new necktie patterns and women's shoe designs have really whipped up my enthusiasm; I am probably a saint, a saint to the bottom of my heart, who is only helpless in the morning because he feels instinctively that in any case nothing will satisfy him apart from God; the whole idea of saintliness is just an exaggeration of a metaphor, a muddled half-dream based on an El Greco reproduction: I am a petit bourgeois who does not have a long enough bed, a shady enough balcony, and a satisfactory number of armchairs in the house, and since he has a certain amount of haphazard cultivation, he elegantly talks up this unpleasant feeling into a theology; I was born a creative artist, & it is due to that that every morning my life is absolutely lacking in topics: and of course it lacks in topic since my business is *not* living but creating outside myself; I am a manual worker, during my childhood I was coached in manual dexterity, and if I could be a blacksmith or carpenter my life would be meaningful; how much undying and more opus-like a key or table is than for instance this work of self-definition.

And so it goes ever-onward every day. Anyone who has experienced a life of total contemplation and total work knows what a pain mornings are. Two nonsenses: to over-*contemplate* a flower needlessly and to over-*garden* a flower needlessly. A writer's contemplation of a flower imagines *everything*: the flower, God, sex, poetry, logic or what you will — it is natural that the infinite freedom of contemplation, the possibility of every possibility, excludes reassuring intelligence; on the other hand, working, the gardening of the flowers, this and that, doing it then and for that reason, is again senseless because it is so *un*ambiguous. If neither contemplation nor work, then what? Only *one* thing would attract me — I am like a chunk of iron in a field with no gravitation, nothing pulling me, nothing wanting me; I have to press out of myself clumsy and crumbling pseudo-myths that I pseudo-worship.

A published fragment of a novel of mine that I find weak: the question of questions arises — should I be a life or a work? I dither with almost mathematical precision between the two poles — I don't live and I am not a 'work'; everything that I write in relation to the biological transition of life and work is instructive merely

of what is between, let's say, Montaigne and Lincoln
Cathedral. I could only shoulder my life completely (as
opposed to the 'work') if it were an ascetic and religious
life, otherwise it is unbearable. Life as 'horrible metaphysics' or a 'giddy metaphor'? An embrace of mine, for
example, or a big scene on the platform of the moral
mystery — the puppet-theatre wires of body and soul,
sin and redemption, Christ and eternity, jerk my tongue,
my arms, my steps — or they are just decorative ornamentation, some kind of harmony of colors, forces, and
irrational forms. The fact is that just as the most ortho-
dox Catholic morality is present in my body in its dic-
tatorial totality and pervades my every second — it is
also just as passive; I transgress it. Thus, I cannot take
responsibility for my life as such as a topic. When I shave
I do not know as yet whether I will be a Spanish mystic, expressionist architect, or a tennis singles partner.

Bad weather: negative. An apartment denuded for
the summer, covered up, mothballed — just like churches having the altar stripped for Good Friday. Home:
does it again not contain all the vital questions? 'Home'
as a Freudian construction: artificial womb & artificial
genitalia — home as eternal peace and archetype of
for-in-Godness; home as a scheme and spatial brother
of my self; home as an idol cage of family & morality;
home as a permanent experimental 'outside world' and
'not-I,' a perpetual milieu; home as 'Geworfenheit'; [32]
home as hastening grave. My home sweet home, how

much I revile you, loathe you, and when you are twisted and covered up this way, how much I love you and am sorry for you. You are a backdrop, permanent, you are time; the one positive inside me, without you I would flow everywhere; an inverse portrait of Dorian Gray: eternally one and the same — you will remain that until I am relativized away into mist. You, lamp, picture, settee, you are my face, my one and only face, and when you are plastered all over in summer, I have no face, only a soul, and I am sick because of that. The start of summer — for me that is always space-deprivation and time-deprivation. I am on vacation, I can do what I want: ahead are two months, and it looks as if I have been granted time, but it is precisely the reverse — I have been radically deprived of time. The apartment has been covered up — I am radically deprived of space. *Oh, charmante poupée de la négativité!* [33]

There are people who supposedly rest during the summer, but I experience the pain of all pains. I am thrown back on my own devices, and one can draw nothing out of oneself. The whole season is a Pascalian horror: not due to external emptiness but to inner emptiness. Metaphysics in the most palpable biological form — that is my summer program. Space, time, life, sickness, morality: those kinds of philosophical concepts *live* inside me, or rather I identify with them, they are embodied within me, I have nothing else with which to occupy myself. From morning till night I am *places*, from morning till night I am *terminations* — *à la* Proust, *à la* St. Augustine. A paradoxical, maddening world of intensity and non-existence, a dual instinct of nihilism and ultra-intellectual analysis throbs inside me. Wild plans to confess, mining for principles — & goofy mooching, impressionist loafing.

Summer is the one season that exists, the other three are calendrical conventions — that is one reason why I should write a *Completa Aestatis Morphologia*;[34] maybe this year. It is the most human time of year. Why do I call it that? Sometimes one feels the most absurd situations, sometimes even the most banal, are felt to be especially human. The summer is absurd. In all its naked structure and impudent poetry, time, for instance, stands before us in summer: repetition, the perpetual selfsame ("We were here last year as well": what wonder there is in these words) existence, traditional monotonous rhythm, and these dreamy pillars, compared with those the eternal stimuli and facts of: a holiday, a 'jaunt,' the great escape, the past is never the past in such a divine manner and so devoutly as in summer (cosmic refrain) — a holiday, a new brainwave, a new flirt, an escapade, are never in such an elementary fashion screamingly new *vita* nuova. Things new in time and things ancient in time: they live in a lukewarm mixture in the other three seasons.

Married couples go to their parents: the invincible and ominous concretes of wife and parent loom up from the metaphysical glass cockleshell of summer. A pack of primitive myths and superstitions, a pack of refined modern experiments, scintillating sophistry.

No experiences at an art exhibition: negative. What a frightful heap of works that have absolutely no impact — a sea of the boring creations of *great* artists. That is the most depressing element of my life. As far as I'm concerned, the unresponsive phenomena of ordinary life & its concomitants are bigger sensations. One of these days I shall define the prerequisites of a sensation for me.

I leaf through books in two bookshops: an achingly deadly tedium. *Don't* search for joy in art: how many times have I said that to myself, and I am such an imbecile that I still always take a look into books and art galleries. I bring home a little book by Emil Brunner, the theology professor in Zurich: *Vom Werk des Heiligen Geistes*. [35] On the bus I look alternately at that and the woman sitting opposite me. Her dress: on the chest there is red wrinkling of her blouse like a half-opened fan. *Voilà* — that, after all, is my element, that has an impact, that is an experience, that pair of *red wrinkles*. My whole being is a gigantic 'phobia'-crystal, sheer antipathy (if there had not been a Freud fashion, of course, I would not generalize so eagerly), and the most important of these is my '*Denkphobie*': that is why I cling on with such frantic enthusiasm and intensity to outside drawings of objects (primarily flowers and women's dresses) because for me a drawing, a colored form, a line is a hundred per cent substitute for thought, or rather an expression of the transcogitative state of the soul: true precision. A drawing is not wrong and it is not true; in a drawing, reality and symbolic openness are one. The doctrine of sensation: that is the great doctrine. My '*Denkphobie*' are oversensitivity and truth at one and the same time.

A child cries and bawls fit to choke: a loathsome synthesis of suffering and stupidity. What is the point in life of these bestial impulses & energies as there are in this crying?

⟸ 30 ⟹

A rationally clarified thought bears the same relationship to a metaphor as a fully-grown human body does to an embryo: the metaphor fills anew the soul's embryonic forms, elemental bends and flexures — metaphors are the tadpole form of reason.

⟸ 31 ⟹

PROUST AND HITLER: I wonder if the dreadful urge to keep myself busy which is at work in me is simply a naïve nostalgia which operates in every intellectual for the non-intellectual, for action, for historical irrationality, or is it a genuine sense of mission, a real ability to be of assistance to humanity?

How close things are to each other in life, just as close in our minds as the houses are in towns: churches, lingerie shops, political posters, and hearses. Those are all obtuse, however: people cross themselves when passing in front of a church but not, for a second, do they feel that it is a fantasticality to beat all fantasticalities that, to start with, God, the one & only Creator, is present on the altar, thirty yards from the bus stop, and for a second thing, that the symbol of God is a device for executing murderers and thieves, a grubby sort of gallows. People go into stocking shops to buy silk stockings, but they don't feel for a moment that stockings are a unification of elemental eroticism and abstract metaphor, biological arching (the foot!) and a mathematical form (squares of a net!), which is to say, two of life's greatest secrets: stupefaction in love & raving-mad *mathesis*, which both blindly steer clear of God. People also read election placards, cast their votes as well, but they don't for a moment feel how grotesque a game all politics is from the perspective of death, what an unbridgeable gap there is between a private individual's private life (his love, his sleep, his illness, his dress, his petty passions) and the apparatus of law, collective arrangements. An artist differs from the man in the street only insofar as the ordinary citizen does *not* take God, stockings, or an election for what they are — whereas an artist simply takes God for really being God, a stocking for really being a stocking. On the other hand, the idea that artistic perception is *plain* perception as compared with an ordinary guy's complete insensitivity is a myth: a God myth, a stocking myth, or a political myth. That's life: either naught or a myth.

 32

'Two jewesses: one for the morning, another for the afternoon.' So schematic, so pedagogically prepared in their structure, that it is a miracle. At times like this it is customary for sharp minds to say that the women were probably not so transparent but my prejudices ("the world's wretched'st word") were excessively simple, and I immediately imposed my own totally abstract scheme on each accent and fragmentary gesture. That may well be, but then it is unnecessary to make a distinction between 'observer objectivity' and 'unbending prejudice': neither of them exists, nor can they, there is *only* prejudice.

The morning woman represented mysticism, *Schöngeisterei*, naïve dogmatism, snobbery, hypochondria, sentimentality, the profoundest humiliation, mindless revolutionariness. The afternoon woman: perpetual self-irony, an inclination to maniacal stylizing and characterizing, sober humanity, humor, gesture, fuming mimicry, a tongue-twisting gift for languages, blind sensitivity. — Nothing is more disheartening than to compare the thousand concrete details of my memory with these abstract nouns reeking of corpses as they do.

How can one portray a person 'completely'? In the first column the scheme: the above nouns. In the second: word by word their speeches as taken down in shorthand. In the third: so as to bring out for each sentence the accent, the psychological and phonetic shade, a simile, first and foremost from the plant world: microscope shots, English watercolors, drawings, colored and copperplate prints, et cetera, e.g., next to the sentence 'as you imagine it,' for its expression of the smile, the cynicism, the idyllic delight, slender to the expression of the raw instinct for making a record — combed, sunlit grasses, all prickly needles, precision, sparkle, springtime charm & poison, in their midst a couple of flowers with spread petals — to transfer harmonies.)

The morning woman lives off the cliché of clichés, an Orphic degree of banality — the afternoon one is all self-deception, scurrying doubt, glittering relativism. Are those not two significant poles of the Jewish people? For one thing, a dogmatic insistence on an idol, whether that be a person, politics, conventional expression, or rite — for a second thing, eternal ferment, criticism, an ironic ever-further subdividing of things. For the morning woman (I suspect) in art it is the 'soul' which is most important & in love, it is 'death' — the afternoon one (for all her poetic interest) treats love as a hygienic, humorous function.

And this constant ebb and flow of the Saint Pauls and Freuds is in their blood: from that stems the loftiest, Christian standard of charity, the great mystery of love — that will always cultivate a relationship with petty family slobbering as well as unexplained and selfish idylls. Eerie as it may seem: the ascetic love of the God of the gospels and a bit of licking of the families of ghetto extras draw on a shared blood. That is one of the lines: from narrow-minded idyll up to the Christian eros of the gospels, whereas the other is in accordance with the Freudian, Proustian, and a host of more primitive literary variants: the dissecting, intellectual, 'uncovering,' compromising line which only 'pays attention to the facts' and sees through everything. What grotesque castings are produced from mysticism and barrel-organ rationalism!

It's a good thing to check women, because in love, bands of reason and mysticism can be experienced as if they were chemically pure.

If kitsch and God are infinitely close in a people's soul and way of life, it is here: was it not from the same blood that God Himself flourished on Earth, and was it not here that Shylock was born? It may be (from an *abstract* ethical standpoint) that Shylock types were born from the blood of other peoples, but there is no other people out of which gods would have come from *this kind* of blood relationship. They are blood relations to the One and Only God: we, non-Jews, can only be chemically positive for God's presence in our bodies if a priest has transubstantiated the communion bread and we swallow it, but even then we only have bread-particles in us, because the new substance, however much it is God Himself, has *no* chemistry — on the other hand, the blood which also circulated in God's body flows in the form of true blood in the blood of Jews: our physical connection with God is a miracle; that of the Jews is biological. Perhaps the reason why they can be as sensual in love & mercantile in social life as they always are is precisely this — because there is that sort of covert biological backing, a half-defined *identity* with God. Their banks are somehow cultic, mystical places — and their eroticism at the beach, the bar, in the weekend, et cetera, likewise has mystical roots. The reason they can be relativists and nihilists if they wish (and a large percentage of them often are) is because the 'truth' is not important, the truth set down by brains in tenets, dogmas, and philosophies is naïve and ephemeral: as compared with the unformulated truth of the inner God living in their own *blood*.

With the Jews rationalism and irrationalism are unequivocal things, or rather their mentality stands outside those two styles: since their own existence as an isolated chosen people was the greatest and sole important concrete aspect of their lives, it was natural for them to be irrational — but when that ancestral (heavenly?) irrationalism meets the mentality of other peoples, it is critical, finds every rationality (being a typically earthly, *non*-divine item) to be ridiculous and superfluous, constantly keeps its errors on record, and that gives Jews a certain semblance of rationality.

Their relationship to the Holy Trinity, for example, is interesting. They condemn the Trinity in the name of reason as being irrational, nonsensical: the matter has every appearance of illogicality being condemned by sober, logical people, though in point of fact the reverse is the case: the doctrine of the Holy Trinity is decidedly rationalist, logically constructed (totally ignoring for present purposes the issue of revelation), a typical product of the reasoning mind, or one might well say the *only* reasoning mind, *ratio pura* — & that is being condemned by the ancient irrationalism of Jews, which senses God as being biologically as it were within itself and compared with that sense of inner blood relationship with God the Holy Trinity, as a logical construction, is alien, superfluous.

Since with the Jews at base a source of irrationalism (to use the old word to make it easier) is constantly bubbling, it is natural that they abhor any definition or scholarly cognition which affects them, seeing in that *ab ovo* partiality & persecution. I know more than one person who lives very much an inward and inwardly directed life, unearthing their every movement and their every word from an embryonically ancient stratum — they, too, desperately flail & battle if I seek to describe or define any one of their actions in the simplest cataloguing manner; nothing is more natural.

I have the two women to thank for the ideal *logical* balance of eroticism between gospel and comedy: one of them, in great amorous humility, immediately disrobes into a 'god' — while the other, in great amorous insatiability, immediately stylizes herself into a mask. A hypochondriac 'deity' & a mask more biological than reality: *quel étalage!*[36]

⇐ 33 ⇒

1. UNEXPECTED freshness at dawn: the greatest secret for the oversensitive, yet it still happens;

2. occupation with a work written long ago: a passage in which every problem of style may be raised, and where the collision between aesthetic & biology is the most intriguing;

3. mourning Jews squat shoeless;

4. a drunk's joviality on the tramcar;

5. a sonata by Mozart;

6. physical weakness, downheartedness, hypochondria;

7. family spat: the 'event' in its completely irrational ceremoniousness;

(all this is the plan or memory, as you like it, of a single day).

with regard to 2 and *to 7*: the *style* is the complete biology, a crude imitation or copy of the innermost irrational rhythm: a total animal nonsense of inwardly directed living;

the *event* is the externality of externalities; accidentality, the moment, the circumstances; impotence and something *faute de mieux*: another nonsense.

A big moral scene: A husband is on his way to his lover at night when, in the garden, he hears and just about makes out his wife disputing and quarreling with bestial and madonnaish Amazonism with an army officer who is an opponent of the husband — no one is more splendid than that wife. Parkland in the evening; big boughs, small leaves; small boughs, huge leaves; the woman is weeping and yelling, her dress is torn and haughtily elegant — her every word is frothy, rabid logic, and fretting, self-dissatisfied goodness, full of faith in her own love, sobbingly skeptical in respect to her husband's love: *beatissima commedia.*[37]

The lover: the moral of morals in the man's life, a perennial cause and source of pangs of conscience, pedantic recorder of the problem of sin;

the wife: the foregoer of a family, tragic directress of the circus of 'strangers';

the lover: 'morality as hypochondria' in the man's life;

the wife: 'morality as deed' in the man's life.

How enigmatic: to go out amid dumb, nocturnal, leafy boughs in a park, knowing that at the same time a huge family wrangling is being waged. To see how realistic the assertion is that a whole bunch of inane rumpuses in life can be avoided — to see that the incredible mystery of simultaneity is nevertheless a reality. Can that be *all at once*? A struggle of ranting, decrepit angels, a thirst for blood, a clashing of lances — and the pastblue, time-peaceful silence of the huge chestnut trees, their unshivering sleep?

The battle of the evil and the good man is tedious, uninteresting — who wins? It is of no consequence. The tragic, big battles (the above novelistic slivers ought to be propped up in that way): when two *goodnesses* of two groups are fighting: both are good to the bottom of their hearts, but in radically different ways, and that is why they slaughter each other.

Big ethics = big murders. Big solitudes = big murders. Sometime one will have to buy a blood-testing laboratory of epics

with a very, very moral husband,

with a very, very moral wife,

a very, very moral wife — with her family,

a very, very moral husband — with his family:

those tightly packed ethics- & solitude-cacti torture to death, destroy each other.

The absolute sins of the absolute *goods*: only that is exciting from a human and a divine point of view. The whole company is full of martyrdom, charity, eroticism, nursing, cash granting, forgiveness, guilty conscience, and hypochondria — but 'events' kill souls and bodies.

Trinity (three kinds of 'goodness'):

wife — goodness as order, destiny, positivity (*God*);

lover — goodness as rapture, happiness, the perfume of sexual ecstasy, a lyrical hypothesis (*poetry*);

parents — goodness as blood, a biological compulsion of blind vitality (*natura naturans*);[38]

that is the big drama: the fight of those three kinds of goodnesses or ethical styles over a man: *mors stupebit.*[39]

What are ethics? where do they grow? always in that ghostly gap which yawns between the million psychological nuances and variants breeding wild and freely in our soul and the one and only done deed — ethics is nothing other than the extent of *foreignness* of deeds from the inside of the soul.

$$\Longleftarrow 34 \Longrightarrow$$

WHAT CAN SOMETIMES LIBERATE (for a short while) writers who have been cramped into anxieties?

1. the start of a love, left as a start;
2. a book which is aimed in polar *opposition* to his personality;
3. a dream;
4. a book's external appearance.

with regard to 3:

Jacob dreamed that he was leafing through a Greek book, a play printed in extraordinarily short lines (probably the memory of old Goethe's poem — one from Dornburg to the best of my recollection — in which he takes leave of *"symmetrische Reime"*),[40] which had the effect that Jacob believed, pathetically, excitedly, with redeeming sensual freshness, with childish optimism, that a book could still be an enjoyable experience — the long essay odes about the barrenness, lack, and tedium of books ceased, it was worth getting up in the morning because there were still stirring, fresh books, such as (one of the piquanteries, among others, of this dream) Schopenhauer. For Jacob that dream was one of the greatest miracles: for the first time in long years he was delighted with a book, purely, idealistically, with sporting eagerness, with radiant rationality. In the Greek text there appeared a word like ωλωλουμευα,[41] which in that context meant 'lover,' knowing (in his dream) that the root "ωλω" meant *being*: Jacob relished that too. It was exactly as one dreams all of a sudden about a woman who loathes one, and whom one loathes in return, that we make love in a park in Sussex, adoring each other fatefully and idyllically, with barbarian sexuality and English fairytale etiquette: in the woman's place it was the Greek text. When Jacob awoke — this is the main point — he *really* did awake in line with the optimism of the dream, feeling a delirious desire (how it had bored him hitherto!) for a text by Schopenhauer.

with regard to I:

Frederick II 'falls in love' with the woman with whom the family had been seeking to seduce Aquino:[42] what might be the element that differentiates an incipient physical flirtation from an incipient 'falling in love'? In an incipient caper with a mistress there is (thereby making it easier to embark on it): great irony, great physical interest, an easy opportunity, having a strong analytical familiarity and knowledge of the woman's external appearance, experiment — its center is 'the woman' as a hazard metaphor, hazard biology, hazard event. The emphasis in the whole affair is on the '*ars amatoria*':[43] it is plastic, scientific, poetic.

By contrast, all those elements are lacking from 'love': the woman is not a statuesque female reality but a misty focus; one's goals are uncertain; opportunities do not help, instead of pegging the woman analytically, one just divides oneself into irresolute scraps of hymns — there is no 'woman,' only some bother between woman and man — melancholic ethical suggestions glide by beside one — one feels the whole thing is unjustified. A mistress-designate is not to one's 'liking,' but desirable — a love-designate is not desirable but is to one's 'liking.'

There is a mistress aesthetic and a love aesthetic: the mistress is a plastic present, colored statue, a ready system, a fixed drama (that is a characteristic of 'desirability,' it seems): a woman of love is hypothetically smeared open, aphoristic, inorganic, and ghost-like: that is precisely why it is capable of releasing, breaking up, a soul stiffened in bands of phobia like a cloud.

One can learn everything from mistresses: what a woman is in love, what time is, what a dress is, and what a soul is, what instinct is and what artificiality, what tragedy is and what a game, et cetera: a mistress is objectivity, the Muse of an eros X-rayed by searchlight; nothing can be got out of a woman of love: no conclusion, truth, or simile is deducible, the whole thing is magical hovering, opium-fueled nonsense, radically torn away from everything. A mistress is always a crystallization of one's normal living conditions: one's manner, one's library, one's provisions, the bounds and map of one's

phobia, one's theories, a direct continuation of one's religion & superstitions: a formula of oneself, and so if
one is a 'bound' soul, a mistress will make one even more
bound, that being the reason one desires her, because one
wishes to see one's boundedness even more plastically.

A woman of love, irrespective of oneself, is — something utterly different, foreignness *per se*, the possibility
that can never be dreamed of, unconcernedness-with-
oneself, unexpectedness: that is why she is the Muse
of freedom. Most splendid of all, in such a liberating
revolution, is that she is tender, rondoesque, quiet: this
discrete anarchy and nihilism exerts an effect far from
the magnificence of psychoanalytic or mystic liberation.

Mistress *Phobie* (the deity of mistress women) &
Mistress *Liberté* (the mysterious deity of the women of
love): how dually two worlds. Frederick II, the Averroist
lover, all at once is liberated: he dares write aphoristically, whimsically — he was overcome by courage and
irresponsibility, he *lost* himself in love (that is the sole
medicine for men) — that denotes a new scholarly and
literary style.

⇐ 35 ⇒

THE PLACE where one is: that is the height of metaphysics and practicalities, a secret from which there is no
escape. During the summer one is continually changing

places; I am often worn right down to the bone from the many changes of place. The constant oscillation between my wife's house and mother's house: I go on foot, sweatily, from the one to the other, not finding my place. Both of them are plastered all over with memories, the colored stamps of time and fate, and both are uncomfortable. The secret of secrets is the unattainability of unattainability: a small room with a big table, a big armchair, a bookcase, and a bed, with a window overlooking trees. Why is that unattainable? The parents' room? If the piano stands in a good position, the table won't fit; if the music is illuminated, then one can't read in the armchair, only a wooden seat without armrests; if I have to open the window, I must first tidy my books and writings from the table, then I have to open the cupboard door a bit as otherwise the window won't open, the piano stool and music have to be pushed to the side, I have to pull out a stack of 'orthopædic' magazines from their stash under the table, the curtains I let hang at an angle and the carpet roll up. What a mystical, salutary experience it must be to open a window without having to undertake three or four minutes of the most maddening Sisyphean labors.

It's the same in my wife's house: there lamps, settees, and baroque wastepaper baskets have to be dragged aside so that just *one* wing of the window may be opened *slightly.* In neither of the apartments are there any sitting places: every single taking one's seat presenting a

separate construction task, an action tied to each constellation of the unfixed, misshapen pieces of furniture.
Large rooms have no centers or inner waves of gravity
— when you enter, you don't see a single point that
would invite or isolate you: the rooms are more open
and scattered than a street or square. The most tragic is
when a homogeneous indifference to space fills an excessively light apartment — there is not a single shaded
focus, a settee, or sofa, a more compact area around
a lamp or table. It is useless being on one's own in an
apartment like that: the uniformity of space, its rarefac-
tion, the aqueous neutrality of the lighting sucks out
one's soul, there can be no question of self-searching.
(That is a cue for the clerks from private firms in cof-
feehouses to make reference to nostalgia for the womb.)

Spaces make me happy (fantastically seldom), and
spaces make me unhappy (fantastically frequently) —
maybe of more interest to me, more than salvation,
more than art, more than anything, the greatest miracle
is: a restricted, lonely milieu in which I would feel comfortable. Spacelessness sometimes maddens me — I
tramp along the streets, lamenting and yelping, weighing up how I might be able to acquire a little room of
my own. The problem of boredom is, first and foremost,
a room problem: the reason I get so maniacally bored
is because only ecstasies are able to draw my attention
away from an empty apartment of corridor-coldness:
if I lived in a warmer, more chiaroscuro, quieter room,

the marvelous magical strength of the milieu in itself would divert, intoxicate me.

Two types of rooms are possible in my book: either a cluttered, average-rococo room in its bounty of mirrors, fireplace, fauteuils, curtains, cushions, pictures, statues, stuccowork, light fixtures, grandfather clock, and candelabrum in all their stifling opulence as if I were loitering about among water weeds, ooze, reeds, & moss lodges (an influence of *English Homes*, the most important book of my childhood)[44] — or else an entirely modern room: having said that, though, I have yet to see a modern interior space (despite devouring thousands of architectural periodicals) that comes up to scratch — for that I would design everything: absolute geometrical strictness and absolute sensual madness balanced to a hair's breadth. A 'modern' home that I have not designed down to the last sliver of mosaic is, for me, an inconceivable absurdity. A room has either been a breathing biological entity for centuries (Proustian times) — or else it is my most personal spatial sophism: there is no third way. But these average rooms, which do not enact either the vitality of a whirlpool of sludge or the self-contradictory tenets of non-Euclidean geometries with histrionic completeness: they torment me, suck my blood.

Just now I spoke about a room which is simple and straightforward, and now I shall put forward posturing alternatives between biological & geometrical rooms — yes, because there, too, as in everything: artistic ambition and bourgeois reticence alternate in me, and I don't know whether my terrible spatial torments are torments of my bourgeois or artistic side? The heroes of my finest dreams are specially illuminated *rooms* & plans: a staircase in twilight, a balcony in the morning, a hall at forenoon, a salon hearth on a winter's evening — a mysterious mixture of wild elegance and a baby's dream, artistic mumbo-jumbo and a bourgeois nightcap. English country-house garden, uterus, Cubist glass hoax — it matters not, only what there is will not be so for long. The most interesting thing is that on the whole it's *not* a matter of money — I could find my room. Why do I not look? I am afraid of change: if I were to stay where I am in my execrable corridors I shall gloss over the thoughts of death; if I swap domiciles it comes to look like I were preparing for my funeral: "It's not worth moving to a new place when it will only be temporary."

36

In the morning heat, Charles II asked his footman whose turn it would be on the stroll: was it perchance his consort, his official mistress, or the № 1 illegitimate or the № 2 illegitimate one? The footman produced some sort of calendar and made reference to the queen. "Let's go, then." On the way he dropped into a bookshop and pulled out the *Summa contra Gentiles* of

St. Thomas Aquinas in a Dutch edition.[45] They walked
on a hillside. Like any man who is quite clear about his
own frivolity and inner anarchy, Charles II was fond
of pigeonholing, classifying, and creating symbolic &
practical systems. That is understandable: a system is always a formal, frame-like entity — the contents always
chaotic, a thousandfold ambiguous, unanalyzable and
unfixable — better therefore to take care of the general
framework.

That morning, for example: around him were leafy
boughs, song-twittering birds, shadows dangling like
masks between the leaves, stones, paths, clouds, or in
other words, on the whole, nature boiled in summer for
the summer — who was able to say what the true sense,
the clear innermost intention, of all the many plasmas
and whistles was? That was 'nature': the word 'nature' itself, this noun which just about diplomatically designates
the thing, was sufficient for the king.

Beside him was his wife, who was reading some fashionable Parisian writer: who knows what is the sense
of sex? Those pale Archbishops attesting to the state of
matrimony among the rays of candles surrounding the
catafalque of Canterbury as they endeavor to place the
whole mystical burden of the Catholic religion and God
on the shoulders of the scraggy bridegroom & scrawny
bride? The love madrigals of birds frisking about in the
trees? A host of cellar and boudoir perversities? Who
would be able to think carefully through the tiring and

not particularly justifiable scale of variants? From marriages for diplomatic reasons and marriages of convenience to love dramas, Romeos & lyricizing odalisques. Much better to accept as a concept, beside 'nature,' that of 'legalized femininity' and then its riddles and nuances; in other words: leave its *content* in peace.

The third element: the book in his lap, *Summa contra Gentiles*. Was it not the gist of that text that "there is such a thing as systematic thinking" — and nothing more? Did it not have the sole role, as justified rationally (*not* out of decorativeness!) that it should represent an order, an elemental otherness as opposed to the confusion of color and form, noise and freedom of nature? That in the final analysis, *in ultima analysi*, there was also plenty of vital Secession in the *Summa* and plenty of rigorous syllogisms in the exotic patterns of fish scales — that did not disturb the king in the slightest as, after all, things do not occur in their *in ultima analysi* condition.

Nature, consort, syllogism: what else was present with allegorical hypocrisy on that royal morning? On the hillside there was a bespectacled Daddy with his infant daughter: the girl was stripped naked down to the waist and was taking a siesta in a stage water sprite's or swimming costume. So, splendid acacia leaf, if you have a *Summa* duplicate, you too, sweet wife, will find your harmonious complement — in the ever-piquant nymphet. That is sex as a surprise, as a momentary *'vue,'* a disclosure: a seconds-long hypothetical golden age &

mythical world on a crevice of an over-organized society. Could we live without such evanescent glimmers of visions? Is not a winking dryad, or a Diana bathing behind a bush as it flutters aside, needed beside the dreadful lead weight of legality? A person can somehow do without passions or deadly earnest loves, but where would he be without those kinds of little piquant medallions?

Charles II spoke a lot with priests, getting them to examine his conscience in accordance with a "*nosce-te-ipsum*,"[46] which was by then halfway towards sinking in the pathological, halfway towards becoming dulled into a bureaucratic routine, so that even now it made him slightly uneasy that he was not exhausting the *content* of things. He was searching for the essence of neither nature, nor Thomas, neither his spouse nor a substitute nymphet, all he wished to do was arrange them ornamentally next to one another: was that not intellectual cowardice, fear of thinking, a self-deceptive keeping-secret of his own stupidity?

He called his wife over and read her a passage from Aquinas: Book I, Chapter 26, in which Thomas sets forth the four motives by which the error of pantheism may be fostered in one. His wife (as any true woman does) examined the content of things very carefully: the one & only meaning of a single sentence, irrespective of any kind of formal background. The king was also gratified by this, it might even have been called a sensual pleasure:

for him it was so unusual not to consider a book as a function of locality that his mouth was almost watering. As the queen spoke that *"cette pensée"* & *"cette autre pensée"* or *"la troisième, je ne la comprends pas"* — it was a special pleasure to see the Thomistic mass (as for him the whole was just a homogeneous mass of systematic 'arrangement') subdivided in a manner whereby there was 'one thing' and 'second,' possibly a 'third.' *"Dites-moi, chérie,"* — he addressed his wife — *"la pensée est-elle grande chose ou petite chose?"* For him, you see, thought in its purity was never familiar: it was either a decoration or a raging anxiety, two baroque neuroses. A decoration: when he enjoyed the *Summa* as a symbol of order — a consuming, emaciating anxiety, a *furor* of associations, self-refutations, further and yet further analyses: when he tried to examine just *one* selected thought. He had never read speculative books in such a way as to pause at any particular thought: a phobia of quite mysterious strength held him back from reading over once again what he had already read once: he had to race on ahead. As a result, he would have a pathetic-irrational inkling about a work as a *'whole'* (though of course not about the whole *work*). If he turned back later in order to comprehend a sentence (he would never have been capable of that when alone in a room: for that a free nature and another person were always necessary), then he always got enmeshed in anxieties, in a bloody network of pros and contras that went on forever: part-thoughts were just as sterile in his brain as the whole. (The relationship between pain and sensuality in examining both a thought-as-a-'whole' and a 'partial-thought' was very interesting.)

The morning sun greatly fatigued the king, as did the sensual pleasure and pain of thinking, so that towards the evening he would be overcome by a sudden weakness. He tried eating lots of bread and butter but that was of little assistance, so he would lie down to sleep beside the veranda windows on a summer-patterned divan. How different sleep stemming from weakness from that due to fatigue. Like a bush with a thick covering of snow from under which Baron Munchausen stole the bush, the new white periwig he had removed would be hanging on a chair. By the time he woke up it would be a dark evening. It was much better waking that way than in the morning: the darkness did not bother the eyes; there was not much difference between opening and shutting them. His heart felt weak — while he was sleeping the whole left side of his chest would 'sink,' as he would say to his entourage: in those days he was so scrawny that there was little in the way of flesh, muscle, or fat between his internal organs and his skin to cover or dampen the secret movements of his lungs, intestines, and heart. Fat around the heart is like the padded doors in a privy council chamber — except it was missing in his case. His heart between his ribs was like a blackbird flitting here and there in a loose cage — his lungs a net dangling in the billows of a lake —, his innards were disintegrating cords tousled by a warm midnight breeze. If he lay down, his organs immediately thronged towards the divan under force of gravity, offering no resistance in the unmuscled body.

In the room next door, the queen consort was waiting for him with supper at a wheeled dressing table. The king staggered in, pretending to be stupid, and started counting the candles in the chandelier; he placed his periwig on a bunch of meadow flowers that had been brought that morning from the hillside. His gums being coated from sleep, he asked for a tot of cognac. The lighting was fine: Windsor Park was completely dark, with just one or two quite pale-yellow lamps roaming between the boughs of the trees — the veranda half-lit by the candles of the salon, and finally the salon itself with its ghostly-sleepy candles. Cardiac pain, dream, darkness: it was natural for the king to tell his spouse about the death of Philip Singward. Philip had been one of his old soldiers, but the king himself had not been present at his deathbed, he only heard about how he had died from his wife and daughter.

The king always displayed a special realism towards scenes about which he was only informed *verbally*, and more particularly by someone who in point of fact was not a good observer but only played the part of an analytical mind and eyes for the king's sake: that shamming *pseudo*-observation so thrilled the king that he saw the scene in a livelier fashion than if he himself had been there, or a truly attentive observer would have related it. Picturing the 'observation' stimulated him better than the object itself.

Right then, during supper, his spouse was seated a good deal higher than himself: the queen was sitting on a long-legged chair on one side of the table whereas he was squatting on a low stool. He (sobbingly) mentioned to the queen two details from the widow's report: one was that on the day the oldster died he had asked for four or five cherries with the pits removed; the other that he had turned quite yellow while he was still living and his nose had become sharply pointed. What a responsibility it must have been to be one of the four or five cherries which had the fantastically significant responsibility of being the last to represent for a dying soldier the world of objects, the physical secret of its colors, tastes, and touch. On the king's table were strewn bundles of files, letters, maps, and budgets, separated from each other by a lady's glove or a fencer's foil: what insignificant bric-a-brac as compared with those four or five cherries. Never had he seen cherries as clearly as those *described* by the widow: one side was pallid, the other a pale red, some were entirely black and with horny, bird-pecked skins, the stems were sticking out to the left and right, the wife plucked the stems off, she heard the pleasant plop of rupture, the hollow where the plucked-out stem had been, the short milling and thick cuff at the other end, and she had then squeezed out the pit, mushily, stained bloodily: if those details existed before the stage flats of death is it worth talking about or making history? How was it that all the widow said was that "his nose turned yellow," and he had immediately seen the yellowness in a thousand details, *instantly*, without fantasizing further, step by step? That jaundice itself was not a ghostly or sickening color, just in relation to the human body: it was more an agreeable, flowery, lyrical color, a golden green like the first leaf shoots of spring. How odd that the colors of humans are not encountered in nature: if a person all at once has precisely the complexion of the freshest meadow flower — then death is sure; if the color of a fruit is like that of the healthiest urban individual, inner disease is already guaranteed.

Having cried his eyes out over Philip's death, the king got out the Gospel According to St. Matthew and read out from it to his wife the part describing the Passion — mainly so as to enjoy the identity in content and the fantastic formal contradictoriness between St. Thomas that morning and the Gospel that evening. Who would have thought that the two — pious Jewish epic and barbarian lordly philosophy — could proclaim the same *one* teaching of *one* religion? A greater difference in style cannot be imagined. Before his wife he threw out the thought in a cataloguist's manner, in the most deferential tones of humility, that he wished to draw up the difficulties of the Catholic soul with regard to the role of Christ, sending these off to the most scholarly bishops and maybe even Rome. "Answer expected" — that should not be omitted at the end. He discussed a couple of difficulties of that sort with his wife. Why did God not also redeem fallen angels? Why does he not give them a chance to be liberated? If we think about God we say: "It is inconceivable that God does or says such contradictory things." Why do we say that? After all, we have no way of knowing whether we should imagine God, precisely on account of His divine nature, as an absolute paradox or, on the contrary, an absolutely consistent logicality.

For instance, people say things like: "If out of His love God breaks the nothingness of nothing by the creation of nature and mankind — then is it «improbable» that He would lead the mankind He loved in such a complicated way towards happiness as do Adam's sin and redemption by way of turning human and by crucifixion: what is the point of the huge range of opportunities and traps on the way to eternal unhappiness, and why the very constant threat of constant doubting in God?"

At the root of that question is that the one raising it pictures God as being 'logical' — but precisely because He is God why is it not natural that he works fantasticalities? On the other hand, how can that be reconciled with his boundless love of humankind — that he acts and speaks in a manner that is so geared towards *non*-humankind? The tragedy of the concept of God is clear; I imagine God either anthropomorphically or in absolutely no way at all. Christianity's concept of God tacks between anthropomorphism (after all, Christ was *anthropos*!) & total *secrecy* of God: between analogia *entis* and mysterium *entis*.[47]

There are *revelations* about God (1°) and there is *thinking* about God (2°), incorporating or avoiding the revelations as part of that thinking. Revelations happened in history, tossed among people, milieus, the biological whims of time, relying on those whims: that biological confusion is apparent. Thinking about God (e.g., scholasticism) is likewise subject to biological laws, though the natural history of thinking differs significantly from the natural history of historical processes. In the face of those biological 'whims' and hazards God says that he will not allow error and looks after the absolute purity of the one and only teaching. But even that divine proclamation is overgrown with a thousand biological (historical, psychological, etc.) parasites and their tendrils, breeding contradictions! — The Gospel represents *revelation* entrusted to the biology of history (1°), whereas *Summa contra Gentiles*, let's say, represents *thinking* about God bound to the human *raison*-techniques of the human brain — the 1° = *vita vivans*, the 2° = *fictio fingens*.[48] ('*Vita*' & '*fictio*' are equally suspect — there is no third way.)

Is it not a decent and seemly thing for a king and queen to talk about such matters of an evening? Their thinking (in that they were in splendid agreement) was always characterized by nervous fermentation and completely down-to-earth sobriety: they did not esteem the so-called 'big' problems because they believed in the sense of the question or philosophizing but because for them, thinking was a human compulsion, an unavoidable sterile mania.

Following that, both of them returned to the small loggia where the king had been sleeping before supper. There was endless silence around them — the queen sat in an armchair, the king, legs drawn up, on an extraordinarily wide windowsill. It had been a long time since anything caused him as much pleasure as that the windowsill was so extraordinarily comfortable and broad: if one finds an absolutely comfortable sitting place in a spot not designed for sitting, one is taken over by a mystical happiness, one of life's most profound, most agreeable joys. The sill comprised three portions: a wooden portion facing the room, a smooth tin part towards the garden (that was *not* slanting!), and beyond that a wide trough for flowers carved from stone in which there were no flowers, it was just filled with soil up to the level of the sill, so that even if the ischium of his hipbone happened to slip from the tin part into the *jardinière* he did not feel even so much as half an inch of sinking. After the theological apprehensions, that was intoxicating for him. What came to mind was what Milton might be doing now, then he looked out into the garden. He was well acquainted with the part in front of the window from the daytime, it was a fairly bare area with few bushes and flowers: now in the evening, by the uncertain lighting of a more distant lamp, the whole suddenly seemed rich and chaotic — out of a leaf an optical trick made three leaves, the analytical scales of the distribution of light made up for the leafy boughs of trees. The most intriguing thing was that the mathematical gymnastics of the light made nature more natural: the sudden jungle was not fictive but genuinely fertile and full-blooded. By day, there was prosaic emptiness between two bushes, but now, due to the two shadows, amplifying and analyzing each other, which stemmed from the moon & lamp, the thousand-hued velvet of the darkness, the unexpected ramifications of perspectives — the bare little garden was richer than the sea-bottom, and marvelous peace reigned over that whole culture of light: instead of an over-illuminated, deaf-and-dumb noonday peace, this was a *seeing*, cool evening peace which breathed freedom. On a fence opposite the window were diminutive, blood-red rambling roses: set up by the four types of force and vocal color of the lamp, the Moon, the darkness, and the inner glow.

Voilà: the first and last word after death, sickness, *Summa*, phobias, and women — those dumb, sharp, positive, and 'formal' roses. Why are nature and music pleasing? Because they are absolutely 'formal' and at the same time absolutely sensual — leaving out the contents that are thinkable and to be thought over; or in other words, fatal imprecision. A thought can never be precise — only 'insubstantiality' can be precise: a flower, a musical theme. Meanwhile, every half-hour a musical clock rang out superbly from somewhere: never had the tragedy and virginal domestic lyricism of time united so perfectly anywhere. The sound in itself was halfway between a hallelujahing Handel theme and the rippling circles around a stone tossed into a lake. After that, both of them retired to bed.

When the king woke up the next morning he sensed in the boundless looseness of his muscles and the quasi-carbonated tingling of his blood that the previous night it must have been infernally hot, and so it was right then, too. The queen was already awake and had straight away started shouting angrily: "What you get up to, Charles, is outrageous. There's a limit to everything! If I tolerate your paramours, if I put up with your scribbling love-letters and pseudo-breaking-off letters, if I praise your gallant *bon mots* — you might at least reciprocate my fantastic gullibility by respecting the boundaries. But no: at six o'clock daybreak — do you hear? —, I was roused from my sleep by a vulgar, insolent female voice demanding you. Have you gone mad, or had the woman you had sent for or who forced her way in gone mad? Who does she think I am? Do you think your bimbos would dare to behave so impertinently unless you had authorized and encouraged them?" "Angel, dearest, you have every right to be outraged like this, but I can assure you that I am much more deeply outraged than you, only I haven't the faintest idea who the lunatic might be who dares to barge her way in here at six in the morning! Stearns, chuck the woman out!"

The king jumped out of bed, while Stearns waited: he suspected that the ejection order was more a gesture to appease an angry wife than a serious command. "Now you're about to go down in your nightshirt to dally with your paramour, is that not so?" his wife asked, rising up from the bed. What a mænadic, horrific thing a woman is *rising* up from a bed that way: one is accustomed to women lying down. "In the end, I, too, am interested to know who the wretch is," said Charles, impatiently helping his footman hoist his nightshirt; he was allowed to see the queen in bed.

By the time the king had got downstairs there was no trace of the woman; she had left long before. He had no clue which one of the *"petite série"* of illicits, as his wife had once called them in a letter, it might have been. In the meantime the queen had also got up, and hardly had she set foot on the gallery that she noticed a servant carrying, without knocking, a pale blue letter into the king's study at the far end of the gallery. The queen had a wild imagination, pumped up by lowlifes: out of the matutinal squawks she had built up for herself, down to the last atom, a female portrait, and from the discreet yet, all the same, glaring color of the pale blue letter, she had built up another. The hussy of the hubbub must have been something like that kind: her skin white as the driven snow, soft, slightly aging; mauve eyelids, mauve lachrymals, jet-black hair tossed in big curly locks over the shoulders, slender boots, riding gloves with huge cuffs, a couple of military expletives, and a riding-switch that swished when applied: that was how she would have stalked up and down the hallway, demanding the king to present himself to her from his wife's bed in the 'black' of dawn; a goddess of insolence. Then there was the blue letter: Oh! that was some sort of lyrical humor, all refinement, death, nervousness and feminine destiny, and snobbery and victimhood of nauseating spiritualism, rosy cheeks, pretentious lisp, tears and belief in the sanctity of suicide.

When Charles had come upstairs, his wife warned him: "Dear, it's not worth working up a lather on account of that vanished nymph — a charming little letter is awaiting you in your room." Charles was a trifle nervous because he was truly tired of his women and wanted to be rid of them so it was ludicrous that his wife had started wrangling with him over them when they meant nothing to him. Had they ever? Rubbish! "Maybe it's from the dawn-raiding woman," said Charles. "Come in anyway. I'll read the letter out for you." "Ah, ah!" said his consort. "What affectation! Still, I might as well hear it."

They went into the study. The king then said to his wife — though not because he had anything to fear from the letter being compromising in its content: "This

113

whole thing is a pack of nonsense. Let's tear it up." "You're again under suspicion just for making that suggestion." In his mind the king twisted daggers ten times over in the hearts of ravening females — who dares to force on him the oafish role of a husband on an escapade? "In any case, I must say that your lovers have chosen a marvelous day for chirruping," the queen remarked. "Today you're going to have to speak or write to my mother about the money she made available to you so you would be able to send ten boats to Holland. You know my mother spends all day, from the morning to night, in the church, she has her meals there and conducts her correspondence there with all those half-blind village priests, and if she knew that you were whoring left, right, and center, not only would she not finance your wars but she would wring your neck with her bare hands. Those little bitches are superb preludes to your chat with her." "I'm a good deal more pious than your ma," Charles riposted. "Sure, I know how the organ-grinding goes: a sinner you were born and a sinner you will die, but there is more ethical stuff and human tragedy in your sins than in my mother's mechanical spleen after her menstruation has ended — were those words to your taste, dear?" "Fine, I'll write a letter. If it comes to that, I'll talk about victories won thanks to the legendary wonder ships she financed, et cetera, et cetera. Fair enough?"

Poor Queen Consort: she was a far more intelligent woman than to have taken sides either with her husband or her mother. It would have been a waste of energy to fret which was the more moral being, both were so, but on fantastically different collision courses. She herself realized that it made one ill even to imagine a dialogue between Charles and her mother. The old lady felt very hurt that the king avoided her and did not even suspect that he was actually fond of her, but he was well aware that they spoke very different languages, and that was why he was anxious to avoid meetings. The old lady was prey to hallucinations and visions: Charles tormented her daughter, was unfaithful, used her, spent her money on all manner of indefinable male misdeeds (a seventy-year-old woman's notion of 'men' — what myths and superstitions): the good queen consort that she was, she spent a good part of her time from morning till evening refuting these, despite seeing them from morning till evening to be largely justified. She also knew, however, that the unfaithfulness imagined by her mother and Charles' infidelities bore absolutely no resemblance to each other.

That very morning the queen had got up with the intention that if Charles was disinclined either to speak or write on the matter of the ships dispatched against the Dutch she would herself go to the dark church where her mother could always be found, and after making some effective excuse, she would herself give thanks on Charles' behalf. It wasn't that Charles was not grateful — far from it! When he had conducted a review of the ten spanking new ships in front of the admiral of the navy he had been sobbing with ecstasy & all but tipping himself in the sea in declaring at the top of his voice: "God bless your wonderful and saint mother." For days on end he had related to his wife like a child who has received a gift from his grandmother how magnificent the ships were: how superbly the prow of one of them was filleted, what a stroke of genius the mechanism of the helm, how elegant the color of the sails, how cunningly the cannon had been placed, and, cheeks flushed after each and every detail, he could not forbear from stuttering: "phantastical mother, dear mad *sanctissima* mammy."

His wife, not expecting either a letter or personal visit to be forthcoming, set off to see her mother. She ordered a carriage to pick her up further away and up till then she would walk along the shaded street. "I'll accompany you" — volunteered the king. — "Don't live in the illusion that I am not inexpressibly grateful to you for giving thanks on my behalf." "And while I am away in church swearing on oath to my mother that you are a saint, with whom will you be cheating on me?" "Confound it!" the king said with a wince, though not to his wife but at the sight of a woman with an enormous hat who was approaching them via the garden gate with an almost derisive spring in her step. She was his official mistress: it was natural that by the time the relationship had become plain for all to see the king had become sick and tired of the whole business. The consort gave

the king a melancholy smirk: "Great sense of timing."
"The thing I don't understand" — the king remarked
with the most objective amazement — "is why you don't
box my ears." When the woman had reached the royal
couple the queen asserted (though not sarcastically or
even out of self-tormenting sadism, more out of quiet
resignation): "Don't accompany me to the coach, Charles
and Lizbeth. Go back into the palace, it's cooler there.
Lizbeth can't stand the heat, and I'm not someone with
whom she'd be preoccupied." Charles snarled candidly
at Lizbeth: "Go home, or pop in on your woman friend
at her villa in Eton. I'll provide a coach." "Don't put yourself out!" the queen rejoined. "That's unworthy of a saint.
In any case I've heard that your master of music will be
directing a wonderful program of Frescobaldi's music
nearby.[49] Get seats in the shade there and have a listen."

Neither mistress nor king responded but like automatons they escorted the queen, who dropped the sarcasm
and protested no further. When the queen's carriage had
raced off, they returned without a word to the palace and
took seats opposite one another, just as wordlessly, in
the darkened grand hall. The king looked at the woman
fainting from the heat: surges of desire alternating with
spells of ironic boredom. "This is where an official portrait of my immorality greets me: fantastic as an armorial
bearing, but tedious as a document." Then, just as wordlessly they departed together to the garden of the villa

in Eton. Charles took with him three of the most urgent
of his papers, sat down at a garden table, and worked
without a break for three hours, while Lizbeth, seated
on a bench beside him, read memos. When the king had
finished they parted.

 37

I AM CORRECTING some of my older writings —
filled by a *furor* of self-criticism. They also need to be
organized in a systematic fashion: my observation relating to my style. The eternal self-examination amounts to
a neurosis, impotence and hypochondria? It is not art?
At all events, it has a strongly ethical character, is magnificently biological — to live in a big ferment of *life &
morality* and bear witness to that (even if absolutely
inartistically) is: important, worthwhile. It would be
interesting to examine precisely the relationship of conceptual and vital inspiration to all sorts of affectation.
Above all, my writings force the issue of style to the
foreground; my subject cannot come into discussion.

38

Two things excite my interest: the most subjective epic
details and ephemeral trivialities of my most subjective

life, in their own factual, unstylized individuality — and the world's big facts, in all their allegorical *Standbild*-like greatness: death, summer, sea, love, gods, flowers. One of the causes of my stylistic confusion is that the subject of my sentence is usually some analytical nicety, a finesse, a pictorial or conceptual paradox — and I pump into the description of the details of those details, in the form of subordinate clauses, compound words and rhythm-killing litanies of epithets, the mythical grand backdrops (sea, summer, death, et cetera). I may write down, for example, the particular shape of a woman's lips, and the even more particular lipstick taste on them, and I load the apparatus necessary for that description with the big, more generally interesting facts and problems of life and death, organs and blood pressure, love and artifice. That too is a phobia: I dare not start off with the 'big,' hence the grotesque sentences: the leaden weight of eternity bound up in the hairs of ephemerality. Rather than ten characters in a novel, I describe a single person, and while analyzing that (cravenly!) narrate ten novels in parentheses. My sentences are: masks; tumors lying immediately (pressed right up against the surface) subcutaneously. All that is important is that a tiny mask, the skin, should be there at the start, at the head: if I see that I wish to speak about *death*, but the beginning of the sentence is talking about the slow dribbling of soap lather (in other words, a bit of epidermis is in place):

then I am perfectly reassured, let the one and only important subject of *death* come in its own expanding ramifications (stretching mask and skin endlessly) like simile, like a playful decoration, grammatically and in terms of sentence-structure subordinating it to the subject of soap lather: a square inch of 'soap lather' (the epidermis), twenty square inches of 'death' (the tumor beneath it).

═ 39 ═

FOR ME it is a much greater pleasure to fester in a lonely room in *summer* (even when a storm or just a gentle breeze is occurring) than in the winter. To look at the storm through loose roller blinds: that is considerably more than watching snow falling from a warm room. (That should be further justified one of these days.)

═ 40 ═

HOW INTRIGUING in Goethe's very early poems (late 18th century, of course) the insipid myth etiquette and naively crude sensuality — on the one hand, "*porzellanene Oreaden,*"[50] on the other, "*Den sonst verdeckten Busen zeigt.*"[51]

⇐ 41 ⇒

QUESTIONNARIUM DORICUM: *Doric* questionnaires, because they are massive, optimistic, pugnacious and, even in their question form, tougher than a good few old yes-dogmas. The endless difference between last year's skepticism, resigned ignoramus mood, self-torturing, naively sadistic relativism & — 20th-century questions, 'ignorances,' the issue of beginning everything from the beginning. The relationship a 19th-century question and a 20th-century question bear to each other is, by and large, that of lyrical pessimism to dramatic tragedy. 19th-century doubts are somehow a merely-rational, merely-psychological, strictly humanistic style of skepticism — whereas 20th-century doubts are an existential, broadly ontological style of skepticism: it is not a response to a given rational question (knowing that is impossible), more a matter of the fact of snatching the 'question' and of questioning from a sphere of the brain of limited logic & conceiving of it as a question of the whole of existence and the cosmos in every biological aspect: it is not a person enquiring about the secret of the world but the fact of the whole world's big, universal question.

⇒ 42 ⇒

Holbein: Portrait of a Young Girl

How should I characterize Chiara? Should I start by describing her body and her dress? By relating the most recent days of my life history, which immediately preceded her? With the vista which ringed around our encounter? With the unexpected lyricism of my own interior? With my metaphors, my dreams, the inconceivable future, my helplessness? How much all that was one: my past, her body, vista, my biological crisis. One moment I would like to tell things in the order of my questions, building architectonically, the next minute I would like to continually crumple the agonizing strangeness of words and facts, life & work, into soft, melting-rippling mass.

Your dress? When I saw you in the afternoon on the steps of the *Scuola di San Pietro*, you were wearing a brown dress, brown coat, brown cap or hat, and you had a brown handbag. Floating round you were all the bestial laziness, Keatsean ripeness, eerie color change of a summer afternoon — from these afternoons are born banal tea parties, it is then that, after a siesta, new brainwaves are hatched, amorous and artistic miracles, then that one becomes unexpectedly decadent or an insensitive onward-toiler at the morning's work —, afternoons send one equally to prose and refinement.

You were standing, with your shoulders a bit shrugging, your long lips drawn apart a bit preciously, with translucent, fish-fleshed hands, and eyes unusually bold-looking due to short-sightedness. It is interesting that a woman's character will 'forever' be what one compiles from the physical traits picked up at the very first glance: it is like a capricious bunch of flowers hastily thrown together from a richly stocked garden. You were a sentimental, sound, discreet figure, timid, but not for a moment fading, an embodiment of idyllic sobriety.

We began talking on the steps: I perched on the broad marble handrail, & we tucked our heads now under the shadow of the columns, now under the warm, yellow pelt of sunshine. That was when I became acquainted with your voice, which to me was perhaps the most important of all. Your long lips snaked and wrinkled profusely and dazzlingly helter-skelter while you were speaking: there was nothing erotic in that lakeside undulation, it was more a homely blending of the homely fact of speech and thinking. You had a big, gleaming white set of teeth without any gaps — just tiny spots here and there where your lipstick had stuck to them. The upper row of your teeth completely covered the lower row: after each smilingly pronounced 'No' you sweetly closed them together, the word hanging in the air before your lips like actors coming forward, close to the footlights, as the curtains whisk together during a change of scenery. Your voice softly purled like a warm spring of water, in your words (and your thoughts as well, of course) all the spontaneity, fresh and easy bubbling warmth and vapor of a spring in the depths of the woods concurred. Is there anything finer than a warm spring of water? The Earth's fire has been turned into gentle, healing heat, yet the water is still crystalline, sparkling, chastely fresh. Your voice was exactly like that, Chiara: full of girlish good spirits, lyrical sobriety, warm naturalness. Not just in its value & content, but also in its rhythm and tone it resembled purling: the words came so readily, they span apart so eagerly in the air, straight in front of your lips, showing the same caprices of sudden speeding-up and pensive slowing-down as a spring.

You did not employ the same vernacular as mine but a trans-riparian one:[52] a bit tense, pronouncing your e's stretched out towards your lips, each 'e' immediately throwing your face into an involuntary smile. What a curious game that was between the perpetual rising and falling of the lips and the cold, regular bone curtain of the teeth — thereby in every word of yours there was something of an odalisque's softness and an oldster's stiff pedantry.

Your eyes were a delight: they were not big, they were grey, but owing to the fact that you wore spectacles to read books (you were known to be studying the humanities, Chiara), there was a stiffness in the way you looked at distant objects, a tendency to excessive fixity: that, too, was an endearing example of how much mental virtues & physical faults are one and the same: what a *faux pas* it would have been to speak separately of short-sightedness and forthrightness, girlishly plain honesty. Nobody looked so frankly into my eyes as you did. Myopia, childish curiosity, self-oblivious faithfulness to the present moment, a teenybopper puritanism, a precious trustfulness in what men say to them, yet at the same time a wild, alarmed lack of trust: would anyone be able to limn out every bloom, every bluntness and Amazonian sharpness of that look? While words poured softly from your lips, billowed like cigarette smoke, your eyes jumped keenly around, zigzaggingly & unexpectedly, with no transition between one striking position of the pupils and the next.

In quite surprising contrast to your frank look were your slightly twinkling smiles: when you laughed your long but scarce eyelashes railed off the whites of your eyes with all manner of van Gogh-like hatched and ragged veils, and the central greyness, the whites and those untidy scribbles, gave the sole silvery, neutral points of cheerfulness; when you unexpectedly switched the word to 'serious' matters (equally, how childish & chic, how tragically playful, that 'seriousness' was), all at once your eyelashes would melt away, there would be no tracery and grille there: only suddenly rounded-wide, fiery and flashing whites from which an unequivocal look would be sharply shot at me.

There must have been odd connections between the movements of your eyes and mouth that I could only suspect but never nail down: it is best if I refer with (perhaps ludicrous) *Sachlichkeit*[53] to the sixth variation of Mozart's (whom you did not know and thus could not like) variations on Gluck's *Unser dummer Pöbel meint* for piano [54] — there one can see the game in that while the soprano underlines the theme in the bass with a single trill like a quiet ship, then later as the bass glides on further above the murmur of the trill the same theme appears with angelic grace in the soprano: if I take your mouth and eyes as alternately now bass, now soprano, I may perhaps have distantly indicated the route which may lead to recognition of their mysterious relationship.

Under your white skin lay a lurking freckliness, but that was gorgeous — there was an autumnal falling of leaves in the greyness of dawn, all full of tiny, flitting leaves, at one moment dense as a curtain, the next scanty.

I loved your gait: you went around from your broad, slightly hunched-up shoulders — what particularly endowed them with a leading role was the blue cape that you had draped on the following evening; that cape was nothing other than the magicking of your entire body into a single darkly petaling shoulder flower — although the material tumbled downward like the narrow belt of a waterfall, clinging close to girlishly slender shoulder blades, here was nevertheless some kind of upward striving in it like in the skyward-pointing petals of blooming flowers — if a bell and a goblet of the same size were to be slid into each other then they would yield a dual figuration of that kind.

How beautiful your three-way stage division was in the evening street: underneath just the steady clacking of walking with the graceful *'Tüchtigkeit'* [55] of trotter heels — in the middle, the terse but dense cloud of the cape, the Acherontic torch and palm-tree of the shoulders — and finally on top the large white panama hat with its great-big near-rigid brim. There were times when you hunched your shoulders that the two opposite rims of the hat & your two shoulder bones touched — everything on that *'paradiso'*-platform was uneasy, endearing horizontality: the brim, the broad shoulders, the extended ovals of your smiling eyes, the eels of your lips.

Yes, that was your second dress: blue, like the true flowers of every true dream. On your neck were little white ruffles of lace — the way that your sweetly obstinate philologist mind pictured Mozart and, with cat-like, voluptuous gusto, continued to misjudge him. Under the lace, reaching virtually down to your shoes, was a blue rectangle of a starched shirt framed by several stitched seams.

Why am I describing your dresses with such pains-taking scrupulousness? Because I am an idolater, and *that* is the nude study of an idol — that is its pagan everlastingness; because I am a Christian, and I know that although body may resurrect, dresses do not: let the glorious nourishment of ephemerality, therefore, be recorded before death.

Our encounter was a chosen and fugitive moment in time: time *par excellence*, the moment *par excellence*, and the *time*-permeated quality of your being, the identity with the moment is not guarded by a nude study of you or your character, but by your dress, your matte antelope-leather handbag. For precisely that reason the driest-as-dust inventory is more lyrical than a lyric poem: there is a vegetative eternity in my sentiments, but your dress was *just* of the moment ("Mozart is *just* Mozart," you said), and the moment, the meek terror and stormy reality of ephemerality is one of those deities whom one always worships, from whom one always fears.

In your whole evening-blue being there was a touch of the wild pansy: a wild pansy is meek and small, there is something tragically familiar and idyllic about a wild pansy — as suggested by its name in German: *Stiefmütterchen*.[56] And you were familiar, 'bourgeois,' in an un-dreamed-of poetic sense of the word: that was implicit in the words with which you talked about dress salons and described the new dress that was being made (every arpeggio, every unexpected chord, racing passage, and sudden pause for breath of the cadences was present in that description: you cast a new gesture of mouth and hands for every word, you interpolated a new tempo for your gait as if the thought of the new dress in preparation had driven you completely crazy and you were going deliriously to pour out every possibility of your mimicry, gestures, and tone of voice into the most ecstatic crowdedness), and it was implicit when you told a story about cooking breakfast and supper; it was implicit in your sweet & modest desire for money, in your playfully stylized baby-doll elegance ("After all, we can be lavish once in a while, no?").

And equally wild pansies are all dark purple and velvet with the mystical sharpness and night of colors: that idyll is — lethal. And that idyll of yours, gentle, chatty Chiara, was lethal: lethal because in it there was goodness, charity, autumn-tinged chastity, the poison of niceness.

Here a bit of a preface from the diary is required — what kind of women were your immediate precursors? Before it was you, who was first & foremost: a *girl*, what kind of women is one talking about (they were all married), and I had not spoken with them for many a long year. How often I spouted about women not meaning anything more to me than the fleeting impression of a body (the shadow of a hair, a silk button left undone, etc.) and anonymous going soft in the head in the black curtain of an embrace. How often did I praise the discerning and levelheaded knowledge married women have about love in contrast with the overhasty and ill-informedness of the drive that girls have for love and getting married. All my wisdoms were annihilated by you in a moment, *girl* Chiara: you were not a few isolated impressions, the tired snacks, the *Imbisses*, of visuality, you did not even awaken my crudely physical routines — you were not a dehumanizing doll, a partly artistic (the impressionist aspect), partly biological (the cohabitation aspect) fiction — no: you were a person, a whole person, a bourgeois, a genuine living partner in life.

Who would have known it? After the poetic rapture of dehumanization (in which instruction was given by the ladies), the rapture of humanization. And this is where 'sensuality' kicks in: where there is *no* bed, no nude figure, just a person, a whole person — with their character, their voice, their portrait. I am *un*familiar with your figure: you were on the steps of the *Scuola* in your long brown coat, the evening of the next day in the dark of the night & the cape — that is where 'sensuality' kicked in. That is why it is possible to be in love only with a girl: a girl's body is a floating entity which, bud-like, is hidden away among the profuse foliation of a human personality. A genuine girl's beauty is always a beauty of 'character,' to employ a fairly lame word: a reflection of the totality of her thinking and her ways of doing things in practice. How wonderful was your invincible virginity (if perchance you were no longer so, the main thing is that you did not as yet live in the sleepy sex office of marriage like the women who had prowled around me before you appeared), and your pseudo-womanly, prematurely old-maidish sobriety — nothing is more lovely than a 'sober' girl ("after all, I'm not a kid," you said with a smile):

how true & justified your sagacity is, how much, when looked at from the viewpoint of the words, they were as if spoken by a married woman, but it was of no use: the Artemisian whiteness of your entire humanity, its moonlit blue-leaved chastity, imbues them — your sagacity is obstinacy.

You were the first woman with whom I had been together until dawn, till sunrise — that was the most splendid five hours of meekness, a crazy, prodigal 'chastity.' At last "I spent a night with a woman," and that night rendered us innocent. Shall we take out our old standard psychology routines, and prattle on about how that 'innocence' was more refined than the perversity of others? No; let's drop it. A girl's imperious profile will not stand it.

⇒ 43 ⇒

A HAYDN-SONATA and a cactus: the difference between the classical-rational structure of a 'work' and biological forms. My own writings, for the time being, belong to the cactus category: if I can have a role in literature it is the direct tangibility of biological lines and forms of instinct in my sentences. "Experimental novel" was said about *Prae* in more than one place,[57] by which one was supposed to understand an anachronistic relic of the old-fashioned mood of the 19th century.

The question is the same as what I said about doubt in general: there are two kinds of 'experiments' — one is strictly rational, self-analytical, & overscrupulous, simply a pathology of consciousness (if one wishes to be petulant about it), but there is a second 'experiment,' namely the perennial experimentation of nature: after all, the fact of evolution is in itself a constant experiment. Biology is so explicitly an experimental domain that no distinction is made between a 'final result' and an 'undecided, exploratory trial': in nature, even the most symmetrical rose is merely a hypothesis denting only an instant in time (an experiment), and even the most grotesque cactus, resembling a caricature of an embryo, is an end result: Racinian 'stringency.' If *Prae* and other works I have planned are 'experimental,' then they are so in a specific biological sense: not an apprehensive, exaggerated self-consciousness, but experiments of primal vitality, which are in a special biological relationship with form (cf. the 'forms' of protozoa: experiment and totality of life are absolutely identical, they coincide).

44

APROPOS Haydn and the unreliability of the human nose for structure:[58] more than once, Haydn was conspicuously free in his treatment of sonata form (throwing the main subject away, et cetera), despite which, I savor his sonatas as form *formatissima* — the sonata structure is retained to the point of bigotry in the works of certain romantic composers, yet they still arouse an impression of disintegrating chaos. My structure-sensitive nerves are *not* stimulated by the structural elements of a work but by other properties.

MUSIC IS THE BEST AREA, of course, for comparing the elementary forms of biological forces and the nature of rational, 'artistic' forms, for investigating their connections and contrasts: musically speaking, most obviously: the fugue. It's a well-known saw: "Fugues are mathematicized music." Readily predictable objection: "Not a bit of it! fugues are rather the most sensual, superbiologized music." Neither is right, both are true. A fugue is deliberate sensuality — a rational technique in order that the sonic character of the voices be sensible and enjoyable from as many perspectives as possible (ever-newer harmonies, which stand out due to the counterpoint, in point of fact their ever-newer perspectives, views, profiles, half-profiles, en-faces, under- and overviews of each voice). Is that not how it is done with love: if one kisses or embraces does one not consider ('mathematicize') the technique that will make the kisses or embraces more enjoyable? Would it not be madness to state (*à la fuga*) that a kiss is: mathematical, an embrace: intellectualism? If it comes to wishing to weigh up and to hierarchize, the fact is a fugue is a thousand times more sonic eroticism than sonic mathematics: the maximum groping of a melodic figure. I recently heard Frescobaldi's *Fuga* in G minor (as transcribed by Bartók).[59] In what an 'experimentally' (*o papillon noir*) clear relationship the three textbook elements of music: melody, rhythm, and harmony are in this fugue. The theme is sounded '*marcato*' in the right hand; this is pure melody in a spatial vacuum. In Bar 5 the theme appears in the left hand while the right hand brings the first counterpoint: at the moment when the first contrapuntal harmonies appear, I cannot even imagine anything more sensual, and richer, more chaotic and more mathematicized. The lonely theme, as I said, is space itself, a single eerie linearity in nothingness: after which the contrapuntal bar is heard unexpectedly, prodigally, almost crazily congested — like a mistake, a sick intertwining of plants, the double vision of eyes before fainting, a heavenly collision of stars: some sort of anarchy which is born of the sensual fact of 'doubling.' The melody all at once dies, vanishes, drops out in a physical perceptible manner, what is left in its place are the pure fact of rhythm and the pure fact of harmony — as if the counterpoint at a single magical touch had drained the color, flesh, & blood of the melody, leaving only its abstract form, above all its rhythm when only 'marcato' had sounded in the right hand, and then, too, it had just been a line, albeit a snaking line, a sensual-sensuous nerve fiber of vitality. Now, however, it becomes a geometrical line: a colorless binding thread of rhythm. At the same time, the harmonies, those sudden cross-sections, signify something a thousand times more expressive than the pure melody, so that the original theme, in which expressivity and abstraction were mildly blended, all of a sudden had broken up to two extreme elements in Bar 5: on the one hand, the abstract world of harmonies expressive to the point of anarchism, on the other, that of geometrical & merely formal rhythm.

For me in this fifth bar (and in structurally similar parts of all fugues) lurks the secret, the marriage and battle of biology & art, of abstract construction and vital 'amorphism': where I sense no melody, only an inexpressive phantom of a melody, the algebraic quanta & spaces of rhythm — along with the dizzying spots of harmonies, the inner sensual unboundedness, with the complex chemistry of the mixing of sounds, running from sexual to theological and back. As if the longitudinal section of each such bar were itself a basic formula of syllogistic order but each and every cross-section were anarchy itself, the swirling formlessness of sensation.

⇐ 46 ⇒

Two motifs:

1) "It is a great star."[60]

2) "I saw the green-black leaves creeping on the golden evening sky like some fanatics kissing and climbing the Scala Santa."

⇐ 47 ⇒

Artists' absolutely *opaque* relationship to their art, most particularly that of writers to literature. How many foreign elements at one and the same time, e.g., I look at the Fountain of Lions in the Alhambra of Granada, a Moroccan Arabic woman's embroidered handbag, a typical hotel room-filler English girl, and I have a recollection, an experience, from yesterday I have a plan for tomorrow, a 'subject,' if you like, which would unify my two basic instincts of Proustian analysis and Websteresque 'gesture + phrase.'[61] There is biology, thought, journal life, rationalist fiction: everything from sex to reason, from dream to impotence — and in every element there is a bit of 'beauty.' Every aesthetically true and honest examination has to proceed from this *compilational* character of beauty. The concept & biological fact of 'decoration' are extremely important: the most elementary ornamentation on the most elementary house; the major lessons of 'stylization.' When one "scribbles out of boredom" (one ellipse after another), and when one "creates."

⇐ 48 ⇒

Now leave me alone, I am alone at last: like a childish blue flower in the sun. I've had enough now of gods: no kind of mythology has any sex appeal any longer. I am deaf & blind to a Thomist *Summa*. I've had enough of the poses and metaphors of Artemis and Dionysos, enough of the transcendences of the Middle Ages: nature's grand and shoddy mantle looks just as bad on the little blue flower as its morally suffocating tether. I don't want to be natural, don't want to be moral; let my corollas turn towards the Sun — o tedious stupor-wombed gods, leave me alone. The mysterious nights, wings of revelations and weight of Aeschylean fate — I need them not, they are no thoughts, no food. The women, too, should go: I need no charisma or carnal delight; which is worse: the cynicism of civilized strumpets or the ethics of lyrical trollops, the latter being composed mainly of their kisses, which are more ceremonious and frightening than the golden oil of extreme unction. Like so many comedies, so many facts: marriage, faith-fulness, death, lies, lovers, neurasthenia — the whole set-up of 'love.' Why the lie for the Flower when he has a

Sun? What stupid company: dumb gods and psychologized women! Just go: an Oriental lover and a Greek god, a Christian neurasthenia and an anonymous bird. Alone, alone, anonymously, aimlessly; "be like little children": so it was said[62] — that is the way I want to be. Nor is there any need for art or justice, and above all there is no need of a *name* for what I am feeling right now & what I want to be now. I was born a virgin: not a sexual virgin, not an intellectual, not a historical, not a floral virgin, I was somehow a virgin in a much more elementary, more infantile way. After all, I truly have had enough of the wreath of moment-to-moment not-wanted acts: of not-God, not-morality, not-freedom, not-literature, not — 'no.' We can't live without a yes-statured and truly yesly Yes: I have the right to a 'yes' at last. I am a flower, an innocent, undemanding flower of my mother that seeks nothing; foreign between the filthy claws of lovers, foreign between the Madonna wings of wives, foreign between the classical impotences of thoughts — finally I want my home, my naked Yes. To flay everything off me, forget everything in Lethe's croaking, cawing, and swooning waves. — I don't want my name, my sex, my past, my future — I am the perfect heretic of everything which is *Me*. I want to forget my language, every human word, every ambition-aping vibration of my routinized soul — I want to be the simplest blue being in the Sun. Let there be an end to the battle between confidence in life & hypochondria, to perennial fretting, so that my life should be merry with or tragic out of incapacity — should I fear disease and death or should I proceed heroically in life: I loathe the opposition of the hero and the neurotic in my life, I want to be freed of everything forever. Should I throw together a scatter-brained catalogue of all the things of which I want to be freed? Why remind myself of my disgraces? I have no wish to see dead myths, dead women, dead morality, dead beauty — to what end the execrable spinning round of 'life-and-death'? Nothing: pure, flowery, babyfying, sun-lit and nameless Nothing. Clear, dewy Insignificance, receive your faithfullest.

49

Is there a separate 'life' and separate 'art'? When I read poems by Goethe (e.g., *Liebesbedürfniss* and *Morgenklagen*)[63] — am I not enjoying the simple fact that "Look here! Somebody also *lived* there": he opened a door, his lips were chapped, he had not had much sleep that night. If I inspect my own 'creative' ambitions — is not a simple catalogue at the back of everything? I was walking along one of the streets on Sun Hill:[64] all arching tree boughs dangling over garden fences into the street — was not "tree boughs dangling over garden fences into the street" the subject for my novel, my poem, my last will & testament, and my moral advice for my child? Nothing more. Maybe that would be the ideal arrangement & separation: a book which would contain simple inventory items like that, with at most a definite article tacked on as a sign of 'pathos' ('the golden sky' instead of golden sky) — and another book which would contain every perversity of intellect and sensation: paradoxes and hallucinations. The reason Goethe is sometimes 'insipid' is because he is more than inventory, less than hallucination.

50

"Our Father, who art in heaven": that duality alone (God and we humans) and the distance (God in heaven, humans on Earth) are problematic. There is God who is infinite and absolutely sufficient unto Himself who creates another being: if He creates it, why so distantly from Himself? Because we are very far from God. It's as if He did not want to create humankind but the fact of *distance* — Adam is not clay & breath but: *realitas distantiæ*. If God created a human-shaped something out of nothing, why not in His immediate vicinity. Why do we not constantly embrace and see Him? Why this eternal desire, nostalgia, sterile apostrophe? I ought to be near God in the way an embryo is near its mother:

not "Our Father" and not "who art in heaven" — but "We" (*without* separate Father and separate I: absolutely together) and "which are in a one and only embrace: where sometimes thou, God, art the trunk and I am the helical parasitic liana, and sometimes I am the trunk and thou, God, are the liana on me." Why did God explicitly create islands of non-divinity like us, humans: Why does God reflect Himself in the non-divine? Why does the divine cause Himself to be wanted and try to ingratiate Himself by the non-divine? God can only live in a distorted fashion in us — Why does a God which is infinitely sufficient unto Himself create such distorting mirrors? And even if they are not distorting — why a human-shaped mirror at all? The creation: God's thirst for a Non-God; the moment Adam is born immediately he *feels the want* of God. Why create *want*? That is an internal difficulty of the prayer: is it conceivable of a being which is infinitely perfect that it should continually have itself sought and apostrophized? If out of love God created humankind in order to quantitatively intensify the fact of happiness around Himself (many salvations of many people), then what purpose is served by this banishment and torture on Earth? Is there not some uneliminable logical absurdity in an infinite God creating humankind, which is to say, in spite of His immortal soul something exceedingly mediocre and, compared with Him, unutterably inferior, primitive, and grotesque and loving that, compared with Him, caricature and non-entity? Eternal happiness: infinite God surrounded by billions of absolutely *non*-divine creatures? Is it possible that an absolute God would need and desire this? The 'heavenly possession of God' of the immortal soul is still an essential, absolute distance from God: what need does God have of this fantastic *foreignness* to God? If God is God, logically that excludes the existence, even the very hypothesis, of humans.

"Hallowed be Thy name, Thy kingdom come": why do we say that? You are holy in yourself in the mysterious solitude of infinity — I am not necessary, you have no wish to be 'hallowed' by me out of gratitude. Sincere thanks are what a petty officer gives to a general for being made up into — a field officer; a priest to the pope for being made up into a bishop; a middle manager to the managing director for getting a thirty-per-cent pay raise but an 'existing' entity cannot offer sincere thanks to God, the Creator, for having elevated him from non-existence into existence simply because: the priest and bishop, petty officer and field officer are the same individuals, two different states of the same person, whereas the *non*-existent means precisely an amorphous nothing, non-existence is not a 'subjective past' for Adam. I *am* — I cannot relate that 'is-ness' to anything, it is an incommensurable solitary fact — that makes thanks impossible. What a strange paradox that is: every bone in my body exudes thanks for my reason for existing, thanks for pain and pleasure (mainly pain) — but when I look at the logic of the thanks, I am neurotically paralyzed. So, am I biologically grateful yet in logic ungrateful? At other times I throw myself so eagerly into the arms of every biological impulse — whence does this taking logic so seriously come all of a sudden? Because as soon as one starts talking about God one senses that the question demands absolutely rational clarity, syllogistic certainty, the God-hunger of primitive peoples is a *biological*, unintellectualized God certainty — and my (and Christianity's, Thomism's) sort of "God is first-and-foremost a need for *raison*, a mathematical requirement of existence" cast of mind: whence that dualism? Papua is normal and the logician is the sick person, or is Papua the hysteric and the logician to God's taste?

"Thy will be done": why did you create humankind — so that your will should have an outlet for expression? When it comes to it the world and humankind are ludicrously tiny matters compared with you — in other words, your infinite will can only be materialized here in a distorted manner, in burlesque miniature like Mozart's will on a penny whistle — in other words, one would be pushed to call Thy will as it is realized here Thy will, so greatly has it been tailored to our pettiness. Why would you have any interest in what joy the fulfillment of your will can offer — after all, only you are truly who you are, and here there can be nothing other than Thy will — why should I demand of you in my prayer a tautology of yourself?

"On earth as it is in heaven" — heaven and earth: why that dualism and hierarchy? Why perturb poor earthlings with your heavenly inconceivability? Why two domains? In relation to you the two coincide anyway, there can be no difference between them.

"Give us this day our daily bread. / And forgive us our trespasses": Oh! Is it possible just to set about paraphrasing these two sentences — the burning-seething complex of the dreadful realities and hallucinations of suffering and ethos? Give our daily bread today — so you are aware that many is the time you do not? Is it necessary for you to draw our attention to yourself with the refined Inquisitional levers of misery, illness, and death? Again making us aware of the *distance*: do you have such a strong wish that patients on operating tables feel in the nauseating totality of their fear how much they are *not* God, just rags; that Jesus Christ on the cross should feel that you had deserted him — do you want that so badly? Can the infinite being want such *danses macabres* of finitude? Is it a particular favor for you to give bread? Would not an uncreated nothing be happier (of course, it is a fairly nonsensical question) than a created person who is hungering, sick, or condemned to die? You can say that I am looking at suffering with the primitive reactions of my primitive instinct for life; that I am weighing it up with finite, short-circuited conclusions of my primitive logic, but what was so good for you about your inoculating Adam with that finite biological cavorting and finite logic-chopping? Your ways are incomprehensible — why do you want that we on Earth should constantly feel that? Why do you want to make us stray from You? "*Absconditus*"[65] — if you do that, and in that way, then why do you love us? Why the 'games': either You should be tangible, as to Thomas,[66] or we should have no idea about you — why did you confuse the two? Why did you create the terrible existential fact of 'doubt'? It is inconceivable that You should either make your creatures worship & glorify you, or that you should make them doubt or deny you.

"Our sins": that is the paradox of all paradoxes, the inextricable tangle of self-contradictions, along with that of 'temptation' and 'evil.' How easy it is to understand, how obvious the heresy which imagined two gods: Satan, not as your creation, one of the cast reckoned with in your creation, a cog, but an autonomous god, your antagonist. Thus, understandably, we are calling on you to release us from him and his temptations — but seeing as how you created the devil then you did not create him as an ornament and backdrop, and it is useless my calling on you to release me from him. Is it conceivable in theory that you have created a Satan, but every single person has vanquished him — it was all just a trial of strength, and everyone passed the test? Hell will be completely empty? No, reality points to something else: the very first person slipped up. And since then billions of people: so should I ask that *I* should not slip up? Anyone who does not ask you leave from Satan, anyone who asks — you spare? Is it possible, that I, finite a person as I am, should love people with a greater love than you, infinite God? No — though that is the appearance: my salvation is no joy if Stalin does not find salvation and everyone also does not — would You, God, be happy up there on high over the barren depth of the well of the damned?

That is how clumsily I think about You, God, simplemindedly, humbly laying out before you my difficulties, and of course the difficulty of the difficulties is that I cannot say with a tranquil and unapprehensive heart "*Veni Creator Spiritus*"[67] — enlighten me, God, in my ignorance as I am unable to believe of a relationship to have been concocted by God such that out of love you created someone in the darkness and you are inclined to show Yourself only after tremendous wailing. There is a biological God instinct & there is a logical surveying of God: the one negates the other, makes it impossible: my God instinct is too nebulous a thing for my intellectual being to be able to satisfy me — my rationalist reckoning of God, however, leads to paradoxes from the beginning and is barren. I shall be saved: I command it. Amen.

⟻ 51 ⟼

INSIDE a candle burned, outside the sky. What a dark world the world of the woman, the lover is — the sweating funeral candle, a symbol of an eerie lie, and of a bliss that softens into a flush as it sways its single prim petal at the table's edge and lets its rapidly diminishing, unseeing tears fall. The ravaged bed — a blanket trampled onto the floor like a tattered Turkish battle pennant, half on the woman, half on the floor like one of Icarus' wings or whispering waterfall: the bulging pillows: on one side puffed up like a turban in a farce, on the other, sagging like a bomb crater in the ground. The window heavily overhung with curtains: a creeper, iron grille, wooden shutters, white roller blind, brocade — one has the feeling one is in a tomb, a madhouse, or prison. How sick love is as well, a suffocating, hothouse flower disease: fidelity here is a gesture on the part of a Parca,[68] desire is malaria and St. Vitus' dance, the peaceful idyll is by now torpor, a kiss the black drip of sin's scorching wax seal. And within eyesight? The room's visual compulsions writhing in one place (while outside the night freely combs its Greta Garbo locks among the clouds!)? These kinds of things: two slippery mossy rocks, ovals, oily and velvety to the touch simultaneously — face to face —, between them a narrow blue stream on which a canoe is darting with its beaked prow towards a bushy bower: there's no knowing if the bower is a creek or a shallow, a parasite-crowned maelstrom or — a bough-peruked jetty. This vicinity unifies every self-scaring petty romance of the rococo and all the biological loneliness of true death. *Rocaille et mort*:[69] the woman's uncombed hair on the pillow, that is every love and physical delight.

Next the window opens, the door springs open: no longer is there a prosaic deathbed, polyp nudity, and closed bower — fresh air flows around the body: air, the true, one and only love partner, warmly-coolly flitting Ariel. One's body is not naked, and thus liberated: a leisurely shirt & jacket, leisurely cravat licking us with unconcealed, joyless love — our hands escape the pincer-like cramping of embracing and swim unbounded in the clear night like a fallen tree branch on the surface of a hurtling river. One throws one's head back, one's nerves are peaceful, one lives only with one's skin, wide as a sail — no lying, no aborting, no pressing of pleasure between our bodies like a rare wildflower between the pages of an encyclopaedia but one looks up at the sky, among rusty shoals of clouds (how lovely the smoldering ruddiness on blue), one's heart driven into the capricious net of the stars — you are better-looking than and preferable to love.

═ 52 ═

INTELLECTUAL contemplation & actions, the Proust-Hitler-antithesis:[70] today I spoke with someone who is absolutely my political adversary. "My political adversary": for me, too, the expression is surprisingly alien on my lips. Yes, even though with me political opinions are substituted by an indefinable historiographic (*O mot rhubarbatif*)[71] musing, there is not one clearly definable political party and principle in the world that I hate. After today's conversation I was surprised at the fanatical, hysterical degree of my loathing — in the morning I had been sampling all the nuances of Mozart's *Pöbel* piano variations, but by the afternoon I had forgotten all about aesthetics, all that mattered were political actions. Actions: which for contemplative souls like me, or rather those like me who, due to their sensitivity and logical fanaticism, their theatrical talent for mimicry, are capable of experiencing both contemplation and action in their own absurd self-identification and delirium of intellectual identity — are very much actions, very much action-shaped actions, i.e., destructive, murdering, combative, inquisitorial, terrorist, and blindly dogmatic things. While I was listening to my adversary the only thought on my mind was the fight against him, just as naturally the only thought on his mind was the fight against me — who cares about Mozart's variations,

Rheims Cathedral, or beauty; just hand me a sword, poison, gas, a bit of cosmic jabber, some symbols, and I will exterminate my adversaries. As to whether this is vacuous hysteria or a hatred of logic against political ignorance, naïve intellectual impatience or mechanical recompense, bestiality or heroism, thirst for God or blasphemy — anyway, since these are all just 'clever' and 'psychological' questions: it is simply a *fight*, a big, insurmountable fact of hostility, a mythical positive 'existibility' which is intact and indelible inside me too. That is why Pope Æneas Sylvius[72] setting off on a crusade is a major topic (so, you see, the writer does finally come out!): an enigmatic human synthesis of absolute gospel truth and absolutely bestial fury.

 53

THERE ARE two kinds of 'knowledge' of human character: the morphological-metaphysical and the moral-practical. I might also call the former medical-poetic (the two are always one otherwise they would not merit being called 'knowledge'), the latter political. Take, for instance, a female spy: an extraordinarily clever man, blessed equally with a poetic imagination and prosaic cynicism, historical blasé-ness and psychological sensitivity, is 'taken in' by her — he allows secrets to be siphoned out of him, in the end his body to be killed:

he did not notice that he had walked into a trap, he had been duped from the very beginning. Another man comes into contact with the same woman: no imagination, no historical cultivation, no medical or poetic observational flair — his one feature is that he's on the watch not to be played for a 'sucker.' The first type of judge of human nature might also be called 'vital' (a so-called deep thinker), the second 'abstract' ('sharp-witted,' as it is called). The two kinds of knowledge intersect awkwardly inside me: there are women whom I enjoy, recognize, & suspect at one moment in their biological floreality, the next in the abstract lines of their actions.

54

ONE CANNOT have enough of the absolute diversity of substance of historical protagonists: what does a petty-intellectual party secretary with pince-nez have in common with a fanatical rabid tub-thumper? what does a shopkeeper called up for military service have in common with a salon diplomat? what does a female spy have in common with a brilliant warlord? what does a university professor of jurisprudence have in common with a raving sewer revolutionary? what do kings ensconced under mystical holy crowns have in common with ecstatic wheat dealers? Still, it is they *together* who contrive historical events, intellectuals, demagogues, warlords and draftees, diplomats and decorative dolls, bearded Tudors & drunken street rowdies, holy kings and light-fingered bag men: what absolute differences in character, yet nevertheless they collaborate. One of these days, a schematic cross-section of an historical event ought to be written from that point of view.

⇐ 55 ⇒

SOCIAL PHENOMENA: either purely biological or purely ethical, but definitely not political. This afternoon I paid a visit on a newspaper publisher, and afterwards on a foreign tourist office. The newspaper: one of the most grotesque, most disgraceful phenomena of our age, an out-and-out *'esse delendam.'* [73] A gigantic house full of people whose goal is to write from hour to hour, the sort of thing that most people will buy — the immense masses of people being masses of ignorance they write similar sorts of things. Wizened porters wait with animal yelps in cellar windows for the printed newspaper: that is life and bread for them. And yawning salesmen or councilors of the buses purchase and read it. A mysterious human reverberation of misery and stupidity! All that paper and all those swimsuited paupers. What passes for 'thought' in a newspaper: that is in principle chemically pure incompetence; as for 'facts' — those are either true blood, true murder, true embezzlement, or primitive lies reeking of bias. In winter these rotary-press pagodas of profit do not stir things up all that much; all the more in summer, though, when I roam around a lot in the street, completely frazzled by the heat.

Demos: When will I become fully aware of it, what will be my ultimate standpoint? Sometimes it is simply amorphousness, the lowest level of life & art, a bestial vitality, a swirling-foaming anonymous Quantum: in this pseudo-intellectual, reporters and newsvendors are equally present. Then there are active separations: the newsvendor as the ethical subject of some gospel-loving mania — the pseudo-intellectual as the victim, jailbird, & cartoon fodder of an imagined elitist revolution. In a press palace like that there is not a breath of air that is not humbug: a tragic myth or comical myth, a well-intentioned lie or a worse business proposition than Sodom's bordellos. Down below are gigantic machines: what do they produce? Affluent managing directors, Communist workers, and fantastic public uneducatedness. As a by-product some little marginal legends about the victory of technology. Physical poverty and logical poverty together like that. Everyone is pushing their own interests, and everyone is unwittingly struggling against their own interests: the engine-building engineer, the financing banker, the worker, the reporter, a bourgeois buying the paper. The machine generates unemployment, the managing director, Communist rebels, the reporter, epidemic ignorance — those things are all bad, equally bad for everyone.

After the dark house of poverty, Mercury and paranoia, I went into the city center: just as I am not seldom willing to consider the poverty-stricken newsvendors and ink-stained petty intellectuals a pure amorphousness (completely dehumanizing such people), so I am able to picture an elegant & rich person (not for long, admittedly) without their ethical context — as the flawless mechanism of an abstract happy end, biological carriers of 'form' and the redeeming 'finish.' I asked for the program of a Salzburg *Festspiele*, a festival like that is a triad of established musicians, established conductors, and established financiers: I don't know which is the more alarming as a social phenomenon or biological hypothesis — the absurdity of poverty or the absurdity of success? I make a comparison of daily newspaper X (an American one, for example) with a Mozart symphony — the former is a professed negation and pursuit of the intellect, of life, and of beauty, the latter intellect, life, and beauty personified. Have they not ended up at the same level 'socially'? Do snobbery, the fashionable '*Fest*,' *Schöngeisterei*,[74] and the technical absolute of perfect *performance*, the civil obligation and nightmare of 'connoisseur-ship,' do they yield place to Mozart — is there any difference between the humbugs of the '*Fest*' and the rotary presses?

Yet for me 'major' concerts sometimes represent the same enjoyment as immaculately fashionable women: they offer the experience of technical 'finish,' of mechanical perfection, in contrast to misery, the amorphousness of art enjoyed and contemplated in my solitude. The *form*, the uniform composition, of a symphony by Mozart in itself gives an entirely different impression of definitiveness from the elegance & technique of one of the fashionable concerts of a Toscanini: the relationship of these two "*fait* accompli" is a constant source of excitement & nervousness for me: the perfect *piece of music* and perfect *concert*. The perfectly composed *piece* leads to chaos, an anarchy of experience — perfect *concert*, on the other hand, is morally mendacious; as a social phenomenon: nonsense. Which should I choose?

⟞ 56 ⟝

OF WHAT DOES a crisis of something consist: a crisis of the suffering body of some art or the internal style of some disease, a financial institution or a love affair? There are simply a couple of decisive factors to its uniform power, to the increasingly conspicuous identity of two or more component elements: in its becoming *obvious*; hitherto vitality and mortality, viability and the ability to die were present in grey hotchpotch: at the crisis point life and death go their own ways, clarifying into themselves, and they hover in eerily faltering balance, awaiting a minimal shove one way or the other — if it then deviated a millionth of a millimeter in one direction it would be sure to plunge in that direction in its entirety — a whole life or a thoroughgoing death. In fact, the clarified essence of every crisis is the separation of certain elements, the direct observability of those clearly outlined elements, and a certain balance, which one knows that it will tip into one-sidedness, an absolute asymmetry. My earlier attitude to a sweaty host of factory workers and the gleaming fashionability of a Toscanini audience is a typically *crisis* observation: in my individual moral and biological life the gang of the poor and the gang of the rich stand in critical separation and also, through the glaring contrast, in critical proximity.

Interestingly, I have no connection at all with the middle class — only the very poor and very rich: I have dealings from day to day with indigent workers, poorhouse old wives, sick domestic servants, craftsmen vegetating at an entirely animal level — but at the same time with the carefree minions of commerce, the naïve priests and poppets of Mercury. It is odd how what I studied so closely in a clutch of 16th and 17th-century English dramas has become my fate in reality: that social scene also consisted of only altogether primitive and grotesque coolies and altogether illustrious and wealthy gentility; this is, by and large, the society of Shakespeare & Ben Jonson. In their time, the 'Queen' is elevated from the peak of the social elite into a heavenly myth — the water carrier sinks into a ludicrous rag of nonsense, a good-for-nothing. That way of looking at things serves equally well for looking at & judging social phenomena from the most avid ethical standpoint and, at the same time, in the most formal or biological manner — in other words, as little as possible according to societal or social nature.

≈ 57 ≈

BUT is it not a human obligation (if not a physiological compulsion) to work actively in the cause of the happiness of mankind in general, rich and poor: to be a *politician?* I have a profound and constant thirst for the practical politics of the *day*, despite all my historical-philosophical and æstheticizing, lyrically selfish nose-sniffing: some day one ought to escape into the service of this fateful human reality — the service of the uncalibrated, perspectiveless, narrow-minded *today*. Perhaps an important feature of the truly great (why should I not flatter myself?) is the desire for the small — just as boundless God felt nostalgia for the bounded, primitive, fiasco-prone, lost cause when he became man: someone who lives in the broad horizons of thought must so immerse himself with elemental desire into the 'narrow' circle of a party — whether pre-existing or created by himself, but in any case standing on a common area of combat with other parties. Only those are fanatical believers in 'wise supra-party contemplation' who haven't the faintest idea of any 'infra,' wisdom, or contemplation. Brilliance has no interest in genius — that is just an obscure metaphysical piquancy & home remedy for the stupid; the excitement, the goal, the subject of genius is absolute *non*-genius: the eros of everlasting truth: a 'constricted' party, a local skirmish, an affair ephemeral to its very marrow.

⟻ 58 ⟾

WHAT disturbs Don Juan is — that one of his lovers is a fanatic of demos, a lyricist of the anti-royal party of the plebs, its harlot, a professional seasonal martyr, even, when necessary, its theoretician: Don Juan loathes that lover, given that he is a prince, a relative of the king. A second lover is an insatiable voluptuary, someone forever bestially wringing the body — what is the eroticist of impressions & numbers to set about with her? A third is blindly in love with Juan; she is no hetæra but a true, ethical partner in love — although she is in the habit of strolling alone in light sunbathing dresses on southern seashores: not that she would indulge in any hanky-panky, but that freedom, that exposure to other men, is unsettling for Juan: the mere possibility, even just in principle, is a greater sin than an actual lover (just as coins are a bigger treasure than the one or two objects that one buys with them). *Demos, lust, solitude*: three let-downs & punishments for poor Don Giovanni.

⇐ 59 ⇒

PHILOMÈLE *und* 'shorts':[75] a good title, don't you think? Let the lamenting songbird of impressions be French, the coordinating conjunction German, and the garment English. Nature and worldliness are two Alphas and Omegas, inspirations, among my themes — only now do I see it clearly, when I glance at the dawn from my loggia at quarter past two, and peeking next to me, willy-nilly, is a girl clad in beach shorts and a sunbathing shawl. The first, the very first bird twitter sounds: by now the sky is light, weirdly silver, as it was not a red or gold Sun which had brought it into being but some silver nitrate on a chemosensitive plate — it is not the day that commences but an abstract chromatic experiment, if it is possible to imagine total abstraction & total coloring simultaneously. What was conspicuous was that this first birdsong in the hollow, exaggerated silence (which at one and the same time was the silence of dream and space, decomposing psychology and the invariable plane of Laplace: at once biological pause & formula)[76] did *not* sputter into the morning out of the lightness but out of the darkness: the first trill was not an awakening but an embodiment in sound of the dream. The night, death. The cool depth of the tree bough, freighted with foliage and balled up by the wind, was proclaimed by that sound; we were ceaselessly looking at the white of the horizon as if the poisoning in a body were spreading ever further — but the sound could not be brought into any relationship with it. How greatly the song, too, was of the night: full of back-loopings, uncertainties, and hesitations — one felt it was not the small strand of the melody of a tiny throat, but the fraying, far-flung waves of a broad black spool. Meanwhile we were well aware all the time that the bird was small and it had woken up: nevertheless the song was surging along & agonizingly giddy.

The impression turned even more tragic when the first cockerel also struck up — the counterpoint of the two 'themes' was musical with such academic precision and not natural that one's breath was taken away. The cockerel yammered at length: pain-masked mourners may well have sobbed like that in ancient tragedies. The little bird harried the ethereal tragedy of altitude, the cockerel the Lethe rebellion of the depths: at times they yelled out together, sometimes they separated, at others they exchanged themes, and at yet other times they crossed each other in an unappeasable fever of disconsolation & *Kunst der Fuge*.[77] The strangest thing of all was that the dawn-time park offered a bad acoustic for this early 'Lacrymosa': the echo was so loud that the voices spilled all over the place as they resounded & got soaked through. Any literary analysis or metaphor was futile: in the boundless silence the color, strength, pitch, and duration of each single sound had its own separate importance — this was truly neither nature, nor litera-ture, but the elemental musicality of death, a *Kunst des Todes*.[78] The throat's first warblings were neither trill nor isolated staccato notes but just the first murmuring of bouncing buds of melody, of song cartridges: foam, spark, tuning, flourishes of fantasy. Then, after an unexpected burst, a long, long protracted note: one did not know whether one was hearing the discovery of a new voice in a new scale, or an old tonality leaping into new com-positions. Had it happily found a redeeming tonic or disconsolately plunged into nothingness on the vertical loudspeaker of a woe is me? After that, sporadic frag-ments of song that pushed the bounds of an '*ad libitum*' tempo: then followed crazy *accelerandos*, glaring pauses, splashing, jabbering, listlessly impressionistic adagios, as if it were investigating the relationship between music and a death rattle — at times it lowered itself into ani-mal chatter or laryngitis only to bound back into an un-accountably polished bar of a song. Was it the death of everything, every single thing, or a rococo singing lesson?

All around was deadly silence and slowly varying visions: ever narrowing clouds and disappearing stars: a star would dissolve in the sky like the tiny crumbs or traces of whipped cream on a woman's lip over which, on their being pointed out by one, they swiftly run a diligent tongue. In the silence the birdcall was not like a piece of music builds into the stillness of a concert hall: that hush is a social & aesthetic peace — this one was at daybreak: an anarchic and mathematical pause. The song went astray in the quiet, sometimes vanishing into it, sometimes amplified by it — it was a quiet like a complex tree bough, every leaf of which was a black mirror, this one enlarging it, another bending it, this one erasing, another duplicating — the song did not find a way out of the thousand-shaped labyrinth of silence. A person could have no inkling of whether the song was nearby or a long way off — the world was all illusion, carnival projection. In the meantime, the sound was constantly also arousing a muddled image of the bird: a given bar would signify the beating of the wings, the black-gloved fingers of a Harpagon of death on the virginal body of dawn. A hummingbird resounding like an organ?

Next to me the young woman with the sunbathing shawl: that was secured with a fastener at the nape of the neck and at the lower end of the small of the back by a hand-tied knot; its pattern: red-&-white zigzags of lightning, lightning-flash slim acute triangles over the breasts, the back naked. Up to her knees were linen shorts. The essence was the red triangle: the fashionable-geometrical 'mask' — is anything lovelier than such scraps of clothing which, by and large, leave a woman wholly naked, but in one or two places nevertheless make room for such an abstract, stylized, and extra-human motif, that *fiction* can sit in triumph over the body's naively boisterous freedom? One is faced not just with a human body and abstract worldliness, but a duality can also be found in the sunbathing shawl itself: the hand-tied knot is nothing but barbarianism, Polynesian — the precise triangles were Chinese masks of Rule (And the bird!).

60

(HYMN TO DESTINY.) Why did you give me a mother? So that when she gave birth she should moan, see on her bed blood that will turn green in its decay and swim on it like a piece of wreckage cast from a sunken ship to the surface? So that she should first tweak and pinch her breasts with wires, rings, & pincers in order to make the milk flow better, which hurts more than the Amazons having their right breast cut off or burned out.[79] For me then to bite and suck them, like the asp bit Cleopatra, like a grunting, red-haired bloodsucker? And only if the gentle velvet of reason finally appeases the animal roving of my eyes, for me then to leave her: her lap still as warm as a baker's deep cellar ovens, but then I light a candle for a never wanted consummation —

in her hands the mimicry of striking still trembles like
a nervous butterfly on an aging tree branch, but I
only exercise a bad form of kisses on awkwardly blind
nymphs. From one betrayal to another: on the evening
of my nuptial, my mother stays up, gazing at the Moon
like at the jeering crown of falsehood, death's discarded
mask wired to the sky, every madonna's ignominious
'I.N.R.I.' — she thinks I have left her, though I am crying out for Mother amid the slowly bubbling, smoky,
bed-begriming torches of the nuptial, and the sobbing,
ignorant nymph I leave intact. Naked, she holds out
towards me through her tears and black hair only an
alarmingly newly wrought ring. To deceive both: was
that why you gave them, withered, marble-faced destiny?

And the father, why? So that when he sees his son
being nudged by the fiery uncertainties of thought into
perhaps untruthful creeks, his soul is enticed like a sea-
serpent-green Laocoön of sentiment to sickbeds and
blasphemous tragedies, thereby offering his young life
as a mad bride affianced to Nothingness: then to have
you, a still young man, jostled away from your work by
stout despots of dissolute forums only to be sent flying
over the threshold like a bad servant? There you stand,
at a premature end to your work, looking with loud
moans or in quiet pain at the torso: like at a statue of
sad, snow-covered Hermes in the garden that a night-
time storm blew over into the mud. And now that fattened servants of the state have taken the kiss-caressed

tablets of work out of your hands you would like your son to sweep with pride toward new Icarus trajectories: but he, racing from bad lovers towards bad gods, is pining in his dreams, awaiting the vengeance of consorts & contagions. O, why do we not go together: you, Father, the end without an end, and I, the beginning without a beginning? Why do we not go into the poison-leafed Delphic gloom in order to bathe our cheated martyr's heads in the billows of Nonsense, the foolish opium of Lethe — or if you don't want that — then let us shatter, rebellious & young, the posturing theater gods and the moronic state? If it did not take care of us, take care of its best!

For what reason, O Fate, did you give the blond child to the father's son: his hummingbird screeches of joy, the soul of his father's eyes similar to a lizard gliding in the sun, Ophelia wreath of love on his blond head, the little railed bed, & sometimes a precocious hard-stoned woe in the throat when dogs or heavy-handed maids chased in a dream — why did you give a child to the anchorless father? So that cheap troubadours or sleepwalking merchants should take him away, so that he should see his young father's legs collapse like a castle of cards swept by a draught from shutting the door? See a lover killing a lover out of love, and the one who brings toys, a flashy doll, and a rattling-shelled sweet, his pale hand — like a nightmare — flourished in and piercing the mystic boundary between two beds, as he points at the desperate signs of love and betrayal? Is that what the child is needed for?

Why the need for a moral madonna, a poetic lover, and a mechanical hetæra — great tax collectors in the night dedicated to the End: I toss the sepulchral farthing of loyalty onto the marriage bed, the believed metaphors of falsehood into the lover's humble basket, the immature wine of unwanted desire into the hetæra's peasant Danaë glass? Why don't you leave me, or if you have had me taxed to death, why don't you leave each other? Why does the holy lover involuntarily pursue the other holy madonna, and why does the seagull-plucky pace of two holinesses become a vulgar sin: blood on the steps, curses, and woe-is-me's on bitterly regretful lips?

And you, distant strumpet, crouching diligent as a gnome, now you have transmitted your body's poison into me, why do you want, O Destiny, that I should decorate virginal bloods with the crippling enigmas of death? What is destiny if it is not the mysteriously close impossibility of the mysteriously close possibility: the frost on the cheeks of an almost-ripe fruit, the shallows before the prow of a ship plowing into harbor, the sightlessness overwhelming one on the last page of a book. That is what I feel, even despondent as I am: in my mother's eyes, fluttering like wild flowers and the gold-glittering zigzagging bees above them, is joy; so justified, so ready, so simple is that joy, yet, all the

same, her time has not come — my father and I burst
in, and the deaf forum and even deafer strumpets do
not want it. The spouse also stands there in welcome
on the church's sunlit, stepped balcony — but the ac-
cursed nymph is standing there already in the dumb
rabidity of solitude to throw her black net on him.

Nothing good will come of it; here no one wants any
good — the children cover their mother, lovers cover lovers in the beggars' rags of affliction: everyone's all holy, all
goodness, joy, & virtue covering the sky as creepers, &
nevertheless together they weave the Parca frieze garments of songless, hideous extinction. Dæmon, dæmon.

⇐ 61 ⇒

WHILE LISTENING TO BEETHOVEN'S Op. 22
piano sonata, in spite of all my revulsion at *literary*
associations with a piece of music. The boat reaches the
harbor with the princely bride brought from a distant
island. The harbor: in point of fact a Venetian street,
a narrow little canal, even though the boat is gigantic.
The water: transparent green, a unification of the mirror, the circle, and infinitesimally tiny bubbles. The vi-
sualization and literature born of that music (the worst
imaginable: but let us be humble — on these pages
the most utopian intention converges with the lamest
possible ability) always displays *schemes* of sensation,

& in that kind of formula of sensation (like, e.g., 'mirror + rings + millions of foaming points'), it is impossible to tell which is the stronger: the sensation or the theoretical cliché. The water being light green: free as air, massive as glass, soft as silk under a woman's hip, statuesque as rock crystal. The boat, in part, hovers over it, leaving its calycularly fraying womb intact, in part, is frozen into it by its black lower body like a scarab in amber. The water itself is clear, far from daylight, far from the Sun's brightness — this is simply the fresh-green inner lucidity of color, the joy of optical innocence over itself, yet all the same the lower body of the boat is black due to it — to water levels, in the air it is light brown, under the sparkling water (which is much more transparent than air!) it is black, like a sluggish fish hewn out of shadows. The blackness signifies weight: one senses the boat's tired dream. However, on the black, submersed part it is also possible to see every plank, every repainting and patching-up and rivet of the ironwork, so that the boundless transparency creates an impression of hovering and weightlessness: the ship is hovering in the air, outside the water, in some enchanting space. The slaves' oars are held up cocked perpendicularly: the boat has already settled, why are the oars not dipped underwater? The way they are being sharply cocked aloft is like arms poised for the attack, guillotines of adverse destiny.

The sea around the boat, in the wake of the raised oars, is alive with white rings — the whiteness is not foam but light —, in places the sun strikes the water in such a way as simply to abolish the water's angelic green, and thus the 'light' looks more like water blindness than the gleaming water. How hair's-breadth-thin the rings are! There are dark ones, too, black ones — the 'shadows' of these can be seen in the interior of the clear water in the shape of white rings of light — tranquil paradoxes of the tranquil creek. What a fateful difference there is in our body between mirror-like transparency & the geometrical, hair's-breadth sense of rings.

Finally, the third element: the spores, acid drops, champagne bubbles.

Sixty slaves are seated in the boat's mildewed belly: dreadful Cyclopean slabs of muscle, vengeance, and brainlessness who on the sea voyage killed the princess' retinue, the woman herself was abused day after day, to within an inch of her life, with fresh tortures & tricks. The princess & the mutinous galley slaves are merely aspects of society's forces: the social classes as botanical hazards — the woman is the 'elite,' the oarsmen represent 'demos.' Every day another slave violated the girl in the bowels of the boat; sometimes she was lashed to a mast, sometimes naked to the prow; at yet other times she was towed on a rope behind the boat; in the evening she would be chained to an oar; when there was heavy swell they left her body bound on the deck to roll and tumble to left and right; while the half-dead woman's body was beaten and tortured to a bloody pulp, many of them fell in love with her, and they would kill each other for her: man's every primitive bestiality & all of a slave's bloodthirstiness deriving from his social conditions were fused on the boat. The fiancé who was waiting did not want the woman: he was a poet, and he had nymphs for lovers — in other words, females who were outside any imaginable social milieu, not peasant hetæras and not princesses, not metaphors, and not the daughters of 'pure nature' — but simply the trembling minimum (and precisely on that account also the maximum) which is necessary for a woman's womanhood and love's lovability.

Abstract nymph and sadist slave brutalized into brainlessness in his social milieu: I was always attracted by that antithesis; love as an extract of an idea, & love as a hapless function of society bound to time and place.

The static boat with the enormous black blades of the lofted oars is all threat: the blades covered in mud, Lorelei mold, which hang down from them in long, watery tangles like ripped-up nets — the water makes the mud heavy, which is why they are with geometrical sharpness vertical. Everything pales into insignificance beside the Damoclean wings of the blades.

Are there two greater extremes in my life than the 'hymnus' — and a *scheme* of sensations like this? The 'hymnus' is a liberation towards poetry — a scheme like that is a shrinking back of my body into physiological monotony, into the barren tautologies of 'vital force.'

⟻ 62 ⟼

WHAT an indescribable difference there is between deaths stemming from disease and those from accident; it is the absolutely *internal*, the physically internal nature of the 'scheme of sensations' that brings this to mind. In one man, death begins to flourish: if there are poets among the cells, then at the first signs of cancer they surely write odes to 'spring': the innermost depths of the body burgeon & be fruitful. How is it possible for the body's inner maturation of death to lead to the same nothingness as a supple stiletto boring through the heart? The incomprehensibility of incomprehensibilities. I wonder how the dialogue of a foliage of tuberculosis (a tree of life!) and a murderous sword goes on over the coffins: the first a solely biological fantasticality and reality, the second an abstract deed, existing only in formulae of *intended* plan and *goal* — the former is nature's internal rhythmic destiny, the latter the human joke of free will, and these foreign things are capable of staging the same one death.

⟻ 63 ⟼

BUT is what ought to be here first & foremost present: the most complete honesty of my life and the most spontaneous caprices of thought? It is immaterial that truth and spontaneous sparks of thought were 'romantic' and unproductive ambitions — even after every romanticism I find it impossible to believe in anything other than the absolute lying-in-wait of my subjectivity — that way it is a theological & positivist method, and the *'innerlichster Brand'*[80] is always: *divine* truth. Ethos and truth: i.e., on the one hand, the absurd completeness of my life, every intention, fiasco, and doubt, every ridiculously minor event and frightfully major falsehood— on the other hand, the most fleeting shadows of my thoughts, the barely perceptible stimuli of their internal determinacy and freedom, the mysterious physiology of the 'brain-wave.' *Morality*: a diary of Freudian-Catholic confession taken *ad absurdum*; *truth*: aphorism taken *ad absurdum*. I have neither. I stylize!

⇐ 64 ⇒

AN ARTIST and a petty bourgeois are at some imagined point in space-time on a single common level: the so-called plane of 'normality.' What is that normality? A *par excellence* 'poetic' collection of exceedingly artistic and stylized masks, conventions, etiquettes, and rites. Petty bourgeoisie strive to make that normality as normal as possible: they rush with wide-open arms towards stylization and art. Artists, on the other hand, notice that the normality adored by the bourgeois is stylized, unreal, and an abstractly constructed entity, and for that reason they rush in the opposite direction to them: *away from* art toward a rather primitive life, reality, and truth. The bourgeois is an explicitly *creative* temperament: their 'normality' is a bigger structure than the Chinese Wall or Rheims Cathedral. An artist runs from creation: he races towards existing, long ready facts, endeavoring to make them as much like those (flower, water, Moon, etc.) as it is possible.

⟹ 65 ⟹

How interesting that architecture & painting (and in some way music, too) — that is to say the arts which use positive materials that already exist in the outside world, & out of those materials they leave their creations in external space: they imitate precisely the psychological & biological rhythms of our murkiest innards, that's what they coax, correspond to, and seek out. Whereas a Racinian tragedy or all perfectly composed literature, the means of which is not the material sensed in the outside world but the reader's soul, with its evanescent, capricious associations, memories, forever unfinished anarchy, creates precisely something 'objective,' independent of us, absolutely dehumanized. The statue and the pyramid: schemes of our innermost physiology. The *Andromaque* playing in my psyche: a reality absolutely remote from me, in an external world outside of some totality. — Addendum:

plasticity & death. The higher a patient's fever the more they hallucinate and have visions, or in other words, the sicker they are, the more abstract the things that they see in color and in their three-dimensional plasticity. Fever makes certain internal *foci* of vitality, our sensory organs, even more vital. What a statue is to a sculptor, a vision or hallucination is to a febrile patient. *Absolute* plasticity: death; absolute abstraction: ideal normality. Interestingly, here art, illness, and eros are interdependent: each is equally in search of plasticity, which is nothing other than forcing onto and into the outside world the hunches about form suggested by our general condition, our inner organs, our blood, skin tension, the slackness of our guts, etc. For eros there are women, for illness visions and hallucinations, for art buildings and statues. If a woman is excessively a woman, a vision absurdly visible, if architecture is infinitely true to physiology: that is death.

 66

Queen Mother,
Charles II.
Lord Reedy,
Lady Ash.

1. Charles II learns from Lady Ash that his mother is willing to give her son fifty thousand guineas for the accomplishment of his most immediate war aims & for

disarmament of his chief internal opponents. Charles is surprised — after all, in recent times he had been in very bad odor with the Dowager Queen. A long time back, Lady Ash had been Charles' mistress, and since he had deserted her she was a blindly devoted servant to the Queen Mother. Now, however, she again falls head over heels in love with him, which hugely complicates her role as intermediary. Charles is skeptical about the gift, but the next time Lady Ash brings a letter from the Queen Mother in which she promises fifty thousand guineas if her son can verify that he will spend it on soldiers and arms. In that letter she makes frequent reference to a Prince Burham,[81] who is actually *her* deadly enemy but she is striving to present this as a bid for Charles' throne.

2. Charles equips a secret army (for the time being through a loan on credit) with which he wants to attack his greatest opponent, Lord Reedy, who also has a military force. Lord Reedy is the aging Dowager Queen's honorary lover, though Charles is unaware of that. Lord Reedy is a young man & feigns being in love — he has to get drunk before going to one of Dowager Queen's macabre rendezvous otherwise he would be unable to play his part in the farce. The old hag is completely in the power of Lord Reedy, who of course laughs at her & has a doctor anæsthetize his lips so as not to feel her eager kisses. When the Lord learns that the Queen Mother wants to lend money to the King, he kicks up a huge ruckus, at

which she, bald-pated through losing her wig, is petri-fied. Lord Reedy decrees that Charles should receive the fifty thousand guineas on the proviso that he inform the Queen Mother in writing, case by case, how many soldiers, how many guns, and how many ships he is seeking to supply against whom, whereat she would cover the expenses. It would be absurd to give Charles the lot in one go.

3. Lady Ash tearfully pleads with Charles to make his peace with the Queen Mother: naïve, she does not know that Lord Reedy wants to use the 'gift' of money to hold the King politically in check. There is a long, heated de-bate between Charles and Lady Ash about the Queen.

4. Lady Ash, again Charles' lover, ditches her plans for conciliation. Beside her bed at daybreak, without being again urged to, Charles writes a letter dripping with gratitude to the Queen Mother: he wants to make up any differences, she should designate the place. In so doing he sends it by special courier, who will ask for something — in point of fact, the whole fifty thousand guineas in one go, because he has soldiers & guns he needs to pay for.

5. Charles is in receipt of the letter that Reedy had dictated to the Dowager Queen, from which he learns that his mother was willing to disburse at most ten thou-sand guineas, and even for that she demanded precise accounts.

6. The unpaid soldiers go over to Lord Reedy's side, and Charles loses five or so castles. Lady Ash — who had tricked Charles into the whole financial business — he cuts to ribbons with a lash and has her kicked out.

a) Lady Ash and Charles: the lyricism & elegance of love (*elite*).

b) Lord Reedy and the Queen Mother: the absolute pathology of love, its repellent nature — the startling impotence of an agonizing body (*death*).

c) Lord Reedy: the perennial Shylock in history (*money*).

d) The unpaid soldiers: the perennially brainless professional butchers in history (*bestial mechanism*).

The psychological difference between the loyalty & the eros, the life instinct, of Lady Ash; she serves the half-mad, rouged skeleton — able to serve her because the whole thing is so irrational and senseless. Her loyalty to the Queen Mother — something half-ascetic, half-nihilistic. She thereby heroifies herself. She would have a hard job emulating Joan of Arc — but she can follow that hysterical shrinking violet, because that is the demon, the secret nonsense of the world, as opposed to the virgin, who is intelligence and value. The alterations in Lady Ash's *womanly* character and consciousness next to the Queen Mother: the jilted lover and the dying mænad. Lady Ash's relationship to the Queen of state, the Queen Mother, the perverted Dowager, the Queen of Death. The lady & the Queen together with the woman's tailor. The complete psychology of people who live and die for the court via Lady Ash: the mysticism of those 'devoted to the royal court.'

Then suddenly Lady Ash again in love — Charles, whom it is *worth* loving: for a girl of the royal court 'value' (a species of *amour sur estime*)[82] is a heretic notion, something democratic and vulgar. A girl of 'services': how suffocating & sensual it is to serve the senseless Queen Mother — boudoir intimacy with death, history, nonsense, dense atmosphere of holy symbols & little idiocies — after which how 'empty', free, and transparent is the service of love, how *non*-erotic, non-demonic. Two watches: one in the midnight antechamber of the sick Dowager Queen, the second before the bed of the sleeping Charles on the eve of his nuptials. From lesbian to self-torture, from heroine to dumb maid. My *dearest* figure: Lady Ash. The Dowager Queen's fits of jealousy: she hits and lashes out at the lady in front of the mirror, then hugs, kisses, & worships her. At last to write an *apotheosis* of aged-dame hysterias. Death hungry for beauty and comedy: that lady and that Queen — they could not exist without each other. A double portrait from one Spanish painter or another: the lady with fluttering hair resembling a huge candle flame, her pallor, the ovals of her enormous eyes — everything on her is flame-like: her eyes, mouth, the trembling of her nose, ears, hands, breasts — each is the fire, oval, evanescence of candlelight. The Queen Mother: the death mask of Descartes with purple, yellow, and red paint, bloody eyes, corpse-crooked nose, a rickety burial mound of a peruke. The two of them wild, biological relativizers of life and death — as against Lord Reedy, a purely mercantile, or in other words a purely abstract man: no trees, women, life, sea, & death, only the immaterial algebra of profit. Charles II stands equidistant from these two poles: distant from the *mathesis* of money, distant from the biological mania of life & death. That is precisely what 'elegance,' true aristocratism, is — mystic distance from both abstractions and the one-sided passions of vital things.

⇒ 67 ⇒

AUGUSTINE got up from the hetæras' table the way a blackbird will suddenly fly out of a bush: the red flowers & steely-selfish leaves chink in its trail — chimes of laughter, wailing? it matters not: Augustine has departed forever. (The perpetual quitters of tables, who would leave behind a yawning chair like a wound on the quivering reptile body of the company: a Judas.) I shall also get up that way one day, just as utterly finally, and it would be useless for the creepers to wave with their Sun hands — I shall go. I shall then have to listen

to and put up with the mockery, accusations, and su-
percilious dismissal that was declared about Augustine
and every other late converting convert: "it was *easy*
to turn to God at a point when he had had his fill of
all pleasures: it was not a triumph over the body
which led him to heaven, but boredom, surfeit, blasé
«for want of better.» That is not a virtue but a mechanism of nature, a shameful, petty-bourgeois business:
first a nice kiss to the point of boredom, then a comfortable insurance with repentance, which after kissing is
frankly gratifying, like a dash of acid wine to a gour-
met's taste buds after a lot of sweet things." I had not
yet got up from the table of the glittering mænads, but
I already hate myself because my conversion — according to accusers — will also be such a conversion,
based on a convenient, cowardly, animal mechanism,
without any heroism, and therefore I seek out beforehand some dead-sure apology. Why mix up the idea
of a heroic choice, self-denial, into the fact of conversion? God was and is in me, and now along come
slave-muscled and diligent harlots, who, with their
snake's grip, will press out, spur above my skin, the
mature God lurking in the bashful bud of my body.
Run over, wine of the sins I have carried: Jesus! A
sinful age & holy age — why the petty-ethical division?
For the time being I conceive of conversion not as a
step from sin into virtue, but one from a covert into a
patent God-carrying: by day the thousand Babylonian

nipples of the stars also shine on the glass chest, only
a humbug of the light does not permit one to see
them — but come nightfall & the many parasites
drop off the breasts, flesh, the light's bad dress, the
flesh's superfluous sightless pillows, and the many,
many needle-tipped buds remain glittering and prick-
ing. Thus, is God's rapier–sharp anatomy separated
out of me through the presser of sins — the excess is
shed from me. The wild grape harvest eats away the
little bullets like a fattened mask from grapes, leaving
a skeleton, the foaming-mouthed rabid wine in the
tub: the hetæras are all vintners, my predestined workers, ankles chained, who strip my flesh, my existence,
down to God. I never fornicated with these hetæras,
just labored with them; without kiss-slobbered, red-
haired midwives God is never born. You brushed off
oak leaves: their green fell off like mendacious ash,
leaving the thousand-veined net of the leaf's skeleton.
Those similes are my apologies if they should smirk
condescendingly around me: "It's easy now to convert
so late." Over-ethical unethical folk like that do not
recognize the biological rhythm of God in humans.
The 'conversion' of an unbeliever and that of a raving
bacchant are quite different: as a matter of fact only
the former is a 'conversion' — a Dionysian lunatic in
sensual delight was simply a vehicle of the demon of
existence, just with the opposite sign, in a negative
direction: fullness with God existed hitherto, as con-

trasted with mute infidel bourgeoisie. Every second of Don Juan's life (pleasure-pursuing, and if totally wild, then pedantic to the point of asceticism) lies closer to salvation than to damnation.

⇐ 68 ⇒

WHY don't I write plays? I thirst so greatly for the lamps of the stage, their black backs turned towards the onlookers, which hide the candlelight like the reddish-brown wing cases of cockchafers — I can hear on the sagging boards the clomp and patter of cothurnus or buckled shoes, in my muscles are a thousand gestures, monologues, duels, demonstrative embraces, universal backstage rags — with every nerve I adore the disguises, bloody dolls, and black masks which dangle on twine in the cellar dressing-rooms, like Malaga grapes in larders awaiting vitalizing sweetness: in an elemental manner, I am dramatic by nature, which is to say, a human mixture of mendacity & primitive facts of life, flashy pose and tragic ever more predestination; to be a great actor was my family's pride and joy; my imagined heroes were all actors — why don't I write plays?

Because I am unable to forego shades of faces, emphasis, & gestures: when I imagine a character (Lady Ash tossing and turning in her bed, the Queen Mother in front of a mirror, Charles among his woodland mercenaries,

Lord Reedy in the tavern before a rendezvous: all 'scenes') I visualize it in such detail that I am unable to begin describing them in words. If the hundred-strong band of actors, the fantastic masks hand-painted by myself, clothes, togas, crinolines and swimming costumes stitched with my own hands, views and houses constructed in my own workshop were at my disposal: if writing plays started off with me not writing but picking out a woman from my gallery, daubing, shaping, and forming her with my own two hands so that the eyes, mouth, endless nuances of hairstyle were present in their plastic, extra-literary biological reality, and I could then remold them for the stage in *commedia dell'arte* fashion and, having done that, just sit in the prompter's box, inhabiting and apprised of the character — then I would be able to set to writing down the *words* that were uttered. For me writing plays and herd coexistence with actors on a stage are inseparable. The moment actors are not present before my eyes in physical reality I am incapable of giving up on analyzing the external appearance of a figure, the special flavor of the lighting, or psychological unraveling. Play*wrigh*ting: for me that is in point of fact self-contradictory nonsense — it's either writing or a play; the two exclude each other in my life. Drama: an existing stage, a 'ready' and waiting existing actor, a gamut of masks lying at my disposal like a piano keyboard. For me the ideal & possible poles are: on the one hand, absolute *commedia dell'arte* (nothing *written*, no literary words, no literature *at all*) — on the other hand, absolute Proustian analysis and Rilke poetry (a thread of pure *psychological* truth, pure magical-impressionistic beauty of *language*: in a word, *literature*).

Interestingly, this complete inability of play*wright*ing may derive from that point in my life, during infancy and early boyhood when I had no familiarity with anything other than dramatic literature — my very first reading matter was the comedies of Kisfaludy and Shakespearean drama,[83] the feverish, deranging experience of my grammar-school years was of daily racing to theatres. I stuck to them like a leech — theatre was my Alpha and Omega. All those pieces, however, I *saw*: for me they were not *literature* but *visions*, though of course not in the sense that I was a visual as opposed to an auditory type: by 'vision' I am also implying the text of a play, the spoken words of the actors that I *heard* — the emphasis was on drama being a plastic, sensory phenomenon of sound & color, not a written creation entrusted to a narrowly literary imagination. Precisely because my thinking is absolutely theatrical and dramatic, I cannot *write* dramas: I want to go on the stage, to move figures *by hand*, evoke weeping from the females in just the same way as bow-wows from dogs by pushing a button.

If I don't have a group of my own actors and masks before me I have to build these up in my imagination, at which point describing faces conceived of as being handled like *vista* miscarries: Lady Ash is simpler as a girl or tragedienne waiting for me in my vestibule than a puppet-theatre puppet — if she's not waiting for me, if she is not living (not living: heaven forbid!) then I have to patch together the primitive non-existing puppet out of words — & one senses the desperate keeping secret and substituting for the puppet's non-existence as psychological over-*analysis*.

These are two dreadful extremes of my artistic life (I am deliberately avoiding the word 'literary'): the concrete living *actor* I have in my power — and the eternal *vista* resolving into analytical nuances, lyrical suggestions, and biological didacticism.

As a matter of fact, it is not only plays I am unable to *write* but *people* in general: it's as if 'people' *par excellence* were an anti-literary device, one that excluded literature; one can only portray humans with people: actors.

In contrast to that, for instance, is the *view* I saw yesterday evening in the sky — a zebra regularity of ash lilac and bright crimson stripes on the horizon; the hills in mist, the tree boughs in grey moldy-patinated velvet; here and there the sun darted its rays on high in sheaves; a few scattered stars like jewels about which a lady of the house hurrying off to the theatre will call back to her maid from the front door, "Put the things I left out on the table into the blue box, dearie," etc.

Until I had seen the sky between branches of foliage in a narrow street — my head was brimful of drama, seething with scenes —, or rather not my head but my hands, shoulders, legs, and hair: the experience with which I was preoccupied was immediately dramatized, with me being the actor, so there was no need for analysis — I danced, gesticulated, uttered an automatic metaphor springing from each *muscle* (cf. Joyce's language: an *absolutely* biologically determined, involuntary *muscle* language of the *commedia dell'arte*). As soon as the insulating black branches had reached an end, sky *vista* took over: that experience was unable to find satisfaction in a theatrical outlet — the view — the view plunged me within an eye's blink into a poetic-analytical behavior, into a world of literary truth and literary grace (a drama is never dramatically 'true' or 'graceful'). Apprehensively, I began to *describe* the features I had felt before on my theatrical visage; drama had died.

⸺ 69 ⸺

SKETCH, sketch: it is of secondary importance whether or not I am a painter, I have to sketch. If I see leaves, the snaky-geometrical slopes and spikiness of forms and colors, when on a plant I sense at one and the same time the skin tone of touch and the optical illusion of perspective, when I do not know what, in truth, intensifies the adored materiality of an adored corolla: the optical illusion implied by the point of view or the nervous rash of the imagined grip in my fingers, I then want to draw and paint, make use of every possibility of contour and contourlessness, gleam and lustrelessness, *sachlich*[84] microscopicness and impressionist blurriness, oily fullness and watercolor porosity, etching precision & chalk haze, in order to reproduce the spatially, chromatically, and tactually lethal reality of the impression. My tongue and glove conform to a garden leaf spotted on such a draughtsmanly drawing like water to a glass' shape: my entire anatomy is paint, brush, & a bunch of technical refinements. I want to draw, I have to draw at all costs — I am a pathological sensor of space & color. The human activity of drawing stands in interesting relationship to the previous opposites of *'living* actor — literary *vista*': *drawing* as action is in point of fact carrying the theatrical, human element of 'action,' the deed, into the otherwise psychological and literary world of *vista* — a certain degree of dramatization of the undramatic.

 70

THOSE simple formulas: on reading my own writings: those over-intellectualized, over-sensualized sentences, I get a feeling of Christian, ascetic happiness: even in the poor quality of the style there is something massively absolute, fatefully and unbrokenly homogeneous — it is like the illness in St. Thérèse of Lisieux in my soul, my brain, and my sensory organs — I have a life-long *disease*, in other words, which (thank goodness) I am able to make use of ethically and penitentially; my impossible, crippled language and grammar is a magnificent example of 'Christian' grotesqueness, 'Christian' sickness and poverty (vis-à-vis 'paganly' classical, well-balanced languages): my style is a rag like St. Francis' clothes; my style is tuberculosis like St. Thérèse's; my style is blood like that of the martyrs — that relationship (despite every painful appearance of affectation) pleases me. — And beside the formula of 'Christianity', another: I listen to an inordinate number of good pianists, partly in order to practice, partly in order to play performance pieces: my ideal is piano *technique*, 'work' on the instrument, the physical engagement of the fingers; the opposite of my sick style is 'healthy', 'uninventive' work on the keyboard. The bleeding skin of a Byzantine self-torturer — and: a perfect E minor scale in sixths.[85]

⇐ 7 I ⇒

A SAINT: a young man living fully committed in three directions — his loves fetter him to his parents, his wife, and his lovers. In his adoration of the parents he senses a tragically unsatisfied idolatry; in his adoration of the wife a semi-morality, an idyll, a self-deluding 'laiciza-tion'; in his pursuit of lovers the sterility of poetry, vi-tality, mechanized lust, and the ethics of feral ones. He decides to become a monk, a Dominican, a saint. One morning he vanishes: he has gone into a monastery. His father is dying — when he learns that his son would rather do penance and pray than attend his sickbed, he curses and renounces God & Christ; with his arms in death agonies he throws out the priest with the last unction and the Holy Sacrament: the house resounds with blasphemy and the vociferous disavowal of God. That is the first effect of the son's sanctity. The father dies as one of the damned. — One of the abandoned lovers in an indignant, manic moment lets slip and proves to the wife that the 'Sainted' husband had still been her lover one week earlier: his wife, who had been almost at the point of herself becoming a nun, or at least a solitary penitent, gives herself up to despair and commits suicide. That is the second fruit of sanctity. The other lover had long harbored suspicions of this one, and when she learns that he had been fornicating with both of them in the same period she kills the first lover. The third upshot. — The 'Saint' preaches to the people: those regions which yield Spain's most savage soldiers are all swimming in ecstatic religiosity — there are no soldiers, half the country are becoming monks. The Arabs are threatening Juan VIII[86] with total defeat:

two of his military commanders laid down the sword and retired to the monastery of the 'madmen' of Al-Acuenza. In person, John goes to reproach the 'Saint': the climax of the story is a dialogue between monk and saint, a war of words. When they part — the 'Saint' is tormented by maddening pangs of conscience, and feels his own holiness is hysterical dilettantism, along-side the diplomatic, worldly, heroic Catholicism of King Juan (in black clothes, of course, as per the scheme followed by the likes of Velazquez in his portraits of Phillip, of course). The king is likewise tormented by distressing qualms: he feels that the 'Saint's' halo is true Catholicism — he goes into battle an unbeliever, driven nuts by his misgivings. He is killed; his dead body is carried straight to the 'Saint.' The Arabs are butchering, the whole of Spain will be theirs: the 'Saint' is to blame. A peasant woman stabs him to death. (*Mémoires*.)

 72

THE CHRISTIAN SOCIALIST: his every minute is a battle, working to improve the lot of the poor. One evening he has a row with his maid: both of them yell and utter preposterous insults — in the yard the girl calls him a sadist who enjoys lording it over others, then races off, sobbing & swearing, to heaven knows where. The next morning her body is found: she had committed suicide. The concierge of the house, other tenants, passers-by in the street had heard the man's abuses; fellow party members smash his windows with stones and he is thrown out of the party. The maid's older brother shoots the man who was the cause of his sister's death. (*Mémoires.*)

73

JAMES I, SOMEWHAT CRIPPLED, had pretty Jane Hobson as a lover in his young days. Ten years later Jane will be a chambermaid to the Queen: she is an insolent, boastful woman, but James is unable to speak to her about it because he considers it ludicrous and disgustingly non-gentleman-like behavior towards a former lover who had once made him happy to play the master, the king — what is more, his wife tolerates everything. Jane has delusions of grandeur to a pathological degree; she believes she is a persecuted duchess and during intimate dinners or while the queen is undressing she shocks the deeply superstitious royal couple with all manner of ghoulish tales of vengeance. Crippled James' idol is the young Duke of Lynnbrook: Catholic, diplomat, poet — that is her love. On one occasion, in the King's presence, half-mad Jane relates some peculiarly startling phenomenon to the Duke. James loses his cool and starts to chide the woman, and when she ripostes, he starts to belabor her with a bundle of manuscripts of the memoirs he is in the process of writing. What is Jane? A lover, employee, and person. James is, with mystic frankness, profoundly grateful to the girl for having permitted a cripple like him into her vicinity: he feels a wild, self-torturing loyalty to her even ten years later. But James is also a mathematically thinking despot: he demands of his soldiers and employees mechanical obedience and precision while they are on service. Thirdly, James is superstitiously Christian, concerning himself a lot with theology and morality: for him Jane is a groping, uneducated person, who is impertinent out of stupidity as well as sickness — he understands that and finds it hard to punish her. — He is ashamed of and hates his temper, regards it as senseless: he sees that all life is humbug, a game, a masquerade if temper can have such a big role in it. He sinks (at least seemingly) before the mystery of senseless anger. Now he is not a lover, nor a despot, nor a Christian, just a blind puppet of momentary wrath. He pursues Jane on horseback as she gallops off on horseback. The king dismounts; he is located the next day. Jane disappears. A parable of disproportionate anger.

⇐ 74 ⇒

*Dedicated to the Compagnie des Quinze theatrical
company of Paris)* [87]

ON THE SEASHORE of a Southern Seas small town
ſtand three houses: in the middle like a shop window
is the house of the town's wealthieſt businessman,
with a prominent balcony & ſteps leading up to it — on
permanent diſplay is the widower merchant's daughter,
who is to be given away in marriage: hideously bad-
looking, hideously daubed, all in all like a made-up
Egyptian corpse or a Nicene masquerade. Every day she
is repainted three times out on the jetty, in full view of
arriving ships; three times the wig is changed, three
times the selection from the dowry that is put out
around her feet is switched, and three times suitors
who are paid to pretend at the busieſt times to commit suicide at the foot of the balcony are swapped.
Very many colored sails, much muddy water, and
many drunken sailors around her; by now the girl's
skin is burning from the noonday sun, she is sick,
barely eating, and is perishing.

The house to the left of that is: a bordello for sailors
— a dreadful antithesis to her 'moral' virginal life,
though in point of faſt it is owned by the girl's father,
& the dowry set out before the virgin's feet had largely

been purchased with income from the bordello — some of the valuable Oriental objects the mercantile father had wrung out of a carousing ship's captain with his own hands: he could be seen on the stage carrying things from the whorehouse into his daughter's showcase. Afterwards he has the inhabitants of the bordello & their visitors publicly anathematized by the township's hedge priest (the merchant's hireling), a vagabond parson. For all that his hideous daughter does not land a suitor.

The third house, the one to the right of it, is a stock market & store, a holy and virtuous hall of trade: the bordello is daubed Satanically black and red, the Bourse with its statue of Mercury, lilywhite & decorated with rococo lutes & flowers, Vestas modestly covering their pudenda and figures of blindfolded Justitia — just like a coy maiden's room. Here, however many crates of goods a merchant sells, a servant will paste up on the crate with a huge brush a colored 'portrait' of the marriageable girl: a reproduction of a famous Spanish Madonna who has nothing to do with the wretched girl. In that way her fame spreads. On the Vestal stock market the old dotard of a trader literally robs a young Italian trader — the young Italian wants to take his own life, but the merchant's raggedy young maid saves him.

It is nighttime, a half-naked painted *statue* of the girl for sale can be seen illuminated on the balcony — the real girl is sleeping. Garish ice-cream-pink wooden breasts with vermillion nipples. The lamp above it is ten times lighter than the flickering lamp of the lighthouse beacon. The little scrubber of a maid has grown into a lovely woman: the senile goat of a trader would have kicked her out long ago were she not incomparably smart and sharp-witted. She is invited in by her screeching master; the Italian is again left on his own. He's enticed into the bordello a few moments later and his last treasure, an enormous diamond ring, can be seen on the hand of the wooden doll: the merchant, wearing a nightshirt, slips it onto a finger of the statue. Behind a curtain are standing two men with shotguns — ready to fire should anyone dare to try & lay hands on anything.

A late night ship that has strayed arrives; it is ghostly, mute, dark & huge: it is either death or belongs to the world's richest man. The half-mad merchant suddenly rips the veil entirely off the blatant wooden doll, dims the light to a quarter the brightness: the naked Hottentot wooden Venus hovers mystically in the semi-gloom. The sailors race off the ship, thinking the statue is advertising the bordello — a few of them, whooping, assail it. The guards rush towards them; the priest jumps out onto a balcony cage of a taller than tall house as thin as a tower — scattering imprecations on immoral humanity & tossing the corpses of Babylonian sinners into the sea: plop, plop.

The ship's master disembarks: in pitch-black clothes — he is the most mystic money, the deathliest death, absolute deceit, the world-famed Mercumorte. He is

attracted to a girl, he says, who sleeps on the balcony
in her virginal solitude; he is minded to buy her — not
for himself but for his absent younger brother. The
haggling commences. The lamps on the balcony are
doused and the real girl is brought out. She, poor thing,
is barely alive; in the background, on a staircase, two
death's head doctors of clownish appearance pump her
with injections (one from the left — the other from the
right). Mercumorte does not spend much time looking
at the girl, he merely has the doctors check her fertility,
could the family be sure about the possibility of having
heirs to the fortune; when they confirm, yes, they could,
he immediately sends the dying girl back. Then comes
the turn for checking the treasures, invoices, debts, in-
comes, houses, properties, stocks and shares, bills of
exchange, columns of money, et cetera — in the end
on one side of the stage the business books & money
build up into such a castle that the merchant and Mercumorte completely vanish behind it.

Day breaks — the Italian exits from the bordello,
covered in lesions & blood from the infections he picked
up there. The young maid quickly sets him right with
a pair of mudpacks. Overjoyed, the looted Italian vows
that he will truck no further with women, he wishes to
be a saint: in ecstasy he rushes off. That is all witnessed
from the balcony by the fake priest: he casts bawled
curses at the maid for having taken the side of sin by cur-
ing sexually transmitted diseases. The maid flees indoors.

Servants bring the corpse of the merchant's daughter; he does not know of her death. The maid puts on her clothes and she is taken onto the ship by Mercumorte. When by glaring morning sunlight, however, she sees on Mercumorte's chest, on the ship's sails, and on the sailors' clothes, a coat of arms bearing a death's head alongside a money-bag, amid hysterical screaming, she slays Mercumorte; with the liberated sailors, who tear off their black garments, she lays siege to the rococo Bourse, beats the cowering traders — the stage is cleared, the fake priest casts off his disguise, hauls the wooden statue off the balcony, takes up position in front of the curtain, falls to his knees in a characteristic pose of veneration, kissing the statue's inscription: "*Omnia vincit amor, virtus agitat amorem.*" [88]

75

IS THERE a more condemned-to-die situation than a sick man and a lover who is willing to sacrifice her own life for the man? Disease makes one selfish and lonely, submerges one into the most anarchic, most private depths of the ego — there and from there every foreigner is a fantastic burden: while the loving woman stays up for the man night after night, he feels suffocated by her & hatches plans to murder her. What is the point of an 'ego' — that craziness, the deadly luxury of subjectivity?

And what is the point of 'love' — that other craziness? Total disappearance into another person, the non-ego? Which is the more shameful fiction: an ego of all egos grubbed up by fever or a predestined other of all others? The man is tormented most by doing ill to the woman, and wishing ill of her, out of nervousness, despair, and impotent sadism: he wants to kill his nurse even as he worships her (with abstract-theological gratitude). Holy, holy, holy: he continually reiterates to his despondent, sick self, and turning to God: holy — my God, do something with her because I am going to kill her. It is the caring lover I have to thank that I am genuinely, concretely ill — otherwise I would wrap myself up in 'human suffering,' 'the tragedy of the body,' and other generalities of that sort — she, on the other hand, is charity gone mad: debased into a patient. Madness, madness. The girl has masses said for me, receives Holy Communion every day: thank God, that will make it easier to kill her. Yes: that person will kill his lover one night when she dozes off during one of her self-denying vigils. What is the point of an *ego*, the point of an *other*: logically there can only be that one consequence.

⇐ 76 ⇒

EACH AND EVERY marvelously harmonious dream: a landscape, for instance. Although the image is grotesque as an image and asymmetrical: its tone is nevertheless idyllic, 'morphine classic,' poetically tranquil. A recent image showed an equestrian statue, but the horse had been wheeled so its head was tight against a wall — rather bizarre yet all the same there was something tranquil about it, complete satisfaction as with a slight breeze in a heat wave. In an image like that, as it happens, at the time of the dream, the phenomena of the external world (the impression) and the dark biological inner world of one's body (general condition) are in singular balance: the impression loses the brutality that its foreignness & accidentalness give it; the general condition loses the sense of nausea, fainting, & secret which is bestowed on it by its perennial unfamiliarity, its being within one and yet far away from one. After all, there are two *unfamiliarities*: the vital heart & core of one's own body and the not inevitable pageant of the external world. Is either needed? Do we need a large intestine or a yellow narcissus: do we need an inner life and outside world? Both, if one perceives it radically: weirdly indigestible, unwished-for things — things which drive one to distraction. These dream images dull the mystery of the inner body, dull the mystery of the bleak outside world, and those two deadenings unite: that is why they are harmonious. Two painful irrationalities of life balance out with the assistance of pastel-like blurring.

THE WEALTHY businessman's daughter teaches piano for money; the son of an impoverished gentry family will not take on work cramming pupils — purely out of 'pride.' How wonderful (*sic loquitur*) that the filthy-rich girl does not wish to live idly: she may go around in a limousine, but she *works*. What virtue! Yet how empty and immoral the pride in which the starving son of the gentry exists to consider work as humiliating. — What naivety & confusion of ideas there is in this idealization of 'work' — which is not a matter of morals, simply the knee-jerk reflex of a merchant's neurosis; just as gentry 'pride' is not pride, but a cult, a rational acceptance, of the divine value of a personality, of outer & inner loneliness, of independence. The 'work' ethic as such is replete with cheap false logic, hypocrisy, old wives' romanticism & neurosis; it is the world's most stupefying humbug. Had it not been for this 'work' hysteria, there would be no unemployment today. What does a businessman's 'work' consist of: whatever will allow him to make money hand over fist, possibly at the expense of the life & health of thousands and tens of thousands, *in such a way* that the whole job, besides being inestimably useful — should appear ethical as well! The 'work' ethic is the root cause of the totally unfettered unethicalness that characterizes today's social set-up.

As far as I am concerned there is just one fundamental ethical concept: the medieval idea of asceticism, the way the Catholics did it. The moment that the place of asceticism is taken by 'sacred *work*' (*quelle farce!*), the moment that a so-called sterile, insane, sickly, comic, antirational Byzantine stylite gets down from his column in order to locate his morality in 'work,' that is when you will also find Shylock. Choose: Byzantine madman or bloodsucking usurer, self-flagellating hysteric or a murdering Harpagon lyricized as a 'managing director'?

How many primitive 'thoughts' teem in the masses around the concept of 'activity': one should do this & that from dawn to dusk, women should also go to work, be productive, telephones should ring, book-keepers' ledgers should swell — but why? To keep active just for the sake of keeping active? Even a blind man can see that humanity derives no benefit nowadays from never-ending production and enterprise. Work is not an ethic; moving just to keep moving makes no sense: the whole thing is in the realms of the sheer romantics of American films.

It is interesting that businessmen are the most sentimental, most puerile-spirited people in the world: ten-year-old girls display more cynicism or realism than these 'leaders' cranking out their unchanging "Chop-chop! On the double!" Ever since work was first falsified as a value and morality by those who derive pecuniary gain from it — an unsuspected rule of *fiction* has got under way in the world. Businessmen have eradicated all sense of realism, prudence, and common sense: the other day I went into a bank and marveled that the officials were not roaring with laughter in one another's face at the sight of the precious chinoiserie of unreality that cocoons such an establishment. The underlying fiction, the first dogma of the imposers of the myth, of course, is that 'reality = money' (or 'reality = office work,' 'reality = sheep-farming,' et cetera, et cetera). Money! That is the blood capillary of everything: bills of exchange, contracts, currency speculation, commercial dodges, the thousand and one ethical masks of fraud. And is a fully-grown man in full possession of his senses supposed to believe this is reality? It is my impression that anyone who maintains that is just joking or dissembling; a person can only say that sort of thing out of self-interest — for money.

And love, death, nature, God: those are 'fictions': in their opinion. The sea, glaciers, flowers, music: they are just holiday fillers, recreations — the complaint of which Bach almost died, a little preprandial entertainment. *Charmant.* With generally educated people speaking about a *'Flucht in die Neurose,'* [89] it would be far more to the point to speak about a *'Flucht in die Fiktion'* in regard to businessmen. A very high proportion of people, indeed the great majority, feel well *solely* in a fiction, in the abstract: they sense reality within an invented form of contract (the most ephemeral of ephemera) and sense only decoration, the games and metaphors of weaklings, in a material sea, material woman, and material death that have been held before our eyes from time immemorial. Those 'Schwächlinge' come in very handy all the same: they goggle at an anemone instead of a bill of exchange & leave others to get on with their work, whereas the fledgling businesswoman, ethicized to death by the work ethic, goes off in her Rolls-Royce limo to give a piano lesson, and meanwhile the poor piano teacher starves to death.

78

THERE are two exciting secrets: the *parents'* secret & the secret of *faraway* lands — the remaining matters between the poles of art and disease are just fumbling on the part of the mind. What is in my mother? What is in foreign scenery? My life is a delirious absorption into the all-excluding parent — & a delirious expulsion from foreign scenery. Parents: deadly eros. Scenery: deadly horror.

79

WHY are wholesalers in the habit of thinking they are Napoleons? The tub maker who in his childhood only ever saw one bathtub at home (if that) now, all of a sudden, sees a hundred or five hundred: very many, very uniform, very new. A canned-food manufacturer or agent at home would have ripped open *one* tin with a sheath knife for supper: now sees ten thousand (yes, all joking aside: ten thousand!) identical cans before his eyes. The monumentality of the quantum and the monumentality of the mechanical uniformity has a dreadful effect on those 'productive' guys. For them 'a lot' signifies 'humanity' — after all, there are *a lot* of people on earth, *a lot* of cans of preserves on a motor truck; that completes the equation between canned food and humanity.

The uniformity of tin cans, however, gives a frivolous illusion of *regularity*, 'mathematicized sociology,' 'mathematicized humanity' — the sense that one is face to face with the most essential aspect of 'humanity' (or what he considers as such): its '*multi*plicity,' and they treat that large mass mechanically, with regular uniformity — a feeling which Napoleonizes them. It does not even enter their heads how insignificant *one* bathtub or *one* can of food is in *one* person's life. How insignificant those 'indispensable' articles, materials, and forces are in our lives. Could we exist without waterworks, electricity plants, or gasworks? Barely. But who cares about water, electricity, or gas? The 'indispensable' things are insignificant, unaccented, like 'free' air. As for bathtubs and cans of food!

⇐ 80 ⇒

THE opposition between 'WORLDLY' and 'unworldly.' And is this 'worldly' not precisely the 'unworldly' and the 'unworldly,' the 'worldly'? Frederick the Great and Bach in church at night, up in the organ loft, both in shirtsleeves, with a big jug of wine, their wigs dangling beside them from the seats: the organ resounds and roars. Behind Bach, his numberless brood, his 'worldliness'; behind Frederick the Great is the army, the state administration, his 'worldliness.' But at night, in shirtsleeves, bald, and in an emerging toccata they forget about all else. They drink, become delirious, chatter: Bach is a perverted lecher, a Don Juan, an atheistic libertine; Frederick is a regicidal nihilist, a revolutionary, a traitor. By the morning everything has grown quiet: Bach prays with his family, Frederick rides on horseback in front of his soldiers. The only thing preserving the memory of all that is an organ toccata. (In olden days the genres were so 'romantic' that it would have made no sense to *live* romantically in addition: all the 'anarchy' went into the work instead of life. That was hygiene!

⇐ 81 ⇒

I AM READING a description of a girl, with its analysis of one type of sensuality, in J.C. Powys' *Jobber Skald*

(p. 114).[90] With certain extraordinarily intense (sensually and rationally *equally* intense) persons it is interesting how a wild corporeality to the point of perversion and enjoyment of the female form almost to the point of Platonism are present in isolation: the two extremes of sexual biology and sexual aesthetics. With an average person, lust is merely a mechanical, well-timed operation of the nerves, and the enjoyment of the forms, delineation, and beauty of the female body is not two isolated extremes but they mix. For me, too, the 'vision' woman & the 'contact' woman are two alien persons. That duality is naturally a consequence of solitude; the duality of narcissism and salon life. As to which is the more sensual sensuality: the enjoyment of beauty or the enjoyment of lust, that would be hard to decide.

⇐ 82 ⇒

CARACALLA WAS in the habit of going at dawn not to the bath of the imperial palace but to the public thermal baths[91] — at a time when, naturally, they were closed to outsiders. At that time of day, the walls were bluish white in the nuance-banishing and nuance-inviting alcohol of silence, the indigo-pallid palms as if they were unused, decayed buds of the night — they dangled their numb blueness, creased & smeared in front of the vast cubistic walls. The emperor was greatly preoccupied by the question of why there was a group of cattle on both sides of the main steps and at the top of the steps, inside the building, a lonely statue of a vestal, slim as a breath Venus. That day he understood for the first time why. The emperor's daytime love affairs had become exhausted in perversities: most recently he had gone through the members of the animal kingdom like over a chromatic scale. Although his fantasy would move on every second to newer and newer animal species (underwater love, et cetera), & he had drifted off to sleep with visions of them — at night he never dreamed about those things, but about young girls to whom he would bashfully pay court as a youth, and the greatest physical sensation was being touched by the girl's fingers, a tunic lifted from the shoulder by the wind, the falling of the hard stones of the ankles from the frayed fruits of a skirt.

The two thermal-bath statues signified the two extremes of love: the diurnal animals, which were symbols of rational, abstract lust 'theory' & lust 'construction,' and the chaste-ecstatic nocturnal child's dreams, which kept watch over the body's primitive, childish, and adolescent desires, the conventional practice and wee mythology of the body (to avoid the words 'normal' and 'healthy,' considered 'inelegant' in recent times). Of course, for a perverse individual, the conventional way of making love after a while denotes the perversity of perversities: though that feeling does nothing to alter the fact of the triumph of convention.

This evening, for example, Caracalla dreamed something of this kind: an enormous number of men and women were bathing on the sandy bank of the River Tiber in the summer heat when suddenly everything went gloomy, a light breeze got up, which blew the sand from the bank onto the Tiber, where it did not sink but carried on dancing in petaloid aerial waves as densely plumed fans, which grew up high from the water. The gloom and that cooling fanning of the sand all at once lured the whole crowd towards the Tiber: everyone was drawn like chess pieces that a single sweep of the hand pushes to one side of the board. There was something typically dreamlike in the airiness and magnetic unanimity of the migration: it was more an abstract-sensual scheme, a rhythm without subject, of a 'change of scene' than a human movement of people. The interesting thing about it was that the curious gloom, and the spiraling of sand, gave the bathers such an impression of extraordinariness that the women took their swimsuits down — not completely: they kept themselves covered with big terrycloth gowns, the trains of which they pulled behind them in the swirling dust, not being sparing with the use of hands & rubber swimming caps. Such a clear oscillation between 'bashfulness' & 'shamelessness' he had never seen before: on the one hand, the freak of nature made the staid, unrevolutionary forgetting of modesty self-explanatory — on the other, the women's whole social modesty routine gathered renewed strength after the initial nonchalant stripping. Visions of 'semi-nudity,' classic 'piquancy,' of that kind are concomitants of adolescence: in the old roué's life it acted like a sunlit glass of water: cold and brilliant.

In dreams there are *merely* schemata and *merely* nuances: these two things never unite in the way they do as in daytime impressions. In this case, for instance, the drawing to the river, the drifting of people, was a self-sufficient schema: a scheme of the motion of the waves, relaxation, stupefaction. However, each female hand, sand rose, or Tiber sail was *merely* a detail, not part of the whole picture but a fragment without a whole.

The most natural style of nature & the most human style for human beings could never be fumed up in a single common picture like today's dream did: with what flower-like, gentle, uninhibited automatism did the women discard their clothes (slowly, *not* bacchically) in the presence of the wonder of nature — "if the sand does not drop into the water, then there is no morality": yet how rococo the poses in which they covered themselves, how elegantly they shrouded the Delphic shade of the pudendum.

That is why there had been that group of combative oxen and the Vesta-Venus slim as a bud in front of the baths: that is why Sun and water exist in order that one may be freed of both. Both the ox & Venus fall within the amplitude of a single local nerve — sunlight and water are meant for the whole body —, and a *whole* body can scarcely be called a body any longer; where the whole frame has an interest in its synthetic homogeneity (like in sunbathing or under a warm shower), the distinction between body and soul is lost: distinctions cannot be made under the cascade of water; we are uniformly St. John Christians (souls) inclining to the mythical compulsion of Christianity and water voluptuaries exposed to all manner of little physiological reactions — it is impossible to make a distinction.

83

I ALWAYS have one subject, and it is always this: a total embryology, the bodily and spiritual life of an embryo from flash of spermatozoon to birth — and the fancy counter-ornamentation of history, battles, bulls, armorial bearings, ideals, kings, popes. In other words, the very innermost of the innards of a person's body, the most primitive, most principle rhythm and structural minimum of its vitality (the beginning), and thereafter the use of that vitality in history, the life of action (the end). On the title page: a cross-section of an embryo and a contemporary portrait of Charles VII. [92]

⇐ 84 ⇒

ONE ASKS 'stupidities' like that and yet suspects that they might nevertheless be in touch with great truths: which is the 'right'-er flower? Would that be the daisy, the rose, or the cactus? The daisy is 'right' if the criterion of rightness is a certain transparent, clean, and simple symmetry of the basic elements (corolla, stamina, stem): the daisy is the most logical, most philosophical flower. The rose is right if one sees the essence and rightness of a flower in a certain sumptuousness, luxury, and melancholy aesthetic. Finally, the cactus is 'right' if one regards biology, the primitive nonsense of vital forces, as being the most flowery quality of a flower. *Geometry, beauty, anarchy*: nature already produces exoticisms and oppositions of those sorts even in the manifestation of a single detail, the flower.

⇐ 85 ⇒

RAPHAEL'S LIFE was difficult with the four madonnas. On taking one stroll he saw a woman — he found her extraordinarily attractive, she inspired him, drove him wild, and he wanted to paint her. The first Madonna was therefore a genuine model, with a genuine background in a neighborhood and street. The second was the one he showed as an altarpiece to the pope in sketch form.[93] The third, about which he told his lover at the time, and the fourth was the way he imagined her, in his moſt selfish, moſt personal vision. A diariſtic ſpecific, a hieratic obligatory ſtylization, a lie, and an individual vision: how many artiſts experience a tiring, complex, ſtifling fourfold life like that.

⇐ 86 ⇒

A PERSON GOING away: not-being-there and its mementoes. Memories are always objeĉtively concrete — non-exiſtence, not-being-there, is always metaphysics, a myſtic ſpace, an incomprehensible absurd. To what a fantaſtic degree the one not-being-here is not here, yet at the same time the moment when we are thinking of the one not-being-here, how *exaĉtly* the same, like when our partner is here. This is one of the moſt unsettling things in reſpeĉt of a person going away: the lack is *more* than non-exiſtence; absence in a mathematical sense is a nuller entity than null — the zero of deficiency lies juſt as far in the opposite direĉtion from the zero of 'normal' as an infinitely large number. At the same time, the life of a person who ſtays there remains absolutely identical with their life up to that point: even though they may possibly have loſt their 'all' in the departed person all of that person is nevertheless ſtill on hand.

Take a person x belonging to one: he or she takes leave of one, goes away. A couple of minutes later they will be invisible. What does that signify? In part I know it concerns nothing more than the most prosaic change of place. The train wagon will pull the person from here to there, there will be no change in body or soul, for the person in question. For herself or himself she or he will be just as much a material reality as hitherto, perhaps — but what about for me? The two viewpoints are irreconcilable and maddening. For me, he or she will be a pure nonentity, a never born-ness, a metaphysical nullity beyond a numerical nil. But I will have colorful memories, microscope slides, and snapshots of him or her — & yet nothing, the material of pure negation, of non-existence prior to the creation. I do not know for a moment which viewpoint is the more real, the more sensible, and the more justified: the one emphasizing his or her non-existence or verifying his or her existence.

That is the most critical state of life, the relationship between the stay-at-home & the goer-away — that is where it turns out that neither the positive nor the subjective illusion has made much of an impression on one; one doubts both equally.

My relationship to memories is intriguing: to keepsakes for one thing — to places where we were together for another. Place: for example a street of homes with gardens by night where we took a stroll; a white bench on which we read together; apartments where we dined together — those places evoke nothing in the way that it is impossible to evoke anything for a person who truly feels things intensely: a person like that is far more materialistic than to make do with 'memories.'

But even as I say such things I still go off to places. What is the most excruciating of pains? It is not so much that the woman is not there, but her 'not-thereness' is also not there — it is not so much that she is missed so much as the *lack* is lacking; when the person went away one imagined it was on the basis of some equitable swap and in place of herself she would leave, as positive material, crystal, or puppet, or physical force: the 'not-being-at-your-place'; on the streets where she no longer is, there will be a flower planted there, or the 'absent' sprayed as a scent. That 'absent,' however — this is the most painful surprise — is not there. The property of commonly visited places which floated before my eyes, was a *second-degree* emptiness when I spoke shortly beforehand about a 'more radical' metaphysical zero lying behind the numerical zero.

And that lack is merely a *thought*, not a real lack. When I think of the woman being no longer with me, then only her going away is 'true,' otherwise not. What is left behind by a person going away is not a physical hole, a chemical alteration in objects, it is just: I *know* she went away. I am in the habit of meeting a person on Mondays & Thursdays and let's say today is Tuesday:

I would be just as likely not to see him if he were in Budapest as not seeing him if he were sitting in his train somewhere around Zermatt. Despite which there is a huge difference — a difference because I *know* (I think) he is far from me.

If a friend of mine goes away for two months then in every second I think of his absence; the whole two months is compressed in the way that a whole room along with all its figures and any possible views onto the sea, will fit in a keyhole.

It is interesting that even though I know the other person longs for me and is pained just as much as I am for him I can still only visualize him as 'usual': even in his gone-away state I treat him in my imagination as he was during his existence-with-me, the faraway place & faraway time I always picture as only my most one-sided personal attribute: although it is he who has gone faraway it is *me* who is distant, or rather I am the lyrical chunk and caryatid of distance. I experience it, I imbibe it, it transforms me — in point of fact (this is the way the imagination works): it is he who is at home. I picture him in the train amid the snowy alps: the picture I see (snow, dining car, English fellow-passengers, the rhombus of the collector bow at the front of the train as it makes a turn) is a *pseudo*-image — the distance does not permeate my friend; it is in me; despite all those glacier backdrops he stands untouched in my ego of yesterday.

One is at a total lack of attitude vis-à-vis the departed: it is impossible even to hanker after them. Every movement is incongruent in respect of the absent one: there is something humiliating and shameful in that. How interesting the first day spent separately: a day that does not have the character of time or passage. If that evening somebody (possibly oneself) says by way of humorous consolation: "So, one day down already..." — one looks at him as at a liar or cretin. Down? Has one advanced toward the date of the return? Nonsense: one has simply done a circuit in the bondless fabric of 'absence,' & in the evening we are at exactly the point we were in the morning. Oh, redeeming hours, when we shall begin to sense that each day is not so much a circuit, not a crazy limbering-up on the spot, but a linearity, a deviation towards a goal: the circuit loosens at some point, and the line no longer returns into itself but a millimeter further on.

Thus, there is 'nothing' at all behind the faraway person, even a space is lacking. That completely paralyses one — neither a thought nor a feeling strikes one, though every now and then a wave of feeling overcomes one: at those times one's soul is tormented by music, crying, scraps of memory, & God in chaotic solidarity. Indeed, the one and only 'feeling' in my life that can justifiably be called a feeling — the others: my worshipping of my parents, my hypochondriac visions, my hatreds, my artistic shocks, and my social hysterias, all lie far, infinitely far from my state of mind sprawling behind the departed person; those others all run between phobia and a wish for narcosis — that, however, is a free, clean, wavering, and gigantic pain in which theological deliberation & individual selfishness, conceptual paradox and bestial simple-mindedness, truly fuse — I am lost in that sentiment, in that there are beauty and sadness, which is something very different from turbulent-technicolored visions & neurotic fears. That feeling is inexhaustible just because 'non-existing' is at its core, because its subject is 'nothingness' or a special 'not present.'

In front of me are trees: them I can describe. But how should I describe them in such a way that it should be apparent that someone is not present? After all, they haven't altered in the slightest. What is nevertheless tangible? That someone is 'not present' (1°) and that is bad for me (2°). But I cannot leave the matter there — something is perpetually amiss, there is a logical and sentimental error in the whole thing but I don't know exactly what and where. That is what is really bad. Pain for the absent is a highly subjective matter, which is part of the reason I feel the feeling explicitly as *the* feeling. Whether I hate him or her or am in love with them, then the other person and my actions are absorbed among the objects and phenomena of the outside world: now, however, there is something inside me which exists for me alone, only I need it, it is not evident anywhere.

I am sitting alone in a room where I am together a lot with the other, and also a lot without the other. The room is totally alien: the most familiar objects might as well be the utterly strange furniture of a Sumatran hotel. But I know that is only my *impression*; it is not true. The same goes for my subjective impression that a flower is more colorful than it is in reality as when, for instance, I am in love or I return home from a rendezvous, but then I do not feel that is humiliating, ridiculous, and frightening. I don't feel it is the isolated mania of the personality. Now I do.

Somehow I always feel the pains caused by an absent person as being *senseless*, though it is possible to adduce very simple reasons for it. Why, in that case, the sense of pointlessness? Is the fact itself an unfathomable paradox? The fact that a 'prosaic' two-month absence awakens an impression of *absolute* termination is, from one point of view, a totally sober impression and is not sentimental hyperbole, to wit, when at one moment I think of the person who has gone away and I wish he or she were with me right then: at that moment it is absolutely impossible. The person left behind at home does not feel two months *time* as being livable, for her or him there is no time problem: for them a duration of two months consists of a million such 'absolute *impossibilities*': the trouble is not that the absent person is not there but that it is totally *impossible* for them to be there. What separates me from my accustomed room is not the woman's lack but her impossibility: in that '*non posse*' from moment to moment I collide with suicidal stubbornness like a wasp against a window's glass in a closed room.

Those two completely alien fabrics: 'real time' (if that is not in itself self-contradictory — does time have anything to do with reality?) and 'impossibility,' the very consistency, dimensions, and direction of expansion are uniformly absolutely alien from each other: the two fabrics are contending within me, deadly tiring to my body and soul.

That is my summer vacation ever since I remember as a young boy: weeping, lamenting over others going away. My primary schoolmates went away, my grammar schoolmates went away, rich girls at university went away, writers went away, whereas I stayed here in the Budapest heat wave — with what? In a world of space, time, feelings, thoughts, and objects. For me, since childhood, nature (first and foremost the top of the Lesser 'Swabian' Hill in Buda and Margaret Island in the Danube between Buda & Pest: dirty brown 'open country' and analytical-Keatsean park) has been identical with time and 'somebody absolutely impossible.' During my summers I am a different person, a different writer than otherwise — I am transformed, manically, hypnotically, I fall into the 'somebody impossible' unavoidable somnambulant predestination, my feelings, appetite, and literary plans change utterly from one second to the next, I am not my own until autumn. The 'absolutely impossible' itself is unreal, 'time' in July and August is unreal — the former is logical, the latter almost chemical, fluid-like, melancholically playful, mythical.

Those things are borne by the trees, by the little man in the rear tramcar (in winter I go around by motorbus or in the front tramcar). In summer the million natural nuances of Margaret Island and the sweating plebs merge — the two nonsenses, which are worthy of the unanalyzable perennial nonsense of 'someone went away': the park's thousand impressions evoke for me a thousand analyses, the indecisiveness of sensual paradoxes and logical *perpetuum mobiles*, true ultralace and sick tautology, Proust-Valéry japes, the end result of which is statements like "every thought stretched to its extreme and to the very end = nonsense," then the milling throng of sweaty proletarians with cucumber salad in their shopping bag, the result of which are statements on the order of: "the whole of social life is a sadistic comedy." Are the hobbyhorses of my summers not tasty?

Oh, if only my *Completa Aestatis Morphologia*[94] were to come off one of these days & I were able to systematize my summer ego, that selfish, domineering person, who operates independently of me with a demonic mechanism. Either chip it apart into pure aphorisms or compose it in hierarchical form: just let it be done with, like this diary entry — that is also my wish, unarticulated experimentation, oscillating between aphorism & system. It would be possible to debate the logic, physics, and lyricism of the missing person — and those would not be trumped up chapters at that.

1. Margaret Island. 2. Lesser 'Swabian' Hill. 3. Last impressions: meeting in nature in the open air; meeting in my room; meeting in her room; meeting at the railway terminal. The carriage, train wheels, the departure of the train *without* a whistle. 4. That day without her. 5. The first day-after. 6. The tyrannical birth of the 'new,' the 'summer' person over me, outside me, in me. 7. The conceptual paradoxes of absence. 8. The lyrical effect of absence: the feeling of the one & only feeling-shaped conclusion. What makes a feeling a feeling? 9. Time and impossibility: two irrealities. 10. My summer style: the barren endlessness of compulsive analysis, the zigzagging of impotence and 'revelation.' 11. My summer reading matter: the material role of a book; time for reading; literature as entertainment & destiny. 12. My pilgrimages to my parents: the Bacchic victory of my childhood over me. 13. The transformation of other women in the street. 14. Open-air swimming pools: the relationship of sensuality and a distant person. *That* woman in the time of the *other*: experiments. 15. Proletarians; the fashionable & ragamuffins as vehicles of time nonsense.

⇐ 87 ⇒

THE SUMMER connection between a sick compulsion to analyze and 'someone went away' is quite natural: a style of analysis is not a vital necessity where there *is* a topic but where there is not. Analysis fills the emptiness of absence, lies its nothingness into something. A person who lives aphoristically to extremes, to an almost perverse degree (in logical & poetic aphorisms) and at the same time is constantly bellyaching for a system, for strict composition: as a matter of course that person falls into one or other neurotic form of analytic style.

⇐ 88 ⇒

ONE cannot serve two gods at the same time: truth and morality, art & morality. Of course, I do not mean that in the idiotic sense of "An artist cannot be bound by morality": that is nothing. More in the sense: someone at some time committed a major sin against his parents — having regretted that and confessed to it, he feels a burning need to set down that sin in its full profusion of psychological nuance, in all its ethical, biological, etc. ramifications: but he can*not* do that as it would mortally offend his parents. And Saint Don Juan has a hundred such cases: he is always having to lie about all of his women to all of his women.

⇐ 89 ⇒

THE UNBRIDGEABLE, disheartening difference between: my writings and my thoughts. I stroll at speed
between trees on St. Gerard's Hill:[95] a thousand sensory
impressions, a thousand metaphors, a thousand logical
sparks. I go through lengthy ranges of ethos, play through
long comic and tragic theatrical roles, plan murders, I
am contrite for lovers, enrich parents, outline theories:
by the time I have got back home and reach for a pen,
only the most foreign, most mendacious, meaningless
repertoire of styles is left in my hands. One of these
days I shall have to write a rather sad obituary, a hymn
of death, about my prolific, active, fine, rich rambles in
which one gets to play every fleeting caprice, I and a
chestnut branch, I and a vivid green patch of sky, the
evening color of the Danube and a garden fountain, et
cetera: in other words, my entire real, plastic, healthy
life, speaking from person to person.

I see a tree stuck to the sky: I play, *dance out* the light,
the foliage, the edge of twilight, the foliage's death, the
tree trunk's crookedness, the ball-like dynamic of the
branches, the groping constellation of the stars, & what
I picture along with the *dance*, that most expressive of
expressions, is some sort of abstract line-music, some
kind of drawing between architecture & kaleidoscope
blotches. But to live from morning till evening in the

rude health of that dance life and to write from evening till morning deadly mechanical pseudo-analyses like those about the absent person is: unutterably painful.

Dancing is in my blood, acting is in my blood — the beauty of the moment I can only feel as beauty when I play it, when I fashion a mask of it for my body, a mask of gesture and architecture, which makes me happy as long as I coexist, face to face, with the phenomenon.

And yet, like a senseless disease that turns one pale, a desire to 'immortalize' on and in me, which may be nothing more than a simple inheritance of my father's passions for collecting mementoes, theater tickets, foreign tram tickets, cinema programs, hotel stationery, serviettes, et cetera — no craving for artistic creativity, just a souvenir mania. What do I perpetuate? My unstylish style.

My experiences? They are perpetually disregarded: my poetry, my brainwaves, my truths, my prayers, my vanities, my subjects, my deeds — they have perished and perish in the blind maelstroms of dark woodland moments. Did I ever utter an honest word about what truly excites my soul to the roots? If I wanted to be frank, radically so, what was the outcome? As at my confessions as a grammar-school boy: frenzies of anxiety, sterile heart-throbbing analysis, a somnambulistic and bloody preciousness of self-rebuttals and question marks. Yet there is in me, besides a terrible sobriety, prosaicness, and mystic penchant for self-torment, a levelheaded bourgeois self-appraisal & 'bureaucratic' heroism — I feel that my business on earth has not been completed with my bad technique of writing & examining my conscience. I feel distinctly somewhere the possibility of a pure 'classicization' of myself and my life. But in my writings: did I ever talk to God about the way I feel about God from one day to the next, from one minute to the next? My relationships to my priests, to scholasticism, my evening prayer, confession, my sins: have I clarified those? No. First and foremost out of shameful, outrageous laziness I haven't; I avoid rationally transparent articulation of a complex matter. I ought to make a lot of corrections to my manuscript, and deletion has associations with death, with absolute, fateful barrenness. I haven't written those things down because I feared that a whole lot of people would be aggrieved. Have I written about my loves, about the personal epic of sexuality before and after Freud and Lawrence? Never. Why not? I detest scandal, a non-Catholic appearance, 'blunder'-anathemas.

If only, one of these days, I could describe in tragic-laboring proximity my whole, whole, whole experience of, and desire for, God — & my experiences of women, and my ideal. What would I have to do with romanticism & realism, æsthetics and morality? What would I care whether it was a diary or philosophy, kitsch heresy or dry pedagogy, self-redemption or the mask of all masks: if only I could one day be freed of the inane cages of maintaining silence and mendacity, of cowardly stylization! Now all such desires are open-handed self-compromise — when it comes down to it: 'total freedom' — that is just a truly obsolete, naïve ambition in art. An artistic question? Ethical question? Personal hygiene? What would I know: 'freedom' — after all, it is only a word; and it could be that it is the very worst, perhaps I want exactly the opposite: indeed, can I want anything else but its opposite? If my ambition, my flagellating phantom, is the reality of realities, the frankness of franknesses (not in a lyrical but in an ontological sense), is anything else awaiting me other than: asceticism?

⇐ 90 ⇒

SEARCHING out exact analogies (there is an innumerable multitude) to 'someone went away' a) in the plant world, b) from mathematics, c) from the area of medical chemistry, such as from anæsthesiology — all scenery is unchanged, absolutely unchanged after, in the wake of, the departed: after a spot of local anaesthesia other sensory organs continue to sense perfectly, yet nevertheless — they lack something, etc.

⇐ 91 ⇒

SUMMER is on the one hand the greatest chaos, and on the other the greatest order. Order: everybody has gone away, there is no work, no concerts, no friends —— in other words, time can be apportioned in a regular fashion, like in a sanatorium: playing the piano and stroll in the morning, reading, writing, and stroll in the afternoon. On the other hand, due to the intensified solitude, I think & fantasize much more wildly, much more, more intricately, more maniacally. That is how it has been since infancy: in the summer I was the most orderly (regular snacks!) and the craziest. An 'orderly' life is not all that orderly anyway: the evening walk which takes place every day between 8 & 9 o'clock can easily, precisely on account of its regularity, become a myth, a rite, and those rites do not calm me down but inflame me, bring me into ecstasy — like every refrain: a mystical mixture of fugitive time and crystallizing pillar. Dissolution and crystallization occur *together* in July and August: stupefaction down to zero (in morale, in my physiology, in my logic equally), stiffening into the statuesque stillness of a philistine. A Philistine likes his order, his *Spieß*-order,[96] because he is smart and knows that more trances, more morphine happiness, and more myth griffins, can be gained from that than from anywhere else. In summer, I would be unable to draw a distinction between hygiene & decadence: my skin tanned, my cheeks fleshier, my limbs somewhat drilled, and my head full of all-reviling Art Nouveau, hypothesis, and lunacy. Am I feverish or sunburnt — burning due to my digestion or bacilli? Am I orderly or chaotic? — A crystal: a swimsuited lady on the beach: all contours snapping like a bowstring, vivid colors like a foreign poison trickled onto the tongue, *exactly the one* special sound which is flattering to an absolute pitch; here sex bears the same relation to Narcissus lyric as a womb-scraping instrument does to Eve's womb. This is one form summer takes. The other: sludge, splishy-splashy puddles, relaxation, fraying, tattered nets, hormones palpably melting like sealing wax, the brain's slow disintegration like a mosaic losing its frame.

92

How preposterous it is for a novelist to describe a person even on the very first page: one has already long ago pictured something else — the tablet of the book, the smell of its print, the letter font, the form of the page numbers, the touch of the paper, a title long retained in the mind, the pressure of the chair in which one is sitting, the shadow thrown by the roller blinds, the wall, door, or picture opposite: these have all once and for all time, absolutely indelibly traced the protagonist's face (even if it is not directly visible).

⟸ 93 ⟹

THESE DAYS, I am hearing a lot about a 'Fräulein Vollen-weider':[97] odd — it's as if a '*g*' sound were missing from somewhere in the name, a '*g*' in the middle of the whole word, its center of gravity, its milling depth and root — yet it is not there. This '*g*' is present around the word like the physical center of gravity of a snaking 'S' or paragraph-shaped iron objects lies *beyond* the object (it was this sort of thing which made physics truly 'scientific' for me): a whole host of words (in English!) suggest a similar 'gravitational' sound, which does not occur but is called for. In Joyce's language a myriad of words are calculations of, and a bringing to the surface of, 'centers of gravity' of the kind — a cross-section of the sound-generating muscles at the point, or in the plane, when they are just midway to the sound, or when they would carry in the same direction beyond the sound.

⟸ 94 ⟹

FROM THE HOURS of young Bonington:[98]

1. He waits on a summer loggia with a friend for a woman; he is reading — a novel full of mythical worshipping of nature and decadent psychologizing. The relationship of the girl who is awaited and the love poetry of the novel.

2. In trio: the girl inspects El Greco & Turner; she is talking to the other boy on the loggia — Bonington is looking at the girl's stockings and shoes. These two extreme aspects of life for Bonington: the 'modern' girl's technological externalities and the El Greco fantasies. Absolute Spanish mysticism (*s'il existe*),[99] absolute silk stockings. He strolls alone around the piano in a dark room. The fate and lesson of sensation: colors; sounds. Madonna-plans (poppy-crimson, poppy-purple) and scenery plans.

3. Evening scene, evening love: Moon and the black leaf mosaic growing on it: "like the plastic thoughts of an inquisitor and the loosened bowels of a Maenad," etc.

4. Daytime cocotte and her relationship to 3.

"I love a woman for ever, insanely — yet I could part from her like one does from a whore; I left a whore but I could love her for eternity: everything in love is — *circumstance*."

≈ 95 ≈

WHAT a mundane subject, what a secretive reality, the difference between truth and imagination, object and feeling, diary life & artistic life, the girl and El Greco. Before me is the painting of the Crucifixion from the Church of the Hospital de Afuera in Toledo,[100] and before me are the girl's silk-stockinged legs, resembling bronze filigree-work, made even darker and more gleaming by zinc white summer shoes. To both an ecstatic-elemental relationship is attached.

The picture — writes twenty-year old painter Bonington — portrays nothing but non-existing things: is not this quasi-'common' attraction to the decidedly uncommon, the non-existing, marvelous? There are two extremes: the absolutely accustomed reality and the absolutely alien miracle. This El Greco painting, however, is neither of those, nor is it a compromise between the two — "a new constellation combined of 'real' elements is a naïve blunder, there can be no question of that."

What is the 'conventional mystery' of, for instance, such a Crucifixion? Why do I also think of another composition for the Crucifixion — the most supreme of fictions? How we have got used to great painting portraying the non-existent, what a realistic acquaintance unreality is: the Madonna on a marble throne; Jesus in the wreathe of his apostles, in a ghostly plane with an oval table; violins & pineapples at the edge of a table covered with a velvet bedspread, etc. If those are miracles to surpass all miracles — why don't I rejoice? If they are conventional, commonplace articles — why do they not leave me indifferent? Has anything been said already about the true relationship of dream and prose? In one picture we have a mitred bishop elevating Christ's body to heaven: when the girl opposite

looked at that in raptures all that was in my head was
— "It's *not* true, it wasn't like that" (not in a theological
sense, of course, but in terms of the spectacle).

Today was the first time I tumbled to the elementary
unreal nature of the subject matter of painting without
the psychological fact of imagination being able to offer
any explanation.

Facing me are lilac flowers running up a fence: each
corolla is like a musical note on Gregorian or modern-
day staves. I take up my pencil and draw strokes in the
shape of such a flower, Jesus' hair as a flower, the dove of
the Holy Sprit as a flower that has dropped from its stem,
clouds — its title is *The Crucifixion* in the first instance,
The Automatism of Flowers in the second, *A Graph of
General Mood* in the third. Why is it so prosaic, natural, as everyday as having breakfast or knotting a tie,
so self-evident that I should paint the crucifixion of
Christ? Where does that direct, unhesitating reaching-
out for the non-existent, for fiction & myth, come from?
And if a miracle is portrayed — why is it nevertheless
so natural?

It's not that I am obsessed — despite being taught that
a person with hair made of lilacs, a flower being turned
into a bird, water composed of flower corollas: those were
crazy. And how can a vision like that be splendid — if it
differs so much from everything else? Am I recognizing
something in them? Do they exist somewhere; do such
things exist all the same? What role does unreality play

in a person's day-to-day life? Is there an unreality — isn't the whole matter of 'unreality' unreal? Is the El Greco painting simply feeling and man's physiological inner surplus with regard to mundane reality? How interesting that most artists take the antithesis of 'reality' and 'style' as a fully-fledged postulate, and they create a style with no further qualms. But why is it that El Greco's so-called vision is such a *natural*, accessible, and absolutely familiar thing to a young woman? What, in the end, am I supposed to marvel at: the commonplaceness of the vision or precisely its extraordinariness? Dying Madonnas, the great whore of Babylon,[101] the apostles with tongues of fire,[102] angels with ruffled feathers, gods issuing edicts to the world: these are everyone's most intimate friends, only people don't talk about them? A young woman who was scarcely predestined for art recognizes herself better in El Greco than in her Angelo photograph or her hand-mirror.[103] Why? To me as an artist those visions are indeed natural, but natural as *visions* — to that girl, however, it is all in the course of things and workaday; for her it is not a vision but prosaic, the mystery is how well & truly implanted in that prosaicness she feels herself.

How natural it was already for the first caveman artist, when he painted or presented, to paint or present the non-existent. This is not a matter of my drawing up apologies for myths, a defense of unreality: it is the case that I still do *not* know what the distinction is between reality and unreality.

For that young woman, whose vision of El Greco is 'homely,' what is her relationship to her dreams — the other type of vision? Dreams are full of realistic elements, and it's all nonsense — a painted sacred image is full of unreal elements yet the whole thing is a simple, daily, human reality? (It's too schematic to be anything.) What is going on, what, between El Greco & dreams? Dreams are realistic and are laughing at us; we don't believe them — pictures are unreal (what never-never clothes! never-never nude figures! never-never get-togethers!), and we believe everything we are told. All the same, it is nonetheless strange that the most likely antelope shoe is quite incredible in our dreams, and Holy Spirit, angel, God the Father, and Spanish evangelists are quite credible, as if that sort of thing passed off twenty times a day in the street before our very eyes!

If the young lady feels so much at home among El Greco's angels — why did I sense such a difference between the love poetry of the novel I had been reading and her social, physical, and individual reality? Then why is all the flirtiness and hide-&-seek: if for her the Apocalypse "ça va sans dire," [104] why do I nevertheless treat her like a figure at a tea party, and why does she treat herself that way? Why is not everybody a Greco radical and a vision radical and tries to live in accordance with the angel, the whore of Babylon, the apostles with tongues of fire, and the Mary Magdalene of the boundless purple robe?

Why have we not already got it clear whether our instinct for reality or unreality is truer? Were we born into the world for what is or for what is not? And which is the real 'what is not'? For me the distinction between a man in the street and an artist was utterly hollow, insignificant, and meaningless that afternoon — there was no difference between El Greco and the girl *sub specie* whatsit.[105] She was 'on the spot' beside Christ in the impossible water, and El Greco wanted nothing other than to be precisely like a chit of a girl who had never painted: no mistake about it, I could see that.

Hostility to visions, a life incongruent with El Greco's, is only elicited from people by social coexistence: people on their own live like El Greco, everyone is unreal and mystic.

The two looks: when she looked at El Greco (which is to say, in her solitude she reflected his solitude) — & when she looked at me (which is to say, with the external appearance that she knew I was looking — looking with her for-others mask at the for-her mask of the other). Art is nothing other than "forgetting about others, about sociality (dreams are helpless, desperate floundering *in* sociality: the cancan of dependence): there is no reality and unreality, separate El Greco & separate chit of a girl, only masks of loneliness and companionship."

What is one's own attitude to the theory of 'social being,' I wonder? A person's sufferings, pains, the king-

pin of all neuroses, are always on account of 'others' —
could it be that *instinct* sought the sociality from which
ninety-nine per cent of sufferings derive? Is one truly
a social being? Or is the pack mentality just a chance
episode, and the El Greco instinct will win out — there
will come a time when the world will be studded with
solitary people. In point of fact, there is so fantastically
glaring a difference between solitude and social being
(cf. love!), the rupture between El Greco affirmation &
tea-party etiquette is so profound that one cannot find
it to be natural: for solitude to be natural and social
companionship to seem a sickness like the epidemics
of plague in the Middle Ages.

Of course, it is never possible to decide with such
questions as to what is natural and what, unnatural. I
stand for either absolute biological fatalism or intellec-
tual-hygienic optimism.

From a biological point of view, I have to say: it may
be that social life is an aberration & sickness, but then
on the other hand life seeks aberration and sickness
just as much as health. Happiness is not a goal of the
elemental biological impulse; in some cases it takes the
side of El Greco, in others, companionship; individual
and herd are its equally lovable and indifferent products.

If I am a psychoanalytic doctor and a humanitar-
ian, then I can say let girls be handed over *entirely* to
El Greco and release them from the deceitful prestige
of the tea-party: but if I am in the least smart next to

my psychoanalytic inclination (after all, a lot happens in nature) — *dare* I make happiness a principle of life? Dare I struggle for something (for happiness) if it looks very much as if happiness does *not* feature among the goals of the whole apparatus of the world? Do a couple of accidentally successful individual human happinesses entitle me to counterpose my entire view of the world against life's basic tendency? If happiness (which in the present case is identical with complete inner freedom of solitude, El Greco-style indulgence) is *not* a basic element of the entire natural existence — why bother with accepting a struggle that is condemned to die?

It may be (indeed, it is certainly so, given that there *are* curable optimists) that nature even wishes some of its products, like humankind, should want the kinds of things which are aimless & meaningless; life wants failure to comprehend life, indeed that may be its ultimate goal: to make humankind absolutely misunderstand itself.

⇐ 96 ⇒

A GENEALOGY of the sufferings of 'Charles VII':

1. An overly idyllic childhood: warm coverlet, warm dash of milk, warm fireplace — Orphic petty-bourgeois mentality. Absolute dependence on parents.

2. Childhood ascetic mania, self-tortures, apprehensive confessions.

3. First bordello shocks — ineradicable fear of syphilis (on moral grounds).

4. Early marriage; the background being: *a*) monotonous sensuality; *b*) ferocious political disputes, battles with statesmen of the princess' lands. Sensual mechanism, fanatical hostility: *à quoi bon?* [106]

5. Continual nostalgia for a heroic and artistic life: he would have liked to be: *a*) a Dominican preacher & *b*) a cathedral-designing artist.

6. Two people fight for him — a lover and a holy woman.

⇐ 97 ⇒

How dazzling and excruciating the three worlds are: someone in the neighborhood is practicing the piano at a staggering tempo; I read a novel; I meditate on my fate, my ailments. The music is technically almost flawless: the keys fly away from the body of the piano like pearls of water from a fountain — a statue to health, non-dizziness, qualm-free cleanness of elements, immaculate fitness, objective work, optimistic progress unacquainted with death, barbaric material beauty, and puerile positive unanimity. Such an antithesis to my present mental & physical condition that it is scarcely conceivable that on Earth we could fit so closely to each other. The book is full of mysticism, Freudian-flavored fears, superstitions, incest, bloody myths, & the English poetry of 'ambigu' spring loves — in short, a sea of pain and uncertainty, but that chaotic, milling imprecision is nevertheless already formulated, elevated into a work: happy desperation & readiness for death, which is able to find such classical form. Last of all, me: all cross-eyed, dizzy, stammering, gloom and nausea, deaf and ear-ringing hypochondria, far from the plastic forms & salvations of God, love, and artwork — simply the amorphousness of suffering, an unlyrical, undesirous, unrebellious idiotic tatter.

⇒ 98 ⇒

WHEN young Bonington is standing before the 'Pays de Caux,'[107] unable to paint due to sickness — to what should he turn his hand? In the yellow sky, which is like a chemically brutal sleeping pill changing everything to lemon: simultaneously wounding & paralyzing, covering up into blood and lulling to sleep — in that sky the Sun is only a white hole, sudden color blindness, fog, eye white, printer's error, melting snow on human fingers:

how he would love to paint how he feels the exciting duality of metaphysics and brushwork which betokens inspiration; how he feels in the very material of the sky itself with what brush, with what diluted paint, on *exactly* what granulation of paper, drying for how long before painting on it, he needed to work, and in that unity of 'phenomenon and representational technique,' where there is no difference between his own arm muscles, the powdery-proximate-dispersing-massive-lethal-wrap-like reality of the sky and the obedient-inventive chemistry of the paint — in that unity he feels his life's sole possible gesture (not 'meaning'): one that he is unable to make. The illness deprived him only of precisely the creative *urge*; every metaphysical and technical nuance of creation, the themes & ideas, the precise goals, ultra-logical plans, all remained completely intact — all the suffering completely shredded was the nerve which ought to have been whispering in order for him to walk from his couch to his worktable — in order to pace roughly one yard. What is he to do, then? Three attitudes are possible, but he does not feel true encouragement, hard-edged self-selection, in any one of these.

One of them: to accept the disease fatalistically and not be sick by *happenstance* but as a vocation, like a rose is a rose.

Second: to accept the disease not biologically but ethically — to make use of the body's blind absorption-in-pain to accomplish an El Greco-style religiosity, even holiness: to pray, pray, pray, to push in among the wings of angels and the blood of martyrs, to be fantastically Catholic.

Third: to rise up from the couch, go down to the seashore, and speak to, kiss the girl who is sitting there on a stone, thereby making acquaintance and enjoying once and for all with never-known love (it is probably enjoyable) until he rolls over dead into the water, when the girl will still have time to make a prudent choice of husband. Yes — the most dreadful thing in life is if a person is not born for anything in particular: at any moment I can be an idiotic suffering machine, a mathematized puppet, a metronome; I can be holy, a Byzantine virtuoso of prayers and virtues, a gourmand tidbit for splenetic priests; I can be crazily in love: a hidebound youth of a pastel-like powdering embrace, loosely buttoning kiss and alcoholic 'belief in women' — nostalgic wanderer of nocturnal gardens on account of an unattainable girl.

But why does God bring into the world people to whom he has not given a vocation? Should I be holy when I could be a better troubadour? Should I be a mindless padder-out of clinics when I could be a second Loyola? Should I be in love with a girl when tomorrow I shall need to be familiar with death's every technical grip on an operating table? The fact is today I won't paint — God speed 'Pays de Caux'!

⇐ 99 ⇒

THE INDIVIDUAL'S ailment and society's ailment: a
hypochondriac's pain and poor & lowly people's pain
under fantastically unscrupulous social arrangements.
If I wish to express the duality of 'pain and vitality,'
and 'general biology & ruinology,' one of the volumes
will be 'Hormonology and Nerve Histology,' drawing on
palaeozoology & palaeobotany with particular regard
to embryology — Volume 2 of which will be 'Tragedia
dell'Arte' — in which the most sadistic, most sumptu-
ous, and most colorful social satires will be collected,
danse' macabre and grand guignol. Possibly, I will cut
the two volumes down to one (to the appalled expert
horror of so-called 'experts'): one chapter on a hormone,
alternating with a satanic social parody: adrenaline, cor-
ruption, cortin, troop transport, pituitary gland, pseu-
do-democracy, thyroid gland, title hysteria, etc. What
fine pictures of 'life': gigantic X-ray & colored micro-
scope-slide backdrops, expressionist-precise maps of
life & death, bacillus tapestries, blood baldachins, and
in front of them the parade, the thousand nonsenses,
the quid pro quos of war, commerce, bureaucracy.
What a dense fabric of suffering, of boundless, irresistible suffering, irrational to its very roots.

What other attitude can I have but the medical and
the parodic? I can be an apostle — found a party, curse
for decades, get myself imprisoned and criticized by

those who are born blind & dilettantes, say catechism for brigands, but then what? If perchance I manage to do something for the wretched people? Every measure of mine is grown to my person; after my fall or death my activity as an apostle will be disregarded. Or I could be a poet (I have lying in front of me a poem by D.H. Lawrence with the title 'Corot'), but the moments of contemplation are so rare in this kitschy tempo of suffering, and I have no wish to kid life that it is fine. I know it is fine alongside every sadism of hormones and society, but it still does not merit my painting it as Lawrence does in 'Corot': that would be to be far too sure of one's hostile 'élan.'

Next to my hormone scheme a social scheme of the following type: Old Sandro has saved all his money for a new seminary to be constructed in Rome (16th century). He dies suddenly, leaving a last will that is curt and fragmented. His lawyer sets out for Rome with the money but spends it all *en route*. He receives a loan partly from Turkish merchants, partly from pope-mad Guelphs.[108] Rome is in chaos — the pope is dying. A wholly villainous secretary takes charge of the inheritance. With the money his first business is to entice a Spanish courtesan with a reputation as a mystic, saying that she will become a huge asset for Italian diplomacy. It will be worth more to the Church if Italy reaps more political success than if it has three or four smarter priests. The courtesan's sea voyage; a chorus of starving seminarists. One of them rebels against the secular secretary's machinations, the secretary gets him into trouble with a cardinal (with forgeries) — the seminarist is forced to commit a heresy. The secretary explains the dying pope's visions as meaning that heaven also intended the courtesan as Italy's savior. The Ghibellines threaten to destroy Rome. A young governor seeks to dismiss the aged, sick, half-dead, long-past-it generals in order that young talent should step into their places; the matter is entrusted to the lawyer, who is now hard pressed by his Guelph and Turkish creditors. He therefore does not discharge the truly geriatric figures but his own personal enemies, offering the vacated positions at exorbitant prices to Ghibelline spies. The pope's valet murders the courtesan — the corpse is made up to look like the Holy Roman Emperor and taken before the pope's deathbed: "The Emperor has been vanquished" — let the pope die in that belief. The next moment the Ghibellines and the Emperor break in.

⇐ 100 ⇒

WHEN WERE THOSE two hymns set down? The first: "To all the Impossibilities of all love" — and the other: "I will not tolerate your not saving me." With the Impossibilities of all love, & also with the second hymn, the basic uncertainty of my life is raised: should I actually write hymns about those topics, or novelistic catalogues of data?

The impossibilities of all love: I can express with *metaphors* the evanescent illusion of love, redeeming only for moments, and the impenetrable blackness of pain that sweeps down on one afterwards: a large cloud half covers the Moon — the space between Moon and cloud, full of luminous emptiness, quivering, silk-misty distance, space and flowering, perfume evaporation & dense light moss like beauty itself; the face of the Moon which is turned to Earth, however, is all inflammation & poisoning-like black, basalt and death, the blackness of which has no relationship to the darkness of shadows, which is, after all, loosely woven on the inside — that is much more concentrated, more fossilized, like the pain felt on account of the impossible girl. Or a poppy corolla and its opium-lilac inner part — the corolla's waving, its evanescence, and its bloody redness in itself are the impossibility of love: the color swims without contour in the air, and the leaves fall easily, very easily; the poppy's fumes, the lilacness, the greasy velvet of the shadow, the smear of poison, are the crystal of pain, its chemical element.

But with the data of the *everyday* I can also express, for example, a girl's unhappiness: her lover has just left her; she was not all that fond of him, only parting magnifies the business — she does not trust in the boy who would stand in as the new lover, he is not needed, nor can he be, because *a*) he is married; *b*) the rumor is that he toys with a lot of women at any one time and in succession; c) his wife is a good friend of hers; d) marriage is still a current, keen ambition, but in this case there is no hope of that; yet inside she, too, like *everyone*, without exception, is: star, sky, bough, a human being hiding Moon & sea, but she does not, cannot, have the strength to stand beside boughs & stars on account of the a), b), c) & d)'s.

The poles! It seems this will be my fate: the first possibility is the *just* metaphor; not a hymn, not a poetic whole, but only a colored formula, the one and only synthetic scheme of my whole inner constitution; the other possibility is not a novel but a dry-as-dust *inventory*, some sort of literary record of reality. I shall be lost unproductively between the non-touching poles of absolute subjectivity and absolute objectivity.

Where is the center of amorous impossibility? No matter if its roots are poetic or psychological, primitive-ethical, or play-social — I want to locate it. Maybe what is decisive is the antithesis between the absolute inner statics of beauty & the all-muddling movement of the I-want I-don't-want of life?

What singular types of inspiration there are: themes conceived in illness, during the second movement (with variations) of Schubert's *Piano Sonata in A minor*, in love, under social abuses, are always of one type, with exactly the same genre or mannerism corresponding to each such separate inspiration. The same clichés of impossibility as well!

Love: among very dark green and steely smooth, puritanical, giant leaves, a couple of berries with the severity of a point and a small thimbleful of the dynamics of a popping in advance, among them a pair of blackbirds — blots, the softness of quills among the edges of the leaves. A nocturnal well: a flat basin virtually to the point of horizontality; all around it, like a blue curtain, water plunging into the depths — no way of telling whether what gushes from it is a deafening orgy of 'S'-es or a nocturnal hush: blueness, monotony, helplessness, gravitational tautness (like a knitted shirt on a woman), tyranny, eternity, symbol, peace, secret, light, sound, loneliness, & destiny radiate from it. A woman's face, listening to music with closed eyes: the fine mystification of a Caola advert, eyebrows & eyelids flowing gently into a point at the base of the nose: a millimeter before they meet the two arches are still quite far from each other, but then they are also quite close together, like confluent brooks, without having suddenly arched — that must be how parallel straight lines meet in infinity. A slightly immature sensuality: rather a kiss reminiscent of Koh-i-noor pencils sharpened with a pencil sharpener ("I suppose one graze of the lips is alright"), a fragment of an arm, a sizzling bundle of moments from the biting haystack, nothing more.[109]

That is not poetry, however: thrush, well, face, and the grounds of touch — a hymn is not begotten of that. What is missing? Some sort of 'idea' — when I look at

poets of old times there is always a primitive, but specific train of thought in their poems, that is always the
significant thing, not the metaphors or vision. For me
there is no 'idea of mine' apart from the words of 'impossibility of love.' I see the whole tragedy of the situation
at one go; it has no beginning or end, no development
— no 'course' is perceptible. I am infinitely *descriptive*
by nature — I am incapable of utilizing forms of sentences (questions, exclamations) in a poem: I feel that
is constructive, fictive, a lie. The relationship between
the whole hunger for reality and total opus neurosis (I
could probably also call it: a total neurosis about reality and total 'work of art' hygiene) — this is what it all
hinges on. Is it possible to square such an apparent circle:
to make a real work of art from my anti-opus nature?

⇐ IOI ⇒

THERE is something eerie about John Cowper Powys'
Jobber Skald, to wit its impressionism, its death smell of
infinite sensitivity to nerves and sensation. On account
of which so many of us feel ourselves to be artists: infinite sensitivity of eyes, nose, and ears — that is precisely where the death of art is, monotony, nothingness.
This is an altogether creepy matter: to see art's poison,
the most hazardous spores of death, at its very center
(at least many of us considered the ultraprecision of the

sensory organs and myth-freighted qualms about reality to be that). In Powys and now me, the sensibility of eyes, ears, nose, fingers, and memory (the latter is also sensory, bound to an internal sensory organ) has become a *curse* from which one should run and avoid: either because one wishes to live or because one wishes to be an artist. One can no longer set about anything with sensibility: it is death in life, death in art. One's prayer can only be: *not* to see sharply any more, not to hear clearly any more, not to feel, not to remember with mythic-magical sensitivity, with plasticity, with analytic complexity.

The privilege of unhappy, full of death, sex-distorted souls is sensory sensitivity: those who scent smells, visualize colors, touch memories and objects with octopus-gluey hands are those who have no need of a sense of smell or light, memory, or object, those who have lost touch with life, those who are unreal. The supreme impotence of the soul, its sex-fiasco, its taking leave of reality: it can be established precisely from knowing all the nuances of the world, of reality: "you *know* the world = you are *far* from it, you are not made for this life." The secret of secrets: only a soul replete with death is able to see and smell life — a person who, on the other hand, is from and in this world does not smell and hear that particular this-world. Sea, sunlight, trees, memories, girls' legs: with what plasticity they are catalogued in Powys — all the same, that raises an impression of decadence, nauseating decay, unreality. The ultimate reality of reality = inauthentic fiction of neuroses. That is absolute tragedy — in the individual and in the work (if I were healthy then I would *invent* sensory nuances, that would be a quasi mathematics — from which the atmosphere of 'reality = corpse poison' would be lacking).

⟸ 102 ⟹

IN JUST THE SAME WAY as artistic impression is lethal, there is just as much death in the simple fact that there are individual faces in the world. One gets tired of them, both of oneself and of others. For what good are all those individual fates, models of fortuities, ethical negatives on the face, the most authentic seal of death: a portrait? Let us get rid, to the maximal extent possible, of both biological & social destiny — let us seek an opening in our organization, in our hazardous civil situation, through which we can fly at the speed of light towards an 'objectivity', an unpsychologized state, irrespective of any formation and civil role.

Here are three figures, three incomprehensions, three sufferings, because they obey the death trap of the physiological frame, the mental nuance, and the social role; the first is extraordinarily intelligent, the second moderately so, and the third hardly at all. Of course, if one takes the word 'intelligence' seriously, portrait-like and with medical apprehension, its lexical and its ordinary meaning do not have much in common.

I think of the first woman: what might 'intelligence' mean in connection with her? To begin with (to begin chronologically), indeed the lexical meaning, for in point of fact, as a result of her parental-terrorist, blind-snobbish upbringing, it meant a broad knowledge of a whole bunch of subjects, languages, musics, literature and lands, in a word: much Renaissance. If the woman happened not to show herself as being a genius, the most extreme catastrophes might have been the result of a cultural incest like that. The woman is sensible, how-ever — she lives amid sensations of Powysian odor & remembrance —, there is no chaotic mosaic and cross-ings-out as the immense philological precision and the hysterical, disorderly, lyrical-sensory impression in the woman's brain. The whole encyclopaedia and the whole sleepwalking, the ever-more-disquieting catalogue and the ever-dottier nonsense strophes bloomed in her all at once (a Joycean tongue was the woman's *body*). All urban neurasthenia and, at the same time, a wild desire after a life of Byzantine stylites and Swiss cows: it could be that those desires are nervous nostalgias par excellence, but I heard few culture-nervous people loath culture so soberly-sadistically, wish for sanctity, and follow bestial-ity as with her. The cultural style of a cultured person: with her that was not on a regular nerve track, it did not play out in a *'combat avec l'ange'* [110] setting but in a very childish, very concrete, honest manner like a peas-ant girl tidying among the mixed-up plates and dishes.

Fears, dreams, moral insanity, the occasional star whim, a load of conventional truisms: *that* was her intelligence, a perpetual vibrating, an undefinable ethical-botanical constellation, windswept tree-boughs: shade, dew, leaf, emptiness, branch-bone, sunlight, rustling, mass, analytical dividedness, monotony, withering, paralysis, shivering, beauty, nonsense, humility, bluff, freedom, a mysterious and ever-restless compilation of diseases. (These kinds of listings of a *'jeux de Pantagruel'*-nature have the neither-nor flavor, if they occur in a serious sense.)[m]

But then I don't think it is a matter of intelligence but of unhappiness. She grapples with a man on the foolish path of illegality. Why does she grapple? Because she is partly bound to her impressions, partly to an Elysian myth, partly to Proust, partly to Byzantium, partly to the Moroccan *'Stadt der Tausend Frauen'*[112] (as it says in a brochure for sea cruises), partly to St. Thérèse of Lisieux. That duality does not mean sin & virtue, sickness and health, subjectivity & objectivity, psychology and inhuman primordiality, are in permanent contention, that this is what makes her life problematic — no. Those poles unconsciously shade and influence her life; those contrasts are in the air we all share. But neither her intelligence, nor the complexity of her morality, *have credence any longer* — let us not call it tragically human, St. Augustinian, a spooky roulette-pattern of fate, because the moment we think that it truly is, we shall straight away have recognized it and set her even more in her pain.

Let us call the ethical or mental dilemmas non-existence, nothing, a lie, a ruse, bordello aesthetics: everything which is individual variation, that is to say, the entangling knotting of loneliness, has to be forgotten.

Forget the mirror image, face, memories, man, parents, and forcibly be drilled into the absolute foreignness of something — *not* 'towards the one and only metaphor,' or in other words, get entangled in the excruciating monogram of the individual lyric, but out, out of the world of metaphors, impressions, fate, the world of life, into a radical, eternally heretical not-I. What bellyaching, beating about the bush, when a woman like that moves towards happiness: mild narcotics instead of amputation. Suicidal molting — that is the only medicine.

There is the second figure: a meekly, slowly old maid, melancholic in a Jewish way. Her intelligence is like an oily puddle by the roadside — it reflects the trees and clouds much more scintillatingly, with a warmer charm, with more erotic objectivity, than a neutral white glass mirror does, but in this mystic-boudoirlike clairvoyance and sticky, muddy plasticity there is prosaic regret, sleepiness, 'sleepy' pessimism. How difficult to hold even myself back from the stylizing-schematizing enjoyment of the individual human variant: I get gooseflesh if I think of the previous woman's windswept tree bough-life & the life of oily-brown reflection in a sheet of water of this one — what a harvest of clichés would open for me. True, it would not be of no pedagogic value were I to manage to designate the personality of those women as 'beauty,' because I can already see that even to a lay person's eyes in beauty there are such glaring signs of unhappiness and barrenness that I would achieve my goal of bringing an end, once and for all time, to the examination of individuality and noticing individual fates.

Why do you accept the mask? — that is my sole Elizabethan-era question to the melancholic woman when, holding out both arms, she distractedly places them on my shoulders, only cupping her hands round the nape of my neck (what a marvelous gesture of life that is: feline stretching and ironic embrace, yawning onanism and charity perfume) — "why did you take the mask, Lemuriel?"[113] Why are you so brown, so thin of hand and so black-haired, so myopically inquisitive and so gluily sticky of voice, sleepless, and an enemy to kissing: why did you not daub your skin purple, pluck your hair out, smash your lorgnette and your nose, make your vocal cords bleed with shards of glass in order to make your voice *different*, so as not to be you? This is not theatrical dehumanization à la *Compagnie des Quinze*: that will not make you happy, that is still beauty, so it cannot be a pellucidly transparent, empty-objective Lethe. Why did your lover leave you? Why daren't you start with a poet? Because that's *you*! because every morning you want to train yourself afresh into being you with your mirror, your memories, and your Bach preludes.

Believe me, a person's fate is not 'one's fate': I can also see you and your mother, the two of you, like an extraordinarily tall and slim tree with silvery white foliage (scaly and bewigged, fluffy and birch-like, at one and the same time), and you as green, vivid green, blackish-green grass at the foot of that tree. The aging mother is the slim pole of a well sweep, the pivoted pole of a well, not a tree, a flirtatious bubble shot up on high, and you, the young one, the girl, the healthy: you grow wild, thicken, become tragic, at her roots, knowing that jungle-like breakneck fertility and hormonal generosity are more tragic, more lethal, than withering. Mother and daughter: a silver-thin '*cri*' and a minor-black explosion of grass — why do you put up with that? why accept it? why believe it? everything that people call 'the way things are' is the lie of lies: an empty dodge. Reality-Hetæra's most inane formula for seduction.

What about the third woman? An English girl's face: moleish stupidity, Salvation Army idealism. Keats-nostalgia, one pound of rouge and virginal 'daisy,' a bundle of real nervous troubles, a bundle of mannered gestures as per the job description for a 'nervous woman.' All affected tragedy and contrived problems, but they pay off so well that either she bursts into tears or else they are so tiring as likewise to make one cry. The emptiest life, no inner fate: one might believe that, Lo and behold! this is the chosen handmaid of objectivity. Yet of the three women she is the least. Precisely because she has no fate, she is a tabula rasa to the point of imbecility & unused graph paper; precisely on that account, with frantic stubbornness and greed, she *wants* an individual fate — a biological self and a social mask. (Let's not play with words: an empty woman with no individuality is something just as individual and charged as a strong individual — obviously.) Such a woman is like a kaleidoscope — she has a few elements that were stolen from somewhere such as fashion-sense, beach, intellectual-poetic or dreamy-mercantile man, philanthropy, liberalism, children, 'it's important to have a home,' and to these she has a few primitive operational tokens to add (likewise thrown into the kaleidoscope): plus or minus, times, in-out. The dialogue begins, life gets under way (the two are identical, with engineering precision): that is, without any enthusiasm she starts to shake the kaleidoscope. She checks to see what is in it: mercantile man a minus, philanthropy a plus. OK: that'll do for five minutes. The partner in the conversation or the sex go along with it, either agreeing with or refuting the girl, but that becomes tedious for her: nervously, with the motions of a three-year-old child, she gives the kaleidoscope another twist. What's in it now? A plus next to mercantile man, a division sign next to children. An ode to business commences and also another ode to birth control, whereupon she again leaps into the sea after Shelley, & does not marry in order that she may become directress of a kindergarten. That is her bio-

logical Lemuriel-mask — so what about the social role?
Old, money-hungry ladies push her to marry — a squirt
of a clueless fool: among aging bankers, textile manufacturers, lawyers. But plump, 'eligible men' like that have
no need of a busybody baby kaleidoscope like her on
any account; what they are looking for is, for one thing,
an upright & pretty wife ("smart and *Tüchtig*": Father
forgive them, for they know not what they say),[114] a
temporary appurtenance somewhere between a lackey
and a woman of pleasure, a secure currency and a tasty
morsel, an obedient pet animal and a valuable signet
ring; for another thing, a dancing girl for the occasional
evening as, after all, even Shylock has his 'moments.'
The moral for the 'eligible bachelor': the slobbery-blood-
stained private property denoted by the term 'home'
along with the wife symbolize this home lie to him; to
the same gentleman love is: an escapade, a clumsy, cack-
handed sex caricature, an aping of the gentry. What
chance do you have when those are stacked against you,
wee kaleidoscope? Though it lies within your powers
not to accept your fate & thereby avoid unhappiness
once and for all: turn blind, you too!

If you were listening, all three of you would say that
I am talking through my hat: in my shifty literary fashion I got a real kick out of using your personalities, and
the things I have said in denying your individuality are
just empty words with no practicable moral or hygienic
content. That's true. But it is irrefutably the case that

in no way, no way at all, do I wish to acknowledge the authority of subjective fate, and every spiritual reform cannot *de natura*, know exactly *what* it wants in the place of the old: one cannot want an already *known* thing — as soon as it is *known*: it is no longer a reform, but automatically a convention. The pace of development is this: I want something unknown, and afterwards I am already bored about something old. Known and wanted exclude each other.

103

FACTA, *facta*: solitude in the study; roller blinds fastened open, hush-hush throughout the house, a northerly late-afternoon murk consisting of moss, mist, orange, interconnecting doors, which may be speaking about the curious relationship between space and quiet, gallery and solitude, a long novel completed not long ago, a melancholy leave-taking from its main characters and its author, child gone away, wife gone away, a girl, eyelashes dripping with mascara, trying on a silver *lamé* dress in the maid's room; a brisk stroll; difference between the circling of Naphegy Square & the straight-lined stroll of Orom Street,[115] the unexpected blooming of a yellow sunset, horribly long shadows, insane golds of lateness, *unheilvolles Spätgold* [116] (mysticism knows no mother tongue); the hills under the Sun are porous like some airy dull-mesh women's dress materials; yellow, yellow, storm-yellow, the yellow of history, the yellow of peace, the yellow of irrationality, the yellow of fruit (Habsburgs — disease, pineapples — secrets), little acacia balls in a light summer-flirtation breeze, which may be very strong, but there is not the faintest chance of a squall; the bonces of thick-haired young girls under attack from Don Juan, when he is just playing and meanwhile thinking of another woman; the shadow-leprous square, projecting here and there and still under the Sun's terror, and the antithesis of my deserted, long-dark home, with a buzzing, invisible mass of bees on its green-creepered walls, fleetingly musing over how an exact photograph of something and a Quixotic similitude bearing absolutely no similarity to the thing manage to be *equally* realistic and hit its essence (viz. 1. a rose = a rose, 2. a rose = Lemuriel's shoulder slipped into a blouse): lies are also new aspects of the truth, indeed, the truth about a thing — once again home is solitude, oscillating between prayer before a crucifix, windowless fluctuations of mood & immersion in some old memory; an atmosphere of a green boudoir jungle, the melodic birth of 'time' from the components of the hush twisting around me like spider's legs...

That is the point at which I speak with a friend about two things, as it happens the two greatest imaginable contrasts of this *absolutely* impressionistic distribution of algae: war and number theory matters. We live through the war in the dark, scenes of beſtiality, wholesale trade, heroism, nonsense, *civitas Dei* and dumb indifference,"[117] so that those have cuſtomarily intereſted intellectuals, wavering between biological, fataliſtic acknowledgement & naively obſtinate rationaliſtic critique, jumping from current events in Abyssinia to morphology, from hiſtory of philosophy to the adminiſtration of the League of Nations. Is that also a human matter? My evening impressions of weightlessness and the pseudo-nationaliſt deal-fixing of tank manufacturers, poems by Keats, & the plans of a Mackensen?"[118]

Then the other counterpole of my tinkering-bout in solitude (which might well be the heroism to beat all heroisms): mathematics. War: physical death, selected figurations of agony; mathematics: a never-maſterable infinite-alien cerebral arrangement, the empire of incomprehensibility. What is that? Fate wished to punish me because I lived for my impressions in ſpite of my decision and therefore, with a regularity fitting a morality play, it sent me as a ſtone gueſt, death and incomprehensibility, *war* and *mathematics*.

We talked about Landau's books,"[119] he recommended as a preparatory ſtep Knopp's wee *Funktiontheorie*,[120] explained the difficulties in proving Goldbach's conjecture (every even integer can be expressed as the sum of two primes), including the attempt of the Muscovite Schnirelmann,[121] as well as the number theory ſpeculations advanced by Hardy & Littlewood[122] with the assistance of the Riemann hypothesis:[123] the reason why I am putting in all those names here in such a naively theatrical doll's house shop-window is because I want extremes of the human mind like my impressionist nihilism (nihilistic precisely because of its maximal objectivity) and mathematics to appear together in at least the form of clumsy vignettes. The mental effort that I had to put in, after the total impression hedonism, in order to understand these sorts of propositions ("any integer greater than 1 can be expressed as a product of primes that is unique up to ordering") — I am barely in a position to analyze; obviously, asceticism of that kind is fruitless and that playing of impression and *mathesis* against each other here as 'literature' can only raise the impression of a game. In my life, however, as raw a contrasting afternoon as this is, is more significant than that — anyone who has not examined the fantastically different mental dispositions of these two worlds knows little about the category known as 'possibilities.' Having looked at what the psychological cause of the wild interest in number theory might be, we stated something to the effect that behind the apparent 'order' of numbers there is a yawning gap of anarchy, chaos, irrational leaps, and wobbling (to make use of distorting literary expressions in a layman's hair shirt); Littlewood said of Ramanujan, "Every positive integer is one of [his] personal friends"[124] — and indeed in number theory the digits 1, 2, 3, 4, et cetera, lose the grey faces of homogeneity or uniformity and are given an individual profile, an almost biologically irrational individuality — again to put it in a somewhat shamefully literary fashion: 1 = apple, 2 = tuna, 3 = Joanna the Mad,[125] 4 = a *tic-tac*, et cetera: one senses the difference in that way. A string of numbers will also not be a monotonous step but a rippling shadow, dunes, hills and dales, a compacting & thinning band. But in this territory every metaphor can only be tasteless.

⇐ 104 ⇒

I WISH to be liberated from the barrenness of the self, lyricism, subjectivism, hypochondria, impressionism and psychology. I can have two programs: either an ascetic-Catholic morality of Grecoesque form and Gonzaga-content — or 'sacrificing my whole life to mathematics.' Either St. Sebastian or — to take a watchword from a book by Eddington that is lying in front of me — "waves of ψ." [126]

Mathematics — I have not completely clarified it for myself inasmuch as I can not mean by it: "I shall be a mathematician," but also that I do not perceive my life and material reality from an aesthetic and biological point of view (*'Philosophie des Organischen'!*)[127] but from the viewpoint of theoretical physics — looking at the excited or quelled hormones of my illnesses & loves not as 'life,' but as an area of atomic physics or quantum physics. My left ear is buzzing: hitherto that was a metaphoric and physiological fact: (1) a dark green funnel rose was continually rolling up within itself, & I have, so to speak, heard that internal friction of the petals boring into my skull like a corkscrew — and (2) *irritatio labyrinthi.*[128] — (1) and (2), the metaphor and clinical definition, are in agreement in that they affect my self, my human nature as a human, they portray me as a human — it is precisely of that I wish to be freed because it has made happiness impossible for me in my life, and a closed, uniform opus impossible in my creative plans.

What has Greco-style asceticism to do with my ear? That perceives it as suffering, that it affirms like a relationship to Christ, like wings which will straight to God. In suffering it is no longer a matter of ears or roses or an X-rayed brain — it is not me who is present but *the* suffering, the pure theological gesture, it does not so much as enter my mind that I will miss the finest love on account of my earache, or I am unable to read the books I have purchased at the cost of sacrifices and I am unable to write how I would know what kind of work: suffering perceived in a Catholic manner immediately dehumanizes me, absorbs me into God. If I 'give up,' do I not give up the things that were the main sources of impressionism and nervousness: love, money, travel? A woman: if I am a saint — I actively smash her image, tear her down, limb by limb, if I am a mathematician — then I simply regard her as non-existing, and anything which does not exist does not have to be torn down. Sainthood is continual smashing, active taking notice, & active battling with the 'adversary'; mathematics, by contrast, is living in a totally separate world; there is no question of a fight, and it does not recognize my woman, does not know what that is.

Colorful caryatids, steadfast carriers of neurosis and art: should I slay you? Turn your corpses around in the eternal blood of morality — or simply annihilate you in the Lethe of *mathesis*? I must try out both possibilities, and the Gonzaga-attitude will not be less Gonzaga in God's eyes if the taste of 'experimentation' remains at the beginning. I'll smash my clock — what need of time that awaited you, seductive caryatid? I shall exterminate the trees, which spoke in whispers about the whispering of your stockings and hair while I was waiting for you; and gave you a shadow, when you gradually appeared at the end of the road, and strangled the wounds that were left on me in the wake of your departure with metaphor gauze until the blood of memory broke through anew. To what purpose the trees? They stand in time, like spoons left in the poison cup of suicides. To what purpose time? to what purpose day and night, the bicolored metaphysical clowns' pantaloons of sex: one leg white, the other black — what are they to me?

Almost everything was impossible: not the miracles
but the simplicities — two of us in a quiet room, far
from the red wells of sin, money, parents and instinct
— a walk in the woods, a melancholy-sure exchange of
glances, a harmonious kiss (a resting bird's wings flattening onto its warm body "as if they had been made
to measure") — *those* were the impossible things: your
loveliness always remained a wild fiction, you were
never able to live in accordance with your dreams, you
clattered your human role, your occupation role, your
child's role, blindly and with a maid's blaséness. What
madness it was to make any attempt at all with it: to
grow wild day by day in the sterility of neurosis of
myth, to cling to you ever more fatefully, day by day,
in the frames of convention, grey embroidery, or as a
confessed malefactor, which are killing you as well.

What can one be next to you other than a Gonzaga or
Gauss?¹²⁹ Why bother with pursuing to distraction the
antithesis of a tatter of myth and prose: the nauseating
incongruence of female vision and female fact? Only one
thing is possible: rip asunder the caryatid along with its
whole milieu and associations. I will tear out your hair,
poke out your eyes, spatter your skin with mud: all without any sadism or *Grand Guignol* gourmandism — simply like a sad and sober workman when a new regime
takes possession of the Gothic town hall and the old statues are useless. Get lost all of you — flowers, women &
all; women, fountain and all — I'll tear you from your

mossy niches & toss you down from on high into the depths like fruit from the highest branch. Shatter into pieces — and as the dialect of workers is simple: drop dead! Lead me, Gonzaga, along your corridor, where everything is black, only your cheeks and the candle are Habsburgishly-Acheronian yellow,[130] I am free... *Nous allons voir si les mathématiques...*[131]

When I see myself, covered with wounds, lined with hallucinations, in Spanish steams of prayer, hanging about among skeletons and relics (for one thing, the ethos only wants the shell, the outline scheme, the minimal formula of death — for another, in a relic, an animated body part with a woman and her decorations made large, extra-human: both equally 'wholesomely' — anti-psychological), squeezed between the label of saints & the Rabelaisianism of devils — then I think agitatedly of the possibility antithetical to El Greco, the 'observer,' about whom I read things like this in Eddington: "Now you have a picture of him. He has one eye (his only sense organ) which is color-blind. He can distinguish only two shades of light and darkness... The sensitive part of this retina is so limited that he can see in only one direction at a time." Elsewhere: "... we stripped our ideal observer of most of his sense organs": leaving him with the happiness of "part of an eye in order that he might observe coincidences" — not living in the crowded bloody drama of ethical agony but between reading a scale and formulas.

Some sort of 'artistic' reflex jerk is inevitable for the time being, however: I would like, one of these days, to give symbolic-absolute expression to an *ascetic* denial of impression and a *mathematical* denial of impression.

The religious expression can only ever be the dead body of Christ: a repetition of the Pietà creatively-blindly for evermore. To carve, kiss, play it with my own undressed body. What do I care if some wee psychoanalyst acts out his own causality little cooking at the foot of my white statue — or if someone from among the official neo-Catholics naïve-politically condemns me or forces on me that I am a kinsman? Whether this statue of Christ is a Narcissus mask or holy Puritanism of my morality, an aesthetic game or a neurotic routine, a chance forced association or a plain gift of grace — what can I care? What I have: a God as nostalgia (whatever the motive), a suffering as a *fait accompli.* And this Pietà is exactly that: God and destruction, an absolute solution, absolute death, the one and only God in whom one can believe because He is the one and only God who was disappointed in God — "My God, my God, why hast thou forsaken me?"[132] If I were to build an Escorial — this would be at its center: a narrow church full of statues portraying the dead Christ; like the branches of the weeping willow or bunches of grapes, lying like tumbledown columns or patients on an operating table, dangling in disorder, topsy-turvy. That would not be mystic-reined death gourmandism: it would arouse a much simpler, more positive impression. Oh, why is there no clay or paint at hand: how I would struggle with the clay, wrestle with it, with the statue preserving no more than a negative of the Sisyphean-movements, already a Pietà — my incompetent pawing of clay would willy-nilly carve a portrait of God.

⟫ 105 ⟫

Boston Weekly,[133] Thursday July 20, 1935:

1. Wolf-Heinrich Graf von Helldorf was named Police Chief of Berlin; Helldorf's imagined milieu: a horse track, gentleman-riders. Bright green turf: nature, poison, engineering symmetry. Wealthy manufacturers, elegant women. A jockey's dithyrambic nirvana sensation while galloping — the psychology of ultimate Bacchanalianism & ultimate nothingness *re:* the industrialist counting in the box; police terror *re:* worldly woman. Secret prison and boudoir, rubber truncheon and perfume, martyrdom and *Die Dame*-illustration,[134] legal hearing and flirt-dialogue: stretch these two extremes to the utmost.

2. Japan turns against Italy — a mystic priest dreams of the union of all colored people. A Black Buddha idol or an X.-Y. idol: the nature mysticism of Oriental religion and Japan's diplomacy, ancient legends & trances,

and the modern foreign policy of rearmament. The whole convention-burdened regional backdrop of Japan with its whole convention-burden: Japanese painting, Hokusai-essay. Immersion in nature and race myth — from fakir ethics to pantheistic nationalism.

3. Göring's actress wife[135] in her dressing room: the dramatic role — worldliness between the acts —, the husband lording it over the world: 3 German-flavored female *Räusche*.[136] German woman and fashion — chic Hegelianism.

4. Rosenberg[137] bathes in the North Sea with a crowd of immigrant Russian boys — mood of a Bachian '*nordische Passion*'; ascetic nudity, erotic nudity, hygienic nudity, battle nudity, philosophical nudity, myth nudity: all that being given expression with gestures on a cold afternoon beach as dusk is falling.

5. A Chinese cocaine and opium smuggler's ship in Odessa. Owner: a worldly, bemonocled Europeanized Chinese *grand seigneur*, his wife a Hollywood film actress. Distributing drugs among hundreds of thousands of starving, tatterdemalion orphans — description of a poverty-stricken juvenile gang of that kind — the film actress in one such cocainist & syphilitic rabble. The relationship of child and crime, child and 'ultimate' pleasure. Two poles: nineteenth-century positivist-

mathematizing history (superstition-sociology and su-
perstition-materialism) — and this disease and dream
caravan made up of these moribund children. What
has more or less in common with living real-humanity:
nineteenth-century social 'science' or this drooping-
eyed, ochre-tongued, cocainist juvenile mob? *Civitas
Dei, Civitas Dei, Die Vernunft in der Geschichte* [138] —
what is sociology, what is a dying flock of children?
The 'concept' of history, the university or editorial 'system' of intellectuals: that is higher nonsense — half-
dopey children hovering deliriously between sickness
and lust: that is lower nonsense. The distinction between Black Sea at Odessa and the German North
Sea; two colors, two kinds of mythology. The world
of theoretical male nudes of the North & the filthy
sailors' quarters of cities in the South. The depravity of
idealisms; a Byzantine residual holiness of decadences.

6. The opium-smuggling Chinaman finances the international society known as 'Liberté,' which is currently
waging propaganda on behalf of Abyssinia against Italy.
A typically human, historical matter: a savage African
land, where, let us suppose, the most bestial slavery and
torture of the poor reign — this country is defended
by a society which owes its existence to cocaine-addict-
ed Russian children, who scrape along between hired
killing and Dreamland: 'humanism' gets rich from child
syphilis — a so-called civilized country attacks a sadistic

slaveholding country (this is just schematic, not 'factual'), and 'attacks' — that is to say, kills & destroys in the name of charity. And that 'charity,' if it is accomplished: will be *summa injuria*,[139] apart from making the 'civilized' country rich. Who can a 'philosopher of history' sated with ethics stand beside?

7. Lemon still life: there are no lemons in London because Italy is using them to make up for the lack of water of their soldiers in Africa. In part, a continuation of Goethe's poem "Mignon" — *sachlich*-metaphorical,[140] natural historical-fantastic 'citrology,' in part: as if there were nothing else in the world than lifeless *objects* — a withdrawal reminiscent of Powys from an unaffirmable chaos of history.

8. Chorus of Berlin Jews. Without choruses there is no '*storia dell'arte*':[141] SA-chorus, morphine-addict children's chorus, Italian army chorus, Berlin Jews' chorus, Hollywood girls' chorus, Abyssinian slaves' chorus, Odessa sailors' chorus. If all of that is God's honest truth as sought by God, then it is: kitsch — if it is not the truth, not living, not of topical relevance, a posh 'solution' of the problem, then: art. In any event, what is the most fitting expression for the masses of the '*radikales Nichts*'[142] of modern history? Primitive naturalism or pathetic stylization, the bored mumblings of stage extras or a puppet theater caricature? Or a bit of

each style, all mixed up, indicating the vegetation of this mass that is beyond style. The dual attitude: the self-sacrificing Catholic love of the poor (Christ, 'the poor man!') and the ethics-independent viewpoint of the comedy writer and biologist (which are the same), the atmosphere of the 'Narrenschiff.'[143] An Old Testament analysis.

9. An Abyssinian missionary will be beatified in the Vatican. The relationship of nationalism and Catholicism. Two big scenes: one of which is the missionary in the jungle. Cf. Le Douanier Rousseau's naïve paintings of flowers and fruit; the saintly living priest and prehistoric animals and plants. An exhaustive 'mock-analysis' of fern forms and lizard colors, white monkeys, butterfly fish, red lianas, cucumber canoes — the world's inner, prehistoric semblance of atheism. Afterwards the prayers of the saint: the faith, man, primary in importance. The other scene in the Vatican: a disputation of scholarly priests at the proceedings in which beatification is debated. Three inorganic, heterogeneous worlds (that is what history consists of: there is history because each and every milieu and state is *de natura* absolutely *alien* from the other): the world of canonists, ecclesiastical *diplomats*, and moral theorists — the prehistoric, pre-human world of *white monkeys* — the lonely mysticism of the missionary, the *saint*.

⇐ 106 ⇒

I. *Dream*,

II. *Inner city*,

III. *Flowers*.

I cannot omit those elements — I live with them, & I shall die with them. If my life comes to anything, if there is an oeuvre out of it, then it will be these, only they can be its decisive elements: *a*) the biological formations as they're outlined in dreams through adhesions of memories (shards of memory here provide a service to the biological ground plans which in point of fact points to the abstract ornamentation like the condensing drops of water in a Wilson cloud chamber, marking the tracks of electrons & positrons: making them visible and plastic)[144] — *b*) worldliness, ultra-impeccable women, luxury autos, milliner's shops, business in men's fashions, tourist offices, hotel halls, open-air pools, brochures and fashion magazines, the formal world of casinos and expensive call houses (but *solely* as a *formal* world, excluding any ethical, practical, or psychological consideration) — *c*) the forms of flowers: petals, stamens, mushroom caps, clusters of leaves. Powysian 'sea-weeds,' mold spores and cross-sections of tropical lianas, including aspects of artificially constructed gardens, water, grass, reeds, stones, every infuriating and wild combination of water lilies and thorn-georgette.

There are three such elements. — As the first, a dream that I might call a '*pirouette à* Freud,' as the thing has the character of naïve-regular homage — all the elements that the Freudian soul-rococo was in the habit of sewing into his own little feminine Gobelin tapestry. There occurred in it two moral extremes: experiencing the holiness of the sanctity of marriage and experiencing the very early childhood sexual uncertainty, the dilettantism of the topic — the first was represented by a friend of mine who moved to the country and was going to get married there: I would visualize a farmstead garden (is there such a thing?) in fog, with pine trees, the fog grinding specks of mold in my throat, dispensing the idyllic fevers of warm sleigh rugs and fire hearths into my limbs, precisely this ascetic and bourgeoisly sleeping-capped mixed impression giving the sense of sanctity (that is not a definition!), a lyrical-impressionistic making one's way in the murk, in the forest, renouncing everything as if a future would no longer be possible, only memory turned material anew (that is something entirely different from the usual morphine-swift regaining of memories in dreams: in the present case I had no sense of that redeeming stupor — I simply saw and felt that the surroundings and my mental state were literal copies of the old, and everything else which was not them was just a 'dream'): at other times I had scarcely ever felt such an odd of mixture of prosaic hopelessness & bird-warm all-resolvedness.

Whereupon I awakened — the intermezzo was that fanatic moment totally kindred to madness when there is nothing in one, only a black awareness of sex similar to the heart stopping or a knife wound, a *reductio absurda ad genit.*,[145] a naïve-Orphic nostalgia after a positive amorous 'no further,' the almost murderous clairvoyance of being half-asleep.

Afterwards, of course, I immediately fell asleep, and the other smeared sex tableau appeared: a flourishing swimming pool from when I was eight years old. At that age a friend and I were always playing Odysseus, which was a mixture of a swimming race, adoration of towels, and confused love chattering and being active *"wie es im Buche steht."*[146] In my dream I labored with the sweet adult satisfaction in the naïvely mistaken belief that a love life by day was to be regarded as a closed business when in fact here was "indeterminacy" (last night I read Eddington's chapter on 'Indeterminacy and Quantum Theory'):[147] an extraordinarily rich but extraordinarily light and airy bunch of flowers (this may have been re-orchestrated into a vague feeling of the concept of a 'neutron') hanging onto the pale green rings of the basin. Someone next to me used exactly the same stresses as when it is *apropos* women: "What a superb *figure* the water has!" — obviously with reference to the rings. There is a possibility that *this* is love: the flowers dangling from spun candy and a Versailles-chandelier combined and the continually onward-rippling & flitting rings of water. "There is a possibility": that sober-sensual phrase has preserved Eddington's Anglo-Saxon empiricist and playful logic, its matter-of-factness, combined with *Alice in Wonderland*, which fitted so well with the phantasmagoria of the dream.

Sanctity — cramp — whatever: those three states of sex might be set out one after another in an encyclopædia. Then came the other kindred elements & officially permitted metamorphoses: the grandmother, a faraway city (area, foreignness), death, guilt, a female figure. The city was a composite of Ghent and Venice: a carnival mask of agoraphobia in eternal readiness, fears of traveling & fears of thinking becoming manifest. Meanwhile continual reassurances: "How far I am from home, yet I feel at home here" — of course, that was not as a result of psychological acclimatization but a tactile memory of home being rigidly retained in my skin, a tactile eruption as it were. At one point my grandmother, whom, somewhat surprisingly, I addressed familiarly as 'thee', attracted my attention, irritated and amused at my naiveté in taking her death seriously when she was alive (thinking back on it, how many times I dreamed of it "in vain") — all her swoonings and her death had been just games. Then someone really was buried: the big, craggily, and leafily landscaped coffin stood in a darkened church in the midst of a restless public — a long flight of stairs led down to the low-lying church, & at the bottom of the stairs, in a place reminiscent of a cloakroom and a museum interior, the person who was to be buried could be seen, though the person was not dead, but a repentant sinner riddled with disease: the body was propped up against some kind of counter in a floor-length shirt, loosely belted with a cord, in a single sloping line from head to toe, paying no attention to a few surrounding bystanders, who acted like powerless dressers around a sick actor behind the scenes. That figure was my sense of moral responsibility, my contrition, my paralyzing dejection on account of all my parodies of sex. Moral heraldics: a midnight church 'piebaldly-blind' (points of light as on a lake at midnight if a wave happens to form in such a way as to reflect a star that until then it had absorbed; Sun among dense boughs; black variants: shiny, dull, like silk, like a tree bough, et cetera: it was almost daylight due to the multitude of variations), the yellow steps, the repentant sick actor.

The other element is a city at daytime in summer. Lighting effects: above a shop window an awning with yellow and grey stripes. Under that a gold-colored, half hall-like, half metaphorically *feuille-morte* light, Spanish paint, goldfish scales and kid-glove softness, kid-glove precision. What was poetically dissolving in the light was offset by the Amazon-steadfastness of the window, the show-off asceticism of cubism. The milliner's: the background of the shop window was a rococo wooden decoration, the seemingly eternal raw material of 'elegance' — in front of it a huge blue ſtraw mushroom, rough meshes, fine polish, the sloppiness of meadows and urban cynicism of chemiſtry — the red tape might be the pathway of poppies towards sleep, its trace, a train of rouge in the breeze — but it is 'city'-stylized by a sadiſtic ſtumble, ribbon, or tear. Woman after woman: abſtractions of abſtractions, beſtialities of beſtialities. On their wriſts, gloves with huge cuffs, ſpinning tops, torpedoes, colossal rotating cones — above them the big lettering of the ſtore, Mercury's neon-light ſpelling book. Crazy commerce, crazy lazing about, affectation, ignorance of love, social injustices: nevertheless, redeeming, fateful true forms. Abyssinia, Abyssinia — the newſpapers cry out — what will these lovely women have to do with war? What fantaſtic diversity — from ſtock-market ſpeculator to count, from sun-tanned ſports ball to aging watercolor courtesan, from a sober and neat woman in her forties (in that certain dark-blue dress with white polka dots and a red belt!) through to bubbly-*mam'selles* expanding into blondeness, from ſtarchily, thickheaded-myſtically lounging cocottes to *millefleurs*-printed-fabric sisters: what maddening, breathtaking fineness of characters and textiles. What excites here: love? textile-technology? the meaning of hiſtory? a crisis in morphology? the psychology of swindling? The fact is that if I go along Petőfi Sándor Street & Váci Street

(I am incapable of going down *just one* of them):[148] I am overcome by an indescribable excitement, joy, the scenting of problems & optimism about solving them — in deliriously splendid waters of delirious fish-beatitude.

The third determining pillar of my *Catalogus Rerum*: plants — perhaps sometimes even more particularly plants photographed from close-up, *in the German fashion*, as living plants. The Germans make the best metaphysicians and the best technologists (irrespective of the extent to which metaphysics and technology are 'good' things in themselves): obviously, they are likewise masters of the art of 'sachlich' photography, which combines these two elements. In that marvelous inner city I purchased a picture book like that, which positively blessed me to bits for one morning with its external appearance. *Das nieverlorene Paradies. Aus deutschen Wäldern, Wiesen und Gärten. Ein Bilderwerk vom Pflanzenreich.*[149] The title page alone is "sweetest madness of a self-in-flowered lake": the counterpointing of concentric ripples of water, a latent interweaving of several subjects of light and shade from end-to-end: what from the front seems to be horizontality is verticality on the horizon, etc. The contrast of splash ovals and sun-baked leaf atoms; impartiality, idyll, jungle, precision, vegetation. Inside: giant white peonies in the foreground, forest lungs relaxing into grey dream sponges in the background — a marvelous expression of the awful blissful fact of the 'garden' —

of a world which runs from a perfume salon near the Vendôme to the plant masquerade of the most ancient prehistoric age. In addition: *"Atmende Algen in der Dorfquelle"*:[150] self-servingness, apoplectic time, thousand upon thousand underwater amulets of grotesque passivity. To all that theatrical nonsense of life, the physical & mathematical sharpness of the photograph, the book's human and mechanical printing-smell.

⇐ 107 ⇒

Two castles and two parklands lay next to each other. *Comme il faut*: one landowner has a son, the other a daughter. The son's father is dying — his sole wish is that his boy will marry the neighbor's girl. The boy's dowry: a perpetual linkage, the identity of death and the maiden; the unequivocalness of autumnal park & a heap of old weapons: the father's legendary heroism and the park's abundant melancholy: *one* & the same; a jumbling of armorial bearings, flowers, 'home,' and a little Venus-niche in the child's head. For years this is the sole topic of conversation in the boy's life: a maniacal cult of park and property, the dying father's eternal agony, the future as the 'bride,' without the girl or love ever once coming to mind. For him, war lives in his imagination without any moral or pathological aspects; the park's flowers & vitality do not yet so much as touch on the world of instinct whereas his fiancée is at most a confused grave cult. The time comes when he gets to know the designated girl — she immediately divulges that her father also wants to give her away to the boy for them to become spouses. The girl's father is an old skinflint: a regular Harpagon, a mythologizing merchant — he looks on marriage as a business deal, though not in the modern sense of business but in an ancient sense of 'religious business' stemming from the great age of immigrations, which is a big difference.

The dotard of a father lives in a permanent game of tarot, and the bridegroom's fate will not be the girl but the other three members of the card party — a curate, a hunter, and a sick man. He hardly ever meets the girl, all the more with the three nuts — the guest for a couple of days now of one, then of another.

The crude scheme of things works out as follows: the priest sets the boy ascetic ideals, playing the organ for him and teaching him to sing — he speaks of marriage as of retiring to a monastery. The hunter freezes him rigid for hours on end in forest hides during wintertime, meanwhile relating piquant stories to warm 'the cockles of his heart,' smutty anecdotes about peasants and kings, and similarly baffling phantasms about immorality without any relation to 'sin' or 'decadence' coming up. What about the sick man? He spends his time with the painting out of pessimism, women's complaints, hysteria, the pains of childbirth, menopausal melancholies, and misfortunate births; his library is full of pseudo-medical atlases, a colorful repository of grand guignol operations. The tragic morphology of provincial life: the endless æsthetics of the park — grace, gentility, tradition, poetry, silence, death harmony: that is the background, the stage. Overgrowing this solitude, the superstitions, manias, and these actors: sacristy neurosis, Rabelaisianism, and lechery in phobia-laden diseases.

What is a marriage? — the boy scratches his head. A mythical commercial purchase and sale? a cult of his father's death? sodomite body clattering? monastic gardening of virtue? or some sexually transmitted disease, the body's disgusting fate? He is barely able to think about the girl, barely able to be bothered with her — his every minute is taken up with selfish tarot playing.

The boy is versed in the world of medicinal plants — on one occasion he is called out to a sick woman, Farlenza, a friend of his fiancée. That is when a new chapter in the boy's life begins. Farlenza constantly entices the boy, though he is bound by his late father's wish, and anyway has been made melancholy by the troubled pedagogy of the tarot party. He now makes an acquaintance with the 'unrealizable dream' and the reality of 'impossibility.' He revolves around two poles of love — one is Farlenza's skirt, always slipping to a little above the knees, and the slightly thinning to white of her black silk stockings in the flexures of the knees — the other:

Farlenza's planned trip to the island of Formosa. A lot of men are courting her, but she wishes to have the medicinal herbalist. The boy's life acquires a rhythm of lying — at midday he has lunch with his senile governess in the castle in a candle-lit dark dining room and afterwards strolls on a long lakeside path to the recovering Farlenza, where he chats, courts her, suffers, strokes her knees, disconsolately feels jealous about the approaching trip to Formosa, eaten up by his own cowardice. Why does he not give up everything and go with Farlenza? A time comes when the Formosan wholesaler, to whom she will be traveling to work, sends her a wonderful Japanese tea service, which Farlenza unpacks in front of the boy, and they eat a snack from it. Everyone around Farlenza is nice to the boy, her older sister, father, and mother — as if he were the fiancé *here*. Furniture, vases, Farlenza's dresses and the path from Farlenza to the fiancée's castle (between two thick evergreen hedgerows — virtually purple they are so dense and on account of the late afternoon sun): for the boy that is the eternity of the reality of the unattainable, insoluble dream, hitherto unknown to him. The late afternoons & evenings he will spend with his fiancée.

At night he looks for hours at the Formosan ship in the harbor — getting to know its sailors; on one occasion he swims over the sea in order to carve her name on the boat. He does not dare stand beside it, however. Why? Why? He is able to visualize every nuance of missed opportunity that is 'on his lips.' Formosa: a lethal alienation, whether he is to go there with the girl or she is to go alone. He recounts a great deal to a sailor about the girl who will be traveling with them: as if she had long been his lover and he were glad to be getting rid of her. 'Still,' he recollects their pleasures well. He is somehow comforted to have turned the sailor on — better him than a stranger: at least there is *one* known person. He is now living practically for that sailor — he, in turn, is greedily devouring the 'piquant' stories. The time for *'embarquement'* comes round, the time for the wedding too — the ship sets sail two days beforehand. The young man lives on the ship, avoiding Farlenza as well, as if he has committed a crime against her. Of an evening he tipsily embraces and bites his fiancée. He had not been present when the ship set off — he went to a prenuptial confession. While the wind is gradually embracing the virginally unfurling sails by the right of *nox prima*, the boy is stepping into the confessional, treading, milling, and poisoning reality into nothing. Among the gifts after the wedding is a gorgeous atlas of flowers, with dedication, that is brought to the boy's house by Farlenza's kind old father.

⇐ 108 ⇒

Henry 'the Merchant,' King of England (45 years old),
Philip 'the Pallid,' King of Spain (22 years old),
Queen Ydoleza of Spain,
Princess Ucia d'Avar of Spain.

1. The ships of sickly King Philip, a ferocious Catholic but weak-willed, are pillaged by English pirates. Philip wishes to declare war, but his wife (who has sacrificed her whole life for her adored husband) is well aware that such a war would betoken Philip's death. Ydoleza therefore puts herself at the head of a delegation to England with the aim of sorting out the business peacefully even though she hates Henry much more fiercely because when she was in her girlhood, he had gravely insulted her more than once. Henry is a Henry VIII type, fat, arrogant, vulgar, lacking only romanticism and neurasthenia. Left alone with Ydoleza: after just two words he utters the crudest of insults to the queen, vilifying Philip and Spain with all the abandon of a loose-tongued drunk. Ydoleza won't take that any more and attacks him with a dagger but is able to inflict only a minor wound. Henry is overcome with disgust, fear, and suddenly inundated with melancholy: he quietly tells Ydoleza she should leave, he has no wish to see her, he does not want war, he wants nothing. On the ship bound homeward, she thinks constantly of her

visionary, semi-sacred, semi-poetic husband and decides that she is not going to report to him the English
king's dockworker vituperations.

2. Princess Ucia d'Avar, who is living on her own
in her castle, is violently in love with Philip the Pallid. Philip is a weak man: sometimes going out to hunt
with her and alternately spending poetic days with
her in the depths of the forest (mushrooms and ferns)
— at other times cursing and driving her away as the
epitome of immorality, a Satanic spider of the Catholic crown and the Catholic bed. She is living in exile
at present — but manages to slip back. Ucia's greatest
torment is that the king treats her as a symbol of sin:
she debates pedantic arguments from one end to the
other with the most fantastic heretics, with Arab and
Jewish philosophers, in order to refute the principle
of the sanctity of marriage: for all her blind manias
she does not wish to be a *maîtresse* of anathemas but
'legality.' Neither heretics nor Jews manage to convince
her: she sends the king to sleep, has him kidnapped
to her castle, and there, at a sham wedding with her
younger brother dressed up as a bishop, has herself
wedded to him. Ucia d'Avar's monologue to her seemingly dead 'husband': the profoundest instinct for ethos,
the profoundest instinct for games, the profoundest
rhetoric of female vitality.

3. Ydoleza returns home — she keeps Henry's vilifications secret. From his spouse's sickly melancholy, however, Philip suspects something is wrong, with the concealment sometimes irritating him to the point of driving him crazy. The whole of Spain is seething against England: England, however, is mighty and Spain weak as a nag on the point of croaking, down to skin and bones. Its government is in Ydoleza's strong hands. Her dilemma: if she were to allow Philip to govern, he would go to rack and ruin the next day — now that she is there to ensure that would not happen, she is making her husband look spineless, which is gnawing away at him. He is not eating — he tussles for days on end with impotent hatred with a shade of Henry grown to mythical proportions. His Catholic ethics forbid that magical hostility — but those same ethics dictate that the heretic mercantile land be punished for its despotism. Ydoleza herself goads Philip into loving Ucia d'Avar in order that he should not be tormented by his visions.

4. Spanish rebels kill the Queen. Philip is left alone with two sins — his hatred of mythical Henry and his blackly selfish love. He is incapable of entering a second marriage even though he is cohabiting with the princess. Spain breaks apart into oligarchies. Philip secretly voyages to England on a French merchant vessel in order to have it out with Henry. He is captured

in London — Henry has him taken, in chains, to the black salon where he had scuffled with Ydoleza. The interview is brief: he abuses Philip, mocking and denigrating him as an immoral rag, sick, a heretic, a poseur and poet. He then has his soldiers toss him into the sea as if he were a madman. Philip, however, survives.

5. Ucia d'Avar travels to London. Posing as a court lady-courtesan, she succeeds in assassinating the English king.

6. The pope's ship is threatened with being sunk by a storm when the sailors discover the dead body of a woman clinging to the leaking side of the ship — it is the corpse of Ydoleza, who had been cast into the sea. The storm abates; the ship has miraculously weathered it. The Spanish queen's body is now carried to Naples by the venerational papal Crusader ships. Philip arrives in Rome at the time of her canonization to sainthood, which is followed by rapturous celebrations. As a secretive Saint Alexius, he prays at one of the altars newly erected in his wife's name: a description of the statue is the first external analysis of Ydoleza.

7. Ucia d'Avar arrives in Rome. Philip sees the canonization of his wife as resolving and redeeming his entire life: there is nothing in him but peace and this definition of the Earth — "It is a great star" (since her penance

in London he has talked to himself in English).[151] That final reconciliation is unsettled by Ucia d'Avar, who with savage joy displays the bloody dagger with which she slew the English King, the vitiator of Philip's life. "Choose: do you need me, who punished the murderer of your soul — or the relics of that secretive, sacred puppet, who tied your hands like a small child." Philip the Pallid abandons the daughter of sanctity and the daughter of killing — he runs off and vanishes.

⇐ 109 ⇒

A PERENNIAL 'questio naturalis': yellow flowers nod over the clipped green hedges in the garden as if they had no stem, or at least the stems that are visible did not belong to the flowers: burning, suggestive ochre rosettes, butterfly hypotheses, umbrellas, kisses mildewed into mist, awakening nipples of nothing — all irrational loveliness, resolvedness, dew-harmony, perfection joyfully from time immemorial… And man, the life of song: morality, suffering, secret, formlessness, knowledge & the life of badly drawn, clumsy death. Both that early-August yellow flower and my physiologically miserable existence are nature — the heavenly grace and fateful quietness of boughs, the distorted looping and sadistic dance of sick souls are the *same* nature. Who can understand that and is able to close the question at that?

The sickbed stands beside the garden window, the sweat of feverishness is closer to the dew on grass than two yachts in the crowded harbor of Naples. While the poisoned scents of intellectual brooding, an intent on moral sacrosanctness, blind desperation, and mechanical blasphemy breathe out of me by turns as I search perplexedly for roles as a patient: a holy patient, Philistine patient, infant patient, listless patient, merry patient, 'normal' patient — out in the garden, newer sunlight brainwaves, newer shadow frescoes, colors, sounds, animal noises, plant whisperings assail one — rain, dawn, wind, rustling of leaves, the splendid color game of flowers opening.

Do both have *one* cause: the well of body and soul desperation, and the well of happiness and beauty? Can *one* God have wanted this? Or is there a world of 'God-man-suffering' & another world of 'nature-beauty-happiness,' for ever and ever independent of that: Did the two of them, my illness and the beauty of dahlias, only accidentally come side by side, blown towards each other by a cosmic wind, like the autumn leaves of far-off gardens on a street? To whom should I listen, be guided by? Should I let my heart yearn for the beauty of flowers like for something realistically achievable, or should I kill those yearnings as the mistake to cap all mistakes: can a prisoner of the 'God-man-suffering' circle ever break through into the 'nature-beauty-happiness' circle — can the one style not learn anything from the other?

Perhaps I am nothing other than a broken-down dahlia, a degenerate flower: a hundred million years later these silver olive trees, sumacs numbed blue by the dawn, lilac leaves downcast like blood-steeped livid and thousand-fold Jesus-hearts will one and all likewise decay until 'consciousness,' into the pathology of 'self-awareness': I cannot for a moment free myself of the idea that thought is a *disease* of life, a false note and decadence — I am incapable of setting about any cogitation while I see mutely triumphant flowers on my bed table and in my window: thinking is comic & *grotesque*; a plus vis-à-vis the flowers, but like a tumor or gaudy skin rash.

In my fever I see that hitherto no one has been a determinist, an absolute, radical, fantastical & suicidal determinist: someone who in every quiver of thought, morality, anti-thought and anti-morality saw a mere curvature of petals, root sores, spraining of spermatozoa & cancer of the nerves. One only has to look over the history of language, etymologies, semantic comparisons, word borrowings, wasting & stinginess of verbal forms, i.e., the most important means of expression of thought: what infantile imprecision, disarray, chaos, absent-mindedness, deception. One also has to look over the thinking in our souls that does not seek linguistic expression: what dreamlike, amorphous sketches, dependent on biological opalescences, nothing but evanescence, perpetual motion, vicious circle. And the thought that I know thinking is like that, something unreliable by nature: that thought is just as unreliable. Or is there inside me a self that without reflection is mistrustful of thought?

Meanwhile I count off decade after decade of *Aves* on my rosary: the Virgin Mary is much less problematical than God. Since perspiring is the central rite of illness, it is above all the sentence "Who sweated blood for us" after the name of Jesus — the habit has remained from my childhood apprehension of imagining every word, or, to be more specific, of visualizing *something* lest it become vacuous — even here I do not see the Christ's sweat-drenched body but his parted hair in bronze or blackish-red like two long hands loosely joined in prayer, the tips of the fingernails meeting. Who would be able to analyze the components of the faltering prayers in a fever? A swinging between any-old-god & dogmatically outlined Catholic Christ, a paradoxical pleading for faith, naïve self-insurance, pastime, cowardice, heroism, experimentation, histrionic nihilism and playroom self-assurance? Undoubtedly, I would have been very religious since long, long ago if I did not feel myself to be of 'religious temperament' par excellence: this determination of mine for religion absolutely inhibits — I feel too neural, biologically prepared to be able to follow. But if I were not religious in character, I could not be religious *ab ovo*.

Shall I truly go to the grave (to cretinous hypochondriacs the grave is a day-to-day tidbit of pain), in such a way that I shall only have *expressed* (and even so that would be the best possible eventuality) the spheres of 'God' and of 'pretty flowers' in life: doing that without having arranged them in a rational hierarchy on a strict scale of yeses and values? Is everything just a domain of questions, but the 'answer' has been all but completely removed from the mental arsenal of humanity? Is it possible to imagine an optimal position for man in which one keeps one's brain, that is, one's ability to think, and at the same time the neurosis to question, metaphysical secretion, is *totally* worn away from it? Hardly. Either the brain: in which case the abiding openness of the problem — or else a hovering happiness of flowers, but in that case no brain.

Why am I an artist, not a 'thinker'? Because I am more attracted by the fact of problematicalness as a theatrical spectacle than by the 'dry' syllogistic of answers? Or because I am very much a *non*-artist but rather a thinker, and I see that the maximum performance of which the human brain is capable is precisely the description of the domains of questions, mythological-hidebound acceptance of them as a closed endowment?

Every circumstance of my illness (the illness itself is utterly insignificant, of course) was a question, so that however much I am *able* to describe only complexes of questions — as for *wanting*, I want answers. That is not going to succeed, as I was well aware in my bed: after all, my chief excitement was the possibility of describing the one whose make-up is that of an 'absolute questioner' — how it might be possible to express in literary terms the sterility of one's cerebral functions in such a way so as not to arouse the impression of either a minor or major neurasthenia (even if it was), but as a species of Greek heroism. It is an old postulate of mine that it is impossible to make a distinction between a neurasthenic question & a logical question; that I don't wish my figure to leave a neurotic impression, that is caused rather by my sensitivity to etiquette — a neurasthenic person is not fit for society, not appetizing, whereas my absolute intellectual martyr has to be fit for society in order for me to carry him around for propaganda purposes.

Describing the entirety of 'consciousness' as being the cause of all troubles. In front of me is a landscape: blossoming trees, semi-neglected garden hillsides — all leafless, dry branches and supple osier lashes, smothered by tiny pink & lilac flowers pouring all over them — all looking as if a surf of flowers were pouring down like rain all the way down the slope, with the branches hastily poking up for air. That is neither an abstract nor a luxuriant image: a million pearls of water without a single sound, a single drop of moisture. The single unswishing sweeping curve of the billow over towards the slope is splendid, and so, too, the flashing into the air

of the unruly branches which intersect it, like an anarchic bishop's crozier at a sanguinary synod. Self-
oblivious prolificacy, sparkling health, the ever-clearer
sounding beauty of the melody could not find a more
expressive god than this image — but if I imagine the air
as a feeling-sensitive *consciousness* then it is in the body
of the air: a painful disease, inoperable lethal prolifera-
tion, death's slow net. If on the other hand I *withdraw*
consciousness from myself, then the rotting basalt of
my guts is not a disease, a weight pulling down the balance of human 'suffering' (which is to say morality) but,
for instance, a gold-footed king mushroom, Cleopatra's
bracelet or the Nile's mud — as it is customary to call
flowers and mushrooms. That is perhaps the hardest
thing about illness: one doesn't know whether to play
the role of the relativist or absolutist before the nurse.

⇐ 110 ⇒

A SYMBOL OF UNPROBLEMATICALNESS: a bunch
of daisies that have begun to wilt slightly. I cannot have
enough of the variation of the curls of the individual
petals — of the kaleidoscope of endearing dishevelment
and maidenly crumpledness. To speak in broad generalities, each of them reminds me of the Dutch millstone ruffs of Frans Hals models as, slightly crooked on
getting out of a carriage, they become crumpled under

the cloak, with the odd iron mounting or spoke wilting. How much enchanting inadvertence, unproblematic child chaos, baby grimace and toy tumbling-down there is in these petal curls.

Here are a few examples or tricks:

1. the petals all smooth out, becoming as straight as an arrow, like Stuart-collars of starched organdie,[152] but one or two suddenly curls up under itself, like the bangs on Katharine Hepburn's forehead: there is an unanalyzable impishness, a white coquetry, in this unexpected little curlicue at the ends of two petals;

2. another flower 'saws the air': one of the petals is rearing up like a pomaded moustache, another is drooping downwards like a maid's legs outwards from a window on the first floor in a Spanish suburb — one up, the other down, with a childish rigorousness of untidiness: one can almost literally hear the sounds that three-year-old infants coax out of a piano if by chance the keyboard falls into their hands;

3. each petal, all the way round, uniformly bends away from the yellow center: that disclosure of the calyx represents the banal affectation of undressing a banal grand cocotte — all immaculate elegance, worthy 'lines,'[153] 'large-scale' pose, hotel-mystique, grandiose falsity. That is how the lady of the camellias moves in a puppet theatre;

4. here, too, every petal participates in the same manner in the 'decaying party': only not in elegant un-ſtitching arches but in tight, turban-like scrolls, they immediately crouch and twiſt at their base under the yellow pillow of the ſtamen. (This afternoon, I saw that geſture being taken to absurdity on the yellow flower of an inner-city flower shop: the pillow of the ſtamen was arching into the air like a fountain, whereas the pet-als — there were only three or four of them — were drooping down, like the drips of a candle falling into nothingness at the foot of a magnified flame.) The yel-low is like a precious gem, the 'curve'-maniacal petals like a medieval ring mounting;

5. yet another variant juſt at random: a squashed ſpider formation, where as a matter of faét every single one of the petals is crushed, wilted, maimed, ripped, or pulled in a different manner: a lot of them are miss-ing, like broken teeth (that might conſtitute a separate 6th variant), the remainder are umbrella ſpokes and tassels in Teleki Square.[154] — When I have been medi-tating for weeks on the internal order of the decay of the individual, sickness, when I meditate, likewise for weeks, on the external order of decay of the colleétive, so-called hiſtory: ſpoliation of daisies is my enigmatic joy, & for me a riddle, not tragic at all, but downright charming, young-missy free and easy, young-missy vacuous.

⟫ III ⟪

ONLY in recent times have I reacted with extraordinary sensitivity to the magical-medicine-man effects of the major languages: on the Orpheus-dance and the Sibylline-hocus-pocus of English, German, & French that millions upon millions of tongues perform in millions upon millions of mouths in 'modern' Europe. And it is not brought to one's consciousness that a language itself is a living creature, a living superstition, a living myth, a living Neander-valley and sacrosanct imprecision, mumbo jumbo. In recent times there has been no literature for me, only language — every book is inundated, drenched, destroyed as a 'work' by the language in which it is written. (That is why Joyce's *Work in Progress* is important above all others: here the writer only wants, or only knows, first and foremost language — though of course such *only-language-language* is no longer language but something else.)[155]

I read Sir Thomas Browne's *Hydriotaphia* and *The Garden of Cyrus* at almost the same time — as well as one of the newer novels by Mauriac.[156] It was possibly those two books, or rather 'language-mushrooms,' which were the cause of my crisis of sensitivity to language. It may be that illness favorably disposes the human body to enjoy 'outward appearances' (there has not so far been an outward appearance in the world about which it did

not turn out that it was the quintessence of essences):
last year my wife read out to me at my sickbed a Powys-
text, & since in her mouth words do not reach the air
by a direct route but after yachting, meandering about,
like a water lily floating on the surface of a lake, rocked
despite the lack of any perceptible breeze: loosely,
sketchily forming the syllables, only grasping each
sound with its muscles like the rather widely spread
green calyx around the petals of an overgrown carna-
tion — maybe that was the reason why I was only able
to pay attention to the savor of the words irrespective
of their meaning. *Savor*: for the time being that is a
good word for it; certainly not, under no circumstances,
the 'music' of the words. "Irrespective of their meaning"
— nor is that quite right as it stands — it was more a
question of my enjoying the meaning of each separate
word, its etymology shucked, *insulated*, rich in semantic annual rings (independent of the sentence and the
writer's 'thought'): a single sentence length in twenty
or thirty cross-sections.

Sir Thomas Browne's language is *archaic*: it is natural
that it can only be conspicuously a *linguistic* experience.
Mauriac, on the other hand, is a contemporary writer,
yet all the same I shall forever feel Tacitus and Virgil in
French — he is a modern writer who still keeps me in
an even more archaic archaism language-mood than the
seventeenth-century Englishman.

How many things a language can be, what extremes: it can be (as it is with Browne) a bubbling archaeoplasma, a silting oil, sticky chlorophyll, congestion, vital mosaic, muddled clump, the material and ground for sporulation of the concrete — and, as with Mauriac, it can also be crystalline, ascetic simplicity, numerical elementariness, glassy geometry & ice preserving reality in symbolic extracts. This does not just concern two *writers*, two individual *styles*, or other such gentlemanly matters — it is a biological issue of the mouth posture, the gingival, lingual, and pharyngeal muscles of two kinds of populaces.

In reading old texts, the greatest delight does not lie precisely in the verbal curiosa but, quite the reverse, the *commonest* words are given a mystic-homely emphasis: instead of 'blue' all one has to write is 'blew' & that banal word becomes at once important, isolated, of great value like the rarest jewel. That is the main sense of archaism: it hallows and ritualizes triviality. It is not just ordinary words which step out before us in hieratic actor's masks but the most elementary grammatical relationships and clause structures: subject — predicate, an attributive and its noun, co-ordination & subordination — all at once pop to the surface in these antiquated sentences like protruding veins or bone structures slipping out of overcooked fish: one sees before one's eyes the embryonic grid of the language's logic, the still flexible wax bones: "how nature Geometrizeth"— as Browne writes.[157]

What is together in this Browne text? Everything that I myself aspire to as 'work' and 'composition' is present there as language, as pitching syntax. In it is time — history's eternal enigma of passing, the historical ambiguity of eternal identity & the withering into nothing from one second to the next, the Janus-paradox of time itself — when he writes: "Oak-apple, pill, woolly tuft, *foraminous* roundles upon the leaf, & grapes under ground..."[158] — all of a sudden I get a sense here of unvarying, *everlasting* nature and its unchanging eternal analyst: humankind, yet I nevertheless sense the experience of a single individual eccentric, perished into a single *past*, never-recurring date, which is so unique as to be almost 'never.' That juicy-melancholy double savor can only be bestowed on that mythical never-never & single 'oak-apple'-idyll running back millennia by the old language, a text matured in its witheredness.

Alongside the indispensable flavor of time there is a second Brownian experience: the *all*. Innocently, picaresquely, without neuroses of synthesis: the *all*. In one of the works, every conceivable burial procedure and corps; in the other, every pentangular and rhomboidal form in nature and art. Today that 'all' is, of course, a *linguistic* all: the mass of concrete facts, historical and medico-botanical data is concrete for me not because it gets at the real objects behind them but because it covers them — *only* words are left, but the masquerade of signs is richer than the masquerade of facts. What an opalinely vibrating rich world are the three or four words of: "folious and stalky emission"[159] — an unbalanced casting of Latin and English words, what a reassuring uncertainty of scientific dryness and popular adjectival designation. Orthography, typographical customs, the etiquette for capital letters & italics all serve to make the linguistic El Dorado more dazzling, more colorful, to make the ancient 'morality' of the English language: the Germanic-Latinate clash stand as nakedly as possible before one's eyes. Here the Germanic and Latinate words — that is to say, the trump cards of vital sensuality and rational sensuality — behave with the shamelessness of a sodomite: "... cretaceous and chalky concretions": the entire metaphysics of 'expression' inheres in tautologies of that kind.[160]

A balance of sense and nonsense can only be found in such old (and at that primarily 17th century) texts (Browne is more Joycean than Joyce): every sentence moves between the life-and-death-precision and overscrupulous naturalism of medical specialist books and what for us are incomprehensible superstitions & humbug words vibrant with resounding vapidities. It is besides the point that what for me is nonsense is precisely the science in it, & what I understand is useless frippery — the main thing is that I always sense the two simultaneously, and can a work be truly captivating if only one of the two elements is present — can, for example, a work which can at all times be fully understood be understood? No. The ideal blend of sense & nonsense is natural where it is a matter of all: the 'much' is equally the experimental ground of reality and the fictitious. A hetæra's phantom, agate monkey, and amber elephant: what is reality here and what fiction? For me a phantom is a more prosaic and down-to-earth reality than agate or amber. When Browne rattles off one of those lists every 'fussy' distinction gets lost in the thousand-jointed undulations of language: language was the first and language will be the last, everything else is immaterial.

I read *Urne-Buriall* when sick with a fever: the language was so visionally tasty that I almost put on weight due to it — I imbibed other-worldly wines poured into graves ("some yet retaining a *Vinosity* and spirit in them"),[161] flame-baked "Metropolis of humidity" (the cerebrum), and "seminal humor."[162] Xenogenesis derivation ("vinosity"), the semi-rhetorical, semi-diagnostic metaphor: in short, the autonomic reflex-jerks of the tongue muscles — for me that was the worldlike world in the bed.

A writer should not feel free to take up a pen without reading Browne (the far madder and precisely on that account much more monotonous Burton is not like that)[163] — it is here, outside *mathesis*, that the functioning of the human brain can be viewed in its most pathological freshness. Either *mathesis* or Sir Thomas Browne — there is nothing else: either a non-existing, non-live self-centered world or a human, live, but totally chaotic breed, jumbled to its last atom. "The sensible

Rhetorick of the dead" — says Sir Thomas:[164] indeed, that can be the only school of literature, its topic for critical self-examination, its book of ſpiritual exercises. Literature is something profoundly grubby as compared with mathematics, and mathematics profoundly 'other-worldly' as compared with literature. In the language of today we do not perceive the 'grubby,' alluvial, shoddy character. But in the language of the 17ᵗʰ century, the prowling in time & ſpace of all languages is perceptible: in the language of the 17ᵗʰ century it is precisely not the 17ᵗʰ century which is sensed but the third, the 14ᵗʰ, & the 15ᵗʰ, i.e., each separate, undigeſted, raw temporal layer, preserved in various words — in Old English it is precisely the English of which one is not conscious but the Danish, the Germanic, the Latin and the Norman.

A writerly writer has to feel, before he ſtarts writing, that his inſtrument is something essentially, fantaſtically different from the musician's, the mathematician's, or the painter's: his inſtrument is materialized inaccuracy, chance reflex cryſtals (which is what words are, after all), a whole lot of debris out of the utterances of big brains & phobia-lashed primitive humans, the muscle-twitchings and cerebral vegetation of a heterogeneous and contourless shoddy mass (that sort of thing is politely called 'word' and 'thought'), the impure cultural sludge of praċtice and sorcery, decorative barking and fallacious sound etiquette: that is language and *that* is the inſtrument of literature.

When I was writing *Prae*, one of my main excitements was caused by this colossal, elemental filthiness of the instrument of literature: the unclarified mixing of word, thought, meaning, and beauty, and my main wish was to knead a basic dough out of the above-named heterogeneous elements that could be handled as being as clean and *homogeneous* as color, sound, or numbers. In *Prae* that was one of the particularly *prae'* things: the chemical hypothesizing of an instrument of literary expression.)

In contrast to Browne is the French language, which betrays itself when infinite poverty (a vocabulary does not count as wealth, of course) has to follow modern technique: at such times it is every bit as ludicrous as those 'classical' Latin texts that grammar school pupils sometimes compose to relate their experiences at a motorbike race or a radio exhibition.

How different, after the Brownian sentences, is this kind of thing: "... *les pins se transmettent pieusement dans leurs branches unies.*"[165] In English, Latin was the same kind of thing as a stolen jewel in the stomach of a cannibal: it became the hocus-pocus of scholarship — here, though: it is a refined, elegant cubism and color diversion that renders reality vitreous, chemically extracted. One could not go as far as to claim that this is 'abstract,' 'logical' *par excellence'* — after all: there is plenty of plasticity in it — 'chemistry' is a fairly good word here — a landscape described in French (e.g., the Bordeaux countryside familiar to Mauriac) bears the same relationship to the real one or to the English as the totality of chemical components laid out in the real one do to a white tale, in glittering bottles, concentrated on plates — besides living trees & lakes. In the end, coal, iron, hydrogen and sodium are not 'logical,' not 'abstract,' not by any chance formulas.

The French text twists and twines in a fever of reality just as much as it does in the English — except we may not have clarified for ourselves, perhaps, what the decisive criterion of reality is: every vital detail, the magnificence of its articulation — or, on the contrary: the entirety, the simple reduction.

"*Dénués de toute malice*":[166] that, too, is plasticity, of the very best at that — but the plasticity of essential, universal, symbolic gestures. It is as a result of this that the 'abstract-rational' French language in point of fact is much more myth-laden than poetic-plastic English.

When I read Mauriac two things were always buzzing around in my head: one was this constant mythical sublimity — the other, the dreadful greyness, consuming cruelty, and vitriolic-prosaicness of Parisian houses, streets, customs: "*… ces deux amours avaient eu une source unique*":[167] the words '*amour*' and '*unique*' are, in part, hollowed out, devoid of content, like a grey frame; in part, though, they are not so much words as Olympian deities: Amor & Unus are mythical participants. The fantastically ascetic profile of the Parisian house, divesting the word of its mythical part, kept only the grey frame, the horrified tenor of generalities, the blind and deaf internationality ('amor,' 'unus'!) that throws everyone to the ground when they visit Paris.

A splendid book on the subject of Browne–Mauriac could be written in the form — *Two Criteria: The Garden of Cyrus and Paris*: where the two realities could be allowed to run on *ad absurdum* — for one thing, as an agglomeration of a million details; for another, as a regular chemistry of the most essential matters, a cubistic ballet of the most essential gestures.

⇐ II2 ⇒

FOR DAYS I have been hearing children crying around me — as if they had conspired to, or as if the crying were arriving like birds of passage or certain fruit in the garden, stars in the sky — it is now the crying season, the season for furious animal wailing. One could not find a more mortal, reproachful, question-impregnated flower of disconsolateness, selfishness, fate-stupidity and fate-indifference than such an almost suicidally ('horror-orgasmic' is a good epithet for it) sobbing child's face. I feel the word 'metaphor' is ridiculous in the midst of that rattling chorus. Towards the one & only metaphor? I wonder if my own fate will not be precisely the opposite: out of a million metaphors towards the one and only — *person?*

ENDNOTES

1 'Intimate countryside of disease.' This, and all of the notes that follow, are those of the translator & were not part of the original Hungarian publication.

2 Friedrich Gundolf (1880–1931) was a German-Jewish literary scholar, poet, & one of the most famous academics of the Weimar Republic. *Shakespeare und der Deutsche Geist* (Shakespeare and the German Spirit), which Gundolf wrote to obtain a university lectureship in 1911, was a turning point in German language and literature studies.

3 Hermann Minkowski (1864–1909) was a mathematician who used geometrical methods to solve problems in number theory, mathematical physics, and the theory of relativity.

4 In English in the original. All further instances of Szentkuthy's own English will be signified with the font Scala Sans.

5 See Genesis 3:19.

6 In French, as in Hungarian, this phrase means that something is introduced out of the blue, incongruously, without having anything to do with what is being talked about. In a word, far-fetched.

7 A grace word meaning essentially *Benedictus benedicat* (May the Blessed One bless).

8 Bronislaw Huberman (1882–1947) was a celebrated Jewish Polish violinist of the first half of the twentieth century.

9 The reference is to the painting of *Susanna and the Elders* by Il Tintoretto (1518–94), a work that also figures prominently in §95 of Szentkuthy's *Marginalia on Casanova*.

10 I.E., weakling.

11 'Sweetness.'

12 Sir Arthur Stanley Eddington (1882–1944), a British astrophysicist of the early 20th century, had a gift for explaining the concepts of relativity. This particular textbook (published by the University of Cambridge Press in 1923) was considered by Einstein to be "the finest presentation of the subject in any language," but his later insights into this and other abstruse topics were gathered into other books such as *New Pathways in Science* (Messenger Lectures of 1934 & published the following year).

13 I.E., with an inferiority complex.

14 M13 (or NGC 6205) is a globular cluster almost visible to the naked eye in the constellation Hercules and was discovered by Charles Messier in 1764.

15 The original Hungarian word here is *"ſportarielek,"* an inventive neologism of Szentkuthy's. He fuses *"ſport"* and "Ariel" (*The Tempeſt*) due to its closeness to "aerial."

16 *The Lady of the Camellias* (*La Dame aux camellias*) is the title of a novel by Alexandre Dumas *fils*. It was published in 1848 & adapted for the ſtage in 1852, thereby becoming the basis of Verdi's 1853 opera *La Traviata*.

17 Charles Gounod (1818–93) ſtarted composing (but never completed) a Suite Burlesque, drawn from music for his opera *Roméo et Juliette* (1867).

18 In Greek mythology, Ananke is the goddess of inevitability, compulsion, and necessity.

19 Praxiteles was a Greek sculptor who flourished c. 370–330 BC and whose works include a ſtatue of a shorthaired Aphrodite of Cnidus (Knidos), copies of which are now held, e.g., by the Glyptothek Munich. Allegedly this had as a model the courtesan Phryne, and the moſt faithful replica is the Colonna Venus (Vatican Museums).

20 The reference is to the main protagoniſt of Molière's play *L'Avare* (The Miser), with Molière himself playing Harpagon when it was originally ſtaged in 1668.

21 The source of the quotation (cited by Szentkuthy in English) is not known but is presumably the Bible, either Revelation or The Book of Daniel 7:3–7: "And four great beasts came up from the sea, diverse from one another… After this, in the visions of the night I saw a fourth beast, terrifying, horrible, and exceedingly strong…"

22 The source of the quote is not known. A literal translation gives: "Dreams are the land of accents."

23 "Midnight, fog haze, sunshine, sailor at sea, day & night, the unbounded splendor … of color and crossings."

The couplet 'Das ist denn doch das wahre Leben…' stands in the middle of Johann Wolfgang von Goethe's 21-verse lyric poem "Wilhelm Tischbeins Idyllen" (Wilhelm Tischbein's Idylls, published in 1821). Tischbein was a German painter Goethe had befriended during a trip to the Italian peninsula from 1786 to 1788 and for whom he sat for what has become his best-known portrait. Roughly translated:

Roses are given birth to in darkness,
it flees, so easily so noble in intent;
the sun shines on its heels.
That is, then, real life's delight,
Where blossoms also hover late at night.

24 Banality and music: what a strange realm!

25 Evidently a play on the earlier quotation.

26 A reference to Charles Frederick Worth (1825–1895) and The House of Worth, a French company that specialized in haute couture, read-to-wear clothes, and perfumes. Worth is generally recognized as the father of haute couture. See also §110.

27 Luxury death.

28 *Zeitlose Kunst. Gegenswartsnahe Werke aus fernen Epochen* (Timeless Art: Close to the Present from Remote Epochs) was published by Phaidon-Verlag of Vienna in 1934. It featured a collection of 132 monochrome illustrations selected & annotated by art historian Ludwig Goldscheider.

29 The very idea.

30 "A very small series of negativities."

31 The idea of the *action gratuite*, the 'gratuitous or disinterested act,' one which has no motivation, was introduced by André Gide in a 1914 novel that was translated into English in 1925 in the US as *The Vatican Swindle* or *Lafcadio's Adventures* (*The Vatican Cellars* in the UK) & later developed by other authors, especially by Albert Camus and Jean-Paul Sartre.

32 *Geworfenheit* (thrownness) is a term used by philosopher Martin Heidegger in *Sein und Zeit* (*Being and*

Time), first published in 1927, to describe our individual existences as 'being thrown' (*geworfen*) into the world. Szentkuthy owned the 1931 Verlag edition of *Sein und Zeit* and his copy is dated (in his own hand) as being read in 1933, 1964, & 1966. It also includes March 10 as one specific reading date, though no year is listed for that date. Hence, he read the book at least once before writing *Towards the One & Only Metaphor*. On the title page of the book, Szentkuthy listed a series of dates — "1933–1964, VII. 26., 1966 III.10." — and drew a bold arrow pointing to this marginal note: "L. Simone de Beauvoir, *A kor hatalma*, 329. oldal." On that page, Heidegger's (as others: Barrault, Giono) name is circled three times & the page contains several marginal notes. For the French edition, see Simone de Beauvoir, *La force de l'âge*, Vol. 1 (Paris: Gallimard, 1960) 363.

33 Oh, delightful doll of negativity!

34 Complete Morphology of Summer.

35 Heinrich Emil Brunner (1889–1966) was a Swiss Protestant (Reformed Church) theologian who, along with Karl Barth, was strongly associated with neo-orthodoxy or the dialectical theology movement. The book in question (*From the Work of the Holy Spirit*) was published by Zwingli-Verlag in 1935.

36 What an (ostentatious) display!

37 Most blessed comedy.

38 Nature doing what nature does.

39 Death will be astounded. The phrase is used in the
     Tuba mirum section of the requiem mass in Latin:

> *Mors stupebit et natura, cum resurget creatura,*
> *judicanti responsura.*

> Death and nature will be astounded, when all
> creation rises again, to answer the judgment.

40 The line appears at the very end of Chapter 7 (Book
     of Timur) in Goethe's *West-Eastern Divan*, a collec-
     tion of poems written between 1814 and 1819, an
     expanded version of which was printed in 1827:

> *Nicht mehr auf Seidenblatt*
> *Schreib' ich symmetrische Reime,*

> No more on silken leaf
> Write I symmetric rhymes,

41 Ololoumena. An invented Greek word of Szent-
     kuthy's own, as the following root.

42 Frederick II (1194–1250), Holy Roman Emperor
     and head of the House of Hohenstaufen, was based
     in Sicily but his influence stretched through Italy to
     Germany. One of his mistresses was Richina (Ruthi-
     na) of Beilstein-Wolfsöden, by whom he had an il-
     legitimate daughter, Margaret, who married Thomas
     of Aquino (Tommaso d'Aquino; † 1251), by then the

first count of Acerra, who in turn was related to St. Thomas Aquinas (1225–74).

43 'Art of love.'

44 A reference to Henry Avray Tipping (1855–1933), a fairly prolific author whose main interest was gardening and garden design, and Charles Latham's book *In English Homes* (London & New York: Charles Scribner's Sons, 1904). Tipping edited and provided analytical and historical descriptions for the book. N.B. In 1917, during WWI, Szentkuthy's father worked as a commander in the Russian compound of Budakeszi (8–10 km from the apt where Szentkuthy would spend most of his adult life). His colleague, Captain Ratkóczy (an inhumane, hard soldier who bound prisoners without remorse), left this book behind in his hut with his dog, which became the Gyuszi dog of the young nine-year's old Szentkuthy. Since 1917, Szentkuthy read and reread the book, which eventually became so entirely tattered that he had a bookbinder restore it in 1979. Incidentally, the bookbinder was a neighbor of Szentkuthy's who restored many of his books. Szentkuthy also used the book as inspiration for his novel on Handel & for part four of the *St. Orpheus Breviary*. Thanks are due to Mária Tompa for this information, which was compiled directly from Szentkuthy's marginalia.

45 The title is often translated as *On the Truth of the Catholic Faith*, and its date of publication has traditionally been given to be 1264, though more recent research puts it at 1270–73.

46 "Know thyself."

47 '*Analogy* of being' and '*mystery* of being.' From the early 1930s on, theologian Karl Barth (1886–1968) wrote about new relationships between God and humans and the 'analogy of faith' (*analogia fidei*) in lieu of the Catholic doctrine of the "analogy of being" (*analogia entis*).

48 'A life lived,' and 'fiction formed.'

49 Girolamo Frescobaldi (1583–1643) was active a generation before Charles II of England (1630–1685) but it may be of interest in view of the significance the Aldobrandini was to play in Szentkuthy's later work (cf. *Marginalia on Casanova*, §73, p. 111 *et seq.*) that between 1610–13, Frescobaldi began to work for Cardinal Pietro Aldobrandini and remained in his service until after Aldobrandini's death in 1621.

50 "But oh! my torment's heard by one / Save porcelain Oread statuettes" — a couplet from "Lili's Park," a fairly long lyric by Goethe (1749–1832) from towards the end of 1775 (tr. John Whaley, 1998). An *oread* was an ancient Greek mountain nymph.

51 A line from "Der wahre Genuß" (True Enjoyment), one of Goethe's mildly erotic early poems to Anna Katharina Schonkopf ("she is perfect, and her only fault is — that she loves me") — composed around 1765 when he was studying law in Leipzig:

> Wenn sie beim Tisch des Liebsten Füße
> Zum Schemel ihrer Füße macht,
> Den Apfel, den sie angebissen,
> Das Glas, woraus sie trank, mir reicht
> Und mir bei halb geraubten Küssen
> Den sonst verdeckten Busen zeigt.

> Vainly would'st thou, to gain a heart,
> Heap up a maiden's lap with gold;
> The joys of love thou must impart…
> Or if at table she'll employ,
> To pillow hers, her lover's feet,
> Give me the apple that she bit,
> The glass from which she drank, bestow,
> And when my kiss so orders it,
> Her bosom, veil'd till then, will show.

52 SW Hungary (known since Roman times as Transdanubia) has a very distinctive dialect.

53 Objectivity. N.B. The Neue Sachlichkeit (New Objectivity) movement, which advocated realism and rejected romanticism in the fine arts, literature, and music, and developed especially in Germany during the 1920s.

54 This was originally an aria in Gluck's comic opera *The Pilgrims from Mecca* in which a dervish makes fun of the pious people gullibly trusting his Order's vow of poverty.

55 Literally, 'qualities, ability,' but typically used of middle-class housewives or girls who are overly prim & proper.

56 *Stiefmutter* means 'stepmother' (*árva*, the Hungarian root which Szentkuthy uses, means 'orphan'), but the diminutive form *Stiefmütterchen* (like the equivalent Hungarian diminutive: *árvácska*) denotes the pansy (*Viola tricolor*). Needless to say, there is no similar pun in English.

57 This large, two-volume novel (his second after *Narcisszusz tükre* (Narcissus' Mirror) of 1933, published one year before the present work) was self-published in 1934 and helped Szentkuthy establish a high regard from discerning literary critics.

58 25 years later Szentkuthy would publish a book entitled *Doktor Haydn* (1959). A short extract from it in English translation appeared in *The Hungarian Quarterly* 50/193 (spring 2009) 80–84.

59 The *Fugue* in G minor for organ & strings by Girolamo Frescobaldi (1583–1643) was transcribed for piano by Béla Bartók (New York: Carl Fischer, 1930).

60 Both are written by Szentkuthy in English, and are almost certainly his own words, though a possible source of the first is ultimately Revelation, e.g., 9:1: "The fifth angel sounded his trumpet, and I saw a star that had fallen from the sky to the earth. The star was given the key to the shaft of the Abyss." Intriguingly, this may be alluded to by the 12th-century nun Hildegard of Bingen in *Scivias*: "I saw a great star most splendid & beautiful, and with it an exceeding multitude of falling stars," she wrote. "And suddenly they were all annihilated, being turned into black coals." Cf. §108 of this book, where the phrase "a great star" is also used.

61 In a short essay entitled *John Webster and the Elizabethan Drama* (New York: John Lane Co., 1916), poet Rupert Brooke wrote: "He may be imagined following doggedly behind inspiration, glooming over a situation till he saw the heart of it in a gesture or a phrase."

62 This plays on Jesus' advice to his disciples after their sternly rebuking those who brought children to him for prayer and blessing: "And He said, Verily I say unto you, Except ye be converted, and become as little children, ye shall not enter into the kingdom of heaven" (Matthew 18:3). See also 1 Corinthians 14:20: "Brethren, be not children in understanding: howbeit in malice be ye children, but in understanding be men."

63 "Need for Love" (written 1776–89) and "Morning Laments" (a longish erotic poem written in August 1788).

64 Refers to Naphegy, which is located in Buda's hilly Second District.

65 Cf. Isaiah 45:15: "*Vere tu es Deus absconditus, Deus Israel, Salvator*" ("Verily, thou art a God that hidest thyself, O God of Israel, the Saviour").

66 "*Tangere me*" ("Touch me"). N.B. In John 20:17, Jesus tells Mary Magdalene, "*Noli me tangere*" ("Touch me not"); but then, later, in John: 20:27, when speaking to Thomas, he says, "Reach hither thy finger and behold my hands; and reach hither thy hand, and thrust *it* into my side."

67 The office begins "*Veni Creator Spiritus, Mentes tuorum visita…*" ("Come, Holy Spirit, Creator blest, & in our souls take up Thy rest…").

68 One of the Roman goddesses of fate (plural Parcæ).

69 Literally *rocaille* and dead, but the term 'rococo' itself may be interpreted as a combination of the word '*barocco*' (an irregularly shaped pearl, possibly the source of the word 'baroque') and the French '*rocaille*' (an artistic or architectural style of decoration characterized by ornate rock-and-shell work).

70 Cf. specifically §31 (but also §28).

71 The phrase is Szentkuthy's own, clearly a pun on the English word 'rebarbative.'

72 I.E., Pope Pius II (pontiff 1458–64), who was born Enea Silvio Bartolomeo. His 1460 proclamation of an official three-year crusade was a complete failure, but on June 18, 1464 he assumed the cross and departed for Ancona to conduct the crusade in person but died on August 14, 1464 just as the Venetian fleet arrived to transport the crusading army.

73 'To be deleted.'

74 Aesthetics.

75 In Greek mythology, Filomela was an Athenian princess who was raped and had her tongue cut out by her brother-in-law, Terius, king of Thrace, and obtained her revenge by being transformed into a nightingale, which sang its lament.

76 The Laplace plane, named after its discoverer Pierre-Simon Laplace (1749–1827), relates to the orbit of a planetary satellite & is to be distinguished from the "invariable plane of Laplace," which is derived from the sum of *angular momenta*, and is 'invariable' over the entire system.

77 I.E., The Art of Fugue, J. S. Bach's great composition.

78 Art of Death.

79 Classical Greek folklore had it that they got their name from *a-mazos* ('without breasts').

80 'Innermost fire.'

81 A totally fictitious figure named by Szentkuthy, although there is, e.g., a village of Burham near Tonbridge and the River Medway in Kent, England, which has a history going back to Roman times.

82 Love linked to *name*.

83 Károly Kisfaludy (1788–1830) was a Hungarian dramatist and actor, the founder of the country's national drama.

84 Objective, factual.

85 When you start & end a major scale on the sixth note, instead of the tonic, you get a natural minor scale.

86 John VIII Palaiologos (1392–1448) was the penultimate emperor of the Byzantine Empire. After a period as co-emperor with his father prior to 1416, he became sole emperor in 1425. He was succeeded on his death by his brother Constantine XI (1404–53).

87 La Compagnie des Quinze, led by Michel Saint-Denis, was set up in June 1929 at the former Théâtre du Vieux-Colombier in Paris, which was originally

set up in 1913 by Jacques Copeau (1879–1949), an influential French theater director, producer, actor and dramatist.

88 "Love conquers all, virtue moves love." The first clause is from Virgil's *Eclogue* X.69, the second is Szent-kuthy's own directly contradictory clause.

89 'An escape into neurosis.'

90 This novel (published in the U.S. in 1935) was an edited version of *Weymouth Sands* (1934) named after the main protagonist, by the English writer and Extension lecturer John Cowper Powys (1872–1963).

91 Construction of a thermal bath complex, which was to become the largest in Rome, was begun by Emperor Septimus Severus in 206 A.D. Inaugurated ten years later by his son Caracalla, it remained in operation up until the 6th century when the Ostrogoths, under Totilla, sacked it. They were popularly referred to as 'the Caracalla baths.'

92 Charles VII Albert (1697–1745) was Prince-elector of Bavaria from 1726 and Holy Roman Emperor from January 24, 1742 until his death.

93 Not named but presumably Pope Julius II (1443–1513), born Giuliano della Rovere, whose patronage for the arts, apart from friendship and support for Raphael, included commissioning the rebuilding of

St. Peter's Basilica, plus Michelangelo's work in the Sistine Chapel.

94 Complete Morphology of Summer.

95 Gellérthegy, a small hill on the near-central Buda (western) bank of the Danube.

96 Also *Spießerlich*: 'narrow-minded, bourgeois, Philistine.'

97 Vollen-weider is a surname meaning 'Foals' Pasture' in Swiss-German, and here it is hard to tell if a specific person is intended.

98 Richard Parks Bonington (Nottingham, 1801–London, 1828), English painter, one of the most important figures of European landscape painting.

99 If it exists.

100 Meaning 'outside,' because it lies outside the Toledo city wall. This is the popular name for the Hospital de Tavera.

101 "And there came one of the seven angels which had the seven vials, and talked with me, saying unto me, Come hither; I will shew unto thee the judgment of the great whore that sitteth upon many waters..." (Revelation 17:1).

102 "And when the day of Pentecost was fully come, they

were all with one accord in one place" (Acts 2:1). "And there appeared unto them cloven tongues like as of fire, and it sat upon each of them" (Acts 2:3).

103 A reference to Pal Funk Angelo (1894–1974), a famous Hungarian studio photographer whose photographs include portraits of everyone from Mahler to Chaplin, Béla Lugosi, Josephine Baker, Picasso and Bartók. Born in Budapest, Angelo studied and worked in a multitude of professions, and traveled widely, studying in Paris with Charles Reutlinger, whilst also working as a fashion and costume designer. In Hamburg, he studied with Rudolf Dührkoop, trained at Aladár Székely's studio in Budapest, and practiced filmmaking under Michael Curtis. He was awarded numerous prizes, including the French Minister of Art award (1961), the Niépce-Daguerre Medal (1960), and others.

104 "It goes without saying."

105 The Latin tag runs *Sub specie aeternitatis*: "from the viewpoint of the eternal…"

106 What's the good?

107 The Pays de Caux is a chalk plateau in France to the north of the Seine estuary and extending to the cliffs on the English Channel coast.

108 A political faction in Italy that supported the power

of the pope against the Hohenstaufen German emperor (he was supported by the Ghibellines).

109 Koh-i-Noor Hardtmuth a.s. is a Czech manufacturer of pencils and art supplies. Formed in 1790 by the Austrian Joseph Hardtmuth, and named after the Koh-i-Noor diamond, in 1802, they patented the first pencil lead made from a combination of clay and graphite.

110 'Wrestling with the angel': refers to the account of Jacob wrestling with the angel (Genesis).

111 'A Pantagruel game': the reference being to the protagonist of the books which comprise François Rabelais' *Gargantua and Pantagruel* (c. 1532–64), a significant aspect of which are his abundant lists of words (many of them his own coining). "Pantagruelism," Rabelais maintained, is rooted "in a certain gaiety of mind pickled in the scorn of fortuitous things."

112 'City of a Thousand Women.'

113 Some people of dubious authority reckon that the Archangel Lemuriel is the most ancient of the Archangels.

114 Luke 23:34: "Then said Jesus, Father, forgive them; for they know not what they do. And they parted his raiment, and cast lots."

115 Orom utca runs on the northern side of Gellért-hegy

('St. Gerard's Hill') & 'Sun Hill' is immediately to the north of it on the Buda side of the Danube in the First District of Budapest.

116 Szentkuthy's own English and his own German translation.

117 'City of God' cf. *De Civitate Dei contra Paganos* ('The City of God Against the Pagans') was one of the major works of Augustine of Hippo in the early 5th century A.D.

118 A reference to Field-Marshal August von Mackensen (1849–1945) who, among other things, accompanied Kaiser William II of Germany to Palestine in 1898 before distinguishing himself with his army service on the Eastern front, before surrendering in Budapest in December 1918 after the armistice.

119 In this context, this refers to Edmund G.H. Landau (1877–1938), a German Jewish mathematician who worked in the fields of number theory and complex analysis.

120 The reference is to Konrad Knopp (1882–1957), a German mathematician who worked on generalized limits and complex functions. The work referred to was published posthumously in English translation as *Theory of Functions* (Dover, 1996).

121 Lev G. Schnirelmann (1905–38). In 1930, he proved

that every even number $n \geq 4$ can be written as the sum of at most 20 primes.

122 In 1923, the English mathematicians G.H. Hardy (1877–1947) and John Edensor Littlewood (1885–1977) set out a generalization of the twin prime conjecture (i.e., a prime number which differs from another prime number by two), being concerned with the distribution of prime constellations, including twin primes, in analogy to the prime number theorem.

123 Proposed by Bernhard Riemann, this is a conjecture that the nontrivial zeros of the Riemann zeta function all have real part $1/2$. Along with the Goldbach conjecture, this hypothesis is part of Hilbert's eighth problem in David Hilbert's list of 23 unsolved mathematical problems. Bernhard Riemann (1826–66) was an influential German mathematician who made lasting contributions to analysis, number theory, & differential geometry.

124 The remark was relayed by G.H. Hardy, in his 1940 book *Ramanujan: Twelve Lectures on Subjects Suggested by His Life and Work.*

125 Joanna (1479–1555) was the first queen to reign over both Castile (1504–55) and Aragon (1516–55), a union which evolved into modern Spain.

126 Arthur Stanley Eddington (1882–1944) was a British physicist and philosopher of science. In 1922, he wrote a paper expressing the view that gravitational waves are in essence ripples in coordinates, & have no physical meaning. Cf. "The propagation of gravitational waves," *Proc. Roy. Soc. Lond.* Ser. A, 102 (1923) 268–282.

127 Title of a book by biologist and philosopher Hans Driesch (1867–1941), who was awarded the chair of natural theology at the University of Aberdeen, Scotland, where he delivered the Gifford Lectures in 1906 and 1908 on The Science and Philosophy of the Organism (published in Germany in 1909) — the first comprehensive presentation of his ideas. Incidentally, Driesch is credited with performing the first cloning of an animal as far back as the 1880s.

128 Inflammation of the labyrinth (i.e., the inner ear) = *otitis media*.

129 Carl Friedrich Gauss (1777–1855) was a German mathematician and physical scientist.

130 The Acheron was one of the rivers in Hades over which the souls of the dead were ferried by Charon.

131 We shall see if mathematics…

132 Matthew 27:46.

133 A fictive title. There never has been a newspaper of that name (cf. *Boston Weekly Advertiser*, *Boston Weekly Digest*, *Boston Weekly Messenger*, *Boston News-letter*); moreover, the date in question was actually a Saturday.

134 *Woman*-illustration.

135 After a first marriage in the early 1920s, during the early 1930s Göring (1893–1946) was often in the company of Emmy Sonnemann (1893–1973), an actress from Hamburg. They were married in 1935 in Berlin.

136 Intoxication.

137 Alfred Rosenberg (1893–1946) was an influential member of the Nazi Party in Germany.

138 *Lessons on the Philosophy of History*, a book (first published posthumously in 1837) by Georg Wilhelm Friedrich Hegel (1770–1831).

139 sum total of injury / affront / injustice.

140 Objective, factual.

141 'History of art.'

142 '[Possessing] radically nothing.'

143 'Ship of fools.' *The Ship of Fools* (*Daß Narrenschyff ad Narragoniam*) is a book by Sebastian Brant

(Strasburg, 1457–1521). It was originally published in Basel in 1494 and included the first commissioned work by Albrecht Dürer.

144 To quote from Eddington's *New Pathways in Science* (see footnote 156): "Plate I shows the tracks of electrons and positrons, rendered visible by Prof. C.T.R. Wilson's method, which causes small drops of water to condense along the tracks. The photograph, due to Blackett & Occhialini, shows a shower of these particles produced by a single cosmic ray falling on copper. A magnetic field was so placed that the electron tracks curve to the left & the positron tracks to the right."

145 An absurd reduction to the genitals (i.e., a play on the usual phrase: *reductio ad absurdum*).

146 "As it says in the book."

147 I.E., chapter 5 in Eddington's *New Pathways in Science*.

148 The two major shopping streets run parallel to one another, in the Fifth (Inner City) district of Pest.

149 Max Mezger & Hans Ludwig Oeser, *The Never-Lost Paradise: Out of German Woods, Meadows and Gardens. A Picture Book of the Plant Kingdom*. This was published in Berlin in 1935 by Verlag der Gartenschönheit (Garden Beauty Press).

150 "Breathing Algae of Village Wells."

151 See §46 for another usage of the phrase — originally in English — of "a great star."

152 A fine, thin cotton fabric having a durable crisp finish.

153 Another reference to C. F. Worth and The House of Worth. Worth's highly original perfumes were popular during the company's lifetime (1858–1956). Szentkuthy is referring to the shapes of his perfume bottles. Cf. §27 of this book.

154 Teleki László tér is a public square in the predominantly working-class VIII™ (Józsefváros) District of Pest, near the Kerepesi Cemetery, which had a flea market.

155 The title under which 'fragments' from James Joyce's *Finnegans Wake* began to appear, in serialized form, in the Parisian literary journals *Transatlantic Review* and *Transition* from 1924.

156 *Hydriotaphia: Urne-Burial or, A Discourse of the Sepulchrall Urnes Lately Found in Norfolk*, was published in 1658 as Part I of a two-part work that concludes with *The Garden of Cyrus*. The discourse entitled *The Garden of Cyrus, or The Quincunciall Lozenge, or Network Plantations of the Ancients, naturally, artificially, mystically considered*, was first published in 1658, along with its diptych companion, *Urne-Burial*.

157 In *The Garden of Cyrus*, Browne writes of the "sex-angular Cels in the Honeycombs of Bees," each cell being "a six-sided figure, whereby every cell affords a common side unto six more, & also a fit receptacle for the Bee it self." He goes on to the patterns found elsewhere in nature before concluding: "... nature Geometrizeth, & observeth order in all things."

158 A quotation from chapter 3 of *The Garden of Cyrus*.

159 Ibid.

160 This phrase occurs in Chapter 3 of *The Garden of Cyrus* in the sentence: "More orderly situated are those cretaceous and chalky concretions found sometimes in the bigness of a small vetch on either side their spine; which being not agreeable unto our order, nor yet observed by any, we shall not here discourse on."

161 A phrase found in Chapter 3 of *Hydriotaphia*.

162 Ibid.

163 A reference to Sir Richard Burton (1821–90), the British explorer, translator, writer, soldier, orientalist, cartographer, ethnologist, linguist, poet, and diplomat, who allegedly spoke over two dozen European, Asian, and African languages.

164 Phrase at nearly the end of Chapter 3 of *Hydriotaphia*.

165 "... The pines piously pass themselves on in their

united branches": a phrase from François Mauriac's "*Le mystère Frontenac*" (1933) 289. One of his lesser known novels, this introduces readers to the Frontenacs, small landed gentry of the Bordeaux region in France, and was translated into English by Gerard Manley Hopkins (published as *The Frontenac Mystery*, 1951, and *The Frontenacs*, 1961).

166 Another phrase from Mauriac's *Le mystère Frontenac*.

167 *Le mystère Frontenac*, 190–191.

COLOPHON

TOWARDS THE ONE AND ONLY METAPHOR
was typeset in InDesign.

The text and page numbers are set in *Adobe Jenson Pro*.
The titles are set in *Charlemagne*.
Photo of Szentkuthy by József Pécsi, 1934. Used with
kind permission of the Miklós Szentkuthy Foundation.

Book design & typesetting: Alessandro Segalini
Cover design: István Orosz

TOWARDS THE ONE AND ONLY METAPHOR

is published by Contra Mundum Press
and printed by Lightning Source, which has received Chain of
Custody certification from: The Forest Stewardship Council,
The Programme for the Endorsement of Forest Certification,
and The Sustainable Forestry Initiative.

Contra Mundum Press   New York · Berlin

CONTRA MUNDUM PRESS

Contra Mundum Press is dedicated to the value & the indispensable importance of the individual voice.

Contra Mundum Press will be publishing titles from all the fields in which the genius of the age traditionally produces the most challenging and innovative work: poetry, novels, theatre, philosophy — including philosophy of science & of mathematics — criticism, and essays.
Upcoming volumes include Josef Winkler's *When the Time Comes*, Pier Paolo Pasolini's *Divine Mimesis*, and Robert Kelly's *A Voice Full of Cities*.

For the complete list of forthcoming publications, please visit our website. To be added to our mailing list, send your name and email address to: info@contramundum.net

Contra Mundum Press
P.O. Box 1326
New York, NY 10276
USA
http://contramundum.net

OTHER CONTRA MUNDUM PRESS TITLES

Gilgamesh

Ghérasim Luca, *Self-Shadowing Prey*

Rainer J. Hanshe, *The Abdication*

Walter Jackson Bate, *Negative Capability*

Miklós Szentkuthy, *Marginalia on Casanova*

Fernando Pessoa, *Philosophical Essays*

Elio Petri, *Writings on Cinema & Life*

Friedrich Nietzsche, *The Greek Music Drama*

Richard Foreman, *Plays with Films*

Louis-Auguste Blanqui, *Eternity by the Stars*

SOME FORTHCOMING TITLES

Miklós Szentkuthy, *Prae*

Emilio Villa, *The Selected Poems of Emilio Villa*

Fernando Pessoa, *The Transformation Book*

Alfred de Vigny, *The Fates*

Jean-Jacques Rousseau, *Narcissus*

PUBLISHER ACKNOWLEDGMENTS

Gratitude is due to Fenyvesi Kristóf for his kind assistance with this publication — even in the midst of dark nights, he remained loyal to the one and only metaphor…

It is however to Orzoy Ágnes, whose magnanimity, devotion, and philological precision were instrumental to our efforts, that we, & many others, are gratefully indebted.

Once again, it is to Madame Fortuna that we very humbly raise our glass — *alis grave nil.*

CPSIA information can be obtained at www.ICGtesting.com
Printed in the USA
BVOW03s0806011013

332600BV00002B/5/P